KILLING ZEBRA HORSES

KILLING ZEBRA HORSES

Caroline Overfield

Matador
9 Priory Business Park,
Wistow Road, Kibworth Beauchamp,
Leicestershire. LE8 0RX
Tel: 0116 279 2299
Email: books@troubador.co.uk
Web: www.troubador.co.uk/matador
Twitter: @matadorbooks

ISBN 978 1 8004 6549 7

British Library Cataloguing in Publication Data.
A catalogue record for this book is available from the British Library.

Printed and bound in Great Britain by 4edge Limited
Typeset in 11pt Minion Pro by Troubador Publishing Ltd, Leicester, UK

Matador is an imprint of Troubador Publishing Ltd

To Mark

ONE

It was a sunny day that held different things for each of them: birdsong, chocolate, conflict and death.

Alison Dobson was fiercely aware of her own happiness as she walked along the riverbank. The cold of a long winter seemed to be lifting and she revelled in the feeling of the sun on her face and the mud beneath her boots. She loved the peace of this walk into town. The dappled light and the cheerful birdsong made her feel more alive, more fully awake. This was her life. She marvelled at that fact. This was her life and she was in awe, constantly, of how simple it was and how happy it made her. When she thought of how it could have been she shivered. She woke in the night sometimes convinced that her life had followed the path she had been born to. But instead she was here. Walking along a riverside path in a quiet market town. Meeting friends for coffee, almost like an ordinary mum. Almost like a normal person.

Something caught her eye up on the Beamsleigh Hill, a movement that was gone before she fully registered it. She held up her hand to shield her face from the sun. Nothing to see – probably a dog or a pheasant. She smiled to herself, nothing to fear. Not here, not now. Not in this life she had so unexpectedly made for herself.

- - -

The man on the hill thought of her as prey. An animal to be culled. She was in his way and she needed to be removed. This was his chance to act, his perfect opportunity. His mother had always taught him that you should take opportunities when they came your way. He felt his pulse racing. He could have called it fear; he chose to call it excitement.

- - -

Izzy Johnson felt her heart pounding. Anger coursed through her. She replayed the argument again in her mind. Mr Riordan had been in the wrong. She shouldn't have sworn at a teacher, she knew that... but he had treated her like a child. Worse, he'd treated her like an idiot. Asking her to stay for extra lessons. After everything. It was an insult. He knew she didn't need extra lessons. She had thought they were... something. Not friends exactly, but something. She had thought they got on. She had thought he respected her.

Evidently not. She wasn't going to stay for any extra bloody lessons and she had told him so. She couldn't believe it when he told her to see him after class. The way he had said it, all calm and bossy like any other teacher. Like she was any other student. *See me after class.* He'd never talked to her like that. That wasn't how they were with each other.

'I don't see the point,' she had said. And he had lost it. Shouting at her like she was a naughty child.

'I am a teacher and you need to show me some respect no matter how clever you think you are. Now sit down and see me after class.'

'Fuck you.' The words had exploded out of her. 'Fuck you.'

She rarely swore. She certainly never swore at her teachers. She never ran out of class either. But here she was leaving the school. It felt dangerous. Rebellious. Exhilarating.

- - -

For the man on the hill the sight of her seemed too good to be true. An opportunity just waiting to be taken. Maybe this wasn't the perfect place, but now might be the perfect time. He could follow. He could watch. And if the moment was right, strike. Strike while the iron's hot. One of his mother's favourite phrases. One of many. Along with 'useless', 'stupid', 'undeserving'. She told him he could have been so much more than he was. She told him he never made the most of things. He never followed through. Well, he would certainly follow through with this.

- - -

Andrea Mills jogged out of her house and up Forest Hill. She took Beamsleigh Park Road and turned onto the footpath around Beamsleigh Hill. There was a little play park in front of the ancient Roman fort, but Andrea turned left to take the more deserted route. She didn't want to meet anyone today. Her mind was on her daughter and her latest petty misdemeanour. Smoking. When had Mary started smoking? And had she really told Mr Banks at the school that it was her human right to do so? Surely he was exaggerating when he said she might be suspended if she was caught again.

Banks was a hypocrite. As if he cared about anyone smoking. Still, Andrea would have to speak to Mary. She was a good girl really, whatever Banks said, and Andrea didn't like the idea of her smoking.

She paused where the path split and leaned against one of the two stiles. She was panting hard already. She checked that no one could see her before retrieving a chocolate bar from her pocket and taking a quick bite. She had read somewhere that sugar helped you run further. Something called glycogen apparently. You had to keep up your levels in order to run efficiently. So really the chocolate was all part of her training. Still, she didn't want anyone to see her eating a Mars bar in her running gear. It might look odd. People were always so quick to judge.

She looked at her watch.

Dom had said he'd be back for tea, but who knew what time that was anymore. Now he was at uni her son seemed to keep very different hours to the rest of them. And Dave was at work so it would be six at least before she saw him. Mary had Art Club on Tuesday nights. She'd be back around four thirty. That gave Andrea plenty of time to finish her run, get herself cleaned up and have a snack ready for Mary.

She liked to be home for Mary getting in from school. She was still her little girl, despite the angry outbursts and the increasingly frequent calls from the school. And the smoking.

Andrea took a bigger bite of chocolate to push the thought away.

- - -

He was watching her. Waiting for his moment. Could it really be this easy? Could he take advantage of her trust so effortlessly? It felt almost ludicrously simple. But then maybe everything was simple if you were determined enough. If you showed that you were strong, maybe the world was yours for the taking. Maybe failure was just weakness or an unwillingness to do what it took. He was never going to be weak again.

- - -

Izzy took out her phone as she exited the school. She knew Robbie would come and he was the only person she wanted to see.

'Riordan's being an arse... I know... He wouldn't talk to me. Acted like nothing happened. Told me to sit down like I was a bloody kid... Yeah, fuck him. Can we meet...? Now. I'm ditching school... OK... Yeah. I'll see you up there in a couple of minutes.'

She began to run.

'Izzy.'

She heard the voice behind her and turned to look, expecting Mr Riordan. Hoping for Mr Riordan. If he spoke to her properly she could forgive him; she could apologise for being rude. It would go back to being the way it had been.

It wasn't Riordan. It was Mr Banks, her English teacher. She ignored him and kept on running. She ran down the steps, around the back of the bike park and out of the school grounds, heading towards the path up onto Beamsleigh Hill.

- - -

Alison was enjoying the weak afternoon sunshine. She was paying little attention to her surroundings. It was a rare moment of relaxed vigilance. She never usually let herself forget where she was, who she was, what she was doing. But today, lulled by the peace and the sunshine and the normality of life, she was walking blindly, seeing nothing. It would be good to meet up with her friends, good to catch up and to forget about work for a while. Ignoring everything but the sunshine on her face was a real luxury. She knew better than to let her guard down, but sometimes it felt good to feel safe.

- - -

He saw the wire on the ground. An old rabbit trap or some discarded fencing, he wasn't sure which. He had planned to use the knife he had with him, but wouldn't this be better? Untraceable. It was luck. Fate maybe. He smiled to himself.

Luck was on his side, the way luck always favoured the brave. He was in the shadows, unseen. He could wait. It would just take patience. A little patience and the moment would be his.

- - -

Andrea stuffed the remains of the chocolate bar back into her pocket, realising with a jolt that it was almost gone. She began to jog again. She wondered if she might see Henry today with his little dog. She hadn't seen him all week. Andrea didn't ordinarily like small dogs, but somehow the little dog suited Henry. She supposed it was a gay thing. Gay men were supposed to have those fashionable little dogs, weren't they? Was that prejudiced? How could it be when she liked Henry and his little dog so much?

- - -

Izzy was alone on the hill. Her heart was fluttering with anger and excitement and hope. She thought of Robbie and smiled. Her boyfriend. Her secret boyfriend. There was a certain thrill to that. Of course they argued sometimes, that was normal. That was passion. She didn't want vanilla, ordinary, sensible, dull. She wanted sparks. She pushed his buttons. She knew that. But you had to break up to make up. And the making up was so much fun. It had been a shitty morning, but she was young and happy to be alive. The sun was shining and soon everything was going to be OK. Really soon.

- - -

This was the moment. He must act now. She looked over when he called her name. No fear in her eyes. It was quicker than he had expected. Easier. He hit her, she fell. Then the wire was around her neck. She fought, but he was stronger. His will was stronger. He smiled to himself. His mother couldn't say he hadn't followed through, she couldn't say he hadn't fulfilled his potential today. His mother had been right all these years, he saw that now. He could do anything when he put his mind to it.

He nudged his prey with his toe. She didn't move. *Cadaverous.* He liked the feel of the word in his mouth. As he turned to go he thought of the last message he had sent her. She had replied with a smiley face, as if he were a child in need of encouragement. She had underestimated him as so many people did. She had no idea who he really was.

Meeting death with a smiley face. It felt both innocent and puerile. He was glad she was gone.

He glanced indifferently at the body on the ground. A carcass now. Blonde hair pastel-tinted with her own blood. Her throat a jagged open wound. A few more precautions, then he turned and left. He forced himself not to run. Breathing deeply, calming himself. He was just a man out for a walk. Just a man but so much more. There were no obstacles in his way anymore.

- - -

Andrea looked up from her plodding to see a man in a hoody in the distance. She plastered a smile onto her face in expectation of a meeting, but the man vaulted a low fence before he was close enough to be recognised. He cut across the grass, probably heading to the Cawpers estate or the back way to the school, and Andrea continued her laborious jog up the hill, forgetting him instantly.

Suddenly she stopped, looking at the simple scene in front of her but unable to take it in.

Her brain seemed to take a full minute to catch up with her eyes. There was someone in front of her lying on the grass like a sunbather. Except it was February. And it was cold. And the young woman she was looking at was not sunbathing. She was motionless on her back, her throat had been slashed and blood had pooled on and around her face, matting her blonde hair to her skull. Dead, undoubtedly and irredeemably dead.

Andrea's brain was numb. Nothing made sense. She knew she should react; she had seen films and knew she should scream, or sob, or throw up. But no reaction came. There was just numbness.

Eventually, she sank to the ground beside the body and reached out a hand to touch the young woman, as though to comfort her. But at the last moment, she drew her hand back unable to make the contact. *Lifeless.* There was no comfort to give or receive now because the girl was lifeless. The word was echoing in Andrea's head as she took out her phone. No signal.

- - -

Alison was in the café with her friends when her phone rang.

'Do not answer it,' Carla ordered.

'It might be the school.'

'It will not be the school. It will be bloody work and we haven't seen you in bloody ages… and she's answering the phone.'

Alison shrugged an apology as she looked at the display. It was indeed work.

'DI Dobson,' she said quietly.

- - -

Andrea sat in the back of the ambulance she had called, shivering. Trying to forget the image of bloodstained hair, white face and staring, unseeing eyes.

- - -

Alison stepped away from her friends and took a call from her sergeant. A body found on Beamsleigh Hill. A body less than half a mile away.

- - -

Izzy Johnson lay cold, unknowing. No longer fully human, just a body now. A case.

TWO

Alison left her friends and walked back up to Beamsleigh Hill. The day was no longer full of hope and sunshine and safety. The walk took her within fifty yards of her children's primary school. Too close.

A body on Beamsleigh Hill just didn't seem real. This was her town. Her place of security. Maybe it would turn out to be an accident or even a suicide. Those things happened, even in a quiet little town. '*Tragic accident*,' the headlines always said, as if some accidental deaths might not be tragic. '*Devastating suicide.*' Again the superfluous adjective.

As she reached the hill Paul Skinner approached. Her sergeant was as eager as ever and she felt a familiar mixture of annoyance and sadness as she waited for him. He so wanted to please her, she had to fight the urge it gave her to be cruel.

She liked Paul. She had begun to respect him over the year they had worked together. She should have known better. Alison was not good with people. More specifically she was not good with men. She always somehow managed to fuck it up. Admittedly this had been a new and spectacular fuck-up, even by her standards, but there was always a pattern to her behaviour. She made friends, she let people get so close but no closer. She hadn't quite realised how close she had let Paul get until recently. And then Harrogate had happened. *Bloody Harrogate*. What a right royal mess that had been. Paul, of course, wanted to talk about it. Like the puppy he was, he wanted to make it better. Alison was not really the talking kind. Luckily the job would take all their focus for a while.

'OK, what've we got?' she asked, barely looking at Paul.

'Young woman. Teenager, we think. Found by a jogger about half an hour ago. She'd been hit pretty hard in the face, probably with a rock, and there's a contemporaneous blow to the back of her head.'

Alison felt her eyebrows go up. 'Contemporaneous!'

'It's a real word,' Paul said. 'Means it happened at the same time.'

'Yeah, I know. You could have just said, "it happened at the same time".'

'Contemporaneous is quicker.'

'Just make sure you spell check it before it goes in the report.'

Paul smiled.

'You sure she was hit with something?' Alison went on. 'Could she have been punched in the face and hit her head on the way down? Could she even have fallen? We sure this wasn't an accident?'

'No way.'

'Yeah,' Alison agreed. 'Pretty hard to fall and hit your face and the back of your head at the same time.'

'It's not that, boss. I forgot to mention…'

'What?'

'She was strangled, or garrotted, I suppose. Looks like it was maybe twine or thin wire. It cut into her throat pretty badly.'

'Kind of an important piece of information that,' Alison said sardonically.

He shook his head. 'I got distracted. After I said "contemporaneous blow", I could see you thinking *what a wanker*, and I just sort of lost track of my thoughts.'

Alison smiled despite herself. He sometimes seemed so young to her, so fresh and tongue-tied. She tried not to find it endearing.

'OK, so she was hit in the face and she was garrotted. Any ID?'

'She's got a bag with her. Schoolbooks and stuff say Isabella Johnson. Her purse is still in the bag but no driver's licence or picture ID but she's probably too young for that stuff.'

'Mobile?'

'Not with the body or in her bag. We're searching the area but nothing so far.'

'Killer probably took it. It's unlikely a teenage girl wouldn't have one.'

Paul nodded.

'Alright. Anything else? Soco found anything yet?'

'Early days. No sign of a weapon yet. No clear footprints.'

'Right. So what have we got? She was hit in the face, probably with a rock or other weapon, but we can't rule out a punch. She was also hit at the back of the head, around the same time. Again she may have been hit with a weapon or bashed her head as she fell. And she was strangled with something thin, probably a wire. So much so that her throat was cut. Yes?'

Paul nodded at the summary.

'Any sign of sexual assault. Was she clothed?' Alison went on.

'Looks like there might have been some sexual activity, but no obvious signs of force. Her clothes were in disarray but...'

'Shit,' Alison interrupted him, pulling her phone out of her bag.

The word disarray had dislodged something in her brain. Mabel leaving the house that morning, her school shirt untucked, one sock up and one down, looking like she had slept in her clothes. Nick laughing, calling her the 'picture of disarray'.

Alison turned her back on Paul as she spoke into her phone.

'Carla, hi... could you possibly...'

'Get Beatrice and Mabel from school?' Carla interrupted, laughing. 'Already organised. And Nick's going to pick them up from me about half five. I told him you got called into work.'

'You are an angel.'

'Gold plated.'

'A gold-plated angel. Thanks.'

Alison turned back to Paul, cutting him off before he could ask about her kids. That was not a conversation she wanted to be having with him.

'OK, where were we? No signs of sexual assault?'

He took the hint. Her family were off limits.

'Nothing obvious, like I said, but we'll do the usual checks. Only other interesting thing is the note.'

'Note?'

If there was a suicide note after all this she was seriously going to lose it. A slit throat and a suicide note? Not plausible, of course. Paul held out the note in an evidence bag for her to read. Definitely not a suicide note.

'Any ideas who this is from?' she asked, handing back the note.

'None.'

She took a deep breath and thought for just a heartbeat.

'OK, first things first. We need her out of here before the kids start getting out of school. I want a PC at the cordon just to make sure none of them come this way. Let's see if we can get someone at the school to ID her before Liz goes and breaks the bad news to the family. Then I want to know who wrote this bloody note.'

'What about the woman who found her?'

'Who was it?'

Paul looked at his notebook.

'Andrea Mills?'

Alison nodded. The name was familiar; her kids were older than Alison's but her youngest had briefly overlapped with Alison's eldest attending Guides. It was a small town.

'You sent her home?'

'Yeah, I sent young Holly to sit with her, at least until her husband gets back.'

Young Holly. Paul was only twenty-five. Alison smiled and didn't comment.

'She see anything, Mrs Mills?'

'Says not.'

'Low priority for now then. Let's concentrate on the school and the family. Mrs Mills can wait.'

'And home in time for tea.' Paul smiled.

Alison smiled wearily back.

'If only,' she said.

She looked at the note again. She didn't like it. It sounded rather too much like an invitation to murder.

'*Meet me as usual. I can explain everything. Please don't tell anyone.*'

THREE

Penbury High looked exactly as a school should look. A bit worn, a bit anonymous, but trying hard to be cheerful. The walls were the requisite cream and green, the paint peeling in places, and there were posters everywhere and examples of students' work. Although she had never been inside the building before it all felt very familiar to Alison. It was much like the school she had attended so many years ago.

They were ushered into the headteacher's office by his worried-looking secretary. The man himself appeared a few minutes later, smiling but wary. Niall Riordan was pleasant looking, in his mid-thirties, tall and thin with a face that looked fitted for laughter. Alison recognised him from a presentation he had given at Bea's primary school the previous week. Her daughter would be starting secondary school in September and Riordan had come to talk to Year 6 about the move. The presentation had been beset with problems, not least a power cut that had trapped them inside the building when the automatic doors refused to open. It could have been a drama, but Riordan had remained calm and reassuring. Alison had liked him.

He showed that same calm now as she explained what had happened and showed him pictures of the girl found on the hill. He was able to confirm that the girl was Isabella Johnson. Or she *had been* Isabella Johnson, before she became a case. A mystery to be solved.

Isabella Johnson. Izzy to her friends. Just turned seventeen. Model student. Gifted, talented. A lovely girl. A full and happy life in front of her. All the clichés. Dead in a ditch. Well, not quite a ditch but still another cliché. Dead at the hands of a madman? Alison hoped not. She knew from experience that madmen are the hardest to catch.

The press loved a madman, it made a compelling story. But most murders weren't committed by madmen. Most murders were simpler, more domestic and more mundane. Alison hoped that was the case here. She hoped the murderer was someone with an ordinary motive, just some small dispute; she hoped the killer was someone that Izzy already knew. That was the most likely scenario. But the location of the attack worried Alison. It was simultaneously too public and too desolate. It didn't seem like the place for a domestic killing. She hoped she'd know more once she'd spoken to the family.

She nodded to Paul as soon as Riordan confirmed the girl's identity. He stepped discreetly out of the office to put in a call to PC Liz Aidan, the family liaison officer. Liz would break the news to Izzy's parents. Alison and Paul would head there next. It was necessary and yet Alison hated it. She hated that she would give her genuine, but completely useless, condolences and at the same time she would pry mercilessly into every facet of their child's life.

'Would you like tea, Inspector?' Riordan asked. 'I think I need…' His voice trailed off. He didn't wait for a reply but went over to the kettle in the corner of the office and made tea for all of them. By the time he had finished Paul was back in the room.

As Riordan returned to his desk with the hot tea, Alison saw that he had shed silent tears and that his hand shook slightly. She understood the shock, but she found the tears surprising.

Would anyone at her school have shed tears over her? She doubted it. Her headteacher had only known her name because she was part of the worst family in town and nothing more. All she had wanted from school was to get out, and get out unscathed.

'We just have a few more questions, Mr Riordan.' Alison smiled reassuringly.

Riordan nodded. Took another sip of his tea.

'Did you know Isabella well?'

'She's in my maths class.' He paused. 'Should I tell the children?' he asked. 'Call an assembly or something?' He was looking at his watch. It was almost three thirty and Alison knew school finished at quarter to four.

'Please don't say anything publicly yet,' she said. 'We're in the process of informing the parents. They have a right to be the first to know.'

'The parents. Oh dear, yes, yes, of course. I'll give you the address.' Alison nodded. He had his secretary pull up Izzy's records.

Alison didn't tell him that Liz Aidan would already have

the address, that she was already on the way to the house. There was some value in letting him feel useful.

'Her mother was here just last week,' Riordan said. 'Parents' evening. Glowing report for Izzy, as usual.'

'And there weren't any problems that you know of? Fallings-out with friends? Boyfriends? Drink or drugs?'

'Isabella Johnson!' He sounded as if she had been suggesting Mother Teresa was smoking weed behind the bike sheds. 'She isn't that sort of girl.'

Alison raised an eyebrow. Izzy was seventeen. Surely all seventeen-year-olds had some issues with friends and boyfriends and the odd drink or smoke. Didn't they? Or had the world changed since her day?

Paul spoke.

'Could you tell me why she wasn't in school this afternoon? Are sixth formers allowed to leave the grounds?'

'Yes,' Riordan said. 'They're allowed off site if they don't have any classes.'

Alison waited; something in his tone told her there was more to it.

'But… she was supposed to be in my maths class actually.'

'She skipped class?'

Riordan ran his fingers through his hair, exhaling deeply.

'She… she left early. We had a disagreement. An argument, I suppose.'

'About?'

'It was nothing,' he said, shaking his head. 'It was stupid. I wanted her to come to some extra revision classes. She's got mocks coming up… only… well… she said she didn't see the point of coming. She was rude… she's never normally rude... and I... lost it. Told her she had to come. I shouted actually, which I never do. She stormed out.'

'What time was that?'

'I don't know, maybe two-ish? I didn't really notice. Not long before the end of period five anyway.'

'And when does period five end?'

'Twenty past two,' Riordan said. 'I had a single lesson with Year 13 and then they had a free study period. Most of them stay and use the library or the study rooms, but they're free to go if they like. Like I say, Izzy left before the end of the lesson.'

'And you just let her leave?' Paul asked.

'What could I do? She's seventeen, she can leave if she chooses to.' He hung his head. 'Christ, it's my fault.'

'I doubt that,' Alison said automatically.

Riordan hid his face in his hands; through the fingers Alison could see he was crying again.

'If I'd kept her in class... If she hadn't stormed out.'

Alison didn't let him go down that path. *What ifs* could send you mad.

'What did you do after Isabella left?'

'I carried on teaching.'

'You were in class all the time until we arrived?' Alison asked.

'Yes... no, sorry, no. I don't have any classes period six on Tuesday. That's two twenty to three fifteen. It's my admin time. Then I always take a form class for personal learning at the end of the day.'

'Personal learning?' Alison asked.

'Prep, we used to call it in my day.' Riordan smiled. 'They have half an hour to start their homework and ask any questions and it basically just rounds off the day. I had Year 7 today.'

Alison's head was spinning, trying to work out the teacher's whereabouts.

'So, you were in class until twenty past two. Then here in your office, then back in class at three fifteen?'

'Yes. Except...' He paused again. 'Except I let the Year 13s out a bit early. After, well, after I had *words* with Izzy I just, well, I needed a moment. I let them out and I went to the bathroom. Washed my face, tried to compose myself, you know?'

Alison nodded. She would have to check on the timeline carefully. Maybe that was a job for Jack Kent back at the office. He'd hate that, which was reason enough to give him the task.

If Izzy had left school just after two, like Riordan said, there hadn't been much time between then and the time when her body was discovered. Not much time to encounter a maniac. Much more likely she was followed. Or had arranged to meet her killer.

'Who were Izzy's friends?' Paul was asking, obviously following the same train of thought.

'Everyone. Everyone loved Izzy.'

'She must have had a best friend,' Paul said smoothly, smiling his natural smile.

'Yes, yes. Lucy, of course. Lucy Jacobs. They came up together in Year 7. Inseparable. Lovely girl, Lucy. Not in Izzy's league, of course.'

Alison gave him a quizzical look and he flushed.

'Academically I mean,' he said, although his blush said otherwise.

Alison hadn't really looked at the body on the hill. She had taken in the youth and the blonde hair and nothing more. Had Izzy Johnson been beautiful as well as brilliant and perfectly behaved? In a different league to the other girls in the school?

'You say Izzy was a popular girl?' she asked.

'Yes. She has... sorry *had*... lots of friends.' Riordan smiled. 'I was rather jealous actually.'

Alison frowned.

'Sorry. God, no that came out wrong. It's just... when I was at school if you were clever you were a nerd. You were laughed at. It's not like that for Izzy, she's popular, I mean really very popular, despite being so very clever.'

Alison said nothing. She glanced at Paul. He understood her meaning as he always did. He took the note in its little evidence bag out of his pocket. This was the sort of shorthand she was going to miss if he had to move on, but after Harrogate she wasn't sure he could stay. Once those boundaries were breached how could they continue to work together?

'We found this note in Izzy's bag,' she said, handing it to Riordan. 'I was wondering if you recognised the handwriting. Maybe a child in the school?'

Alison read the note again as she passed it over.

'*Meet me as usual. I can explain everything. Please don't tell anyone.*'

'I don't teach many of the children,' Riordan was saying. 'My subject is maths so there isn't a lot of writing... but I'll look.'

He took the note from Alison and glanced at it just as the office door burst open.

'Shit, sorry, sorry, didn't know you had company.' A slim handsome man stood in the doorway, smiling and not looking at all apologetic. His hair was wet from a recent shower and he had a studied casualness about him that was instantly appealing.

'Henry, I'm busy... what is it?'

'Just needed to get...' He paused, looking at Riordan's face. 'You OK, Niall?'

'Yes, yes... I'm fine. It's just... there's been some bad news. I'll tell you about it later. Why are you here?'

'Sorry, sorry.' The man called Henry smiled again. 'Just forgot my wallet. Forget my head if it wasn't attached, isn't that what they say?' He half winked at Paul.

'There it is.' He reached across Riordan onto the desk for the wallet. 'Sorry again... Got to dash.' He stopped dramatically looking at the note in Riordan's hand. Riordan drew the note away, half concealing it in his hand.

'My God, are we going to have the whole "confidentiality" talk again, Niall?' Henry laughed. 'I was just being nosy.'

'This is not the time.' Riordan sounded every inch the teacher but the other man cut him off.

'Don't play high and mighty.' He was still laughing and half pouting now. 'I just want to know what Simon is doing writing you notes about meeting up. You playing away from home?'

The idea seemed to amuse him inordinately.

'It wasn't sent to me,' Riordan said.

'Oh.' The young man giggled a high, false giggle. 'Oh, OK then, so I don't need to get jealous.' He swept up his wallet and left the room before Alison could question him.

'Simon?' she asked Riordan.

He looked back at the note.

'Yes, I think he's right. I think it is Simon's handwriting. Very scruffy. I've had words with him before.'

'And is Simon in one of Izzy's classes?' Alison asked.

'No, sorry, no, of course not. Simon Banks. He's Izzy's English teacher.'

FOUR

School had just finished but Banks had already left for the day.

'Is that usual?' Alison asked Riordan.

'Not really, most staff stay until at least five.' He seemed to catch himself. 'But it's not unusual either, not unheard of. There may be a good reason.'

Like a girl he'd been sending weird notes to ending up dead, she thought, nodding.

'We going to talk to him?' Paul asked as they left the school.

'Yeah, only I think we need a word with Izzy's family first. Give Banks a chance to get home and start to worry about whether we've found that letter or not.'

'Bloody perv,' Paul said. 'Bet I can guess what he wanted her to keep quiet about.'

'You can't make that assumption.'

'No? Beautiful young girl, middle-aged teacher. And that note is creepy.'

Alison agreed, but she wasn't ready to jump to any conclusions.

'Not all teachers are pervs,' she said.

'Not *all*. But some.'

They got into Paul's car in silence. He would drive. She trusted him to drive, although she usually hated being driven. Another thing she would miss if they had to stop working together. *Bloody Harrogate*. She wished they had never gone there. Paul broke into her thoughts.

'What about Riordan?'

'What about him?'

'Could he have a bit of a thing for Izzy? All that stuff about her being "in a league of her own"?'

'It was a bit gushing,' Alison conceded, shaking her head. 'I liked Riordan, though. Just because a teacher likes a pupil doesn't mean…'

'And just because you like him doesn't mean he can't be involved.'

She shot him a look, but she knew he was right. She tended to overlook people she liked; she trusted her own judgement. Perhaps a little too well.

'I'm not ruling anyone out,' she said decisively.

Her phone rang as Paul pulled up outside the Johnsons' house.

'DI Dobson.'

She nodded, took out her notebook and wrote a couple of things down.

'OK, thanks. They've gone for analysis? How long? Anything else? That's fine, par for the course. OK. Email me a copy, would you. Thanks for the heads-up.' She hung up.

Paul didn't speak. He would be itching to know what the conversation had been about but he wouldn't ask.

'The initial examination confirms time of death less

than an hour before she was found,' she said, taking pity on his curiosity.

'Riordan said she left his class about two and it must have been about two thirty when Andrea Mills found her so that fits.'

'We can check when the call came in to the ambulance service for an accurate time,' Alison agreed. 'It's a pretty narrow window. Half an hour at most.'

'Anything else, boss?'

'She had had sex before she died, but no sign of force. They've got semen for DNA… so…'

'That'll basically only be useful once we've caught the bastard.'

Alison nodded.

'Only other thing is… they found some undigested pills in her stomach.'

'What sort of pills?'

'Jenny doesn't know yet. Could be nothing, could be significant.' She tried not to sigh as she got out of the car. 'OK, so let's see what the family have to say. It's mum and stepdad right?'

'Yeah, Leanne and Bob Johnson I think Liz said.'

'Johnson? That's odd.'

'What is?'

'Izzy must have taken her stepdad's name. Most kids stick with their birth dad's name, even if mum changes hers.'

Paul shrugged; clearly he didn't think it was important. Maybe a secure upbringing could do that – make you unaware of the importance of a name.

Liz Aidan, the family liaison officer, opened the door.

'How are they?' Alison asked.

'As well as can be expected,' Liz answered. 'Quite calm but you know that's pretty normal at this stage. It hasn't sunk in yet. The stepdad's wanting action. The mum's pretty quiet. No hysterics. Not yet anyway.'

Alison nodded. She appreciated the heads-up.

'She's Leanne, right?'

'Yeah, and he's Bob. Although I think he'd prefer Mr Johnson – seems big on the formalities.'

'Thanks,' Alison said, walking past Liz into the hallway.

The house was modern. A large detached. A nice part of town but without the prestige of the old cottages near the river. The living room, where the family sat, had a bay window to the front and patio doors opening onto the garden at the back. It was almost dark outside now, but none of the curtains had been drawn, or the lights lit. They had been sitting here without noticing the passage of time.

'Let's have the curtains drawn, eh,' Alison said to Liz. 'Keep some of the warmth in.' And the nosy neighbours out. News would be leaking out by now, and Alison didn't want anyone looking in on this particular scene from hell.

'Mrs Johnson, Mr Johnson, I'm DI Dobson. I'm so sorry for your loss. We're doing all we can to find out what happened to your daughter and to catch the person responsible.'

'So why has it taken you so long to get here?' This from Bob Johnson. Alison turned to look at him properly for the first time. He reminded her of a cat puffing out its fur trying to look fierce or a terrier yapping at the Rottweiler down the street. He was a small man, stocky of build, and wearing a suit which made him look rather like a toddler dressed up for a wedding. He looked angry. She forced herself to be patient.

'I understand your frustration, sir. From the outside it can look as if things are moving slowly, but I can assure you we've not been sitting on our arses. Things are progressing.'

'Have you found him?' Johnson asked. 'That's all I want to know.'

'Who?' Alison asked, stupidly hoping for a name.

'The animal who did this, of course.'

'We're pursuing a number of inquiries.' She didn't look at Paul. It was a bullshit answer but what else could she say? She took a deep breath.

'Mrs Johnson…' she began.

'Call me Leanne, please…' she said, smiling politely. Alison nodded.

'Thank you, Leanne.' She turned to Mr Johnson, her eyes daring him to tell her *not* to call him Bob.

'Bob,' he said at last. It was a small victory. Maybe unimportant. But they were Leanne and Bob now and she could get on with her job without all the dick-swinging.

'OK, Leanne. I just have a few questions.'

'Of course. Would you like tea?'

'Thanks,' Alison said. 'Perhaps your husband could… while we get on.' Bob Johnson looked daggers. 'After all, we don't want to waste any time,' Alison said smoothly. There was no way out for Bob Johnson and he got up with a sigh.

'The good cups are in the cupboard over the sink,' Leanne Johnson said. Her husband ignored her.

'I'll help,' said Paul. Alison felt her stomach churn a little; she didn't want tea, but she would drink it because it mattered. It was important to observe the niceties, to be polite even when you were tearing someone's life apart.

'How long have you been married?' she asked.

'Five years, maybe six.' Leanne smiled. 'Been together a lot longer though.'

'He's Izzy's stepfather, right?' Leanne nodded. 'They get on alright?' Alison asked.

'Of course.' She looked affronted.

'She took his name? When you got married?'

'Yes... I thought... fresh start... you know. And they've always been so close. Especially when she was little... she adored him.'

'And now?'

'Well, you know how teenagers are... moody... answering back. But they're still really close... they adore each other... always have.'

Alison nodded again. She wondered whether Izzy would have used the word adore to describe her feelings towards her stepfather. She couldn't imagine that any teenage girl would.

'And what about her real father? Does Izzy see him?'

Leanne blanched. 'No, never. Not since... not since she was about five.'

'Do they keep in touch?'

'He sends birthday and Christmas cards.'

'Could she have seen him without you knowing? That sometimes happens as children get older.' Leanne snorted.

'Not unless she could get herself on a plane without my knowing. He's in the States. Florida. God, I'm going to have to ring him, aren't I?'

'We can do that if you like. If you give PC Aidan the number.'

Leanne nodded, clearly relieved.

'You're sure he hasn't been in touch with Izzy at all, apart from the cards at Christmas and birthdays?'

Leanne was shaking her head in response just as Bob came back in.

'Talking about the dad of the year?' he asked, handing Alison a cup of tea. 'Bastard barely manages a Christmas card. Wouldn't even remember her birthday if Leanne wasn't soppy enough to send him a reminder each year.'

'That's for Izzy's sake. I don't want her thinking...'

'What? That he's a total loser?'

Leanne didn't reply. Alison changed the subject.

'Tell me about today,' she said. 'Isabella went to school as usual this morning?'

'Yes. We left the house at the same time and I drove her to the top of Forest Hill on my way to work.'

'Where do you work?' Alison asked, although she knew. Leanne Johnson was the receptionist at the posh hotel out on the Milbury Road.

'I'm still at the Halfpenny Rabbit,' she said. 'I always drop Izzy on the way.'

'But Forest Hill isn't on your way.'

Bob Johnson gave a huff.

'Bob thinks I spoil her, but if I've got the car out anyway...'

'Kid's got legs,' Bob said. 'In my day we walked.'

Alison interrupted. 'If you dropped her at Forest Hill she'd have cut up Beamsleigh Park Road from there, wouldn't she? And across the Beamsleigh path to school?'

'Yeah, that's what she usually does. She usually meets Lucy at the bottom of Beamsleigh Park. Lucy lives on Westbar. They walk up together.'

'Lucy?'

'Lucy Jacobs. They've been best friends since infants.'

'She's Dr Jacobs' daughter?'

'Yeah, their youngest.'

'OK. And after she went to school you didn't hear anything from Izzy all day?'

'No.' She shook her head, tears rolling silently.

There was nothing Alison could say. She patted the other woman's arm gently, then went on. The best thing she could do was her job.

'My next questions might not seem relevant but sometimes it's the littlest things that matter. Was Izzy on any medication that you know of?'

'No,' she said. 'Izzy's always been really healthy. I mean the usual colds and stuff, but never anything to speak of.'

'Didn't take herbal remedies or anything like that?'

Leanne gave a hollow laugh. 'No, she didn't believe in any of that stuff.'

'And I have to ask this,' Alison said. 'She didn't use street drugs?'

'Jesus, what is this…?' Bob Johnson began.

Leanne spoke over him. 'No, never.'

'OK,' Alison said. Whatever those pills in Izzy's stomach were it was clear her mother knew nothing about them.

'And was she happy in herself? Was everything OK at school?'

'Yes. As far as I know. She's a good student, she's clever, never been in any trouble.'

'What about her friends? Everything OK there?'

'Yeah. She's got a good bunch of friends. Most of them she's known for years.'

'I'll need a list,' Alison said. 'Perhaps that's something you can do for me when we've gone. Come up with a list of all her friends, give it to PC Aidan when you're done.'

Leanne smiled as if she recognised the kindness in being given a job.

'You don't think one of her friends…?' Bob asked.

'No. But someone might know something. Teenagers don't always talk to their parents. They sometimes talk to their friends. About boyfriends, for instance.'

'Izzy didn't have a boyfriend,' Leanne said at once.

'Well, there's Dan,' Bob said.

'Dan?' Alison asked.

Leanne shook her head, as if to dismiss the name, but she spoke anyway.

'Dan Humphreys, he's been on the scene for a while. She calls him her boyfriend but it doesn't mean much at that age, does it? More like friends really.'

Alison took a deep breath.

'Do you know whether Izzy was sexually active?'

Leanne gave a snort, half laughter half horror.

'God no. I mean, she's only just turned seventeen. Well, I know… I know that's not that young but… no… she was so focused on her studies. No, I don't think… No.'

'Mr Johnson?' There had been a look on his face that seemed to imply a different answer.

'How would I know?' he said gruffly. 'She wouldn't talk to me about anything like that.'

'There was nothing *to* talk about,' Leanne said firmly.

'Yeah, only… well, there were the phone calls,' Bob said.

'Phone calls?' Alison prompted.

'It was nothing,' Leanne said. 'God, Bob, it was nothing…'

Alison waited.

'Probably nothing,' Bob Johnson agreed. 'But a couple or three times I walked in and she was on her phone and she put it down sharpish. Face down, like, so I couldn't see who she'd been facetiming or whatever they call it. And she was always a bit... well, a bit shifty about it.'

'It was Lucy... She told you it was Lucy.'

'Yeah... only she's been going out a bit more and staying out a bit later.'

'You think there could be a boy on the scene?' Alison asked. 'This Dan Humphreys maybe?' Bob Johnson shook his head.

'If it was him she'd have let me see her phone. I never had a problem with her seeing Dan. He's a nice enough lad. I reckon this was someone else.'

'It was Lucy. She told you,' Leanne insisted. 'She isn't into boys, too focused on her studies.'

'OK.' Alison nodded.

She'd ask Izzy's friends about a boyfriend. See what came up.

'What about today?' she said. 'Do you have any idea why she might have left school early?'

'Bloody school,' Bob said. 'Should keep an eye on them. *In loco parentis* or whatever it is... So why was she out of school wandering about? What were they thinking of letting her just walk out?'

'She should have had English,' Leanne said, talking over Bob again. 'No. It's Tuesday, it was maths. She loves maths, she wouldn't have missed it.'

'She got on well with Mr Riordan?'

'Oh yes, yes. I think he's her favourite teacher. She... she looks up to him I think. Even walked that dog for them once or twice. Babysitting they called it... Well, they are like babies to people like that, aren't they? Dogs I mean.'

'People like what?' Alison asked.

'Well, you know… gays. Mr Riordan is… well, you know.'

'I think she gets it,' Bob said angrily.

'So Izzy got on well with Mr Riordan,' Alison reiterated.

'Never shut up about him,' Bob said. 'Mr Riordan this, Mr Riordan that… He's the only one she ever showed that bloody maths book of hers to. Like he was the only one who'd ever understand it. Like we were thick.'

'To be fair we didn't understand it,' Leanne said quietly.

'Aye, I know… but still.' He gave a gruff little laugh and squeezed his wife's arm.

Alison interrupted. 'You weren't aware of any disagreement she might have had with him?'

'Mr Riordan? No, none. Like I say, she's always looked up to him.'

Bob Johnson nodded. It was clear this was one thing they agreed on. So why had Izzy stormed out of his class?

'Did Izzy get on with her other teacher too?' Alison asked, thinking of Banks.

'Yes. Like I said, she's a good student.'

'She didn't like that bloody Banks,' Bob said.

'Bob!' Leanne said, her voice outraged. 'You can't say stuff like that. She never said she didn't like him.'

'Called him a waste of space, didn't she? Said he couldn't walk and talk at the same time.'

'She was upset,' Leanne said to Alison. 'She wanted a different teacher. She thought she might do better with a different teacher. Personality clash I think they call it.'

'Yeah, because that fat git basically hasn't got one,' Bob said.

'Mr Banks was her English teacher, right?'

'Yeah.'

'And she didn't like him?'

'Hated him...' Bob began.

'That's not fair,' Leanne said. 'She just wanted to swap classes, that's all. Only it never happened.'

'Did she say why she wanted to leave his class?' Alison asked.

Bob shook his head, Leanne hung hers.

'She just said he wasn't a very good teacher... and there were rumours,' she said.

'Rumours?'

'You know how teenagers are, they said he had favourites, and if you were one of them then you would do alright. If you weren't he could make life very unpleasant. But Izzy has always been a good student, everyone loves her.'

Evidently everyone had not included Simon Banks.

'Had there been any trouble with Mr Banks recently?'

Leanne shook her head.

'She said it was all sorted, and she didn't want to talk about it.' Bob Johnson looked far from convinced.

'Was there ever any suggestion of anything inappropriate?' Alison asked. 'With Banks I mean.'

'You think I'd've let him anywhere near her if there was?' Bob asked. Leanne said nothing. 'Fucking hell, you think it was him?' Bob went on. 'I'll flatten the fat fucker... You think he did stuff to her?'

'No,' Alison said. 'No. Not at all. We just need to ask. We need to find out about everyone Izzy knew.'

Johnson looked suspicious.

'We're just gathering information at this stage,' Alison said, trying to calm him down.

'If it turns out that bastard hurt her you can tell him I'll kill him, right.'

'I think I might pretend I didn't hear that,' Alison said. Bob scowled at her.

'I'd like to look at Izzy's bedroom sometime,' she said.

'Some men have already been and looked. They took her laptop and her tablet.'

'I know, but I just want to get a feel for her, what she was like. You understand.' Leanne stood up as if to show them upstairs; Alison waved her down.

'Not now,' she said. 'You must be tired. I'll come back tomorrow and look. I'll leave you in peace for now.'

She knew it was a stupid phrase. It would be a long time before Leanne Johnson felt at peace, if indeed she ever did again.

'Bloody hell,' Paul said when they were back in the car. 'Talk about denial. Everything is roses and rainbows, isn't it. Izzy loved everyone, everyone loved her. Banks could have had the kids fellating him under the desk and she'd convince herself they were sharpening pencils.'

'Thanks for the imagery,' Alison groaned. 'That will stay with me for days.'

Paul laughed darkly.

'Dad's got a different view, though,' Alison said.

'Yeah, he just wants to rip the balls off anyone who ever went near her,' Paul said. Alison smiled again. She understood that sentiment. God help anyone if they ever tried to hurt her girls.

'And what about this "rumour" that Banks liked to play favourites?' Paul went on. 'That fits with the note and with Banks being dodgy.'

'Maybe,' Alison said, playing devil's advocate, 'but what about this lad the stepfather thinks she was seeing?'

'We sure it was a lad?' Paul asked. 'Couldn't have been someone older and a bit more teachery?'

Alison smiled.

'By all accounts Izzy hated Banks,' she said. 'I can't see him as a secret lover, can you?'

'Nope. But there *is* something going on. It's more than a teacher-pupil relationship. I really didn't like the tone of that note.'

Alison agreed.

'Let's go see what Mr Banks has to say for himself, shall we?'

FIVE

Simon Banks lived in the village of Upper Habdale, about five miles and fifty years outside town. It was a tourist hotspot in summer with the steam railway, quaint tearooms and gentle rambles. In winter it was bleak and inaccessible, with nothing for people to do but mind each other's business.

Banks' house was in the middle of a row of three old farm workers' cottages, close to the beck and half hidden from the road by a ridge of thick gorse bushes. Sheep were grazing on the rough grass outside his gate.

The location was either idyllic or suffocatingly twee depending on your point of view.

Alison walked up the short path to the door and knocked. She was aware of being watched from several of the windows along the street. This was not the sort of village where visitors went unnoticed.

Banks opened the door to them almost immediately and they introduced themselves as police officers. Alison watched his reaction closely. Cautious, surprised but not overly concerned. Far from panicked. He invited them inside.

The interior of the cottage was modern. There was no hint of the character the exterior promised. The ceilings were low but there were no beams and the walls were smoothly plastered. There were no fireplaces. The downstairs space comprised a single large room with the front door opening into the living space, the kitchen to the side and the stairs rising straight up in the centre. Alison liked the look. She wondered how it would work in her own elderly cottage, then dismissed the idea. Nick, her husband, loved character in an old house. He said it was the only reason to put up with the damp and the dodgy electrics and the constant repair bills. He was right, of course. While this open-plan house looked amazing, it wasn't in keeping with the cottage's age and location. And it certainly wasn't cosy.

Alison could see the advantage of an open-plan layout for Banks, though. The man was huge, tall and very overweight. The open-plan layout suited his bulk.

'What's all this about?' Banks asked.

'Just a few questions,' Alison said. 'About a pupil. We were surprised not to catch you at the school.'

'I left straight after lessons ended,' Banks said. 'I usually stay late but...' He offered no further explanation, just shrugged. 'Is one of my pupils in trouble?'

He did not give the impression that he cared about the answer. Indeed, he gave off an air of resignation generally, as if he didn't care about much at all. The air of a man defeated. His shirt was greying and unironed. His hair needed a cut and he had shaved badly that morning, leaving tufts of bristle on his chin and upper lip. He moved as if every step were a great effort.

'We just have a few questions,' Alison said, deliberately vague.

'Who is this about?' he asked. Alison didn't answer.

'Is this your handwriting?' she asked instead, showing him the note to Izzy.

'What?'

'We have reason to believe that this is your handwriting,' she said, handing him the note. She liked 'reason to believe'. People heard it a lot on TV cop shows; it gave her words authority.

'Where did you... Who gave this to you?'

'Did you write the note?'

All the colour had drained from his face. Alison wondered whether he was thinking of lying.

'Yes, but... Did she give it to you?'

'Who?'

'Izzy. Isabella Johnson. Did she give you this note? Has she said...? What has she said?'

'What would she say?' Alison asked, keeping her tone light.

Banks paused, reading the letter closely. Studying it. As if he was trying to decipher its meaning.

'Did Izzy give you this letter?'

Alison wasn't quite ready to answer that. She took the note back from Banks.

'Why did you send it to her? What does it mean?'

'What? Nothing. I just... What has she said?'

'Never mind what Miss Johnson may have said, we'd like an explanation from you, please.'

Banks licked his lips nervously, his fat tongue flicking

out over the pink fleshy chops. Alison found she had to suppress a shudder of revulsion. She kept her gaze neutral and waited for him to answer.

'It's just a note asking her to see me after class,' Banks said at last.

'This is a note asking Izzy to see you after class? Is that what you're saying?'

'Yes. I… Yes?' He made a gesture as if to take the note back, as if he needed to check it over again. Alison shook her head. Taking her time. Sometimes silence had a wonderful effect on people. They liked to fill it. Even if it was to their own detriment.

Simon Banks looked like a man who had something to say. Alison only needed to let the silence stretch between them and wait.

Maybe he even had something to confess. Wouldn't that be something? Case closed. 'And home in time for tea,' as Paul had said.

She waited another second but Banks didn't speak. OK, time for a little push.

'Sergeant Skinner, would you please read the note we found in Izzy Johnson's bag.'

'You found… She didn't give it…?' Banks began but Paul held up his hand for silence as he began to read.

'*Meet me as usual. I can explain everything. Please don't tell anyone.*' When Paul read it aloud it sounded even creepier than it had inside Alison's head. There was a pleading quality to the words. It didn't sound like a communication between teacher and pupil.

'Could you explain that note, please?' There was a hard edge to her voice that pleased her.

Banks shrugged, licking his lips uncertainly again.

'Mr Banks?' she prompted.

'It's just a reminder that we had an appointment… to discuss Wordsworth. She struggles with some of the finer points, symbolism, naturalism… you know the sort of thing. She doesn't really appreciate the Romantic movement. Which is odd because I find teenage girls… you know… they tend to like all that stuff. Byron next term. Girls still love Byron. Nothing new there, I suppose… the original bad boy.' He stopped, aware that he was rambling.

'Meet me as usual?' Paul read again from the note. 'Please don't tell anyone?' Alison waited. Banks said nothing.

'Mr Banks?' She was barely keeping her temper now.

'Sorry. Was that a question?' His smug smile told her he was dying to say something about the syntax of Paul's sentence.

'I'll rephrase that as an interrogative sentence, shall I?' Alison smiled coldly. 'Are you saying that *this* note is nothing more than a request for a pupil to meet you and discuss homework?'

'Yes,' Banks said simply. 'Like I say, I wanted to meet her to discuss…'

'Yes, you said, Wordsworth's poetry. Please explain why you used the phrases "meet me as usual", and "please don't tell anyone"', Alison said calmly. She wanted to add, 'use examples from the text to illustrate your answer', like all her old English exams but she stopped herself.

'I don't understand,' Banks said, his tight smile still stretched across his face, lips pink like pastel slugs.

'The note says, "meet me as usual"', Alison pointed out, knowing that Banks was playing for time. 'Did you usually meet Alison to discuss Wordsworth?'

'Not Wordsworth, no… but to discuss literature. To discuss her work, the course and, well, literature. She's incredibly bright. She'll get an A*, no doubt, but she's also interested in so much more. Not everything in education can be measured in economic terms, you know. Good grades, good jobs all that. Sometimes we teachers still take pleasure in teaching for its own sake. Especially someone bright like Izzy.'

Alison shook her head. He didn't strike her as a man with a passion for teaching, or anything else. There was no fire behind his words. And it didn't explain the tone of that note.

'So you met Izzy regularly? Always at the same time? In the same place?'

'We meet every Monday after school. In my office. I look forward to it actually.' She knew for certain that the last sentence was a lie. Even if everything else was true, Alison could tell Simon Banks did not relish his meetings with Izzy Johnson. His face contorted every time he said her name. It was very clear that Simon Banks did not like Izzy Johnson.

'Did you meet Izzy yesterday?' Paul asked.

'Yesterday?'

'Yes. It was Monday yesterday. Your note said, "meet me as usual".'

'Oh. No. She couldn't make it yesterday. Netball practice I think. I don't remember. She told me in class in the morning.'

'And were you disappointed?' Paul asked.

'Sorry? No, not disappointed. Why would I be disappointed? Plenty of work to get on with.'

'Can anyone confirm that these meetings took place?' Alison asked.

Banks looked suddenly relieved.

'Yes, yes, of course. I spoke to the headmaster before... before I made the arrangement. I mean, alone in a classroom with a female student. Best to be safe... girls say all sorts of things... I wanted it all above board. What has she said, by the way...? I mean why did she give you that note? Has there been any... any suggestion of anything?'

Alison cut across him.

'The last part of your note. You say, "please don't tell anyone". Could you explain that to me?'

'Um... I don't understand. It just means I didn't want her to tell anyone about the meeting.' Paul sighed.

'Oh for fuck's sake,' he said. 'Can I just wallop the bastard and have done with it?' Alison almost laughed. Was he going to play bad cop? The idea was ridiculous.

'Stop being so bloody pedantic,' Paul said. 'We know what "please don't tell anyone" means. It means don't bloody tell anyone. What my DI is asking, as I'm sure you know perfectly well, is why in God's name, if everything was above board and everybody knew about these meetings and you'd passed it all with the headteacher and God and the fucking Dalai Lama for all I know, why were you asking Isabella Johnson not to tell anyone?'

Banks was pale, shaking slightly.

'What has she said?' he asked. 'Has she accused me...?'

'This isn't about what she's said,' Paul bellowed. 'We want to know what the fuck you have to say about it.' Banks looked at Alison, as if hoping she would protect him, as if she would be the voice of reason. No chance. Alison smiled indulgently and waited. Banks breathed.

'Whatever she's said... I can explain... I just...' He paused again.

Alison sensed his panic. Just a little longer and they might reach the moment. That moment when a lie falls apart and the liar realises it's time to tell the truth.

Banks' phone trilled. He took it from his pocket and checked the text automatically.

'Shit,' he said, his face flushing and then turning ashen grey. 'Shit, is this true?' And he fell into a dead faint, hitting the floor with a sickening thud.

'How's the head?' Alison asked five minutes later when Banks was sitting on the sofa with a cup of tea which Paul had reluctantly made.

'Fine. I'm fine. It was just a bump. A shock.' Alison nodded. She had checked Banks' text. It was from Riordan, telling him Izzy was dead. It had gone out from the headteacher to all members of staff. The rumours were circulating and he had taken it on himself to confirm the truth. Or had he wanted to warn Banks specifically about their visit?

'Did you like her?' Alison asked.

'No, I didn't like her.'

Alison was surprised by the honesty. Most people lied when someone died.

'She was a clever girl,' Banks continued. 'But she could be cruel. To the others who didn't get it. To me if I misspoke or made an off-hand remark that she didn't think was quite correct.'

'So why give her extra lessons? She didn't really need them, did she?'

'Like I said before, she was a good student but she could still learn more... There were subtle points...'

'Bullshit,' Paul said quietly. 'No one's buying, Mr Banks. Try again.'

Banks sighed. 'Look, even a clever girl like Izzy can miss some of the subtler points of poetry. Literature, unlike maths, is about more than learning and applying a set of rules. To understand it fully one needs empathy and life experience, both of which Isabella lacked.'

'Oh, I'm sure you wanted to rectify her lack of life experience,' Paul said.

'I don't know what you're trying to say.'

Alison interrupted.

'So, you maintain that the note you sent to Isabella Johnson just referred to extra lessons? A meeting you had arranged to discuss Wordsworth?'

'Yes,' Banks said evenly. 'As I have explained, Izzy was a clever girl but there was a lot I could teach her.'

'I bet there was.' The sneer in Paul's voice was unmistakeable.

'What's that supposed to mean?' Banks asked.

'Extra lessons. Alone in your classroom after hours. She was a very pretty girl.' Banks shook his head.

'That had nothing to do with it... What are you implying?' Alison stepped in, again.

'We're not implying anything, Mr Banks. Simply asking questions.'

'Your colleague seems to be saying...'

'Where were you between one thirty and two thirty this afternoon?' Alison asked.

Banks smiled. Clearly this was a question he could answer.

'I was teaching. I had a double period with my Year 7 class, 7B to be precise.'

'What time was that?'

'Afternoon lessons start at one thirty and as it was a double I had the same children through to three fifteen. Then I had my form class for the last half hour of the day.' He smiled again. Alison remained unsmiling.

'You never saw Izzy Johnson this afternoon?'

'As I say, I was teaching Year 7. Those are eleven- and twelve-year-olds. So no, Isabella Johnson was not amongst them.' Again the smile.

'And you never left the classroom?'

'No.'

Shit. If that were true there was no way he could have killed Izzy. He looked nervous, he was sweating, but he kept eye contact. He could be lying but it was a pretty stupid lie. It would be easy enough to check.

'What was it that you didn't want Izzy to tell anyone? What did she know about you that you didn't want her to know?'

'What? Nothing. What do you mean?'

'Now's a good chance to tell us whatever it is you're hiding, Mr Banks. If it has nothing to do with Izzy's death then we won't take it any further. But we'll find out anyway. You'd be amazed what we uncover in a murder investigation.'

'I'm not hiding anything. It was just a silly note. I've told you it meant nothing... I just didn't want her to tell the others about the extra lessons... Favouritism... You know how girls talk. I... I have nothing to hide.'

Alison smiled.

'We all have things to hide, Mr Banks. Even if they're not illegal things.' She stood up.

'Thanks for your time. We'll be going now.'

The relief on Banks' face was palpable.

'You won't object if we take your laptop, will you? Just routine. We're checking everyone who had contact with Izzy.'

'What... I... Why? I never... I don't contact my students via email.'

'It won't take us long to check then.' Alison smiled. 'You'll have it back in a day or two.' She had already slipped on latex gloves, lifted the laptop and was putting it into an evidence bag which she had fished out of her handbag.

'What? Don't you need a warrant?'

'Do I?' Alison asked, looking puzzled. 'I just want to take a look... eliminate you from our inquiries. Quicker it's done quicker I'm out of your hair.'

'OK. OK.' Banks slumped into his chair. 'Just be careful with it. I've not had it long.' Alison left Paul to give Banks a receipt for the laptop and look about to see if there were any other electronics worth looking at, while she went out to the car to make a quick phone call.

She was smiling when Paul got into the car.

'What?' he asked.

'Alibi's bullshit,' Alison said.

'What?'

'I just called Riordan and, according to the school timetable, Banks shares his Tuesday afternoon class with another teacher. And today wasn't Banks' turn to teach. He had an admin afternoon.'

'So he lied to us?'

'Looks that way. Although Riordan said it's just possible he swapped the session. Apparently the teachers sometimes do that.'

'You want to go back in and have another talk to him?' Paul asked. Alison thought for a moment, then shook her head.

'Nah. If he lied to us let's let him think he got away with it. We can double-check the alibi in the morning, then we can go in guns blazing if the dick really has been lying to us.'

'So what now?'

'Let's go see Andrea Mills, shall we? See if she saw anything important when she found the body.'

'Let's hope she saw a big fat man with blood on his hands, then we really can nail the bastard.'

Alison smiled.

'Glad to see you're going into this with an open mind,' she said.

SIX

Another house, another cup of tea. Andrea Mills was sitting on the sofa looking exhausted while Paul helped her husband, David, make tea in the kitchen. Alison watched Andrea sympathetically, recognising the adrenaline crash. After the shock of finding Izzy's body, Andrea probably felt like she had run a marathon. She had tried to stand up to greet them but even that effort had been too great.

Alison asked as gently as possible for a recount of the events of that afternoon, but before Andrea could gather her thoughts a young man came into the room, followed reluctantly by a girl of twelve or thirteen.

'This is Dominic and Mary,' Andrea said, giving a weak smile. 'They're just heading out to their grandmother's for the night.' The young man looked as if he might protest.

'I don't want Mary here for this,' Andrea said firmly, cutting him off.

'God, Mum, I'm not a little kid,' the girl whined.

'Please,' Andrea said, still addressing her son. He nodded.

'Come on, Mary.'

'Bloody hell, OK. I'll go die of boredom at bloody Nana's. God.'

They waited until the youngsters had left.

'Sorry,' Andrea said, 'I just… I don't want them to see me like this. I'm a mess. Mary's sensitive no matter what she says. So I said right off, you go to Nana's.' She was babbling. Another side effect of shock.

'I'm sure you're doing the right thing,' Alison said. 'There are some things you just don't want the kids to see.'

'That's what I said to David. Best they're not here. He wanted us all together. But I said I just didn't want… I mean tomorrow I'll be right as rain, but just for today…'

Alison nodded, accepting the myth that it would all be OK tomorrow.

'OK, Andrea… may I call you Andrea?' The woman nodded, barely moving her head. 'OK. I know it's been a long day, and I know you've already told someone about what happened but I need you to tell me, really clearly and really slowly, what happened this afternoon. And I need you to tell me every little thing you can think of, no matter how stupid or pointless or irrelevant you might think it is.'

'OK.'

'You were out running, I understand?' She nodded. 'What time did you set out?'

'I don't know. Sorry. I've been trying to think but… I even looked at my watch up on the Beamsleigh. I remember looking at it, but I don't remember what time it was. Isn't that stupid?'

'It happens,' Alison said soothingly. 'Do you have *any*

idea what time you set off? Did you watch the one o'clock news maybe?'

'God no, I never watch telly during the day. But it must have been after two when I set off because I'd been at work. I got home and had lunch, washed up, changed the beds and hung them out. So probably more like quarter past or twenty past, even.'

'OK. Let's say between two and two twenty, does that sound about right?' Andrea nodded.

'Do you usually run at that time? Most days?' Andrea shook her head.

'I call it running. It's jogging really. Maybe not even jogging. I try to go three times a week but it's probably more like two and sometimes not even that.' She patted her slight belly gently. 'Dave's really into his fitness. I mean he swims and he cycles and sometimes I just think... well... you know... you get a bit older and you think, what does he see in me? And I just... well, I suppose I think maybe a bit of jogging will hold back the years.' She half smiled at her own vanity. Alison smiled too.

'So where did you go when you left here?'

'I always just run round the Beamsleigh. I go up Forest Hill, along Beamsleigh Park and over the stile at the top. Then round the mound.'

'And that's what you did today?'

'Yeah. Only I went the back way. I usually go round the front, through the park, but I fancied a quieter run today.'

'And did you see anyone?'

'No. I mean not on the Beamsleigh. I saw someone down on the riverside path heading into town. A woman I think... but I'm short-sighted and I didn't have my contacts in.'

'It could have been me,' Alison said. 'I wasn't on duty this aft and I walked that way. Anyone else?'

'I saw Alice Davis in her car heading up Beamsleigh Park. She lives up there.' There was a note of envy in her voice.

'And that was it? What about once you were on Beamsleigh Hill?'

'Didn't see a soul. With it being such a nice day and after all the rain we've had I thought there'd be folk up there. But like I say, I took the back path. It's always quieter that way.'

'And you didn't see anyone? No one at all?'

'No. Oh, hold on a minute… yeah, I did see someone. But they were a way off and I couldn't make them out. Just coming off the back of the mound as I got to the two stiles. They went over the fence and took that cut-through that goes up to the Cawpers.' Alison nodded. It wasn't a well-used path, just a meander really from the Cawpers housing estate onto the hill. Kids could go that way from town into school, but the route over the stile was quicker.

'Not many folk go that way,' Alison said.

'Well, no,' Andrea said. 'I thought that. Then I remembered that they've put the CCTV up at the back of the school – trying to catch the kids smoking – so I suppose anyone who wanted to avoid that might go the long way round.'

'Did it look like a kid going back to school?' Alison asked.

'I don't know. My eyesight's shocking, like I say. Could have been a kid. I didn't really take much notice and then it went out of my mind, because… well, it was right after that that I saw her.' Her voice dropped away to a whisper.

'This person you saw, were they coming from where you found the body?' Andrea shook her head.

'I don't know. They could have been. But there's a path that way into town, and one onto the river path, so I don't know.'

Alison nodded.

The Beamsleigh was a warren of paths connecting to the main loop. It was possible for someone to come round the hill as Andrea described and not cross paths with Izzy Johnson at all.

Possible. Not likely.

'You don't think they had anything to do... to do with... You don't think I saw...?' Again her voice died away.

'I don't know,' Alison said truthfully.

'I don't think they can have had anything to do... I mean I don't think they could have... have hurt her or been involved or anything.'

'Why do you say that?' Alison asked.

'He was walking,' Andrea said, as if explaining it to herself as well as to Alison. 'He or she I mean, but I think it was a he. He was walking and then he hopped over the fence... and the way he did that it was sort of... sort of joyful. The way he walked it was... calm, I suppose. It didn't look like someone running away or hiding or anything.'

Alison nodded, although she knew better than to trust a fleeting impression from a witness who admitted she had barely seen anything.

Andrea suddenly put her hand to her mouth as if she was about to be sick.

'Oh God, what if... what if it was... what if I saw the person who...?' She couldn't finish the sentence.

'We don't know who you saw,' Alison said calmly. 'It

could have been totally innocent, as you say – a teenager bunking off school or someone from the Cawpers estate out for a walk. Either way I need you to give me as detailed a picture as you can, please.'

'I don't know. He was wearing a hoody, like they all do. I think it was dark, maybe black. He wasn't close enough to see his face.'

'Was the hood up?'

'No.'

'Hair colour.'

'Brown I think.'

'Was he black or white?'

'Must have been white. I didn't notice, but I would have if he was black, wouldn't I? I mean, you do round here, don't you? There's only the Patels and that new family, Gordon I think they're called.'

Alison nodded again.

'Any idea of height? Taller than you?'

'I couldn't tell… only… well, maybe quite tall because he leapt over the fence and it didn't look hard.'

'Fat or thin?' Alison asked, thinking of the bulk of Simon Banks.

'I don't know… not fat definitely.'

'Anything else you noticed?' Alison asked, hiding her disappointment. 'Shoes or boots? Was he carrying anything? Smoking? Anything like that.'

'I couldn't see, I'm sorry. I wasn't really paying attention.'

'Not to worry,' Alison reassured her. 'Whoever it was will probably come forward on their own when they hear we're looking for them. Almost certainly a teenager, like you said.' Andrea nodded.

Paul and David Mills came back into the room. Paul gave a half-nod of his head. The shorthand told Alison that he had talked to Mills and nothing unusual had leapt out of the conversation.

'OK, we're nearly done,' Alison said, taking the tea David Mills offered her and blowing across the surface of it.

'Can you tell me about finding the body? What exactly happened?'

'I came round the mound and she was lying there. And then I saw the blood and her throat. And I knew.'

'Did you touch her at all? Check that she was dead?'

'No, I… Oh God, I didn't even think to help her. God, could I have helped her?'

'No, no, not at all. You did the right thing in not touching her,' Alison said. 'Absolutely the right thing. She was definitely dead before you got there. There was nothing you could have done.'

She had no idea if this was true or not but Andrea Mills had called an ambulance and the girl had been dead when it arrived. If there was anything Andrea could have done differently it was irrelevant now. Izzy was dead. Andrea feeling guilty wouldn't change that.

'What did you do then? After you found her?'

'I called an ambulance. I didn't really know who to call. I had to go back towards the road a bit to get a signal. Then when I was on the line I realised I needed the police too. Then I went out onto the road and waited. The woman on the phone told me to do that, go out onto the road so I could show the ambulance man where to go. Only it was a woman, an ambulance woman. But you know what I mean.'

'Did you recognise her?'

'No, not really. I think it was an ambulance out of Milbury, so you know I didn't...'

'No, sorry... not the paramedic, the girl. Did you recognise her?'

'I think it was Izzy Johnson. I didn't look closely, but it looked like. Was it Izzy?'

'Yes, I'm afraid it was.'

Andrea shook her head sadly.

'Did you know her?'

'Not really. But she's a bit of a star up at the school. Top at every subject, always winning awards. Good swimmer too. Always in the newsletter. Mary talks about her a bit. But Mary's a few years younger than her so... And Dom's older, away at uni...'

'I was her swimming coach for a while,' Mr Mills put in. 'It was a lot of years ago. I used to teach the ten- and eleven-year-olds. Probably not relevant but in the interests of full disclosure...'

'Thank you, Mr Mills. Do you know who would coach her now?'

'No idea, I'm afraid. I left the club when Dominic quit swimming.'

'When was that?' Alison asked.

'Oh, a good few years ago.'

'Dom's at Cambridge now,' Andrea interrupted. 'He's doing really well... Just home for a reading week... I was planning to make it really special... and...'

Her husband shot her a look that silenced her.

'Sorry...' she said, head bowed.

Alison smiled her reassurance.

'That's all for now,' she said, making her way to the door. 'You've been really helpful.'

Definitely not fat. The phrase rang in her head. Whoever Andrea had seen they had been definitely not fat and they had leapt a fence with ease. Whoever she had seen it hadn't been Banks.

Whoever he was, they needed to find him.

SEVEN

'Get a call out for whoever Andrea saw on the hill, will you?' Alison said to Paul after they left the Mills' house. 'Then call it a day. I'll brief the whole team tomorrow. We'll check out Banks' supposed alibi then. Talk to Izzy's friends. See if there *was* a boyfriend on the scene.'

Paul nodded, making a note. Her car was still on the hill where she had left it that afternoon; Paul pulled up behind it.

'You fancy a drink tonight?' he asked, not looking at her.

'I can't... I need to get back for...'

'Just a quick half?'

'I can't... I don't think I should.' She hated that there was almost a stammer in her voice. She should just say, 'No. I don't want to.'

'We ever gonna talk about this?'

She didn't reply. They sat for a moment in the parked car, neither of them moving. It felt both intimate and distant. Alison wanted to speak but the silence remained. Really there was nothing to say. Or rather there was too much to say and it was too difficult. She wished she had never gone to that stupid bloody conference in Harrogate, had never got drunk. But there would have been other conferences, other chances to get drunk. It would have happened sometime, somewhere. She thought for a moment that she might broach the subject, but she had never been good at those sorts of conversations. The sort that started with 'We need to talk...'

'I want the CCTV from behind the school checked out,' she said instead. 'There's a chance it caught Izzy heading out or someone else heading back in.'

Paul seemed to accept the change of subject.

'You hoping for a big sweaty bloke looking out of breath on that tape?' he asked.

'It'd be a start.' Alison smiled ruefully.

Another pause.

'I just want to say...'

She cut him off.

'I'll see you at eight thirty tomorrow,' she said, dismissing him.

He looked at her with an expression of loss that was almost unbearable. She got out of the car and closed the door.

She got into her own car and watched him drive away in her rear-view mirror.

A sudden bang on the window made the glass judder.

'Bloody hell, you made me jump,' Alison said, leaning over and winding down the window.

It was her friend Milly.

'Sorry.' Milly looked amused and not at all sorry. 'Look,

can I have a word?' Alison suppressed a sigh. She was tired and wanted to get home but she opened the passenger door and Milly got in.

'I was gonna call you tonight actually, but then I saw your car...'

'What is it?' Alison said, trying to keep the exhaustion from her voice. Milly was a good friend but when she was working she liked to keep working. She didn't like to be distracted by domestic problems or her social life.

'You had a bad day? God, silly question, of course you have...' Milly had been at the café with Alison when the call came in that afternoon about a body. She would have all the information by now. It was that sort of town and Milly was that sort of woman. 'I don't know how you do your job. I was saying to Carla, I just don't know how you sleep at night, I mean seeing what you must see and... well... everything.'

'It's a job, Milly. Pays the bills.'

'God, but still... I thought I'd had a day of it. We had a cat run over. I was telling the girls after you left the café. That's why I was late. Poor thing ran in the road.'

Milly was a receptionist at the local vet's. Her stories usually made Alison laugh but she wasn't in the mood today.

Still she asked dutifully, 'Is it OK? The cat?'

'God yes. Silly beggar just got scraped paws and a bit of a bash. Luckily the driver saw her in time. But I mean, put your cat in a proper basket when you come to the vet, right? Those wicker things are cute and everything... but it just leapt out. Not that I blame it really, bloody yappy dog. Scared the hell out of everyone.' Alison smiled, despite herself. It was good to be absorbed, momentarily, in the melodrama of someone else's life.

'I hate yappy dogs,' she said.

'God, me too. I could have killed the bloody thing.'

'Maybe not the best way to help your career though, eh?' Alison said.

Milly laughed.

'No, "dog murderer" would not look great on the CV. It was a total pain that bloody dog, though – making the cat run out and get itself nearly killed. Making me late for coffee. Bloody animal. And I mean it was a *bloody* dog, though. I mean literally... it was covered in blood. Poor thing. I'd've felt sorry for it but it wouldn't bloody shut up. Yap yap yap.'

'What had happened to it?' Alison asked, laughing despite herself at Milly's impression of the dog.

'Caught in barbed wire or some sort of rabbit trap. I don't think it was badly injured but there was loads of blood. The owner was drenched in it – probably had to chuck his clothes away. Shame because they were lovely clothes, and he was a lovely man, to be honest. One of those proper gorgeous men, if you know what I mean. Still, all that blood. I was glad I was leaving to meet you lot. I didn't fancy cleaning that all up.'

Alison nodded.

'But compared to your job, I mean... I couldn't believe it when you got that call. I mean, something like that in Penbury.'

They were back where Alison didn't want to be. Talking about the case.

'I can't really talk about it,' she said.

'I know yeah... only after you left we were talking. And then when we found out who she was, well, I said I should

tell you and Carla said you'd probably already know but…
well, here you are so…'

'What is it?' Alison asked.

'I was at school with Leanne, you know.'

'Leanne Johnson?'

'Yeah. I mean we were never friends, she's a couple of
years older. To be honest she was always a bit up herself,
liked the sound of her own voice, you know? But I'd never
wish any of this on anyone. And after all the other crap she's
had to deal with.'

'What crap?' Alison asked, properly listening now.

'That's what I wanted to tell you. You know her
first husband was Andy Steel?' There was a breathless
excitement to the way Milly said the name, as if it should
mean something to Alison. It didn't.

'He's Izzy's real dad. I mean Bob Johnson's no catch but
a damn sight better than Andy Steel.'

'Sorry, I don't know…'

'He was the coach driver.'

Milly delivered her bombshell, waiting for the explosion
of understanding that didn't come.

'Coach driver?' Alison asked, puzzled.

'Yeah. I mean, if it was me I'd've moved. There was a lot
of hate. But Leanne stuck it out. And I reckon people were
finally starting to forget. Only maybe not.'

'Milly, what are you talking about?' Alison asked. 'Izzy's
dad was a coach driver?'

'God, you don't know, do you? He was the one driving
the bus. You know… the crash. The Whitby crash? He was
the one driving the school bus. Most people in this town
will never forgive him.'

'Oh my God,' Alison said, understanding at last.

'Was I right to tell you?'

'Yes. God yes.'

When she walked through her front door ten minutes later it was to the smell of cooking. Nick came out of the kitchen.

'I made a casserole,' he said. 'Wasn't sure what time you'd be back.' She fought off a feeling of guilt. She should have rung. She searched Nick's face for a hidden criticism but there was none. He was just telling her he had made a casserole. It made the guilt worse.

Nick had always done most of the domestic chores and family stuff. He had wanted children more than she had and his job was less demanding. She told herself that as long as the kids were cared for it didn't matter who did what. She fought the notion that she was a bad mother. She wasn't going to go down that route. Her recent conversation with Milly made her think of that crash. Life could be so short; sometimes she wondered if she should spend more time with the kids. She pushed the thought aside. They had Nick. It was arrogant to think they needed her too.

'I got caught up,' she said. It was not an explanation or an apology.

'I know.' He kissed her on the forehead. 'Mabel's just gone to bed, why don't you give her a kiss while I dish up? Bea's just getting a shower, then I said she could watch the end of *Animal Killers* before bed. If we're quick we could have tea in peace before she reappears.'

Alison smiled.

'I don't deserve you,' she said.

'You're absolutely right,' Nick grinned, 'but you got lucky so you might as well make the most of it.'

Alison went quietly up the stairs.

'That you, Mum?' came the voice of her eldest daughter from the bedroom.

'I thought you were supposed to be taking a shower,' Alison said, going into the room.

'I'm just going.' Bea was pulling her sweater over her head as she spoke. 'You'll never guess what Max did in class today… it was so funny.'

Alison smiled as she listened to some story about a loud burp and an outraged teacher and laughed in almost the right places. She suddenly felt exhausted, happy to be home. She kissed Bea and hugged her.

'Get a shower and we can snuggle for half an hour before bed,' she said.

'Tough day?' Beatrice asked.

'Not the best,' Alison said, smiling.

'I'll give you a big hug in a minute then.'

'Thanks, darling.'

As Beatrice crossed the landing to the bathroom Alison went into her younger daughter's room. Mabel was already asleep, her small body curled around the large teddy bear she insisted on squeezing into her bed every night. Alison watched her for a moment, listening to her breathing. Her face was angelic, as the faces of young children are in sleep. Alison bent to kiss her forehead and Mabel stirred slightly.

'Night night, darling,' Alison murmured.

'Nigh.'

Alison felt relief, as she always did, in seeing her children home and safe and happy. She remembered as a child lying awake in bed waiting for her mother to come home. There had been no soft kisses and tucking into bed, but she had always felt a sense of relief knowing that her mother was there and that danger had been averted one more time.

Back downstairs Nick had dished out the casserole and poured her a glass of wine.

'Want to talk about it?' he asked.

'A girl from the comp. Body found on Beamsleigh Hill.'

'Murdered?'

Alison smiled sadly and nodded.

'Shit.'

'Yeah,' Alison agreed. Nick squeezed her hand briefly and after that they ate in near silence.

He understood that she didn't always want to talk.

'I've cancelled the hotel for tomorrow night,' he said after a while. 'Mum's still coming to help with the kids if that's OK. I thought I might as well just go to work, save the holidays for another time.'

For a moment Alison was confused, then she remembered the start of her day. She had been consumed by cleaning and packing, getting ready for the two nights away she had planned with Nick.

'Shit, Nick, I'm sorry... I forgot. I... I could probably still get time off... probably... I could ring Rogers in the morning, reassign the case. It's probably not too late.' She had said probably too many times. Nick smiled.

'If you were going to do that you would have done it straight away,' he said.

'No, really, I could sort it,' she said, shaking her head.

'It's OK. Honestly.'

'I really don't deserve you,' she said again. He laughed and gave her a one-handed hug as he got up to clear the table.

They had just finished the washing-up, Alison washing and Nick drying, when Beatrice came down from her shower. She snuggled beside Alison for an hour watching cute animals being chased and killed by other cute animals. 'It's the circle of life, Mum,' she said whenever Alison complained that her favourite programme was a bit gruesome. Not for the first time Alison cursed Elton John and the bloody Lion King.

She squeezed Bea extra hard as she said goodnight. She wanted to freeze time, hold on just a little tighter, keep childhood going just a little longer, even as she knew it was time to let go.

They went up to bed early; Alison checked her email one last time while Nick locked up and checked on the girls. She often told herself she was going to stop checking her emails after nine at night. She had read somewhere that being too connected to work was ruining family life. Still she checked. Bad habit. Bad wife. Bad mother.

There was nothing important. Holly had confirmed that the 999 call had been made at 2.36pm, which tied in with what Andrea Mills had said. Jenny McBride had examined the body. Alison just glanced at the summary.

COD strangulation with a ligature, probably wire.

Significant force used, causing the skin at the throat to tear. Significant blood loss but ultimately asphyxiation had killed her.

Sexual activity shortly before death but no indication that force was used.

Stomach contents included undigested pills, being sent for further analysis.

She closed her laptop as Nick came into the room. He

stroked her hair when they got into bed, the way he used to when they first met.

As usual, she was asleep within minutes, so when her phone rang, waking felt like surfacing from deep, deep water.

'Paul, what's happened?'

There was a pause on the other end of the line. Alison could hear noise in the background – music and talking.

'Paul...'

'Sorry, I... Can we talk?' He sounded drunk.

'We can talk in the morning,' Alison said, making her voice professional, aware of Nick beside her in the bed.

'I just wanted to say... I wanted to say sorry and... and...' She cut him off, afraid of what else he might want to say.

'Tomorrow at work. Eight thirty. I'll see you then.'

'Yes... it's just...'

'Paul, it's the middle of the night,' she said firmly.

'I need to talk to you.' His words slurred drunkenly. 'Why won't you... You won't even look at me... It's like... like you're ashamed of me.'

Alison sighed in exasperation.

'I am not talking about this now. I'll see you in the morning. Eight thirty sharp.' She ended the call before he could say more.

'Your other man?' Nick asked sleepily.

'Work,' Alison said.

Bad wife. Bad mother.

'What else would it be?' Nick smiled, and turned away. He was snoring again in moments.

Alison lay awake for a long time, staring at the ceiling and trying not to think.

EIGHT

Alison made her way to Milbury police station early the next morning. She had not worked there since she was in uniform and it felt odd to be back. As part of the North Yorkshire Major Incident Unit she was used to being deployed wherever she was needed but she had never been this close to home before.

Milbury was a little over five miles from Penbury, a very similar town but slightly larger, slightly richer, slightly more urban. There was a police station in Penbury but it was mostly unmanned except for the occasional PCSO. The call had come from the Chief Super to use Milbury because it was better resourced. Alison had felt huge relief. Milbury was close to home but Penbury *was* home and the case was already closer than she would have liked.

Paul was waiting for her outside the station.

'Morning,' he said. His voice was quiet and his eyes looked a little red. Ordinarily she would have teased him about the late night and laying off the booze, but not today.

'Coffee,' she said, holding out a paper cup to him. It was

a gesture of truce and she thought Paul could probably do with an extra caffeine hit.

'Thanks.' He sipped the coffee and watched her over the top of the cup. 'About last night…' he began.

'We're not going to talk about it now,' she said firmly.

'Are we ever going to…?'

'We've got a murder case to concentrate on, let's focus on that, shall we?' He nodded. Another sip of coffee.

They walked into the station together.

Alison had brought pastries from the local bakery and she distributed them amongst the staff as she said her hellos and introduced herself to those she didn't know. It was a pain in the arse to suddenly have to share your space with an outside team; most people were good about it, but sugar always helped.

'Your lot are in the meeting room,' Bill Murphy told her.

'Thanks,' she said, holding out the cake box.

He patted his rounded belly. 'I shouldn't,' he said as he reached for a pastry.

'The DCI wants to see you,' Jack Kent told Alison before she was even inside the room. He was smiling, always happy to be the bearer of bad news. Alison suppressed a sigh and squared her shoulders.

'Where is he?'

'He commandeered an office. Third on the left.' Commandeered would be the right word. Chief Inspector Alistair Rogers had never been one to ask nicely. Alison had worked for him for almost ten years and could count the number of times she had seen him smile on the fingers of one hand. He was a decent enough man but he enjoyed nothing more than being bad tempered. He liked Alison under his direct gaze, otherwise she was accused of 'fannying around'.

'Doing your makeup, having your hair done, crying somewhere because you've chipped a nail...' Alison overlooked the sexism because he was equally vile to her male colleagues. They were accused of being 'off ogling women, sneaking a quick drink or having a wank in the bathroom'. She wondered how he thought they ever got any work done if they were all so incompetent.

'So, you've decided to grace us with your presence,' he said when she entered his office. 'Now you're here, any chance of you doing some work today?'

Alison knew better than to answer. All Rogers required was an audience; she was not expected to respond.

'Where exactly are we on this case?' he asked.

'I'm just about to brief the team...'

'And do you want a medal?' Rogers interrupted. 'I don't have time to listen to what you're *about* to do, which undoubtedly involves acres of arsing about, I'm here to tell you this is getting a lot of media. And that means we need to get on with it.'

'Yes, sir,' Alison said, keeping her voice polite. *I was about to get on with it before you called me in here for this pointless conversation.* The thought went unvoiced.

'OK, so why are you standing about in here? Get on and sort it out. Brief the team and for God's sake, Dobson, sort this one. The last thing we need is the effing media.'

Alison left his office, shaking her head, absolutely none the wiser as to why she had been called in to see him at all. Paul was convinced Rogers' aim in life was to deliver at least three bollockings a day, so he liked to get one in good and early. There were days when Alison wasn't sure that was a joke.

She walked into the meeting room. The team were gathered and Paul was handing out folders with all the pertinent information. Holly Webster was earnestly asking questions, referring to her folder and to the whiteboard as she spoke. She was the youngest on the team, a DC not long out of college and keen to follow the rules. Alison thought she might make a decent officer once she learned to use some of her own initiative and started to trust herself. Mick and Miles were more at the other end of the career path, waiting it out for retirement. They did their jobs but weren't consumed by them. Alison often wished that she was more like them. Then there was Jack Kent. Alison knew Jack was merely tolerating his time on her team. The move to the major incident team was a calculated one, designed to get him a breadth of experience so he could move on to bigger and better things. Kent reminded Alison of her younger self. Ambitious and certain that he was right. He wasn't a bad man. He'd work harder than anyone, as long as the work was *seen*. As long as he knew he was earning brownie points with the brass then he would do whatever it took.

He had no imagination, though. For that alone Alison found she couldn't like him. And she knew he had no respect for her. She suspected he knew all about her past. He was the sort of man who would have googled her. He treated her with outward courtesy but there was something close to contempt in his eyes. It was as if her past clung to her like an ancient smell, and he couldn't fail to detect the taint. Still, he was a useful copper and she had dealt with worse contempt all her life.

'OK. Let's get to it,' she said briskly. They all turned to her. 'Isabella Johnson, known as Izzy. Found dead yesterday afternoon at approximately two thirty by a jogger on Beamsleigh Hill in Penbury.'

'Bit close to home this one, eh, boss?' Mick said.

'You have no idea, Mick,' she said. 'The jogger's name was Andrea Mills. Local woman, runs up that way a couple or three times a week. We've already talked to her. Only other person she saw up there was someone in a hoody. She said she thought it was a teenager, but when pressed she couldn't be sure and she didn't see a face. Whoever it was hopped over the fence before she reached them, then she rounded the corner and saw the body.'

Holly's hand was in the air.

'Holly?'

'Sorry, boss, but I don't know the area. You say the body was found on a hill. Isn't that a bit exposed? Visible I mean?'

Alison shook her head. 'Sorry, Holz,' she said, taking up a marker and drawing a rough plan of the area on the whiteboard. 'When I say Beamsleigh Hill I mean this whole area. It's an old Roman site. The mound in the centre has been used to send signals since the Middle Ages. They light bonfires on top of it and there's a whole series of them across the country.'

'They lit them for the royal wedding a couple of years ago,' Mick put in.

'The road here, Beamsleigh Park Road, ends at the bottom of the hill, see?' Holly nodded.

'The path Andrea Mills took actually skirts around the hill itself. She went clockwise, towards the school and then around the back of the old mound. There's a couple of stiles here, where the path splits, left to go along to the school, right to continue around the hill. Andrea turned right. It's actually a little warren of paths up there: some go to town, to the school, to the Cawpers. Most of them don't climb the hill at all.'

Holly was still frowning.

'What is it?' Alison asked.

'Sorry, boss, but when you say the Cawpers do you mean the Mistletoe estate? There's no Cawpers on my map.'

Alison laughed.

'Yeah, sorry. I forgot they call it Mistletoe now. They've built some new houses, hence the name change, but mostly it's an ex-council estate. Been there since after the war.'

'Is it rough?'

'Rough by Penbury standards but mostly just the odd bit of dealing, nothing very serious.' Holly nodded again, making a note in her folder.

Alison went back to discussing Andrea Mills.

'So as I said, Andrea went up Beamsleigh Hill. She was at the two stiles when she saw someone. They were coming from her right. But there's really no way to know where they were going or indeed where exactly they had come from. Most likely it was someone taking a back route into the school but they could have been going into the Cawpers, or just out walking and about to double-back into town. And equally they could have come from anywhere; they may not necessarily have come from where Izzy was found. Even though I said up on the hill, the body was actually found round the back, at the furthest point from the river, the town, the road and the school.'

'So it's out of the way?' Holly asked.

'Yes and no,' Alison admitted. 'It's not visible from the road or the school but people walk their dogs there and kids bunk off school all the time – nip out for a quick fag or a snog. You know how it is.'

She caught a glimpse of Holly's face that told her no, Holly didn't know how it was. Holly had almost certainly been a perfect student.

'Right,' Holly said, a slight flush on her face. 'Sorry to be dense.'

'It's not dense at all,' Alison said. 'I said she was on a hill, it's natural to think that means she's on high ground. It's just what people call it locally. Up on Beamsleigh Hill. But a jury would think like you do so I'm glad you pointed it out.' Holly looked pleased.

'The location's been bothering me actually, because it's not exactly the sort of place you'd plan a murder.'

'Spontaneous then?' Mick asked. 'Could it have been an assault gone wrong?' Alison shook her head.

'Izzy had a blow to the face and a blow to the back of her head. Most likely she was hit in the face and banged her head on the way down, but that's to be confirmed. That could have been spur of the moment, of course, but it wasn't cause of death. COD was ligature strangulation. Whatever was used was thin and hard enough to cut into her throat. No weapon has yet been found.'

'So they brought it with them and took it away?' Mick said. They all knew that meant premeditation.

Alison continued.

'Initial examination of the body found Izzy had had sex not long before she died. No obvious sign of force but we all know that doesn't mean force wasn't used. Also there were some sort of pills in her system but as yet we're not sure what they were.'

'Could they be prescription?'

'Could be, although Jenny McBride didn't recognise them. We'll check with her GP. You can do that, Holz. And find out if she was on the pill too, would you?'

'Sure thing,' Holly said eagerly.

'Anything useful at the scene?' This was Jack Kent.

'Not so far. It had rained more or less non-stop for a week so the ground was muddy, churned up. Loads of people walk their dogs up there, lots and lots of disturbed ground but hard to tell what's relevant.'

'What about Izzy? What do we know about her?'

'Paul?' Alison said, sitting down to let him speak.

'Seventeen years old. Gifted student and sporty. Not a future Olympian or anything just a schoolgirl athlete. She was predicted to get top grades in all her subjects and she was an Oxbridge candidate.'

'Shame,' Jack Kent put in.

'Why's that?' Alison asked, letting her irritation show.

'Well, all that potential. A kid with a bright future.'

'And if she'd been stupid we wouldn't care, is that it? If she was ordinary no one would miss her?'

'I didn't mean...'

'Carry on, Paul,' Alison said dismissively.

'Izzy was last seen at about two o'clock in her maths class. Apparently she had a somewhat heated discussion with Mr Riordan, her Maths teacher. This was unusual behaviour by all accounts. She stormed out of the class.'

'The school didn't look for her?' This was Jack Kent again.

'Apparently sixth formers are entitled to leave the school during the day,' Paul said. 'So no one was going to chase after her.'

'Did she have her bag with her when she was found?' Holly asked.

'Had her bag and her purse but no mobile phone.'

'So robbery's a possibility but unlikely?' Holly said.

Alison nodded.

'We can't rule out sexual assault,' Jack interrupted, as if to dismiss Holly's opinion. 'Just because it didn't look rough doesn't mean... There are other ways to force... A knife to the throat... or...'

'Now, lad, don't give away all your seduction secrets,' Mick laughed.

Paul cut across him. 'Like the boss said, we're not ruling out sexual assault just yet.'

'There was no sign of a condom being used,' Alison said. 'Doesn't mean anything much... but if Izzy wasn't on the pill and there's no other evidence of contraceptive use, consensual sex looks less likely. You know the drill, so far nothing's being ruled out.'

'She got a boyfriend? You talk to him yet?'

'Mum mentioned a boy called Dan Humphreys. He's next on the list thanks, Mick,' Alison said, smiling.

'Sorry, boss, don't mean to teach you to suck eggs, but you know as well as me that a young girl, out in a field like that... Chances are it's sexual. And most likely someone she knows.'

'I know,' she said solemnly. 'Tell them about the note, Paul.'

'When we searched her bag we found a note along the lines of "I can explain, meet me as usual, don't tell anyone".'

'Was it from the boyfriend?' Mick asked, leafing through the document folder until he found his copy of the note.

'It was from Simon Banks, her English teacher,' Paul said.

'You think they were having an affair?' Holly asked.

Alison felt herself shudder.

'He's not a prime candidate for a schoolgirl crush,' she said. 'But it is a possibility. He denied it, said the note was about meeting for extra lessons.'

'Bullshit,' said Miles.

'I know, but if you just read the words there's nothing explicitly to say it wasn't a legitimate meeting.'

'Alibi?' Mick asked.

'He claims he was teaching at the time,' Paul said.

'Claims?'

'He shares a class with another teacher,' Alison explained. 'According to the schedule she should have been teaching yesterday not Banks. It was his afternoon for marking and paperwork apparently. Obviously we need to check that out.'

'Bloody dumbass lie to tell if he is lying,' Miles said. 'I mean, it's gonna take us all of ten minutes to check.'

'Haven't you heard?' Alison asked. 'The police are idiots and they never check anything you say so any old lie will do.'

They all laughed.

'Assuming he's not lying,' Miles went on, 'does it definitely rule him out? There's no question over time of death? No way he could have killed her before or after class?'

Alison shook her head.

'Not really,' she said. 'Even without the coroner's report,

time of death is pretty certain. Izzy left the school not long after two and she was found at around half past. The 999 call came in at two thirty-six to be precise. Pretty narrow window. If Banks was teaching…'

'So who else have we got?' Miles asked.

'No one yet,' Alison said. 'We need to find out who Andrea Mills saw up there. Could be our guy, could be a witness. We also need to check out this Dan Humphreys. If he is Izzy's boyfriend he could have been up there with her yesterday. Stepdad seemed to think there was another lad on the scene too. Someone less savoury. Not the type you introduce to your parents.'

'Any idea who?' Kent asked.

'Nope. We're waiting on DNA from the semen found on Izzy's body but if it's some teenage boyfriend then he's not gonna be in the system. And it'll take a week at least.'

There was a collective nod. Everyone understood DNA analysis took time.

'You're chasing the CCTV from the back of the school, aren't you, Holz?' Alison asked.

'Yeah. It's held centrally over at Northallerton apparently. Their system's down but as soon as they locate it they're going to send me the footage for yesterday afternoon.'

'OK,' Alison said, although she was annoyed at the delay. 'We need to make an appeal for witnesses, anyone else who was up on the Beamsleigh around that time. If hoody guy's not our man he should come forward.'

'I'll get on with that, boss,' Jack Kent said. Alison nodded her head, saying nothing. Jack liked to liaise with the press. And to his credit he was good at it.

'One other thing,' she said. 'It might be nothing, but I

found out last night that Izzy Johnson's biological father was a guy called Andy Steel.'

She saw a look of instant recognition from both Mick and Miles.

'The coach driver?' Miles asked. 'The Whitby crash?'

'Apparently yes,' Alison said. 'It might be nothing, like I say, but it could be relevant.'

'What crash?' Paul asked. 'I didn't hear about it. Was this last night?'

'God no, lad,' Miles said. 'Ten-odd years ago.'

'Twelve,' said Alison. She had looked it up the night before. The images from old newspaper reports were still vivid in her mind. 'It was all over the papers at the time. National as well as local. You might have read about it.' Paul shook his head. He'd been a child twelve years ago, just thirteen years old. Alison sometimes forgot how ridiculously young he was.

'It was a school trip from Penbury to Whitby. A bunch of kids from the primary school. Year 5 or 6 I think. The kids were all about ten anyway. Bus lost control on Blue Bank and there was a horrible crash. Brakes failure officially but a lot of folks blamed the driver.'

'Andy Steel had been out with some bird the night before, I heard,' Mick put in. 'He wasn't over the limit but he was close. And this was hours later when the police took his blood. And he was knackered. Been up all night getting his end away.'

Alison shook her head.

'Whatever happened, he was cleared of any wrongdoing.'

'Were any of the kids badly hurt?' Paul asked.

'Almost all of them. Something like twenty were killed. And some of the others were permanently injured.'

'Shit,' Paul said.

'Yeah, and Andy Steel walked away unhurt.'

'And that was Izzy Johnson's real dad?'

'Yeah.'

'No wonder she took her stepfather's name,' Holly said quietly.

It was a good point.

'You think it could be connected at all?' Miles asked.

'I don't know. It was a long time ago, but it is possible someone's still holding a grudge.' Alison turned to Kent. 'I want you to look into anyone who lost a child in that crash. Anyone who might want to let Andy Steel know how that feels.'

He nodded unhappily. It was background work, no chance for glory. The sort of thing he hated. Alison smiled serenely at him and he looked away.

'What about the rest of us, boss?' Miles asked.

'Interviews.'

She felt the groan rather than heard it. It was dull, old-fashioned policing but it was what they needed.

'We talk to her friends, we talk to the teachers. We see who she might have been having sex with or who might have been wanting to have sex with her. We find out what she was doing outside of school, whether she was intending to meet anyone. And who would have wanted to hurt her.'

'Could it be random?' Kent asked.

Alison shook her head, more to dispel the idea than because she thought it wasn't possible.

'I bloody hope not,' she said. 'But for now we focus on people she knew. We go with that unless we have reason to think otherwise. Whatever DNA we do get it's unlikely to be from someone already in the system so that means we need a bloody good reason to hold someone and get a sample out of them.'

Everyone nodded.

Her phone rang.

Niall Riordan.

'Mr Riordan?'

'I just wanted to let you know I've spoken to Miss Hatcher, the teacher who shares Year 7 with Mr Banks. She confirmed that she *did* swap a class with Banks yesterday. He was teaching all afternoon.'

'Shit,' Alison said, more to herself than to Riordan. 'We'll want to talk to her, of course.'

'Of course,' Riordan said. 'She's in school now.'

'Thank you, Mr Riordan, we'll be over to speak to Miss Hatcher and to some of Izzy's friends a little later.'

Alison was about to end the call. Banks' alibi was confirmed. There was nothing more to say.

But Riordan kept speaking.

'Yes... of course... only... well... I think you ought to speak to one of the children in Simon Banks' class too. She has something interesting... well, she has something to say.'

NINE

Niall Riordan was waiting for them at the entrance to the school. There was a young woman with him – small with dark hair and a long nose. She looked nervous. Riordan on the other hand looked calmer than he had the day before, although his face was puffy from tears and lack of sleep. He greeted Alison and Paul.

'This is Miss Hatcher, one of our English teachers.'

'I understand you swapped teaching duties with Mr Banks yesterday,' Alison said.

The woman nodded nervously.

'I had a lot of assessments to get through. I asked Simon, he was happy to help.' She was looking not at Alison but at Riordan. It was clear she was worried she might have made a professional error.

'I was going to take 7b tomorrow instead. We'll end up with the same amount of classroom time... just... I was so busy and...'

'It's fine, Verity,' Riordan said. 'In future I would appreciate a heads-up, that's all.'

'Of course… of course… I should have told you… I didn't think…' He touched her shoulder reassuringly. She blushed fiercely.

'Do you have any more questions for Miss Hatcher, Inspector?' Riordan asked.

'You said you asked for the swap? Mr Banks didn't ask you?'

'No. It was my idea.'

'And he was happy to do it?'

She nodded.

'OK,' Alison said. 'That's all for the moment. Thank you for your time.' The teacher glanced at her for just a moment, then looked at Riordan for permission before she scurried away down the corridor.

'So Banks *was* teaching yesterday,' Alison said. 'All afternoon.'

'That's really why I wanted you to speak to one of the kids,' Riordan said. 'I spoke to his class first thing this morning. They all say the same.'

'Which is?'

'Maybe you should just speak to Lily. I called her mother in and she's happy to have Lily speak to you.'

'OK,' Alison said, a little annoyed that he wouldn't just give her an answer himself but surprised by his efficiency.

Lily Baines was a bright, precocious little girl, who seemed delighted by the drama of speaking to the police. Her mother, seated beside her, looked equally happy.

'Yeah, we had Mr Banks for period six and seven yesterday,' Lily said in answer to Alison's question. 'That's basically all afternoon. Well, an hour and forty-five minutes actually. We're reading *Othello*. That's Shakespeare.'

Alison cut across her.

'Do you usually have Mr Banks on Tuesday afternoon?'

'No. It's almost always Miss Hatcher but yesterday they swapped. They do sometimes.'

'Was there anything else unusual yesterday, apart from it being Mr Banks instead of Miss Hatcher?'

'Not really. Only Mr Banks did go out for a bit and he never does usually.' Alison felt her heart rate increase.

'What time was that? When Mr Banks left the classroom?'

'About halfway through the lesson, I suppose. Actually it was just before the bell rang for period seven. I remember because Mr Banks wasn't in the room when the bell went and Harry started to pack up his bag. He never remembers that it's a double on Tuesdays. The bell goes at twenty past two so I suppose it was ten past when Mr Banks went out.'

'Did Mr Banks say why he was going out of the room?'

'He went to find Mr Riordan because Ryan was being such a pain.'

'And how long was he gone?'

'About ten or fifteen minutes. I don't know. The boys were messing about and I couldn't concentrate. They all got told off when Mr Banks came back, especially Ryan.'

'How did Mr Banks seem?'

'He was really cross.'

'Anything else?' Alison asked. 'Was he out of breath at all? Or sweaty? Anything like that?'

'Well… not being mean or anything but Mr Banks is a bit… well, he's not the slimmest person, is he, and he's quite often out of breath. So he was a bit.'

'But no more than usual?'

Lily shook her head.

'OK, Lily. Is there anything else you'd like to tell me?'
Lily shook her head.

'No, but… Is this to do with what happened to Izzy Johnson?' she asked.

'We're just trying to find out where everyone was yesterday,' Alison said dismissively, hoping to shut down any gossip.

'You said you spoke to a few children,' Alison said to Riordan after Lily and her mother had left the room.

'Yes. They all said pretty much the same.'

'We'll need to interview them all,' Alison said.

'I'll get you a class list.'

That would be a job for Miles and Mick. Alison couldn't imagine they would enjoy it, and it was probably pointless, but it had to be done.

'Lily said Banks left the classroom to find you,' Alison said.

'Yeah, all the kids said the same. But he never spoke to me on a matter of discipline yesterday.'

'Where were you at the time, when Banks was looking for you?'

'Like I told you yesterday, I let my sixth formers out a little early from period six and I spent period seven on admin.' Alison nodded, no longer really listening.

'Would Banks have known where to find you?' Paul asked.

'Of course. I post my schedule on the office door, so anyone – students or staff – can always find me.'

So looking for Riordan could have been an excuse. To get Banks out of the classroom and give him a chance to kill

Izzy. But would he have that sort of nerve? To kill a girl and return to his class as if nothing had happened?

Maybe he hadn't intended to kill her. Maybe he had seen her leaving and followed her, trying to get her to keep his secrets, whatever they were. But whatever the case the timing was tight. Ten minutes, maybe fifteen. To get to the Beamsleigh, confront Izzy, kill her and get back to class. Could he really have done it? It was unlikely but not impossible. The worst-case scenario.

'Inspector?'

Riordan pulled her out of her reverie.

'I'd like to interview some of Izzy's friends now if I may. You said you'd set that up in the sixth-form lounge?'

'I'll walk you there.'

'I've been meaning to apologise, Inspector,' Riordan said as he walked her and Paul through the school. 'I hope I didn't mess up by informing Simon of Izzy's death last night. It didn't occur to me until later that you might be talking to him as a suspect... I mean I never thought that he would be under any kind of suspicion.'

'This is a murder inquiry,' Alison said, as gently as she could. 'Everyone we speak to is under some level of suspicion.'

Riordan nodded gravely.

'I suppose that includes me,' he said. He paused and bit his lip. 'Yes, I suppose, looked at objectively, I did have an argument with her before she died. I suppose that might make me look, I don't know, suspicious?'

Alison didn't reply.

'If I just hadn't shouted at her. If she'd stayed in the classroom. I just... When I think what happened... when

I think… I just don't understand how anyone could… How do people do such things?'

'I've been doing this for over a decade,' Alison said. 'I don't have an answer to that.' They took a staircase in silence and Alison pretended not to notice Riordan brush a tear from his cheek.

'You were fond of Izzy,' she said.

'Yes. Very.'

'She walked your dog for you, I understand.'

'Sometimes, yes. I work long hours and don't always get a chance and it was a way for her to make a few quid.' Alison nodded.

'Weren't you afraid that some of the other children might see it as favouritism?' Riordan looked genuinely surprised.

'You know, that never occurred to me. I suppose it was favouritism in a way. I liked Izzy. I can't really see any reason why professionalism should stop us liking some children more than others. I like to treat people as individuals.' Riordan smiled sadly.

'It's a shame, I think, that because there are… well, perverts for want of a better word… in this profession the rest of us stop treating the kids like human beings. I think it's actually nice for teenagers to see that adults are human too.' He smiled again ruefully. 'I suppose you think me naive?'

'Idealistic maybe.'

Riordan laughed.

'A polite version of naive but I'll take it.'

'It didn't stop her storming out yesterday, did it, treating her like a human being?' The smile vanished; a shadow crossed Riordan's face.

'No,' he said.

'Any idea why she was so touchy?' Alison asked. 'You said the argument was out of character.'

'It was. Completely. That's why... well, I'm afraid I lost my temper.' He looked broken but went on.

'I pride myself on never losing my temper but it was so unexpected. Such defiance and, well, contempt. I never expected Izzy to look at me with such contempt.'

'And you're not aware of any reason for that? Any change in your relationship? Had you given her a poor mark? A punishment?'

He laughed humourlessly.

'Izzy's grades were amazing and I never had any discipline issues with her, no one did. So no, I don't know what happened. It was like she hated me.'

'You must get that a lot in this job,' Alison said.

Riordan looked bemused.

'Actually, no, I get... respect... humour... liking. Teenagers are wonderful, passionate people. I shall miss that.'

'Miss it? You're moving on?' Alison asked.

'I don't know, possibly. Harvard, maybe. A junior lectureship. It's... it's just a possibility.' He stopped. They had reached a set of double doors that opened into a large room that was a cross between a library and a coffee shop. There were comfortable chairs as well as desks with laptop connection points. Alison took it to be the sixth-form lounge.

'Here we are,' Riordan said, his voice businesslike again.

A young girl was waiting in the room, playing on her phone. She looked up anxiously as they entered.

'This is Lucy,' Riordan said, 'Izzy's best friend. Just let my secretary know when you want to see the other kids.'

Alison nodded her thanks as she and Paul took seats opposite the teenager.

Lucy Jacobs was a pretty girl with dark brown hair and braces. She looked younger than her age.

'You were Isabella's best friend?'

Lucy nodded.

'What can you tell us about her?'

Lucy thought for a moment. Her eyes were red from crying.

'What do you need to know?' she asked. 'I only saw her yesterday morning. I never saw her leave school or anything.'

'I know. We just want a picture of Izzy really. Stuff she might not tell her parents. Like who she was seeing or if she was having any problems or if there was anyone in her life she was worried about.'

Lucy didn't speak. Alison tried again.

'Was there anyone in Izzy's life that made her uneasy? Anyone she was frightened of?'

'Of course not... God no... We don't know people... I mean Izzy never knew people like... like that.' Alison realised that the idea that someone Izzy knew might have done this to her had never crossed Lucy's mind. For the police the most obvious suspects in a murder were those closest to the victim. For friends that idea was always hardest to accept. Killers were portrayed as the ultimate *other*. Not like us, not quite human, monsters even. Yet usually, terrifyingly, they were ordinary people, known to the victim and her friends and family. Alison decided she would go in more gently.

'She was a good student?'

'Yeah, really clever. A lot cleverer than me.'

'And were people jealous of that?' Alison asked.

'No. She never showed off about it. I mean she could run rings around the rest of us, but she was always alright about it. Gave you a hand if you were struggling, that sort of thing.'

This somewhat contradicted what Banks had said about her being cruel.

'She never teased anyone for not understanding something?'

'No. I mean only the "specials" but everybody has a laugh at them. I mean... I know it's not nice but... well, Izzy didn't do it much anyway... and not to their faces. So that's OK, isn't it?' Alison didn't reply.

'What about the teachers? Was Izzy popular with them?'

'They loved her.'

'Anyone in particular?'

'All of them really. Mr Riordan especially. We all take the piss out of the way he practically wets his pants every time she puts her hand up in maths. Matt Browne says Riordan gets an erection every time she goes up to the board to complete an equation. He calls it an equection.' She stopped, looking at their faces in horror. 'Oh God, I shouldn't be laughing. I just... It's not funny.'

'It's OK,' Alison said. 'Tell me a bit more about Mr Riordan and Izzy.'

'Oh no... it wasn't like that,' Lucy said, a note of panic in her voice. 'I mean it wasn't pervy. He didn't actually get a, you know, a hard-on. It's just a saying, it's just what we say.'

'He got excited because she was so good at maths?' Alison asked.

'Yeah. That's all I mean... nothing... Mr Riordan's alright. We all like Mr Riordan.'

'Did Izzy like him? Were they close?'

'She really liked him. Used to go and babysit his dog

sometimes. Henry really liked her, so you know, she was, like, the natural choice.'

'Was there ever anything… inappropriate… in Mr Riordan's behaviour?'

'Mr Riordan? God no. Mr Riordan is great… not like…' She stopped, looked down at her hands.

'Not like?'

'Nothing… no… I mean it's just some teachers… well, you know… there's just some you wouldn't necessarily trust. But not Mr Riordan.'

'Who would you say you couldn't trust?'

Lucy shrugged.

'OK,' Alison said. 'What about teachers Izzy didn't trust? Or just ones she didn't like much?'

'Mr Banks,' Lucy said at last. 'Izzy said he was thicker than cold custard. She said she was sure there were apes at the zoo with higher IQs. She said it was an insult to her intelligence that he was giving her extra tuition.'

'You knew about that?' Alison asked.

'Of course I did. Everyone knew. We all felt sorry for her, closed up in that office with that sweaty old… well… you know.'

Alison smiled.

'And it wasn't like he was paying her or anything… I mean not like the boys…' She stopped again, looking at the ground.

'What boys? What was Mr Banks paying boys to do?'

'Nothing… I don't… I don't know. It was just a rumour.'

'What rumour?'

Lucy looked at her indecisively for a long moment. Alison waited.

'Well, some of the boys would go up to Mr Banks' house at the weekend and help him out. Mow the grass or clear stuff out of the garage for him, and people said he used to pay them with drink and stuff. And some people said... well, some people said he did stuff. Only it's just a rumour and Dan went up there once and he said nothing dodgy went on. Said Banks was just a sad old bloke and he liked the lads around to watch the footy or whatever. And he'd give them beers and stuff. That's what I heard.'

'And it was only boys? Izzy wasn't ever invited?'

'No, just lads. He never bothered much with the girls in class. I mean except those extra lessons for Izzy. She bloody hated those.'

'So why did she go?' Alison asked. 'She didn't need the tuition and you say she didn't like Banks.' Lucy shrugged.

'She just sort of did what she was told. Izzy I mean. Well, she used to at least.'

'Had something changed recently?'

'I don't know, she just said she was getting sick of it. Banks especially.'

'Had she had a row with Mr Banks?' Alison asked.

'I don't know.'

Alison waited.

'I don't know, OK,' Lucy said again, defiantly.

'Were there any particular problems yesterday? Any reason why she might have left school?'

'I heard she stormed out of maths, but I don't do maths anymore, so...' Alison changed tack.

'Mr Riordan said you came up in Year 7 with Izzy. Were you at primary school together?'

'We started nursery on the same day,' Lucy said,

smiling. 'I don't really remember it but Izzy says I went up to her in the sandpit and said, "You have to be my friend now." And that was it really, we've been friends ever since.'

'That's a long time,' Alison said, feigning admiration. 'And you've never fallen out?' Lucy smiled again.

'We fell out all the time when we were little. You know how little kids are. But we grew out of it.'

'Did she have many other friends?'

'Yeah, loads. I mean there's a big gang of us that hang out at school. And she had friends from athletics and outside school. Everybody liked her.'

That wasn't strictly true. Someone had disliked her enough to strangle her to death.

'What about boys?' Alison asked.

'Yeah, some of our friends are boys.'

'No, I meant did Izzy have a boyfriend?'

Lucy paused again.

'It's important that you tell us the truth, Lucy. Even if Izzy told you things in confidence we need to know.'

'She was supposed to be going out with Dan.'

'Dan?'

'Daniel Humphreys. He's in our year. He's my ex, but you know, we're cool.'

'So you and Dan split up and Izzy started going out with him?'

'Yeah, but like I say, we're cool. We're friends.' Alison sensed a well-rehearsed line.

'I'd be furious if my best friend started dating my ex.' A shrug. 'Weren't you angry at all?'

'About what?'

'Izzy and Dan getting together.'

'No, no, it's fine.'

'Really?'

'Yeah. Me and Dan are just mates now. Really. It's cool.' Alison nodded. Lucy was clearly trying to convince herself.

'OK. So Izzy was going out with Dan.'

Paul cleared his throat, and Alison turned to him.

'DC Skinner, did you have a question?'

Paul turned to Lucy, his face showing just the right amount of concern and interest. Lucy smiled at him, blushing slightly.

'You said she was *supposed* to be going out with Dan,' he said. 'What did you mean by that?' *Good point*, Alison thought, kicking herself for not picking up on it.

'Well, it's just… they never seemed to see each other out of school. And just lately, I don't know but I think she might have been seeing someone else.'

'What makes you think that?' Paul asked.

Alison had leant back in her chair, a signal that it was time for Paul to lead the questions for a while.

'It was just stuff she said and, like, stuff she put up online. Like last weekend she put up a picture and she had a caption, "wicked party", and it was just a picture of her but there was someone's arm around her and it wasn't Dan. And no one knew where the party was, or anything.'

'Did you ask her about it?'

Lucy flushed.

'Lucy?'

'We weren't exactly talking.' Tears began to fall unchecked down her round cheeks.

'You weren't talking? You'd fallen out?' Paul asked. So bloody much for best friends and not bickering like they did when they were little.

'Not really. I just… I didn't like some of the things she was doing and so we were just, well, we were still friends. I just hadn't really seen her out of school so much.'

'Since when?' Alison jumped back in.

'Just after Christmas, I suppose.'

'So who *was* she seeing outside school?' Alison asked. 'And what was she doing that you didn't like?'

'I don't know.'

'You don't know?' Alison felt her temper rising. 'You don't know what she was doing but you knew you didn't approve of it?'

'No, I just meant… I didn't know who she was seeing.'

'What was she doing that you didn't approve of?' Lucy paused.

'She's dead for God's sake,' Alison snapped. 'The girl you say is your best bloody friend in the world is dead and you're keeping things from me. If you really cared about Izzy I suggest we stop pussyfooting about saying how bloody perfect she was and get down to the truth. Don't you?'

Lucy looked stunned. Alison expected tears; instead Lucy sat up straighter and took a deep breath.

'I think she was taking drugs and I'm pretty sure she was sleeping with someone, but I don't think it was Dan.'

'Who do you think Izzy was seeing if not Dan?' Alison asked.

Lucy was non-committal.

'I dunno. All I know is it can't have been anyone cool or she would have told us.'

'What made you so sure it was anyone at all?'

'She asked me to cover for her one night, a few months back. I thought she must be seeing Dan only then he was on Facebook talking about a match he was at and Izzy wasn't there. I asked her the next day but she wouldn't tell me. She just had this big grin, like she had a secret.'

'Did Dan suspect she was seeing another boy?'

'God no, he didn't know anything.'

'You weren't tempted to tell him? Get your own back on Izzy for stealing him away?' Lucy laughed, although there was no humour in it.

'I told you we split up ages before she got with Dan. And anyway I would never have told him. He would have gone ballistic.'

'Ballistic how?'

'Shit, I don't know. Throwing stuff and shouting. I mean she was supposed to be his girlfriend. He'd have just lost it if he knew.'

'He ever hit anyone?' Alison asked. 'He ever hit you when you were going out?'

'Not really,' Lucy said.

'Not really sounds like a yes to me.'

'It was nothing… It was my fault really.'

'Tell me about it,' Alison said, feeling sudden sympathy for the girl. 'What happened?'

'Like I said, it was nothing really.'

Alison waited.

'It was ages ago, just before we broke up, I suppose. I got a bit upset one night when he went out with his mates instead of me. I showed up, embarrassed him, like. They were all calling him pussy-whipped. He was really pissed off. And afterwards, when we got back to my room, he sort of pushed me a bit… I mean… he didn't hit me… but he sort of held me against the wall. And he raised his fist, like he was going to smack me. But he never did. I don't think he ever would really. And he said sorry afterwards.'

'They always do,' Alison muttered.

'But he'd never have hurt Izzy,' Lucy said.

'What makes you so sure?'

'He just wouldn't.'

'Even if he found out she was sleeping with another boy?'

'But he didn't find out. I never told him.'

'Izzy could have told him. Or the other boy. Or he could have seen them together.' Alison's mind was running away with her now. The jealous boyfriend. Meeting in a secluded spot. Strangulation was an intimate sort of killing. She'd have to check out where Dan Humphreys had been yesterday afternoon.

'You ever see them argue?' Alison asked. 'Dan and Izzy I mean.' Lucy shook her head, unconvincingly.

'I need you to tell me the truth, Lucy. It might be important.'

'He'd never hurt Izzy.'

'But you did see them arguing?'

'Monday afternoon, near the lockers.'

'You hear what it was about?'

'Not really. She was having a right go at him, saying something about how she was fed up of it. And he was just stood there taking it. I mean, if that'd been me… if it'd been anyone else he'd have…' She stopped herself. 'Well, he might have lost his temper if I talked to him like that. But he just stood there taking it. Because it was Izzy, see… he was taking it because it was Izzy.'

'He wasn't arguing back?'

'No, he was just stood there taking it. Then when Izzy saw the rest of us she sort of pulled herself together. She stopped yelling and just sort of walked off.'

'Did Dan say what the argument was about?'

'No, he just sort of shrugged it off. But see, that's how I know he'd never hurt her. I mean if he put up with all that shit… well…' Alison wasn't convinced. By Lucy's own admission Dan had a temper. Could Izzy's outburst on Monday have tipped him into violence? She decided she'd get no more on that subject from Lucy so changed direction.

'What about drugs?' she asked.

'Drugs?'

'You said you thought Izzy might have started taking drugs.'

'No… I didn't mean…' Lucy shook her head.

'We're not looking to get anyone into trouble, Lucy, we just want to find out what happened to Izzy.' She kept her voice reassuring. 'If Izzy was into drugs where do you think she might have got them?'

'I don't. I didn't mean it, OK. I never saw her take anything. It was just… well, she was a bit moody, a bit manic sometimes, that's all. I shouldn't have said…'

'Your father's a doctor, isn't he?' Alison asked.

'So?' Lucy said defensively.

'So you'd know better than most about the dangers of drugs, even prescription drugs.'

'Yeah, Dad gives me the whole "just say no" bullshit all the time.' She bit her lip, looking wide-eyed at Alison.

'Not that it's bullshit really, I mean… you know… I don't… I wouldn't… I just meant, well, he goes on about it a bit, that's all.'

Alison nodded her head.

'We tend to do that… us parents,' she said. Lucy didn't answer. Alison's phone rang. It was Jack Kent.

'Yes?'

He didn't beat around the bush, one of the few things she liked about him.

'Couple of things, guv. Preliminary look at Banks' computer's come back clean.'

'OK.'

'No, I mean really clean. There's hardly anything on there. No browser history, no email, not even any spam. Like it's been wiped.'

'OK.' That was interesting. 'They going to be able to do anything?' she asked, aware that Lucy was listening, choosing her words so as not to give anything away.

'Should be able to get some of the data back, work some sort of magic. I don't understand it but they said it could take a couple of days. You want them to get on with it?'

'Yes, I think so. Let's find out what the smug bastard doesn't want us to know.'

'Other thing is they've got DNA from the semen found on the body.'

'That was quick.'

'Turns out a bit of media interest will push the case to the top of the queue,' Kent said.

Even in death the pretty girls get it all, Alison thought. Then she decided just to be grateful for the lucky break.

'Handy,' she said. 'So, let me guess, unidentified male, right?'

'Nope. We got a match on the database. Nasty little shit with convictions for assault. Could be we've got the bastard.'

TEN

'I'll call you back,' Alison said, quickly ending the call to Jack.

If they had DNA then they had a suspect. She felt Paul's eyes questioning her but she couldn't talk yet. She needed to get rid of Lucy Jacobs.

'Right, thanks for your time, Lucy. That's all for now.'

'That's it?'

'Unless you have something else you'd like to say?' She paused, opened her mouth as if to speak and closed it again. Alison was impatient to get moving. If they had a DNA match that probably meant they were looking at a known criminal. A serial offender maybe. This whole thing probably had nothing to do with teenage fall-outs, jealous boyfriends or unsavoury teachers. A DNA match might mean it could all be cleared up quickly.

Lucy seemed reluctant to give up her place in the drama but she had no choice as Paul gently ushered her to the door. As soon as she was gone Alison called Jack Kent back.

'OK, let's have it,' she said.

'Robbie Smith,' he said triumphantly. 'Local lad, drug dealer, petty thief, real lowlife.'

'Robbie Smith?' Alison repeated.

She didn't know whether to laugh or cry. She knew Robbie Smith. Everyone in Penbury knew Robbie Smith. He was a Jack-the-lad. And lad was the word. He couldn't be more than eighteen or nineteen years old. She found it hard to imagine he was a murderer.

Then, of course, she knew better than to underestimate what anyone was capable of given the right provocation.

'His DNA was on the database?' Alison said.

'Yeah, he was arrested last year for possession of cannabis.' *Hardly the crime of the century*, Alison thought, but she held her tongue.

'You said he had a conviction for assault?'

'Yeah. As a juvenile. There was an altercation with another boy, the school called the police. He was given an ASBO.'

'Jesus, Jack, a schoolboy fight. You made him sound like Reggie Kray... or Ronnie... or whichever one it was that was the real psychopath.'

'He's got a criminal record for assault and drugs offences, and Izzy Johnson was found dead with pills in her stomach and his semen all over her. Looks like a pretty good suspect to me.'

He was defensive now. Alison knew he was right. Robbie Smith had to be a suspect. It just wasn't quite the slam-dunk she had been expecting.

'You're right, Jack. Good work.'

A recent management course had said it was important to give praise. It hadn't explained how to make it sound sincere.

'We'll interview Robbie right away.'

It was Robbie's mother, Sharon, who opened the door. She seemed unsurprised and unconcerned to see two police officers on her doorstep.

'What's he done now, the little bugger?'

'We just want a word,' Alison said.

Sharon opened the door wider and walked away down the short hallway.

'Get up, you lazy little sod,' she yelled up the stairs at Robbie. 'I've got the bloody police at my door again.' She turned to Alison. 'Three boys I've raised and never once had the police at my door with the other two. Never once.'

Alison felt some sympathy for her. She was notorious in the small town. Loud-mouthed, hard-faced and with a tendency to drink too much and dress too young. But her elder two boys had indeed stayed out of trouble.

Robbie's older brothers might not have set the world on fire with their achievements but they had never come to the attention of the police as far as Alison knew. One was on the dole long term, but the other had a steady enough job stacking shelves at the local supermarket. They had kept their noses clean. Robbie on the other hand had been in trouble as long as Alison had lived in the town. Labelled as a bad boy he had grown up into a bad adolescent. At twelve he was arrested for shoplifting, stealing sweets to sell in the playground. At fourteen he had moved on to nicking cigarettes. There had been a couple of trips home in a squad car when he was caught drinking up by the castle. It was typical of a kid who was rough around the edges and trying to find a way to get by.

That he had finally been arrested for possession was

almost inevitable and Alison supposed next it would be dealing. There was a terrible predictability to most of these kids' lives. The fight that had led to his arrest as a juvenile was playground stuff; she had had Jack Kent read the arrest sheet to her over the phone. The other boy had been hurt when Robbie pushed him to the ground. Nothing really, but the school had a zero tolerance approach so Robbie had ended up with an ASBO and a criminal record. Hardly a terrible crime, pushing a boy over, but there it was. A conviction. And when a girl was murdered, a criminal record for assault was just the sort of thing to throw up red flags.

Alison had to remember that just because Robbie had been a scabby-kneed kid with a cute smile when she first moved here, it didn't mean that he couldn't grow up into a violent manipulative adult. And he *was* an adult now. Legally at least. He was eighteen years old as of last month. A little older than Izzy, although they would have been in the same year at school. When Robbie had ever bothered to go to school that was.

'I ain't done nowt,' he said to his mother as he sloped down the stairs. She clipped him round the ear anyway.

'I 'aven't got time for this,' she said. 'I've got to get to work. There's fish fingers for your dinner.' She looked at him sharply and then said in a slightly softer tone, 'Ring me if you need me.'

Robbie just nodded.

'I just need to ask you a few questions,' Alison said, keeping her voice reassuring. For now at least.

'It wasn't me. I wasn't there. It was like that when I got there.' A half-smile played on his lips as he said it.

'Very funny,' Paul muttered, unamused.

'Cheers,' Robbie said, taking a small bow.

Alison understood the act. Pretend nothing matters and you can't get hurt. She knew it didn't always work. Robbie's performance was already tainted with weariness. She wished his mother had stayed. He looked as if he would need someone on his side.

'You'll've heard about Izzy Johnson,' Alison said.

'Izzy? No, what about her?' This was unexpected. She had assumed everyone in the small town would know by now.

'She's dead, Robbie. Her body was found up on the Beamsleigh yesterday afternoon.'

'Shit. Izzy? You're sure it was Izzy? It can't... I... Shit.' He shook his head, disbelieving.

'You didn't know?' Alison asked.

'Fuck off,' he muttered, turning his head away.

There was no aggression in the words and he used the back of his hand to wipe away sudden tears. Alison hated that she felt shocked by his crying. It seemed like a genuine reaction. Lucy had had time to drape her sorrow in sentimentality; Robbie's pain seemed to be real and undisguised.

'I'm sorry,' Alison began. 'Were you close?' Robbie ignored the question.

'What happened?' he asked.

'We were hoping you could tell us that,' Alison said.

Robbie shook his head.

'She was fine when I left. She never said she felt ill or anything.' Either he was a great actor or he had no idea what they were really asking him.

'Izzy was killed, Robbie. She was murdered.'

'Shit.' Again he shook his head, fighting disbelief and tears. Then Alison saw a change in his face as he realised why they were there and what they were really asking him.

'You're asking me because you think I did it? You think *I* killed Izzy?'

'Did you?' Alison asked.

'Fuck off,' he said again, tears still falling down his face but anger in his eyes now.

'I'll take that as a no.'

Robbie said nothing to that. He wiped his eyes with the back of his hand again and watched her under his long lashes. He had a face that was almost pretty beneath his attempts at hardness. His features were androgynous, delicate, almost fragile.

'Did you see Izzy yesterday afternoon?' Alison asked.

'Yeah, I saw her.'

'Where was that?'

'I met her up at the Beamsleigh… She called and I… We met up there.'

'And how was she?'

'She was fine. I told you already she was fine when I left. I never killed her.'

'How come you hadn't heard about it?' Alison asked. 'It's all around the town, everyone knows.' He shrugged.

'That's not very convincing, Robbie, is it? If you want me to believe you, if you want me to understand that you didn't kill Izzy…'

'I didn't.'

'OK then, convince me. Start by explaining to me how it is that you don't know about the biggest thing that's ever happened in this town.'

'Don't call it that,' he said. 'That makes it sound like a good thing that's happened.'

'OK. I'm sorry. But go on... explain it to me.' He shrugged again. Alison waited.

'After I saw Izzy yesterday I went down to Leeds. I've got some mates over there and there was a party. I was pretty wasted, didn't get back until God knows what time. Early hours. And I just went to bed. I've been asleep all this time.'

'And no one's phoned you, no one's texted you? Your mum didn't say anything to you?'

'I never saw Mum. I went straight to bed. And my phone got nicked. Sometime last night. I was well pissed off.'

'And no one at this party knows anyone in Penbury? No one over there heard anything?'

'I don't know. If they did they didn't tell me.'

'How did you get down to Leeds? You got a car?'

'Nah, I got the train.'

'Which train?'

'The one to Leeds!' he said sarcastically.

'Yeah, thanks, I guessed that. The train from Milbury to Leeds, but what time?'

'I dunno. I just went to the station and got on a train.'

'You bother with a ticket?' Alison asked.

He shrugged. She didn't ask him how he got past the barriers at the station at the other end. Fare-dodging was way below her radar at the moment.

'OK. So how did you get home?'

'A friend.'

'A friend?' Alison asked. 'Does he have a name, your friend?'

'Ben Adams,' Robbie said reluctantly.

'And he gave you a lift all the way back up to Penbury at some ungodly hour of the morning? Must be a good mate.'

'Not really. He's just a bloke I know.' There was something in the way he said it that piqued Alison's curiosity.

'You got his number, this mate? His address?'

'Don't know his address and my phone's been nicked like I said… so…'

'So no phone number. No one who can confirm where you were or when you got back.' Paul gave Robbie a snide smile.

'You think I'm lying?' Robbie said. Paul continued to smile.

'Is there any way you can get this Ben Adams' number?' Alison asked.

'Don't say "this Ben Adams" like I made him up. I'm not fucking lying.'

'OK. So can you get his number?'

'It was on my phone, which got nicked so… Hold on… yeah… he had a card. He gave me his card, ages ago.'

Robbie got up and went into the kitchen. Alison watched him from where she sat. He rummaged around for a while in a drawer and came back with a card.

'There.' *Ben Adams. Management Consultant.* Not the sort of man Alison would expect Robbie to be friends with.

'How did you meet this man?' she asked. Robbie blushed.

'What the hell's that got to do with anything. He's just a bloke I know, OK. He invited me to a party last night and then afterwards he gave me a lift home.'

'A long way to come to give someone a lift,' Alison said. 'It'd take an hour at least.' Robbie shrugged.

'Maybe he likes my company.'

'Must be your charm,' Paul put in.

Alison continued before Robbie could answer.

'OK, we'll contact Ben to confirm you went to Leeds but you're not denying you saw Izzy Johnson yesterday afternoon?'

'Yeah, I saw her.'

'What time?'

'I dunno. I'm not much good on time. I had just got up, had something to eat so maybe it was dinnertime. And she rang and said she'd had a shit morning at school and would I meet her on the Beamsleigh. So I said yeah.'

'And you didn't organise a time to meet?'

'No, I was like "I'll come straight up" and she must have left school straight off because she was waiting for me when I got there.'

'Was there anyone else around?' Alison asked.

'Nah, didn't see anyone.'

'What about when you left?'

'Never saw no one the whole time we were there. Then again I wasn't looking.' A smile played on his lips and quickly disappeared again. 'I can't believe she's dead. You sure it was Izzy? It couldn't be a mistake?' His pain was tangible.

'I'm sorry,' Alison said. 'There's no mistake.' Robbie took a deep breath. He wasn't going to cry anymore.

Boys like Robbie didn't cry. Instead they pretended to be tough. Alison had seen young people like that many times before. Hell, she had even been one once herself. Maybe it came from growing up knowing that crying was more likely to get you a clip round the ear than bring you comfort.

'What did you and Izzy do when you met up yesterday?' Alison asked.

'You know… we hung out.'

'I need details, Robbie. It's important.'

'Yeah, 'cause you want me to say we had a big row or something and I stabbed her or whatever. But I never… I wouldn't.'

'So what did you do?' Paul interjected, his voice dripping with contempt. 'Talk about her application to Cambridge? Discuss the finer points of English literature? You help her with some particularly difficult maths equation?'

'Yeah, I get it,' Robbie said. 'No need to lay it on with a trowel, mate. She was too good for me. She's like this superbrain who's going to get out of this shithole town and get herself a brilliant job and probably, like, change the world someday. And what am I? Some little scumbag.'

'I didn't say that,' Paul said, his tone emphasising that that was exactly what he had meant.

'Yeah. Well, I'm gonna get out of this shithole town too. You see, me and Izzy we're different. She might be super smart but she was sick of it too.'

'Sick of what?' Alison asked.

'The whole thing. Being the best student in the school, being the perfect bloody daughter and friend and everything.'

'She was feeling the pressure?'

He barked a laugh.

'What pressure? Izzy could do that shit with her eyes closed. She could have passed her A-levels like three or four years ago, maybe more. There was no pressure on her. Exams and getting into uni and all that is just easy for Izzy. No problem.'

'So what was she sick of?' Alison pursued.

'She was sick of being the great white hope. She was sick of being her mother's chance at redemption, the school's great chance to look good because they produced this genius. They put her on the prospectus, you know. Izzy's smiling face telling all these little Year 6 kids, "come to this school and you'll be like Izzy Johnson". She's like a celebrity in this town. And it's all bullshit. She's the way she is despite that school and her flaky mother and this shitty little town. Despite it not because of it.'

Alison waited until the tirade ended, and then gave him a moment before speaking again.

'How long had you been seeing each other?' she asked.

'We got together just before Christmas.'

He smiled at the memory of it, his face suddenly younger than his years. Alison caught a glimpse of the little boy he had been.

'I was in the Old Swan and she just came up to me. Came up and started talking like we were old friends. And we just sort of got off together. I thought that'd be it, you know, a one-night thing. Some of the girls round here they do that, see what it's like being with a bad boy. Most of 'em never talk to you again afterwards. Which is fine with me. But Izzy was different. She texted me the next day and we just sort of got together.'

'None of her friends seem to know about you and her.'

'Yeah, well, I don't suppose she was proud of me, was she? I'm not the sort of boy you take home to meet the parents.' Alison didn't comment. She wondered how she would react if one of her girls brought home a boy like Robbie in a few years' time.

'Were you supplying her with drugs?'

'She didn't do drugs.'

Alison raised her eyebrow. Did he think she was stupid? 'She didn't do drugs,' he repeated.

Alison made no comment. They still didn't know what the pills in Izzy's stomach had contained. It was possible they weren't street drugs at all. She decided to move on.

'You sound like you knew her pretty well.'

'Yeah. We're pretty tight.'

Paul huffed.

'What?' Robbie asked angrily.

'I don't buy it,' Paul said.

Robbie gave him a hard stare.

'Maybe she was slumming it,' Robbie jeered. 'Good girls like a bit of rough, you know. Maybe she just liked the taste of my dick.'

Paul looked vindicated. Robbie Smith, low-level drug dealer, dropout, loser. Playing the part Paul wanted him to play. Alison wasn't often annoyed with Paul but she was furious with him right now.

'Tell me about yesterday,' she said again, trying to get Robbie back on track. 'Was she upset when you met her? Did she tell you why she left school?'

'Weren't much talking going on,' he said. 'Our tongues were otherwise engaged if you get my meaning.'

Alison wanted to slap him. She had seen his tears, she knew his relationship with Izzy had been about more than sex. But he had brought the shutters down on his emotions. No one was listening when he opened up, so his best protection was to pretend he didn't care.

'You had sex?'

'We fucked, yeah.' He seemed to want to shock her. She wasn't easily shocked.

'OK, so you fucked her. Then what happened?' He faltered.

'I had to go. I had this party in Leeds. She was fine when I left her.'

'You didn't have a row?'

'No. And I didn't fucking kill her.'

This was directed at Paul.

'How long were you up on the Beamsleigh together?' Alison asked.

'Long enough,' Robbie said, trying for a leer that didn't quite work.

'How long?'

'Dunno. Ten, fifteen minutes.'

'Last of the great lovers,' Paul mumbled.

'It's long enough if you know what you're doing, gramps,' Robbie shot at him.

'Yeah, cos speed is what girls value,' Paul began. Alison held up her hand.

'So, you met Izzy, you were together for ten minutes or so and then you left?' Robbie nodded.

'Can anyone corroborate that?' Alison asked. 'I mean can anyone back you up?'

'I know what bloody corroborate means,' he said.

'OK then,' Alison said quietly. 'So can they? Was anyone else up there on the Beamsleigh? Anyone who might have seen you leave, might have seen Izzy after you left?'

He shook his head, looking down at his hands.

'I never killed her… I told you she was fine when I left. She was OK.'

'But you had had an argument, hadn't you?' Alison said. 'Why else would you leave so quickly?' Robbie shrugged, unwilling to answer.

'A shrug won't do it, I'm afraid, Robbie. We need to know. Did Izzy end it? Was that why you went to Leeds? Why you got so drunk?'

'Like I need an excuse to get drunk.'

'You haven't answered my question. Did Izzy dump you yesterday?'

'No.'

'But you had a row?'

'No comment.' He smiled but it was a miserable smile.

'We just want the truth, Robbie. The quicker you tell us the truth the quicker we can stop looking at you and maybe find the person who really hurt Izzy.'

'Yeah right,' Robbie said, glowering at Paul. 'He's already made up his mind it was me. Makes no difference what I say.'

Alison opened her mouth but Paul spoke over her.

'Here's what happened,' he said. 'Izzy had her walk on the wild side or whatever it was. She'd had her fun and she decided to ditch you and go back to her real boyfriend. Only you weren't having that, were you? You weren't about to let her show you up for the low-life little maggot that you are.'

'Yeah, brilliant, you worked it all out. Except that's not what happened. She never ditched me. And she never went off with no other bloke. Who the hell is this "real boyfriend" supposed to be, anyway?'

'A nice boy. A clever boy who was doing A-levels too, heading for university like Izzy was. The school hunk. Exactly the sort of boy she *could* take home to her parents,' Paul sneered.

'You mean Dan Humphreys?' Robbie said with a hard laugh. 'Dan wasn't her boyfriend.'

'That's not what he thinks. Not what her friends seem to think either,' Paul said.

'I don't know what her friends think but Dan sure as hell knows he isn't Izzy's boyfriend.'

'What do you mean?'

For a second Robbie smiled, then he shook his head.

'Nothing. Maybe I don't know jack shit. You're the great detective, you go figure it out.' Alison decided it was time to intervene again.

'Are you maintaining that you had nothing to do with Izzy's death?' she said calmly to Robbie.

'I'm maintaining that I didn't touch her, if that's what you mean. She was fine when I left. We… I had this party to go to in Leeds. She didn't want to come so I left her there.' He shook his head slowly. 'She was just stood on the Beamsleigh when I left.'

'How did you leave?' Alison asked.

'I levitated,' Robbie said sarcastically. 'How do you think I bloody left?'

'I meant which path did you take?'

'I went straight back from where we were down the path to Beamsleigh Park Road.'

'You didn't head to the school?'

'Why would I go there?'

If Robbie had taken the direct path then he must have left before Andrea Mills arrived. Otherwise he would have passed her directly.

Unless he was lying. Unless he had killed Izzy and left in the direction of the Cawpers. Unless he had been the figure Andrea had seen vaulting the fence.

Ten minutes to meet and make love and part again

seemed like a ridiculously short time. But who knew, teenagers were passionate, irrational. Alison had had her share of upright shags when she was that age. She had her share of quick, soon-forgotten blazing rows too. Robbie could have left like he said, after sex and recriminations and tears. Or he could have killed Izzy, walked away and vaulted that fence.

'What were you wearing yesterday?' she asked him. Robbie held out his arms indicating the grubby T-shirt and jeans he had on.

'Just that? Or did you have a jacket or coat?'

'I had on a hoody. Didn't sleep in that though, did I?' he said, as if the idea was ludicrous.

'The sergeant will go with you while you get changed so he can take those. And I want you to stay where we can find you, OK?'

'Well, that screws my plans to go to Monte Carlo this weekend,' Robbie said, attempting a smile.

ELEVEN

'Little scumbag's lying,' Paul said when he caught up with Alison outside Robbie Smith's house a little while later.

'You think so? I'd never have guessed.'

'Come on, you're telling me you buy all that shit? How close they were? And none of her friends knew?'

'What about the stepdad? He suspected a lad on the scene. And Lucy Jacobs? Oh yeah… and the semen found on Izzy Johnson.'

'I'm not saying he didn't have sex with her. I'm just saying, all this romantic crap is utter bollocks.'

'Well, whether it was true love or not, he doesn't really have a motive to kill her, does he?'

'No. But he was there, the last person we know to have seen her. And what if she wasn't as willing to have sex as he made out?'

'You're saying he raped her as well as killed her now?' Alison asked. 'You really think he's got that sort of violence in him?'

'Who knows?' Paul shrugged. 'Someone did it.'

'He seemed to really care for her,' Alison said. Paul made a sceptical huff.

'What?' Alison asked.

'I don't buy this whole act about them being soul mates, that's all.'

'He never said they were.'

'Look, I get that she might have fancied a bit of rough, but if Isabella Johnson was interested in a kid like Robbie Smith it wouldn't be for his sparkling personality. It'd be his drugs connections she was after. And he says she wasn't interested in drugs.'

'Yeah, well he would say that, wouldn't he?' Alison said.

'So you admit you think he's lying.'

'About that maybe. Even Lucy said she thought Izzy had started taking drugs. And if so, Robbie's her most likely source. But maybe he's not her only source. I mean whatever she took yesterday hasn't been identified yet, which means it's not run-of-the-mill stuff. I get Robbie dealing a bit of weed or coke, but would he have access to anything more unusual?'

'Who the hell knows? Drug dealers are slippery customers.'

'OK, but even if he gave her the drugs, it doesn't mean he killed her. Maybe he met her like he said, they had sex, he left, someone else killed her. It's plausible.'

'We have to treat him as a suspect,' Paul said.

'I know that,' she said angrily. 'I *am* treating him as a suspect but just because he's from a shitty home doesn't make him guilty.'

'And it doesn't make him innocent either. It's not the same as… I mean they're not all like… they're not all rough diamonds.'

'Thank you, Sergeant, I am aware of that.' There was a cold silence between them for a moment.

Alison didn't like the way they always looked at the rough kids first. She didn't like the way that good manners, a nice haircut and clean clothes always gave some people an advantage. It was easier to believe ill of the scruffy, undernourished, foul-mouthed kids. She just didn't want that always to be true. But she knew Robbie had to be a suspect. His DNA was the only concrete evidence they had found so far and his alibi, or lack of it, sucked.

'We'll get his clothes examined, get Holly to check CCTV on the trains down to Leeds, make sure he really did go down there, then call this "friend" of his, Ben Adams, and see if we can tie down what time he got back. Then we'll take it from there.'

'And in the meantime?'

Alison was thinking over her answer when she saw Niall Riordan walking up the hill towards them.

'DI Dobson, hello.'

'Hello,' Alison said. 'Skipping school?'

'Guilty.' He smiled. 'Actually I was heading home for lunch. Thought I'd take the long way round, get a bit of fresh air.'

'Actually I could do with a quick word,' Alison said, making up her mind. 'Would you mind if we talk at your place?'

'Not at all.'

'What are you playing at?' Paul whispered, holding her back for a moment as Riordan went ahead.

'I want to talk to him a bit more about Dan Humphreys and about Banks,' Alison said.

'Anyone but Robbie, eh?' Paul said.

'What?'

'Just saying. It looks like you're looking for this to be anyone but Robbie Smith. Just because he reminds…'

'Do not tell me how to do my job, Sergeant,' she said, cutting him off as she strode on to catch up with Riordan.

Alison looked around Riordan's flat appreciatively. Penbury didn't really do loft living but this old converted mill was as close as it got. The windows looked out over the river which cut through the centre of town. The flat was industrial, exposed brick and steel. A fashionable place for a cosmopolitan thirty-something. A little out of place in a small market town. Rather like Riordan himself.

She thought that Penbury was probably just a step on the career ladder for him. He was young for a head and he was already looking to move up. He had mentioned America; she imagined he would be happier there.

A handsome young man came into the living room wearing tracksuit bottoms and pulling on a T-shirt. His hair was tousled from a recent shower. Alison knew she had seen him before but for just a moment she was thrown by his beauty. It seemed to stop her brain in its tracks; her reaction to him was almost visceral. There was something unsettling about his presence. He moved like a piece of performance art. His actions held a certainty of being watched. Alison found she didn't want to look away.

'Sorry, I just got in from a run,' he said, his eyes lingering on Alison, a smile playing at the corner of his mouth. It was as if everyone in the room had been waiting for him to arrive and now he was here and ready to be celebrated. Alison found herself smiling at him.

'This is my partner, Henry,' Riordan said. 'Henry, this is DI Dobson and DS Skinner. They're here about… well, I guess you wanted to talk about Izzy?'

Alison nodded, still watching the beautiful man. She finally placed him. He had come into Riordan's office to get his wallet the day Izzy had died. He had recognised Banks' handwriting. She had not looked at him properly then. He had been rushed and harried; there had been none of this studied casualness about him. He had looked almost like a different man. Almost ordinary.

'Did you know Izzy, Mr…?' Alison asked.

'Chapell,' he supplied. 'I know. Henry Chapell. Sounds like some sort of medieval hall at Oxford or something, doesn't it? I'll meet you at Henry Chapel.' He smiled, a charming easy smile, and then seemed to recollect himself and replaced the smile with a small frown.

'I knew Izzy a little,' he said. 'She came and babysat occasionally.' Alison raised an eyebrow.

'Henry means dogsitting,' Riordan corrected.

'Well, strictly speaking of course she *is* a dog but to me she'll always be my baby.' Alison didn't reply.

Chapell smiled as he held up a small dog for her to admire. Alison smiled politely. She wasn't a huge fan of small dogs. Her eyes followed him as he carried the dog to her basket and put her down. He really was a beautiful man. A creation, an idea made manifest. A truly aesthetically appealing human being. She didn't know why but beautiful people were different from the rest. They were golden. This man was golden; she couldn't imagine he had ever had a real problem. Maybe Izzy Johnson had been like that in life. Maybe that was why few people had a bad word to say about her. We need beautiful people to be good and pure, it offends our sense of justice otherwise.

Chapell was, of course, aware of his beauty. There was no way to look the way he looked, and to have the effect he had on people, and not to know it. He was watching Alison watching him. Appreciating her appreciation, yet at the same time bored by it. A man who was used to being adored.

'I'm sorry, Mr Chapell, but we just need to ask your partner a few questions,' Alison said, pulling herself together. Chapell pouted.

'Can't we just have lunch? I see so little of him. All this wretched business has just made it worse.'

'It won't take long, Henry, I'm sure,' Riordan said reassuringly.

'You always say that. When was the last time we had lunch together?'

'Yesterday,' he laughed gently.

'That doesn't count. Sandwiches in your office. I mean a proper lunch like grown-ups have.'

'We won't be more than a few minutes,' Alison said.

'Fine,' Chapell said, smiling at her but tossing his head like a spoilt child. 'I'll take Angela for a walk if I'm not wanted here.'

He flounced theatrically from the room. On a lesser man it would have looked pathetic; on Henry Chapell it looked charming, ironic, playful. Beauty was transformational; it even transformed bad behaviour into good.

Riordan turned to her with an apologetic smile on his face.

'It's all just an act,' he said, indicating Chapell's behaviour. 'He's actually very upset about Izzy. He was fond of her.'

'We just have a couple of questions, Mr Riordan,' Alison said, changing the subject.

'OK, but call me Niall, please.' He was giving them his full attention now. Professional. The tears of yesterday were gone, though the marks of a sleepless night were obvious.

'We've found out that Izzy was seeing a boy by the name of Robbie Smith. Do you know him?'

Riordan smiled.

'Every teacher in the school knows Robbie. Although of course he's left now. Officially left last summer but I doubt we'd seen him more than half a dozen times in the year before that. When you say Izzy was seeing him, you mean they were going out?'

Paul gave his trademark humph of disbelief.

'My colleague here finds it very hard to believe that a girl like Izzy would ever date a boy like Robbie,' Alison said pointedly. 'I was wondering what your opinion was.'

'God knows what goes through these kids' minds. Then again I could say that about many adults I know. I mean there's no accounting for taste, is there?'

'What did you make of Robbie?'

Riordan thought for a while. Alison liked him for that.

'I liked him actually. I mean he was probably the worst-behaved kid in the school, but it's a pretty good school so, you know... Compared to the teenagers you get in some places he was an angel.' He gave a gentle laugh. 'Actually, no, you could never have called him an angel. But there was no badness in him. No malice. He broke rules, he swore, smoked, skipped school, but I never saw him bully a kid or lie to get another kid into trouble. And when he got caught he was always one of those kids who just admitted it, straight away, whether he was sorry or not. You've got to like that.'

'Were they ever together at school? Izzy and Robbie? Ever in the same class?'

'Not that I know of. I could check the records, but even if they weren't in the same classes they'd've seen each other. I mean we have assemblies and sports events in year groups. They'd've been in the same year, so they'd definitely have known of each other even if they weren't friends.'

Another smile and a small affectionate shake of the head.

'What?' Alison asked.

'It makes a sort of sense actually. They were probably the two best-known kids in the school for different reasons. Both stars in a sense. And Robbie isn't dumb. I mean he didn't do well academically but you could tell, just talking to him, he's a bright kid. A shame really.'

'What is?' Alison was prepared for a barrage of the usual insults about Robbie's family.

'We let him down, I suppose. The school, the town. Let him be the bad boy because it was easier than finding a way to make him engage.'

The honesty surprised Alison and she found she respected Riordan all the more for it.

'What about Dan Humphreys?' she asked. 'He was supposed to be Izzy's boyfriend. You know anything about that?'

'I heard the rumours,' Riordan said ruefully.

'Which were?'

'Which were "OMG Dan is so gorgeous, OMG I'm so jealous." That sort of thing.' Alison laughed.

'What did you think of the relationship?'

'Have you met Dan?'

'Not yet.'

'Well, he's a nice enough boy, very popular, but I couldn't see him with Izzy somehow, to be honest. But then who knows what kids get up to outside school.'

'She ever mention Robbie?' Alison asked.

'Once or twice actually,' Riordan confessed. 'She never said she was going out with him. His name was just dropped into conversation once or twice. The way you do when you like someone. I didn't pick it up at the time, but now you mention it...'

'Can you give an example?' Alison asked.

'Well, last week we were talking about determinism. Free will, that sort of thing. And she said something about kids like Robbie and how they could be anything they wanted despite being written off by society. I thought he was just an example, but now I think maybe she was being more specific. Maybe she just wanted to talk about him. You know how it is, young love. You sometimes just want to say their name.'

Another humph from Paul.

'I doubt it was love,' he said.

Riordan shrugged.

'Who knows, but I can't really see Izzy wasting her time on anything less.'

'What about Dan? Wasn't she wasting her time with him?' Alison asked.

'I suppose. Except... well, I think that relationship probably had its uses. It suited them both for people to think they were together. Particularly Dan.'

'What does that mean?' Alison asked.

'Nothing much, really, just that it was good for his image. For both their images, I suppose.'

'What d'you make of Dan?' Alison asked. 'We've been told he has a temper.' Riordan laughed again.

'Seventeen-year-old boy has a temper. Not exactly a newsflash, is it?'

'He ever get in any trouble?'

'Not at school, no.'

'And out of school?' Alison asked, picking up on the distinction. Riordan paused, as if deciding whether to speak.

'I saw him out in bars once or twice where he shouldn't have been. I tried to talk to him, let him know it wasn't a good idea.' Alison nodded. *Seventeen-year-old boy visits a bar.* That was hardly a newsflash either.

'Would you know if Dan was in class yesterday afternoon?'

'He isn't in my maths group,' Riordan said. 'I could get my secretary to check his timetable.'

'If you would, please.'

There was a pause.

'Oh, you mean now,' Riordan said. 'Of course. Yes.' He phoned the school, spoke to someone on the other end for a moment, then held the receiver away from him, covering it with his hand.

'Dan had history yesterday afternoon. Karen's just putting me through to Miss Walsh, his history teacher.'

Alison nodded her thanks. A few more minutes and Riordan was off the phone.

'Yesterday afternoon was a revision session. Dan was there at first but cut out before the end of the session.'

'He give a reason?'

'Liz says he just said he had an appointment. She didn't push it. We like to give the sixth form a bit of freedom and since it was only a revision class... He didn't come back before the end of school.'

'Could she confirm what time he left the classroom?'

'I'm afraid not. I did ask her, but like I say, we're pretty relaxed about letting sixth formers come and go.' Alison nodded, then shook her head. So Dan could have been out of school when Izzy was killed.

'And he has a temper,' she said almost to herself.

'You can't think he had anything to do with...' Riordan began.

'If he found out about Izzy and Robbie he might have been jealous.' Riordan shook his head.

'I can't imagine he'd be that jealous. I mean I don't think... Well, he just wasn't that interested. I think he was with Izzy more for show than anything else.'

'What makes you say that?'

'Dan's, oh, I don't know. It was the impression I got, that's all. I don't think he liked her that much.' There were tears in Riordan's eyes again.

'I know it seems ridiculous,' he said. 'I was just her teacher after all but... I was very fond of her. Both Henry and I used to joke that if we had a daughter we'd want her to be like Izzy Johnson. I'm not sure her parents really understood how special she was.'

'Her mother idolised her.'

'Oh yes, I know that. I'm not saying... Only that perhaps she would have idolised any child, just because she was hers. You know how mothers are. But Izzy was remarkable.

I mean her brain... the way she thought... the way she saw things. The girl was a genius. And I don't use the word lightly. I've seen some remarkable maths brains at work, in academia, but I've never been so totally thrown by ideas like I was by Izzy's. She just saw the world in a different way. More clearly, I suppose. What she might have done...' The tears really were threatening to overwhelm him now.

'She was applying for Cambridge?' Alison said. 'Her mother said you were helping her.'

'Hardly,' Riordan said. 'I introduced her to an old colleague of mine, that's all. I was doing him a favour rather than her. Every college in the place was desperate for her and of course she could have gone abroad. There was no question she could have gone anywhere she wanted to.'

'You say an old colleague?' Alison said, intrigued. 'You used to teach at Cambridge?' Riordan flushed.

'For a while, as a postgrad student,' he said, 'before I was lured away by the promise of riches.'

'In Penbury?'

'No, no. I worked in the City for a while. Big bucks. Designing algorithms to try and beat the stock market. I was something of a wonderkid myself.' He smiled self-deprecatingly. 'Needless to say it didn't last.' Something in the sadness of his expression persuaded Alison not to ask why.

'It must have been something of a comedown to end up here,' she said before she could stop herself. Riordan laughed gently.

'Henry felt it more keenly than I did. I was never very interested in the money. It was the maths that interested me and then, suddenly, it didn't. Teaching was my saviour in an odd way. And Henry stuck by me, which was a blessing.'

It seemed like an odd thing to say, but Alison didn't want to pry. Instead she ended the interview, thanking Riordan for his time.

Back in the car her phone rang. Holly this time.

'Just wanted to update you, boss. Robbie's alibi checks out as far as it goes. CCTV has him on the three o'clock train to Leeds. The footage isn't too clear, but he didn't look agitated at all on the station, and his clothes look clean enough.'

Alison took that to mean no visible blood.

'And it seems like he stayed in Leeds all evening,' Holly went on, 'so he might be telling the truth about not knowing that Izzy was dead. Assuming he didn't do it, of course. I rang Ben Adams, you know, the guy who gave Robbie a lift back after the party.'

'And?'

'All seems above board. Bit weird though, Robbie having a friend like that. He's a businessman, a bit older than Robbie. Got a bit of money behind him, nice car that sort of thing.'

'Nice car?' Alison asked.

'I got the reg, checked it out,' Holly said. 'BMW. Really nice car, 7 series. Expensive. Got it on camera coming up the A64 about three thirty in the morning. So that fits with Robbie's account.'

'That was good thinking, Holz,' Alison said, genuinely pleased.

'Also checked out if he's got any priors,' Holly said, clearly pleased with herself.

'And?'

'Nothing. Car was stopped in the red-light district of

Sheffield in an operation over there a couple of weeks back. But it wasn't Ben Adams driving. He loaned the car to his cousin apparently. The cousin and some other bloke took it out cruising.'

'Nice cousin,' Alison said sarcastically.

'Absolutely,' Holly agreed.

'Any other reason to think he's not a straight-up guy?'

'Not really, boss. I mean, the way he talked about Robbie it was... well, it was a bit creepy... I mean he obviously really fancies him.'

'Nothing necessarily wrong with that,' Alison said, 'Robbie's an adult. You get the impression he was lying for Robbie, anything like that?'

'No, boss, and the CCTV confirms everything he said... so...'

'So the guy's just a bit of a creep. There's a lot of it about.' Holly didn't laugh.

Even with Adams' corroboration Robbie didn't really have an alibi for the time of Izzy's death.

'There was one more thing, boss.'

'Yes.' Alison listened. 'Shit. Really? Well, that's interesting, isn't it?' She ended the call.

'What?' Paul asked.

'I think it's time we had a talk with Dan Humphreys.'

TWELVE

Dan Humphreys was a handsome boy in that arrogant way Alison had found irresistible as a teenager. He had a long fringe which he kept flicking out of his eyes and a way of stroking his hands across his taut stomach which was self-conscious and deliberate. *Here's me looking sexy.* Alison found it faintly disturbing.

'You were Izzy's boyfriend, I hear.'

'Who told you that?'

'Most people,' Alison said. He smiled.

'We hooked up sometimes. Nothing serious,' he said.

'What does that mean, nothing serious?'

'Well, you know, it wasn't like love or whatever. It was more… she was the hottest girl in the place. You know? It just sort of made sense.'

'Because you were the hottest boy?' Alison asked, holding back a laugh.

'You got eyes, you tell me.' He sat back in his chair and looked through his long lashes at her.

'OK, you can cut the gangster act. This is Yorkshire,

lad, not LA. I am a woman old enough to be your mother and I am a police officer investigating the death of a girl you were supposed to care about. Now, you might want to act like a dickhead in your own time but please don't waste mine.'

She felt Paul watching her, suppressing a smile.

Dan looked a little humbled and Alison was satisfied.

'So you and Izzy were going out. Yes or no?'

'Yes.'

'And before that you were going out with Lucy Jacobs, Izzy's best friend?'

'Yes.' He looked contrite. Good. Keep it that way.

'So when you started going out with Izzy did that cause any friction?'

'No, not really. Lucy was cool with it. We stayed friends. I mean, she's still got the hots for me, but I moved on yeah. We were cool.'

'OK. So you were going out with Izzy since when?'

'God, September, I suppose. Start of the year there was this party. We just sort of, like, got off and then that was it, you know. Nothing serious. We fooled about a bit, that's all. If you get my meaning.' The flirtatious look was back in his eyes; Alison ignored it.

'And Lucy didn't mind?'

'I never asked her,' he said. Then seeing the serious look on Alison's face, 'I'm pretty sure she was cool about it. Me and Lucy were well finished, she knew that.'

'Were you and Izzy having sex?'

He paused, blushed slightly.

'She wouldn't,' he said, at last.

Alison let that remark sit for a moment. 'You want to

tell us about your sister now?' she asked, getting to the real reason for this conversation.

'What's my sister got to do with anything?' His voice was quiet; he wasn't looking at Alison anymore.

'Well, you see, I just had a very interesting phone call, in which one of my officers told me Izzy Johnson's father was responsible for a crash that killed your big sister. Don't you think that's worth talking about?'

'Not really,' he said flatly.

'Don't you think it's a bit odd that you ended up going out with Izzy, after what her father did?'

'It was a long time ago, and it had nothing to do with Izzy.'

'How do you think your mum would feel knowing you were dating Izzy?'

'Leave her out of this.' His fists were clenched, a muscle in his jaw working.

'She died too, didn't she? My officer said she killed herself. I'm sorry for your loss. It must be hard. You live with your dad?'

He shook his head, before answering.

'I live with me nana, OK. Dad's long gone and good riddance.' Alison felt a stab of pity for him but she pushed it under. The worse his life was, the greater his motive to hurt Izzy. She had to remember that.

'You must have resented Izzy. Perfect Izzy with her perfect life. Her father caused all that mayhem, caused you to lose everything and there she was swanning through life like the universe owed her a living.'

He took a deep breath, the air juddering into his lungs.

'It wasn't like that,' he said. 'Izzy was cool. All that other shit happened a long time ago. Ancient history.'

'It didn't bother you at all? Her father is the reason you lost your sister and mother. *Izzy's* father. That didn't cross your mind? Even when you lost your temper?'

He shrugged.

'You see, Dan, I've heard you've got a pretty bad temper,' Alison said.

'Who told you that?'

'Would you say you have problems with anger management?'

'Who told you that? Banks?' Alison was surprised but went with it.

'Why would Mr Banks tell me that?'

'It was one time, right. The old perv deserved it... I never thought... Bloody hell, it had nothing to do with Izzy.'

'What happened with Banks?' Alison asked. Dan eyed her cautiously.

'Was it him who said I had a temper?' Alison didn't reply, hoping he would draw his own conclusions.

'Look,' Dan said at last, 'I was up his house one day and he got a bit, well, he got in my face. I told him to back off, that was all. I might have said I'd floor him, but I never actually touched him, right?'

'You make a habit of going to teachers' houses?'

'Course not. It was just... Look, Banks gets lads up to his house sometimes. He gives us money to help him out. Odd jobs and that. People say he's an old perv but I just reckon he likes to hang out, you know? We usually watch the match or whatever after.'

'And what about the day you lost your temper?'

'It was nothing, he was just having a go. He wanted me to up my grades a bit. I lost my temper, that was all.'

'Did Banks ever ask you to do anything inappropriate?' Alison asked.

'Fuck off! I would have floored him. Seriously.' Alison didn't speak.

'Look, he's alright really, old Banks. Just a bit of a loser. He gives us beers and stuff, you know, trying to be cool.'

There was an emphasis on 'trying', as if Banks had abjectly failed in that attempt.

'I'll need the names of the other boys there.'

'Shit, man, it ain't got nothing to do with Izzy.' Alison shook her head, wondering if it was worth explaining to the boy that grooming was a process. Maybe the boy was right, maybe Banks was a lonely man trying to be cool. Maybe he was a paedophile grooming teenage boys. Maybe he was a murderer. She shook her head. They hadn't quite ruled anything out yet.

'Was that the only time you ever lost your temper?' Alison asked. 'Never lose it with Izzy?'

'No.'

'Even when she refused to have sex with you.'

'Look, I'm chilled, man, I'm ice cold. Ask anyone. If Izzy needed a bit of time then I was gonna wait, I mean it's not like we were exclusive. You know? Plenty of other fish to fry, you know?'

'And that worked both ways, did it? You'd be cool if Izzy was seeing someone else?'

'Why would she do that?' Dan asked, running his hand through his hair and smiling. Alison ignored the flirtation.

'Did you have a fight with Izzy the day before she died?'

'Who told you that?'

'Is it true?'

'There was a bit of a disagreement, no biggy.'

'Was she dumping you?'

'No.' His voice was defiant.

'Did she tell you that all the time she'd been refusing to sleep with you she'd been having sex with Robbie Smith?'

'What? No.'

'She was dumping you, wasn't she? Was she going to tell everyone at school that she was choosing him over you? Was that what it was all about?'

'You've got it all wrong.'

'So set me straight.'

'No comment.' He smiled at her. Thinking he was clever.

'Izzy was heard telling you she was fed up of it. What was she fed up of, Dan? Fed up of you? Fed up of pretending when the one she really liked was Robbie?'

'No. Comment.'

'See, here's what it looks like to me, Dan. Just so you understand. Just so you can make an informed decision about how long you want to dick me about and when exactly you might decide to start telling me the truth. It looks to me like you had a row with Izzy the day before she died. She told you she was dumping you and that she'd rather go out with Robbie Smith. Now, I imagine that hurt your ego quite badly. I imagine you'd do quite a lot to stop that from happening, stop your friends from finding out your girlfriend preferred another boy. And so it's not much of a stretch to imagine you followed Izzy when she went out of school yesterday and you saw her up on the hill with Robbie, you lost your temper and you killed her. Does that sound about right to you?'

There was silence.

'Maybe all those years of seeing her living her perfect life, all that resentment had something to do with it too. You'd been man enough to forgive her for what her father did and there she was shagging someone else. Not just someone else but a druggy scumbag like Robbie Smith. I mean, what the hell was that going to do to your reputation around school?'

Still more silence.

'So you lost it. Understandable really. You saw she'd chosen him and you couldn't have that. You couldn't have people knowing that. So you hit her. Maybe you didn't mean for her to die. Maybe you just lost your temper. Was that it?'

He was shaking his head now, looking at his hands.

'Is that really what you think?' he asked. 'You can't think I... Come on, man... I never...'

'Where were you yesterday afternoon?'

'I was in class. I had history with Miss Walsh.'

'You sure about that?'

'Yes.'

'Try again, Dan. You see, we already checked. We know you left class early. So where did you go? You follow Izzy out to the Beamsleigh?'

'No, I... No, it had nothing to do with Izzy. I never hurt her... I wouldn't.'

'So tell me what happened.' He seemed scared now. And she was glad. She wanted him scared. She wanted him to realise that his big man act wasn't fooling anyone.

She waited.

'We did have a row,' Dan said. 'But it wasn't about Robbie, at least not like you think.'

'She admitted to you that she'd been seeing Robbie Smith?' Humphreys gave a hollow laugh.

'There wasn't anything to admit. I knew. I never thought she'd sleep with him, but, well, I knew they were together. That was the whole point.'

'The whole point?' Alison asked, confused.

'I was cover. I was the nice boy her parents could approve of, that her friends could be jealous of. I fitted the image. Image mattered to Izzy. I suppose after what an arsehole her father was, she was trying to make up for it somehow. I mean after what he did. She didn't want to be tarred with that brush.'

'And you went along with that? Even though what her father did cost you your sister and your mother?'

'That wasn't Izzy's fault.'

There was something more, Alison could sense it. It seemed like now he had begun he really needed to talk so she waited.

'Image is everything at our school,' Dan went on. 'Literally life and death. Like it's social suicide to go outside the norm, man. I know kids, kids who I hung with in primary school, and they do one really uncool thing and bam, they're labelled as weirdos and that's it... end of.'

'End of what?'

'Life, man. I mean no one invites you to parties, no one wants you on their team, no one to sit with in the lunch hall, total annihilation. Total.'

'But that never happened to Izzy, did it? She was popular, right?'

'God yeah, she was like the most popular, and she acted like she didn't care. But she did. I mean she was a bloody

Einstein. How the hell she made that cool I will never know. And all that shit with her dad, I mean that could have been the end. Would have been for most kids, but Izzy rode it. She got away with it. But this crap with Robbie Smith… I mean, come on, that would be the end.'

'Isn't there something cool about being a rebel?' Alison asked.

Humphreys looked disgusted.

'Have you seen the tracksuit he wears? The guy is the pits. He's got loser written all over him.'

'Maybe Izzy saw through that. Maybe she liked the person underneath.'

'I've got no idea what the hell she liked about him, but that's not the point. She wanted to have her cake and eat it. That was Izzy all over. She wanted to get her kicks with some low-life druggy, but she wanted to be liked at school and she wanted her mum to think she was little miss perfect, all at once.' Alison thought of Lucy Jacobs and Robbie both telling her that Izzy had had enough. Was this what they meant? That Izzy was tiring of the endless pressure to appear perfect whichever audience she played to? Cool for her friends, a good girl for her mother, an ideal student for her teachers?

'Where did you fit in with this perfect image?'

'She called me camouflage,' he said. 'Going out with me gave her cover to do what she wanted without anyone noticing.'

'And what did you get out of it?'

'I got to be the guy dating the hottest girl in the school.' The boast sounded hollow.

'Yeah, but you knew your girlfriend was seeing someone

else. The hottest girl in school was screwing someone else. That must have been pretty frustrating.'

'I coped.' Dan smiled sadly.

Alison suddenly remembered what Riordan had said, about seeing Dan in bars where he shouldn't have been. And the way Robbie had smirked when he said Dan knew he wasn't really Izzy's boyfriend. Now everything made sense.

'Are you gay, Dan?' she asked.

'Do I look gay?' he asked, holding out his hands.

Alison shook her head. What was that supposed to mean? Who the hell looked gay? The answer was too quick. Rehearsed. It might work on another teenager. It wasn't fooling Alison.

'I don't know many straight guys who'd be happy to date a girl who was sleeping with someone else,' she said.

Dan shrugged, but he couldn't quite pull off the nonchalance he was going for. There was something close to panic in his eyes.

'What did you row with Izzy about on Monday, Dan?' Alison said.

'I told you it was nothing.'

'If it was nothing you can tell me,' she said reassuringly. 'If it has nothing to do with the investigation it'll go no further.'

He looked at her for a very long time.

'There's nothing wrong with being gay,' she said. 'Surely you know that, right?'

'Been a long time since you were at school, hasn't it?' Dan said quietly.

'What did you argue with Izzy about?'

Another very long pause.

'Robbie knew,' Dan said at last.

'Knew what?' Alison asked; she needed him to say it.

'He'd seen me in Leeds last week. There was a man he knew... He told Izzy... told her the guy was bad news... told her to tell me to stay away from him.'

'And you argued because...?'

'I lost it, I didn't want *him* knowing... I didn't want him thinking... shit, I don't know what he thought... but I... I thought she'd told him, at first, and I was angry with her. Then she said maybe it was time... maybe we should stop keeping secrets.'

'And you didn't want that?'

'No... that's why I... That's why we argued.'

'Izzy had known all along? That you're gay I mean.'

'I'm not... I mean... Just don't say that word, OK? I'm not... well... whatever this thing is with guys... it's not...' He shook his head. 'Anyway whatever it is, Izzy knew.'

'You told her?' Alison asked.

'Nah, she just knew. I don't know how she figured it out. She just knew. That's why she said we should go out. It was after I dumped Lucy. Lucy must have told her I didn't... that we hadn't, you know... done it. So Izzy reckoned if we went out we'd be doing each other a favour. No one would ask questions if I was going with the hottest girl in the place. And it got her parents off her case, so she could go out and stuff without the constant interrogation. They loved me. If she said she was out with me they never asked any questions. Then when she got together with Robbie I was sort of her alibi. Whenever she wanted to go out with him, she'd say she was at mine.'

'But she was sick of the pretence?'

'I don't know. She said maybe it was time to tell the truth. But then Monday night she texted me and said forget it, she wouldn't tell anyone.'

'I'll need to see that text.'

Dan nodded and removed his phone from his pocket at once.

'*Soz for today. I won't drop u in it if ur not ready.*' It was hardly eloquent but it backed up Dan's story.

'Who were you with in Leeds last week?' Alison asked.

'Sorry?'

'The man Robbie saw you with. I need his name.' He blushed again, a very deep crimson this time.

'I don't know... it was just... it was a club... They're... well... they're pretty anonymous. You can just... just do stuff.'

She nodded.

She'd been there, as a young woman. She'd known the sort of self-loathing that meant you ended up 'doing stuff' anonymously in clubs. She wanted to tell him that he could have so much more than that. She stopped herself. She wasn't his mother or his friend. It wasn't her job.

'Where were you when Izzy was killed?' she asked instead.

'I had an appointment.'

'I'm going to need more than that.'

'It's private.'

'Yeah, I get it... but until I find out what happened to Isabella Johnson nothing is private.' Dan scowled at her for a moment, then pulled a business card out of his pocket.

Ridgedale Counselling Services.

'I go once a month now, used to be more when Mum first died. I don't really need… I'm a lot better these days… I just go because… well, I just go. Usually I go in the evenings, after school, but my counsellor was busy this month and that was the only time she could fit me in.'

Alison nodded.

'I'll have to check that you were there.'

Dan nodded.

'I'll ring her and tell her it's OK to talk to you.'

'Thank you,' Alison said.

He seemed like a different young man now. She suspected that she was finally talking to the real Dan Humphreys and she liked him a lot more than the image he was trying to portray.

She got up to leave.

'School doesn't last forever,' she said from the door. He smiled at her.

'I know… it just feels that way, that's all.'

THIRTEEN

When they got back to the station Bob Johnson, Izzy's stepfather, was waiting for them.

'You arrested him yet?' he asked, as soon as Alison had taken him to her office.

'Who?'

'Robbie Smith. I heard it was him.'

'We're still making enquiries. So far we have a number of people we're speaking to.'

'Yeah, well they've been a scourge on this town ever since they moved in, that bloody family. And that Robbie's always been a wrong'un. And what were the school doing letting kids out to meet up with drug dealers in the middle of the day? And the police... you know what they're like, that family... but no one does anything.' Alison took a breath, holding her temper because she understood his impotent fury.

'Mr Johnson, we're doing all we can to move the investigation forward, and we have a number of people to speak to in connection to your stepdaughter's death, but just because someone comes from a less than respectable family doesn't mean...'

'So what about this then?' Johnson asked.

He took a small plastic bag from his pocket. Inside were half a dozen round white pills. Alison took the bag and raised her eyebrows at Johnson questioningly.

'I found that in Izzy's room.'

'When?'

'About a week ago.'

'A week ago? And you didn't think to tell us about this yesterday?'

'I didn't want... Look, Leanne thinks the sun shines out of Isabella's backside. Only child, and after all that shit with Andy and the crash it's a miracle Izzy turned out as well as she did. But no one's perfect. Only Leanne couldn't see it.'

'What did you do when you found these?' Alison asked, holding up the bag of pills.

'I asked Izzy about them.'

'And?'

'She said they weren't what I thought they were. I don't do drugs, so I have no bloody idea what they are, but I know they're not bloody aspirin. So I asked her where she got them.'

'And did she tell you?'

'No.' He shook his head angrily. 'But it must be him. Robbie Smith.'

'Why have you kept these? Why not get rid of them as soon as you confiscated them?' Alison asked.

'I wanted some proof, in case... Well, Izzy could be devious. Leanne never saw any bad in her, never believed...'

So he wanted something over Izzy. So much for adoring her.

'Look,' Johnson went on, 'Izzy promised she wasn't taking anything, so I said I wouldn't tell Leanne. I just kept the pills so I'd have some proof if I ever... if Izzy broke her word.'

Alison shook her head.

'But those pills don't prove anything. Izzy would just have to say she'd never seen them before. You have no evidence you found them in Izzy's room.'

'You don't believe me?'

Alison sighed.

'Yes, I do believe you. I'm just saying Leanne probably wouldn't have. And Izzy probably knew that.'

Johnson shook his head.

'I hate bloody clever women,' he muttered.

And I hate dumb-shit men, Alison thought. If Izzy was taking drugs, then Johnson confiscating her stash would mean she had had to get more. The questions were what were the drugs and where was she getting them?

'Were you aware of any changes in Izzy's behaviour? Anything that might suggest she was using drugs?'

He flushed, shook his head.

'Mr Johnson, please... if you think you're protecting Izzy you're not. I don't care what she may or may not have done, all I care about is finding the person who killed her.'

'I found the pill.'

'The contraceptive pill? In Izzy's room?'

'Yeah.'

Alison refrained from asking why he hadn't mentioned that before. She really didn't have time.

'Did you confiscate those too?'

'You joking? Last thing we needed was a teenage pregnancy.'

'So what did you do?'

'Told her I knew. Told her to keep it a secret from her mother.'

'What did she say to that?'

'She laughed. Said she knew her mum would kill her if she found out and she didn't have a death wish.'

His eyes widened.

'It was just a figure of speech... I mean Leanne would never...' Alison interrupted him.

'When did you find the contraceptives? Last week when you found the other pills?'

'God no. No, it was ages ago. Back in the summer, I suppose. I mean she was sixteen, but still, it's young, isn't it?' Back in the summer. Before Robbie came on the scene.

'Did you ask her about any boyfriends she might have?' He shook his head.

'Not my place, is it? But she was seeing a lot of that Mills boy back then. Andrea's lad... you know the one who went off to Oxford or Cambridge or whichever. He was supposedly tutoring her. But when in hell did our Izzy ever need tutoring? She's been smarter than me ever since I met her and she could only have been about seven then.'

He almost laughed but it turned at the last moment to a tear. His first real sign of emotion.

'Did you remove anything else from Izzy's bedroom?' Alison asked. Johnson shook his head.

'I haven't been in since... since it happened. Her mother's been up there but she just sits on the bed. Your guys searched, of course. I don't know what they took away.'

Alison nodded.

She would have to go through the findings from Izzy's

room, but if there had been anything significant she was sure she'd have heard by now.

'Did Izzy have a diary of any sort? Somewhere she'd write down appointments or who she was meeting, that sort of thing.'

'I don't think so. They all use their phones for that sort of thing. Only time she ever used pen and paper was for her maths journal, she always had that with her.'

'A journal? Would it have personal information in it?'

'I don't think so. It was all equations. Squiggly marks I couldn't even tell you the name of, let alone what they're supposed to mean.'

'You say she'd have had it with her?'

'Yeah, always kept it with her. God knows why, but it meant something to her. Absolute gobbledegook to anyone else. Except maybe that Mills boy or Mr Riordan up at the school. Maths geeks basically.'

'OK, Mr Johnson, thanks for bringing these in,' Alison said, holding up the pills. 'Unless there's anything else?'

He shook his head and Alison ushered him out.

The Mills boy.

Had Izzy really been seeing Andrea Mills' son last summer as her stepfather suggested? Alison had barely looked at him when they had met at Andrea's house. Could he be connected somehow? Another boy who might be jealous of Izzy's relationship with Robbie? She decided it would make sense to pay him a visit. First, of course, she needed to get the pills analysed.

She saw Holly as Johnson left the office.

'You went and had a look at Izzy's room today, didn't you?' she asked Holly.

'Yeah.'

'Anything interesting?'

'Nothing. It was just a typical teenage bedroom. Except…'

'What?'

'Nothing.'

'Spit it out, Holz.'

'Well, everyone says how unusual she was. A big genius and everything but there was no evidence of it. It was… it was almost too ordinary.'

Alison thought about what Dan had said. Image was important to Izzy. But if even her bedroom was part of her managed image where was the real Izzy? On her missing phone? In the notebook full of gobbledegook?

'Thanks, Holz,' Alison said.

'It's stupid, isn't it?'

'Not at all. Izzy was extraordinary. You're right that we need to keep that in mind. But it doesn't mean the reasons she died can't have been pedestrian. If you hear hooves you think horses not zebras.'

'Got it,' Holly said with a smile.

As Alison headed out the door Debbie on reception called her back, holding out the phone.

'You might want to take this,' she said. 'A guy called Ben Adams? Says he's got some information about the case.'

'Ben Adams?' Alison said.

'He's the guy who gave Robbie Smith a lift back up from Leeds. I spoke to him earlier,' Holly said. Her tone betrayed her fear that she had missed something. Alison took the phone.

'Mr Adams. This is DI Dobson, how can I help?'

'Are you the person in charge? Looking into the killing of that poor girl?'

'Yes. You have information, I understand.'

'I was expecting a man… is that awful of me? In this day and age. Not that I mind a woman in charge. I rather like a powerful woman. The idea that she could dominate me… rather delicious, I find. I'm quite charmed to speak to a female… even given the circumstances.'

'How may I help?' Alison asked, reminding herself of the disastrous summer she had once spent as a receptionist when she was a student. She had never quite been able to pull off that phrase without sounding insincere.

'Has anyone ever told you you have a charming voice? I'm sure they have. I've always been quite a sucker for a northern accent.'

Alison waited, unsure how, or even if, she was supposed to respond.

'Sorry, inappropriate under the circumstances. I'm desperately influenced by voices. Robbie has a rather wonderful voice, don't you think?'

'You said you had some information for us?' Alison asked again.

'Oh yes. Yes. Well, no, not information as such…'

'But you have something to tell us?'

'I've spoken to Robbie… He's… well, he's understandably upset. He rather doted on the girl… Lucky her. Anyway, yes he's rather upset and he told me that he had told you his phone was stolen and that you, or rather the police generally, seemed disinclined to believe him.'

'Do you know anything about his phone?' Alison asked.

'Yes. I was with Robbie on Tuesday evening. I can

confirm that he had definitely lost his phone. Perhaps it was stolen, or he misplaced it. I offered to buy him a new one, but you know how young people are… their lives are on their phones. He was unhappy about it all evening. My offers to cheer him up were not appreciated.'

His tone was lascivious, almost predatory.

'I'm glad to say he has now accepted my offer… of a new phone I mean. My offer of comfort is still currently being rejected, I'm afraid, but I live in hope.'

He chuckled in a self-satisfied way.

'Is that it?' Alison asked, more sharply than she had intended. 'You're confirming that Robbie's phone was stolen?'

'Yes. And I wanted to tell you… well, I just *know* Robbie couldn't have had anything to do with it. He's a good boy. Well, no, not good. But who wants good? So dull.'

'When you saw him on Tuesday, how did he seem?' Alison interrupted.

'Fine. A bit quiet, a bit upset. I think that's why he was so angry about the phone. They'd had a row, him and the girl. He kept saying his photos of her were on the phone.'

'They'd had a row?' Alison asked.

'Oh God, am I making it worse?' Adams said lightly. 'God, look, Robbie's a bit of a lad, but he's sweet. Sweet as a peach in fact. He would never have… I mean surely you have other suspects, more likely suspects than dear Robbie. Even in a sleepy little place like that, Robbie can't be the most likely?'

'Thank you, Mr Adams.' Alison cut him off. 'If you think of anything else please call.'

'I shall, even if it's just to hear your rather delicious voice.' Alison ended the call.

She didn't have time for this. She wanted to speak to Dominic Mills. But before she could get out of the building Jack Kent appeared with a gleam in his eyes.

FOURTEEN

'The big boss wants to see you,' Kent told Alison.

'Did he say what about?'

'Nope. Just said you were to get your bloody arse in there whenever you decided to finally make an appearance.'

'His usual cheerful self then,' Alison said, trying to smile. A summons to DCI Rogers' office was never a welcome part of her day. She knocked on the door and waited.

'Come,' Rogers barked at last.

Alison couldn't help smiling. She and Paul had often joked that that was probably what he shouted at his wife when they were making love. But Alison had met Rogers' wife on a number of occasions; she was far from the sort of woman anyone could bark at. Janice Rogers was confident, outspoken and prone to laughter. She was a well-respected academic with strong opinions and a willingness to express them. Alison had even seen her on TV on a few occasions talking about education and feminist issues. Maybe Rogers felt the need to be such a bully at work because he would never get away with it at home.

'You wanted to see me, sir?' Alison said when she entered the room.

'I know that,' he said, choosing to be pedantic. 'I presume what you meant to say was "why did you ask to see me, sir?"'

Alison didn't reply. There was no point. Rogers enjoyed being annoyed.

He pushed the intercom on his desk then shouted so loudly that it made the action unnecessary.

'Could you get that bloody woman up here? DI Dobson has finally shown her face.' Alison heard Sarah Jones' quiet reply through the intercom. Sarah had worked for Rogers even longer than she had; she must have the patience of a saint to be at his beck and call all day. Sarah was good at her job – efficient, presentable and not known for 'fannying about'. Although Alison had never heard Rogers praise his PA she had never heard him actively criticise her either, and coming from Rogers that was a huge compliment. He turned to Alison now.

'OK, so fill me in. The girl died practically in your own back garden. Piss-ant little town like that one, it can't be that hard to solve. Someone must have seen something.'

Alison didn't rise to his bait but simply began a calm summary. She liked to do this. Going through the facts for someone new could often help to clarify them in her own mind.

'Isabella Johnson,' she said. 'Seventeen years old, a student at the local comprehensive school. Found by a jogger, Mrs Andrea Mills, at approximately two thirty on Tuesday afternoon in a popular dog-walking spot a two- or three-minute walk from the school Izzy attended. She was dead when the paramedics arrived. It appears that she was garrotted using a thin wire of some sort but forensics haven't found anything at the scene that could be the murder weapon. Jenny McBride is in charge so it'll be a thorough job.'

It suddenly occurred to her that she had heard some complaints recently about people setting rabbit traps around the town. A wire rabbit trap might fit the description of Izzy's murder weapon. She made a mental note to mention it to Jenny.

'Go on,' DCI Rogers grunted, impatient of any pause.

'Initial examination of the body found traces of semen, but no evidence of force being used. There were some partially digested pills in the victim's stomach but we haven't discovered what they were yet. Her stepfather has just handed me some pills he found in Izzy's room weeks ago, so I'll send them off for analysis to see if they match the stomach contents.'

She paused, expecting Rogers to comment but he said nothing.

She continued.

'Izzy's schoolbag was with the body when she was found. Her purse was inside but her mobile phone is missing. The only other thing we found was a note which implied she had been planning to meet a teacher. It talked about not telling anyone and how he was able to explain.'

'This is the note from Mr Banks? Her English teacher?'

'Yes,' Alison said. 'We spoke to him and he had an explanation for the note, although in my opinion not a very good one.' Another humph from the DCI. Alison's opinions clearly didn't count for much.

'We took his computer and it's blank. I mean really blank, like it's been erased.'

'Lack of evidence cannot be taken as evidence,' Rogers pointed out. 'You know that.'

'I know. And he has an alibi. He was in class for all but a ten-minute window yesterday afternoon. But I still don't like it. The guys in the lab are looking at the computer seeing what they can discover.'

'Not anymore.'

'Sorry?'

'There is much for you to be sorry for, DI Dobson, I'm sure. However, what you mean in this instance is "excuse me but I don't understand".'

He waited as if expecting Alison to repeat the phrase. She remained silent. Rogers sighed.

'Mr Banks hired a lawyer this morning. She argued, quite reasonably, that since her client had an alibi for the time of the killing and no motive whatsoever for wanting to harm Isabella Johnson and since he had explained the note which was your only reason for suspecting him – however unsatisfactory you may find that explanation – and since we have found no evidence on his computer of any connection to this killing, there is no reason to examine it any further.'

'You let him have it back?' Alison asked, astounded.

'As I have just explained to you, there was no logical reason for us to keep it,' Rogers said. 'So after you wasted an inordinate amount of time with Mr Banks what did you do next?'

'We talked to Izzy's friends.'

'I'm not asking about your social life. I don't want details of every person you spoke to and what you had for tea or when you went for a shit. How has the case progressed?'

'The DNA results for the semen on Izzy's body came back to a Robbie Smith.'

'Local drug dealer and general lowlife.'

Alison didn't ask how he knew that. DCI Rogers had his faults but he knew what was going on locally wherever his team were working. He made a point of it.

'Robbie admits to meeting Izzy yesterday. He says they had sex and then went their separate ways and he spent the night with friends in Leeds. He certainly seemed shocked when we told him about Isabella's death.'

'When I want an assessment of a suspect's acting abilities I'll ask a film critic,' Rogers said. There was a knock at the door. A pause.

'Go on,' Rogers said to Alison. She glanced at the door but Rogers kept his eyes on her.

'We checked out Robbie's story. He was certainly in Leeds but it doesn't really give him an alibi. The time of death would have been just before or just after he says he left Izzy. But equally he doesn't have any real motive to kill her. We think they argued but he says he left her amicably enough. We've taken his clothes to check for blood... Actually I was just about to chase that up.'

She paused, but again Rogers didn't speak.

'The only other person of possible interest is Dan Humphreys, Izzy's *supposed* boyfriend. He has a bit of a temper and they had argued the day before she died. He wasn't in school when she died but he's given us an explanation of where he was. DS Skinner is checking that out.'

'And Humphreys would kill Ms Johnson why?'

'Couple of possible reasons. They had an odd relationship. Dan's gay and desperate to hide it. Dating Izzy gave him cover. And she was using Dan to hide the fact she was actually seeing Robbie. Izzy was heard telling Dan she was fed up, or words to that effect, the day before she died. Maybe she was tired of dating him. It's possible that he feared she was about to expose his secret.' Rogers looked sceptical, as if unimpressed with this possible motive.

Alison pressed on.

'Also Dan Humphreys' sister was killed in the Whitby coach crash and Izzy's father was the driver. He must have resented Izzy...'

'Long time ago that crash,' Rogers said.

'Yes, sir, but...'

'Anyone else look likely?'

'Not really, sir. I've just found out Izzy has been on the pill since the summer. She was friendly with a boy called Dominic Mills around that time. Andrea Mills' son as it happens. If they were intimate and if he was jealous it might give him a motive. I was about to go and see...'

Rogers held up his hand for silence.

'Sounds like you've been busy,' he said. 'You sound *almost* as if you actually know what you're doing. But all this other stuff is a distraction, surely. Robbie Smith has to be the focus. Come in.'

He barely raised his voice on these last words and Alison took a second to register that they were directed not at her, but at the person behind the door waiting to enter the room.

Nothing happened.

'Come,' Rogers bellowed, making Alison jump. The office door opened, and a tall woman in a very expensive-looking suit entered. Alison recognised her vaguely, although she was sure they hadn't met. The woman was carrying a briefcase that screamed lawyer, but her smile was friendly enough. She stuck out a hand.

'Marianne Downes, Media Liaison,' she said as she walked up to Alison. 'You must be DI Alison Dobson, the face of modern policing in North Yorkshire.'

There was no hint of sarcasm in her voice, although Alison was sure she must be joking. She took the woman's outstretched hand, which was warm and firm. A good handshake.

'Right, has DCI Rogers briefed you on what's going to happen?'

'Sorry?'

'DI Dobson has a habit of apologising rather than communicating directly,' Rogers said. 'I think it's a female thing.'

And you have a habit of being a knob, which I imagine is a male thing, Alison thought, although she said nothing.

'I was getting up to speed on the case before letting the DI know about our little jolly this afternoon.'

'Right,' Downes said, seemingly undaunted. 'As I'm sure you're aware, the Isabella Johnson murder is attracting a lot of media attention. Beautiful young woman, model student, idyllic rural location.'

Alison thought of the dog-shit-strewn hill in the middle of town where Izzy had died. In her opinion it neither qualified as idyllic nor rural, but she said nothing.

'There are rumours of sex and drugs. There are rumours

that this may be a motiveless killing. The press are baying for a "Moors murder" part two.'

It wasn't on the moors, Alison thought, and anyway these were different moors. Still, the press liked alliteration.

'We need a quick result. Be seen to be doing something. There are spending cuts in the offing and we do not want to be on the wrong side of them. Sure you understand.'

Rogers was scowling at Downes but Alison knew this was exactly the sort of thing he would have said to her himself. Without the smile, of course, or the reassuring nod.

'We always strive for a quick result,' Alison said. 'But we have to do things right. Sometimes that takes a while.'

'Yes, absolutely. The right result. Achieved in the right way. God yes. I mean we absolutely cannot get this wrong with all the press looking on. And of course if it's not done absolutely by the book, well, the trial would be... You know all of that. I mean shouldn't make any difference if anyone's watching or not but...'

'It *doesn't* make any difference if anyone's watching,' Alison said forcefully. Marianne Downes smiled.

'With all due respect, Inspector, I do think that's a little naive.' Alison blinked. It was a very long time since anyone had called her naive.

'The media is a huge power in this country. If it decides that you're not doing the job fast enough or well enough or whatever... well, let's just say it can be detrimental to one's career. And ultimately the whole force can suffer. It's my job to prevent that.'

'I don't see what this has to do with me.'

'Be seen to be doing everything we can. That's the main

point. Keep the media happy. The press like justice to be *seen* to be done, and done swiftly.'

'And is the "swift" part of that sentence more important than the "just" part?' Alison asked.

'Of course not,' Downes said, continuing to smile. 'But I understand you have a suspect. An arrest would look very good about now.'

'Robbie Smith is just one line of inquiry. We have other people to speak to.' Downes cut her off.

'Would arresting Robbie Smith in any way prevent you speaking to other possible suspects?'

'No, but… I'm not sure Robbie did…'

'I'm not saying he did it. I'm saying an arrest would show that the investigation is moving along, it would show us doing something.'

'Is doing *something* more important than doing the *right* thing?' Alison asked again.

'Surely arresting a viable suspect *is* the right thing to do.' Downes smiled even more widely. 'After all, an arrest doesn't have to lead to charges. An arrested man can always be released. A suspect can be vindicated and a new suspect found. The press understand that.'

And fuck Robbie Smith, Alison thought. Fuck his chance of being presumed innocent. A new suspect could always be found, but no one would ever forget that Robbie had been arrested. The taint would stay with him forever, and not just in this town but everywhere if the national press got hold of it.

Downes looked at her watch.

'I'm giving a news conference this afternoon, it would be super to be able to say an arrest had been made. I would have liked you to make the announcement, but DCI Rogers assures me you're far too busy.'

Alison said a silent 'thank you' to Rogers for that.

'I'll rely on you then,' Downes said. 'And announce the arrest this afternoon.' She shook Alison's hand again.

'Excellent.'

She was still beaming as she left the room.

'Media Liaison making the decisions for us now, sir?' Alison asked.

'Certainly looks that way, Dobson,' Rogers replied, his usual bluster gone and a look of genuine disgust on his face. 'Just arrest the little toe rag, will you. Then get out there and find some bloody evidence. Either prove it was him or prove it was some other fucker. OK?'

'Yes, sir.'

'I don't want any fannying about on this, Dobson, I do *not* appreciate lessons on how to run my team from some jumped-up toffee-nosed media consultant. Get the bloody job done, so I can get her out of my hair.'

FIFTEEN

Alison slammed the door to Rogers' office.

'You OK?' Paul asked.

She wanted to turn to him like she had so many times in the past year. She wanted him to let her rant about Rogers until she saw the funny side, and then agree with her that he was a dick. But her relationship with Paul had to be nothing but professional now. Because of a stupid drunken night in Harrogate.

'Rogers wants Robbie arrested,' she said.

'OK. Let's go.'

'Jesus, you don't need to sound so eager.'

'I'm not… I just… Well, it makes sense, doesn't it?'

'Why does it make sense? Because he was a naughty boy and he's done a bit of dealing? That makes him a killer?'

'No… but everything points…'

Alison cut across him.

'Holly,' she called.

Holly came over.

'I want you and Kent to arrest Robbie Smith.' Holly looked surprised but pleased with the responsibility.

'OK, boss.'

If Paul was surprised or disappointed not to be making the arrest, he didn't show it.

'What are we going to do?' he asked.

'*You're* going to carry on checking the whereabouts of everyone Izzy knew. I want to talk to Andrea Mills again. And her son Dominic.'

Put him in his place and keep him there. No special treatment. No matter how many drunken late-night phone calls and requests 'to talk' he might make.

No one had yet come forward identifying themselves as the hooded figure Andrea had seen on the Beamsleigh Hill. Alison wanted to see if Andrea had remembered anything more. If she was honest with herself she was hoping for some detail that might rule out Robbie Smith. She was also keen to speak to Dominic and find out about his relationship with Izzy the previous summer. It was a long shot, but he might also know something about the little white pills found at her house.

Paul had made it very clear he thought the trip was a waste of time. She was glad he wasn't with her.

'DI Dobson, come in,' Andrea said as she opened the door. She looked better today. She had her hair tied into a ponytail and she was wearing a little makeup. 'Coffee?'

'Thanks,' Alison said, following her into the kitchen so they could talk while Andrea made the drinks.

'This is my son Dominic,' Andrea said, nodding towards the young man sitting up at the breakfast bar.

'We met briefly,' Alison said, looking more closely at Dominic Mills.

He was slim and pale. A rash of acne covered his cheeks

and he blushed slightly when he said hello to Alison, not quite meeting her eye. His mother had said he was at university, but he looked younger than his years.

'He's up at Cambridge,' Andrea said, her voice emphasising 'up' just enough to make Alison aware that she wasn't yet used to saying the phrase.

Alison had never understood why people went 'up' to Oxford and Cambridge and came down from there on graduation. Just as one went 'up' to London, not down. It made no sense to her as all three places were 'down south' as far as she was concerned.

There was a hint of satisfaction in the way Andrea said the sentence now though, as if she was proud of mastering the syntax as well as of her son's achievements.

'You having a break?' Alison asked him.

'Yeah, I'm on a reading week. I was going to go back this morning... but I thought... with Izzy and, well, Mum... I thought I might stay around... see if Mum needed me... go to the funeral... show my respects.'

'He's always been a thoughtful lad,' Andrea said, ruffling his hair as if he were a child. She busied herself with the coffee and Alison sat down opposite Dominic.

'Did you know Izzy well?' she asked.

She had had the distinct impression from Andrea the last time they met that no one of her family had really known the girl. But Bob Johnson had mentioned Dominic tutoring her. He had hinted that their relationship might have been more than that.

'You must have been a couple of years ahead of her in school,' Alison went on.

Dominic laughed shyly.

'I'm a couple of years older than her, I wouldn't say I was ahead of her. She ran rings around me really. Some of the stuff she had in her journal, I couldn't make head or tail of it.'

'You're too modest, Dom,' Andrea put in. 'Always have been.' Dominic didn't reply to his mother, instead he addressed Alison.

'I was supposed to mentor Izzy, last summer. Mr Riordan set up this programme. He wanted some of the ex-pupils, those of us who had got into good universities, to sort of encourage the most able kids in the school. A way of getting more kids into the top universities, he said, and it'll look good on our CVs too. Izzy was great, but it was really obvious from the start that I couldn't teach her anything. Not about the subject anyway.'

'And that subject is maths, right?'

'Yeah, that's right. That's what Izzy's doing too. Sorry, *would* have done. She got an unconditional offer last year. I knew she would. She was due to come up to Cambridge in October.'

'An unconditional offer?'

'It meant they didn't care what A-levels she got. They had seen what she was capable of and they wanted her no matter what.'

That might explain why Izzy had been happy to take her eye off the ball. Happy to play at bad girl with Robbie Smith because she already had her future lined up.

'I'm sure you mentoring her helped her get that place, Dominic,' his mother said, turning around from the kettle and beaming in pride at her son.

'First to go to university in our family and goes straight

in at the top. You don't get any better than Cambridge. I mean, seriously, it is the best place in the world.'

'OK, Mum,' Dominic said, although he half smiled indulgently.

'So you knew Izzy quite well?' Alison said, interrupting.

'Yeah, I guess. I mean I'm away at uni most of the time but we kept in touch. Facebook and Snapchat, you know. I was really pleased when she got her offer, but like I say, I knew she would. I told her, just show them your journal and they'll be blown away.'

'This is a maths journal?'

'Yeah, a place to jot ideas and stuff. I have one. Lots of maths students do. Mostly they're full of rubbish, generic stuff anyone could come up with. But Izzy's was just full of all these amazing proofs and stuff.'

'Would it be of any value to anyone else?' Alison asked. She had had a quick look at the contents of Izzy's bag; the maths book seemed to be missing.

'No, not really.'

He looked upset.

'Izzy would be devastated to lose it. All her best ideas were in there.'

'You were fond of Izzy,' Alison said. Not really a question.

'Yeah. I liked her a lot.'

'When did you last see her?'

'I saw her when I first got back, last Saturday. A few of us were in the pub. Then we were supposed to meet Thursday, just for a catch-up, but she ended up having to go see Mr Riordan so that got cancelled. I can't believe someone would... I just can't believe what happened to her.'

'What about Robbie Smith? You know him?' Andrea whipped around but Dominic answered smoothly.

'I know him by sight. Everyone does. I've probably been to one or two parties when he's been there too. Seen him in the pub, that sort of thing.'

'Dom!' His mother looked scandalised. 'I've always told you to stay away from that family.'

'I didn't say we were friends, Mum. I've just seen him around.' Andrea shook her head as if lost for words. She picked up the two coffee cups and gestured to Alison that she should follow her through to the living room. Reluctantly Alison made to stand, just as the house phone began to ring.

Andrea looked annoyed, but she said 'excuse me' politely and went into the hall to answer the call.

Alison took the opportunity to be alone with Dominic.

'You ever see Robbie with Izzy?'

He thought for a moment.

'Not that I remember, but like I say I'm not here most of the time.'

'Would you be surprised to hear they were going out together?'

'Not really. Nothing much Izzy did would surprise me.' There was real fondness in his voice.

'Your mum gave me the impression she barely knew Izzy,' Alison pressed on, 'but she must have seen her a lot last summer, if you were her mentor.'

'Yeah, she was in and out of here all the time.' Dominic frowned. 'I think Mum thought I was in love with her.'

'Were you?'

He shrugged.

'Maybe a bit. We fooled around a couple of times, but I always knew she was out of my league. Mum's old-fashioned, she doesn't really get the way people date these days. She thinks that people are either together or they're not, and if you're together that means, like, marriage and kids and the whole thing. She probably acted like I didn't know Izzy because, well, I suppose she probably didn't want you to think… She wouldn't want any gossip, I suppose. Izzy being younger than me and us not really being an item – officially I mean… Mum didn't really approve. But Izzy was sixteen last summer. So it was all… well, it was all OK.'

'What was OK? Are you saying you slept together?' He nodded, blushing furiously.

'And your mum knows?'

'I think she suspects, although it's not the sort of thing we would ever talk about.'

'So that's why she gave the impression she barely knew Izzy? Because she didn't want to admit…'

'To admit I'm the defiler of young girls?' Dom laughed, his face beetroot. 'Sorry… that's just what Izzy used to say, that I had defiled her, taken her maidenhood that sort of thing. It wasn't like that though really, we were both… both virgins. It was lovely actually.'

'And Izzy ended it?'

'Yeah. Like I say, I knew she would. She was nice about it though, said we could stay friends and we have sort of. I mean I haven't seen much of her, but I'm away, so…'

He didn't sound angry or jealous. He sounded like a boy recounting a pleasant time in his past. If he was capable of passionate rages there was no sign of it now. Alison waited for him to say more.

'Mum cares a lot about family reputation,' Dominic continued. 'She wants me to be the perfect Cambridge undergraduate. I suppose fooling about with a schoolgirl doesn't fit into that image for her.'

'I guess you knowing the local drug dealer doesn't fit that image either,' Alison said. 'She looked horrified when you said you knew Robbie Smith.'

'It's almost a superstition with her, keeping us away from bad influences. Robbie's probably her worst nightmare.'

'You ever buy drugs from Robbie?' Alison asked. Dominic looked at her for a long moment, as if deciding whether to lie.

'I bought pot from him once or twice,' he said in the end. 'Everyone does.'

'You ever buy anything else? Pills?'

'No. I never saw Robbie selling any of that stuff.'

'And you never knew Izzy to take pills?'

'No. What sort of pills? No… I never…'

Alison nodded. He was blushing again. He could be lying, but he blushed so often it might mean nothing. And why would he lie?

'Would your mum recognise Robbie Smith if she saw him?' Dominic smiled.

'I think everyone in town would recognise Robbie, even Mum. She might not want to admit it but she *does* know who he is.'

'Why wouldn't she want to admit it?' Alison asked.

'That superstition thing again. Plus she's sort of an ostrich. You know, head in the sand. She wants the world to be roses and rainbows, especially around here. Robbie doesn't fit her image of Penbury at all.'

He paused, thinking.

'If she'd seen Robbie yesterday though, I mean with something as serious as this, I'm sure she would have said. She wouldn't bury her head about something as serious as that. If she recognised him she'd've said. Only, well, she's blind as a bat without her glasses or contacts so...'

'So it could have been him, Robbie, up on the Beamsleigh? Your mum just might not have been close enough to see?'

'Do you think he did it?' Dominic asked.

'We don't know, we're keeping all options open.' It was a police-speak answer but what else could she say? She didn't know whether she thought Robbie did it or not. And so far she had no proof either way. Andrea popped her head back round the door.

'Sorry, Inspector,' she said. 'Coffee's in the lounge.'

Seated in the lounge opposite Andrea and her son Alison repeated most of her questions. Why hadn't Andrea made it clear how well she knew Izzy? Would she have recognised Robbie if she saw him? Could she see well enough to say it definitely wasn't Robbie on the Beamsleigh?

Andrea gave basically the same answers to those her son had given.

She hadn't known Izzy well. Yes, she had come around to the house when Dom was mentoring her, but last summer was a long time ago and she herself had barely spoken to the girl. Yes, she knew Robbie although she wished she didn't. She'd definitely recognise him, but she couldn't be one hundred percent sure, given the distance, that it wasn't him she saw vaulting the fence.

'If I could be sure it was him I'd say so,' Andrea said.

'Everyone's saying he killed Izzy and it could have been him I saw. But honestly, Inspector, I'm not sure.'

'They can be a rather intimidating family,' Alison said cautiously.

Andrea gave a derisive snort.

'I'm not afraid of people like that,' she said fiercely. 'It's one of the problems with this country – too many people afraid to stand up to folk like that. But not round here, we don't stand for it round here.'

'Don't stand for what?' Alison asked.

'Anti-social behaviour, drinking and shouting, selling drugs to little kids.'

'You ever suspect Robbie of selling drugs to little kids?'

'I did more than suspect, I saw him, and I reported him up at the school for hanging around outside and offering them to the kids as they left.'

'Mum.' There was a warning in Dominic's voice.

'I'm sorry, Dom, but I couldn't just let it go.'

'You know that wasn't... Robbie had nothing to do with...'

'I know what I saw. I saw him hanging around and he's a drug dealer. So I told Mr Riordan about it. He sorted it. Never saw that Smith boy up there again.' She paused. 'His mother didn't like it though. Cursed me out in the Co-op next day. Told me to mind my own family and let her deal with hers. But that's the thing, isn't it? If Sharon Smith had taken care of her own family we wouldn't be in this situation now.'

'Mum, you can't say that. You don't know it was Robbie.'

'Well, no, maybe not, but still.'

Alison finished her coffee quickly.

It had not been a very productive visit. Andrea had agreed to come into the station later in the day to look at some mugshots, and compile an e-fit. But what use would that be? She had barely seen anything. Still, it needed to be done. Another item ticked off Alison's to-do list. It didn't feel like progress.

Time to interview Robbie.

SIXTEEN

News of Robbie's arrest was already on the radio as Alison drove back to the station. They referred to him as 'a local youth believed to have a substantial criminal record'. It was the truth, but it didn't reflect the reality. She felt for his mother. Whatever he was he would always be a little boy to her.

She pulled Paul aside to discuss the case with him.

'What do we really think of Smith as a suspect?' she asked.

'Apart from being low-life scum, you mean?' Paul said.

'I was hoping maybe we could be a bit more objective than that.' Robbie Smith reminded her of her younger self. She knew Paul knew that. Hearing Robbie called scum felt like a personal affront. And Paul would never understand the power of those words. Despite how well they had got on, despite Harrogate, there were still so many things Paul didn't understand about her. Like how close she had come to having Robbie Smith's life. She didn't want to discuss it now.

'Case against Robbie,' she said. 'He was with Izzy right before she died. He has no alibi for the time of her death. He's a known drug dealer and she had drugs in her body.'

Paul interrupted.

'Nothing like what Robbie usually deals though. He deals dope, and Izzy had pills in her stomach. So if Robbie gave them to her where did he get them?'

Alison nodded, but continued.

'Robbie's also got a record for assault.'

'Nothing like this though,' Paul said fairly. 'A schoolboy fight. Hardly in the same league, is it?' Again Alison nodded.

'Motive's weak, but it's possible he could have lost his temper if they argued or she threatened to break up with him.'

'Looks more premeditated than that,' Paul said, acting as devil's advocate again. 'Whoever did this brought the wire with them, and took it away with them too.'

'Yeah, but I've been thinking about that. Could it have been a rabbit trap?'

'A what?'

'A rabbit trap – it's a trap for catching rabbits,' Alison said, raising an eyebrow.

'Yeah, thanks, I worked that out. But is that likely? Would someone set traps up there? Does it match the injuries?'

'Don't know,' Alison said. 'We'll check it out. There have been traps set up there before. Carol Burgess will know. She's the local community support officer. And you can ring Jenny McBride, see if a wire trap would fit with the injuries.'

'OK,' Paul said, making a note.

'It makes more sense for whoever did this to use something they found up there. I mean the location has been bugging me. Too many people, too exposed. It smacks of spur of the moment, but then the murder weapon seemed to point to planning. If the weapon was just something someone found, we're back to spur of the moment.'

'And that puts Robbie squarely in the frame,' Paul said. Alison had to nod despite herself.

'One other thing's bothering me,' Paul said. 'If Robbie killed Izzy, why would he admit to being with her before she died? As far as he knows no one saw him, no one knew she had arranged to meet him. He could have told us he hadn't seen her in days and was none the wiser.'

'True,' Alison said. 'Apart from the semen, the DNA. He might have known that would give him away.'

'Is he clever enough to think of that? And we got lucky there, didn't we? Normal investigation we wouldn't have had DNA results for a week at least. If it hadn't been for the press interest…'

'Yeah, but a lad like Robbie wouldn't know that. On the telly they do a montage and get a DNA match in about thirty seconds.'

Paul smiled, acknowledging that she was right.

'So if Robbie thought we'd get his DNA anyway, it makes sense for him to admit seeing Izzy. Covering his tracks.'

'OK, but if he *is* clever enough to think like that, why is his alibi so rubbish?' Paul asked. 'He was in Leeds, but not until after Izzy died. Wouldn't he know people who would lie for him, give him a better alibi than that?'

'Maybe he thought Izzy wouldn't be found for hours, by which time he'd be safely miles away. The party in Leeds would be a perfect alibi if Izzy was found a couple of hours later than she was.'

Paul nodded, satisfied. But Alison had her own problems with the case.

'My issue is, how did he do it unseen?' she said.

'Maybe he didn't. Maybe Andrea Mills saw him.'

'True. She said she couldn't be sure either way. The figure on the hill might have been Robbie, but it could have been anyone.'

'So there are three options as I see it,' Paul said. 'Either Andrea saw Robbie and was too far away to recognise him. She saw someone else, someone unconnected to the case who hasn't come forward yet. Or...'

'She saw our killer, and it wasn't Robbie,' Alison finished. In other words, Andrea Mills was no help at all.

'If it's not Robbie who else do we like the look of?' Paul asked.

'Banks?' Alison suggested.

'No real motive and everyone agrees he was only out of his classroom for ten minutes or so.'

'I still don't like him,' Alison said. 'All that stuff Dan told us about Banks inviting kids up to his house and paying them to do jobs. He's dodgy.' Paul nodded.

'What about Dan Humphreys?' Alison went on. 'He could have a motive if Izzy was going to "out" him, or even as revenge for the crash way back.'

'I checked out the counsellor,' Paul said. 'He *was* there yesterday afternoon, but his appointment wasn't until three.'

'So if he ducked out of school early he could have had time,' Alison said. She ran her hands through her hair, feeling exhausted. 'No one in this bloody town seems to be where they're supposed to be. Everyone's got an alibi and all their alibis have loopholes.'

'Always suspect a perfect alibi, didn't you tell me that?' Paul said.

'Yeah, I think I got that from Morse or someone.' Paul smiled.

'The drugs are bothering me,' Alison said. 'Could we be looking at it all the wrong way round? Could the drugs be the key? Whoever sold her the drugs killed her?'

'Any results from the lab yet?'

'Not yet.'

Holly knocked at the door. Alison waved her in.

'Robbie Smith's clothes came back clean,' she said.

'Too clean?' Alison asked.

Holly shook her head.

'Filthy actually, but no blood, no evidence of anything that shouldn't have been there.'

'OK, thanks, Holly,' Alison said. 'Have we got anything back from Northallerton yet, the CCTV from behind school?'

'Not yet. I'll chase them, shall I?'

'Thanks, Holz,' Alison said. 'Good work.'

Paul was smiling as Holly left the room.

'What?'

'If that had been me you wouldn't have said, "Good work". You'd have said, "Might be a good idea since they might have a video of our killer dripping in blood".'

'Maybe I just expect more from you,' Alison said, laughing.

'I'll take that as a compliment.'

Rogers opened his office door and barked at them.

'Dobson, Skinner – get your arses in here now.' Alison looked at Paul, her mind whirring. Rogers' default mode was shouting, but he seemed angrier than usual.

'It's a bloody balls-up,' Rogers was saying into the phone as they entered his office. He cut off the call without saying goodbye.

'Right. Get your arses down to interview room one and speak to this Robbie Smith of yours.'

'Haven't Holly and Jack taken a statement?' Alison began.

'Yes, the children have had a go while you were getting your nails done and pretty boy here was doing his hair, but now I would like you to do the bloody job you're paid for, instead of foisting it off on kids who are barely out of short trousers.'

Alison didn't point out that kids didn't wear short trousers anymore, nor that both Jack and Holly were capable of taking a statement. She knew better than to try to defend herself.

'With respect, sir, we were just going over the case, deciding the best approach to take when questioning Robbie…'

'With respect?' Rogers spluttered. 'You're talking out of your arse as usual. If you had actually been here doing your job, you might have realised that a lawyer has arrived for Mr Smith. A very eminent criminal lawyer from the metropolis.'

'London?' Paul asked.

'Leeds,' Rogers spat contemptuously. 'Apparently your Mr Smith has friends with money. Who knew? His lawyer is talking harassment.'

'Harassment?' Alison said. 'That's bollocks.'

'Thank you so much for the astute assessment, DI Dobson, I'll bear it in mind. However, as we discussed earlier, if you can remember that far back, this is a media-sensitive case. The last thing we want is coverage about how heavy-handed we have been with a grieving young man who has lost the love of his life. Just because he has a bit of a reputation and some petty arrests on his record, does not mean we can go in guns blazing.' Alison took a deep breath. Hadn't that been her point all along? That despite the circumstantial evidence there was no real reason to arrest Robbie yet.

'This is what I tried to tell that Downes woman,' she said.

'What, that Robbie would get an expensive lawyer? You suspected that did you, Dobson?'

'No, sir, I meant that we were moving too fast in arresting him.'

'Maybe Ms Downes is unaware of the quite inordinate amount of time you are able to spend doing sweet FA. Perhaps she assumed that once you had arrested Mr Smith you might try to find some actual evidence.' Alison didn't rise to his bait. She hadn't wanted to arrest Robbie and neither had Rogers. They had been persuaded into it by fear of the media, and now it was fear of the media and some hotshot lawyer that was bullying them into... what? A speedy interview and release? All for the sake of appearances.

She was buggered if she was going to let that happen.

'Let the lawyer cry harassment,' she said to Rogers. 'I can handle it. He doesn't have a leg to stand on.' Fuck it, she was not going to let anyone tell her how to run an investigation. Except of course her senior officer.

'That's very noble of you, DI Dobson,' Rogers said, his

voice a syrup of sarcasm. 'You can handle it, you say. All very well, but it won't be just your arse on the line if his lawyer gets the media on side. You want to be reading about police incompetence and racism over your cornflakes tomorrow?'

'Racism?'

'Robbie's father is a gypsy apparently.'

'Oh for fuck's…' Alison began.

'Quite.' Rogers cut her off. 'You are to go down to interview room one. You are to interview Robbie Smith, as courteously as if he were your own grandmother. And unless you get a gold-plated confession from him tied in a bow you are to let him go. Understood?'

Alison nodded.

'I'm sorry, I didn't hear that. I asked if you understood?'

'Yes, sir.'

Robbie was already in the interview room. Sitting beside him was a well-groomed woman, every inch of whom screamed money. Money used as intimidation. Alison hated to admit that it made her nervous. The woman reminded her of their own 'media adviser', Marianne Downes. Another woman more interested in appearances than in the truth.

Alison took care of the technicalities, introducing herself and DS Skinner, making sure the interview was being recorded, making sure that Robbie knew his rights.

'Hortence Mitchell,' the lawyer introduced herself loftily. 'Of Hargreaves, Mitchell and Webster. I will be representing Mr Smith.'

A partner, Alison noted. That would cost someone a very pretty penny. She thought of the man who had given Robbie a lift back from Leeds. Ben Adams. The predatory note in his voice had worried her. She wondered how Robbie might be expected to pay for this lawyer.

'Can I ask who is paying your fees?' Alison asked innocently.

'You can ask,' Mitchell said with a faint smile. 'But I am not at liberty to answer. Suffice it to say Mr Smith is entitled to legal representation and my firm will be representing him. Shall we proceed?'

'I didn't do it, DI Dobson. I told you how I felt about her. I wouldn't do it.' Robbie looked scared. Alison found that it surprised her. She had to remember that he was only eighteen. The big man act was nothing but an act. He was a naughty little boy suddenly accused of something very serious.

'I want you to tell me again what happened with Izzy yesterday afternoon,' she said.

'I told you. Then I told them other two what asked me.'

'I'd like you to tell me again, please, Robbie. Everything you remember.' His story hadn't changed. Izzy had called him from school. She was having a shit day and wanted to meet up. He had met her on the Beamsleigh. They had talked a little and then made love. He called it making love this time, Alison noticed. Afterwards he had told her he was going to a party. She wasn't too pleased. She didn't like the people he knew in Leeds.

'So you argued?' Alison asked.

'No, not really. She just said she didn't like the people I knew over there. So I left.'

'And you didn't see anyone else?'

'Didn't see any mad axeman if that's what you're asking. You think I'd've left Izzy up there on her own if I thought there was someone what was gonna hurt her?'

'We found Izzy's bag but no phone,' Alison said, changing pace. 'Did she have it with her when you saw her?'

'I never saw it, but she must have had it to ring me, mustn't she?'

'So whoever killed her took it. Any idea why they might do that?'

'It was quite a nice phone,' he said. 'But nothing special. Not the latest one or anything.'

Alison paused, deciding what to ask next. But it was Robbie who asked a question.

'Was any of her other stuff missing?'

'Not that we know of. Her purse and schoolbooks were there.'

'What's going to happen to it? Her stuff I mean.'

'Once the investigation is over it'll go to her family.' His shoulders drooped.

'Why?' Alison asked.

When Robbie finally spoke it was with the saddest of smiles.

'She had a picture of the two of us. She printed it off, like the old days. She kept it in the front of her journal. I haven't got no pictures, seeing as I lost my phone. I thought maybe I could... but if it's going to go to her mum... she'll probably burn it.'

Alison didn't know what to say to that. She watched Robbie for a few moments.

'Can you describe her journal?' Alison asked, not sure why.

'Yeah, it's this notebook with owls on the front. Purple. Owls represent wisdom and good luck in Buddhist culture apparently.'

He smiled fondly at the memory.

'And she always had it with her? This diary?' Alison said.

'It wasn't a diary,' Robbie said fiercely. 'It was a maths journal.' Full of squiggles and gobbledegook, Bob Johnson had said. It had definitely not been with Izzy's possessions. Could a jealous boyfriend have taken it in order to destroy a photo of Robbie? Dan Humphreys? Dom Mills? Robbie was still talking fondly.

'She's such geek, Izzy. Imagine having a book just for maths. Mental. But she proper loved it. I couldn't understand any of it, but she said it was her way of understanding the world.'

'And it just contained maths?'

'Yeah, calculations and stuff.' He paused. 'None of that matters to me though. Her mum can have all that... If I could just have... if there was any way I could have that picture out of the front...'

Alison shook her head.

'The journal appears to be missing,' she said.

'She never went anywhere without it,' Robbie said, frowning.

'Did she write anything else in it?' Alison asked. 'Notes, dates, that sort of thing.' She was wondering if the journal could have been of use to anyone. Or whether it might have been incriminating to the killer.

Her mind flew to Banks. If Izzy had written anything about him it was most likely to be in a journal of some sort.

Robbie shook his head.

'She didn't write anything in it but maths. No good to anyone else. Even Riordan up at the school didn't really get it, she said.'

Alison thought for a moment. Was this relevant, or was Robbie trying to throw her off track? Derail her questions?

'What were you wearing when you met Izzy yesterday?' she asked. Back on familiar ground. He scowled at her.

'I already told you.'

'Remind me.'

'I had on jeans and a hoody.'

'Colour?'

'Dark blue jeans, pale blue hoody. You took 'em off me. Your bloke here watched me get undressed like some old perv. Probably got off on it. I know his type.'

Alison ignored his comments. She had already asked him about his clothes. They had been tested. She was spinning in circles.

'You have the clothes my client was wearing yesterday, Inspector,' Mitchell said calmly.

'I have the clothes he says he was wearing, yes,' Alison said. 'They appear grubby but quite new.'

'They are new. I only got 'em last week,' Robbie said.

'You buy a lot of new clothes, do you?' Alison asked.

'Not really. Ben bought me them.'

'This is Ben Adams?'

'Yeah.'

'He must be a good friend, Mr Adams, giving you lifts, buying you clothes.'

'What can I say, he likes me.'

Mitchell interrupted.

'I can see no relevance to these questions,' she said. 'My client has discussed his clothes *ad nauseam* so unless you have any *new* questions,' the emphasis was on the new, 'then I think you need to charge my client or let him go. And given the *evidence* presented so far I suggest the latter.'

'Thank you for the advice,' Alison said. 'But I do know how to do my job.' She was pissed off because she didn't *have* any new questions. Robbie had no alibi, but he also had no motive and there was no forensic evidence that he was the one who killed Izzy. He had explanations for everything that tied him to the scene, but every explanation could be a lie.

'Did you give Izzy drugs?' she asked.

'I advise my client not to answer that question,' Mitchell interrupted.

'OK. Do you know whether Izzy was taking drugs?'

'I already told you. She didn't do drugs,' Robbie said quietly.

'Was she on any prescription medication?' Alison asked.

'What?'

'Did she take any medicine that you know of?'

'Not that I know. She was on the pill, but I don't think she took anything else. She was never ill.'

'And you didn't give her pills? Or sell her pills?'

'I have already advised my client not to…' Mitchell began.

'Look, you ask me if I smoke dope or sell it I'm going to tell you "no comment". Ask if I sell a bit of speed, same answer. But ask me if I sold Izzy pills and I'll say "no way". You get me? I didn't give her pills, I didn't sell her pills. She wasn't into that sort of crap.'

Either he was telling the truth or he was a clever liar. Alison didn't know which. She changed the subject.

'You admit you argued with Izzy yesterday afternoon. Did she dump you?'

'What? No. Like I said, it wasn't an argument. People fall out, it doesn't mean it's over.' Mitchell began to shuffle the papers in front of her. She was clearly ready to draw the interview to a close.

'Do you know Andrea Mills?' Alison asked.

She felt Paul shift beside her. She ignored him.

'No,' Robbie said immediately.

'Dominic Mills?'

'Name rings a bell.'

'You sold drugs to Dominic Mills on a number of occasions. You must have called at his house, probably saw his mother.'

She was guessing, but Robbie couldn't know that.

'I advise you not to answer that, Robbie,' Mitchell said calmly.

'Andrea Mills once reported you to the head at the school, suspected you of dealing drugs to children there.'

A look of recognition spread over Robbie's face and he opened his mouth as if to speak. Mitchell held up a hand and Robbie remained silent.

'Must have annoyed you, that. Sure as hell annoyed your mother,' Alison continued.

'I wouldn't know,' Robbie said, eyeing her wearily.

'Sure you don't know Mrs Mills?' Alison persisted.

'No.'

'Well, she knows you, Robbie. She'd certainly recognise you if she saw you running away from a murder scene.'

Robbie went white, but he spoke very quietly.

'I never ran away from no murder scene. Izzy was fine when I left her. She was fine. And if this Mrs Mills woman is saying anything else, well, she's lying. I never...'

Mitchell put a hand out again to stop Robbie from speaking.

'If DI Dobson had a witness who put you at the scene of the killing at the time of the killing I don't think we would be having this conversation, Robbie. I suspect you would have been formally charged already. Am I right, Inspector?'

Alison knew when she was beaten.

'I'm letting you go, Robbie,' she said, as if she had a choice. 'Stay where we can find you.'

'That was a bit of a risk,' Paul said.

'What?'

'Revealing that Mills might have seen him.'

'Oh for fuck's sake, Paul. Robbie's hardly an assassin. If he did kill Izzy it was a crime of the moment. He's hardly organised enough to set up an intimidation campaign to keep a witness quiet.' But she knew she had made a mistake. She hadn't even thought it through. She should never have mentioned Andrea's name. Except everyone knew Andrea had found the body. And Andrea was no doubt also telling the town that she had seen a man in a hoody running away. Alison hadn't told Robbie anything he couldn't have heard anywhere else in Penbury.

Mitchell stalked out of the interview room behind them.

'It was a pleasure to meet you, DI Dobson,' she said, shark-smiling. 'I have a feeling I shall enjoy working with you.'

Her tone implied that much of that enjoyment would come at Alison's expense.

Jack Kent made his way along the corridor towards them.

'Jack, it's been a long time,' Mitchell said coolly.

'Hortence. Hi.' Kent looked surprised.

'We really must catch up. It's been an absolute age. I had no idea you were up here in the wilds… How splendid.'

Before he could answer she had swept out.

Alison raised an eyebrow questioningly at Kent.

'We were at school together,' he said. 'Never could stand her.' Alison laughed at that.

'You looking for me?' she asked Jack.

'Rogers sent me to find out how it's going.' Alison nodded.

'Tell him it's going absolutely perfectly and we're letting Robbie Smith go.'

'Letting him go? What the…'

'Your choice, Jack, you can either ask Rogers or your friend Mitchell for an explanation as to why.'

'Thanks,' Jack said. 'That's like having the choice between taking swimming lessons from a shark or a piranha.'

Alison laughed as Kent slouched back up the corridor.

'Let's get out of here,' Paul said. 'I'll buy you some tea and we can talk.'

'I want the team upstairs in ten minutes,' Alison said. 'Let's go over where we are before we call it a day.'

'We have to talk about this sometime,' Paul insisted. 'We can't just pretend Harrogate never happened.' As far as Alison was concerned that was exactly what they should do.

'Upstairs. Ten minutes,' she said.

SEVENTEEN

Alison had to pass through reception on her way up to the meeting room. Andrea Mills was just leaving.

'I just finished with the e-fit,' she explained. 'I don't think I was much help though. I really didn't see much.'

'It's OK,' Alison said, hiding her own frustration. 'If you didn't see anything then you didn't see anything. Were you able to give a description of his clothes and height at least?'

'I think so. I hope it helps.'

'I'm sure it will,' Alison said. Privately she thought quite the opposite. They were no further along.

She accompanied Andrea to the door.

'We really appreciate your help, Mrs Mills,' she said.

They waited in the doorway for a man in his thirties to shake out his large golf umbrella.

He apologised and held the door open for Andrea to pass.

Alison looked out after Andrea as she rushed to her car, head bent against the chilly rain. Just two days ago she had been an ordinary mother and now she would always be someone who had found a body. It would never leave her. Just as losing a child would never leave Leanne Johnson. Some things changed you, no matter how subtly, and those changes couldn't be undone.

'Could I see Robbie Smith, please?' the man with the umbrella was asking at reception. 'I understand he's been arrested.'

'I'm afraid we can't allow...'

'Of course, you have your petty rules.'

'I can't allow...'

'I understand,' he said, speaking over the receptionist. 'So please may I speak to someone who *can* allow me to see him.'

'I'll handle this, Debbie,' Alison said.

The man turned, smiling, ready to be charming if he could get his way.

'I'm DI Dobson,' Alison said. 'Can I ask who you are?'

'Ben Adams.' He held out his hand and shook hers. Confident, firm.

She recognised the voice now. The man who had given Robbie a lift home on Tuesday night; the man who had bought him new clothes and a phone; the man Holly described as having 'a crush' on Robbie.

She hadn't expected a man like this. She found herself assessing him.

Good looks just beginning to fade. Self-assured, arrogant even. Well dressed, tall. A man used to getting his own way.

'We spoke on the phone this morning,' she said. 'You're a friend of Robbie's?'

'What a terribly quaint word. Friend. Are we friends, Robbie and I? Well... I suppose perhaps we are. But friends is such a pedestrian word. Robbie and I are more, far more than that.' She had imagined someone a little more pathetic. She couldn't see Robbie manipulating a man like this and the knowledge unnerved her. If Robbie wasn't the one doing the manipulating… 'How is Robbie?' Adams asked.

'Robbie's fine,' she said, as she steered him away from the desk. 'He's being released as a matter of fact, it's just a matter of completing some paperwork. Since you're here, Mr Adams, I wonder could we have a quick chat?'

'Of course, of course. Anything I can do to help. Robbie would never… whatever you think… I know Robbie would never be involved with anything like this. He's not violent.'

Alison didn't reply but steered Adams into an empty meeting room.

'I know you gave a full account to my colleague,' she said. 'But I'd like you to just run over the events of Tuesday evening with me again if you would.'

'Certainly. I met up with Robbie at a party. Mutual friends. That word again. We spent the majority of the evening together. As I think I told you he had lost his phone and was rather morose. Not great company to be frank. A little boring. Robbie is rarely boring. It is one of his finer qualities. Anyway when the party ended I agreed to give him a lift home. Offered him a bed at my house actually, but he refused. So up the A64 it was. All rather dull. We got here about three thirty or quarter to four in the morning.'

'And what did you do then?'

'I went home.'

'Forgive me, Mr Adams, but it's a very long drive, at that time of night, all the way from Leeds. Must have taken about an hour.'

'About that, yes.'

'And then you just turned around again.'

Adams smiled, looking almost abashed.

'I'm a bit of a sucker where Robbie is concerned, I'm afraid. I find it hard to refuse him anything.'

'I have to ask, Mr Adams, are you and Robbie in a sexual relationship?' Adams smiled again. She didn't like the smile. It felt like a weapon. Deployed against her, intended to disarm.

'Robbie's a young man who is not yet comfortable exploring all aspects of his personality.'

'That hasn't answered my question,' she said evenly.

'I'm sorry.' Adams paused. 'I'll be clearer. No, our relationship is not sexual. I will admit I find Robbie very attractive. He *claims* not to feel the same way.'

He inclined his head as if he questioned that 'claim'.

'I endeavour to be patient,' Adams went on. 'And in the meantime I enjoy spoiling him whenever I get the chance. I enjoy the chase.'

Like a hunter, Alison thought.

'Were you aware that Robbie was seeing Isabella Johnson?'

'He may have mentioned it,' Adams said. 'I wasn't very interested.'

'Were you aware that he was sleeping with her?' He laughed.

'DI Dobson, is it?'

Alison nodded.

'DI Dobson, you seem to think that such information might shock or upset me in some way. You are mistaken. In fact it doesn't even interest me very much. I don't believe in labels, Inspector. I don't believe in gay or straight, and I certainly don't believe in monogamy. If Robbie was attached to someone else that has no bearing at all on how attached I am to him.'

'And how attached is that?'

'I would say that at the moment I am a little infatuated with Robbie Smith. A little in love.' Alison was surprised and it must have shown on her face. Adams laughed gently.

'Again, don't misunderstand me. I fall in love very easily. When I am in the throes of a great passion I am capable of many grand gestures but once the passion is gone I lose interest very quickly. Robbie intrigues me at the moment. It may not last. I have numerous relationships. Some last longer than others, some are more intense than others. None are ever exclusive and nor do I expect my lovers to be exclusively mine.'

'Robbie isn't your lover,' Alison said.

'Not in any crude sense, no. But he likes spending time with me, he likes the favours I do him and the little gifts I give him.'

'So you're planning on buying his affection, or at least his body?'

'My goodness, no. Quite the opposite. I do not wish to buy Robbie. I don't pay for sex. Not my thing at all. Money is so grubby, so sordid, don't you think? I don't want to pay Robbie, I want to persuade him. I want to seduce him. What a lovely old-fashioned word. Seduction. That is my game. Seduction. Believe me I am rather good at it. When I set my heart on something I tend to get it.' He smiled at Alison as if daring her to contradict him.

'I like to buy him little gifts and I like his gratitude. And

I like his curiosity. And I wonder if one day, when he has tired of the unaccomplished fumbling teenage girls can provide, he might not decide to be a little more adventurous. And if that day comes I will be there to oblige.'

'And if he isn't interested?'

'Oh, Inspector, we're all *interested*, aren't we? Currently Robbie tells me I'm a "dirty bender" and that "blokes don't do nothing for him". But he comes back. He calls me. He may not yet be ready, but he is *interested*.'

'How can you be sure it's not just your money he's interested in? He may just be using you.' Adams continued to smile.

'Well, perhaps he is and perhaps *I* am using him. But don't we all use each other? Isn't this conversation, pleasant as it is, just your attempt to get information from me? To use me to further your case? Likewise I am trying to convince you of Robbie's innocence. I am using you for my own ends. I want you to believe in Robbie's innocence. After all if he ends in prison I might never get to fulfil my many fantasies regarding him.' He laughed.

'And now I have shocked you, Inspector. I apologise. But Robbie and I are consenting adults and however we choose to "use" one another is our business. If he chooses to think that I will drive him halfway across the country indefinitely without asking anything in return then he is naive beyond measure.'

'Did you ever meet Isabella Johnson?' Alison asked.

'Oh my,' Adams said. 'I reveal myself as a pervert and suddenly I'm a suspect?'

'That's not what I was implying,' she said.

'I never met Isabella. She would not have been my type

anyway.' He saw Alison's expression and went on, 'I don't say that because she's a girl. Nothing so simple. I don't limit myself only to beautiful boys, although I would say they are my preference. No, Isabella, from all I have heard and read in the press, was perfection. Beauty, brains, popularity. Such people are hard to like, don't you find? One can admire them, they may even inspire passion from some people, but they are rarely loved.'

'Izzy was well loved.'

'Was she really? Or is it just that no one has yet told you how they really felt about her? I believe Robbie may have been capable of loving someone like that. His self-esteem is low enough that he might even enjoy not being good enough for her. Maybe that's where I've been going wrong, treating him too well. Maybe the poor lamb is so damaged he can't appreciate my kindness.'

'I think I've heard enough,' Alison said.

'Really?' Adams asked. 'I was just beginning to enjoy our little chat. I have a suspicion you and I might have a lot in common.'

'I think not,' Alison said. 'Thank you for your time.' She stood up. Adams stood too. He shook her hand and held on to it, turning her palm up in his. She knew she should pull away but found herself watching his thumb as he stroked it along her wrist.

'It leaves marks, you know,' he said gently. 'Not just these,' he stroked the almost invisible scars on her wrists, 'but scars you can't see. It makes us different to other people. You can fight it, you can try the whole love and marriage and settled thing, but people like us, damaged people like us, somehow we find each other.'

His eyes were dangerously blue. Alison swallowed painfully, watching his face and feeling his thumb still stroking back and forth along her wrist. There was a bang on the door. Alison wrenched her hand out of Adams' grip. Paul put his head around the jamb.

'Ready upstairs when you are, boss.'

Adams gave a chuckle.

'I better let you go, I suppose. Thank you so much for your time, DI Dobson,' he said smoothly. 'I know where to find you if I *need* anything.'

Subtle emphasis on *need*.

EIGHTEEN

It felt like they were back at the beginning. Gathered together like they had been that morning.

'OK, so Robbie's been released on bail,' Alison told the team. 'He's still our main suspect, but we need to tread carefully. He's got a Rottweiler lawyer who would love to sue someone for harassment.' There was a collective groan.

'So far our only forensic link between Robbie and Izzy is his semen at the scene, and he admits having sex with her. His clothes were blood free, as were swabs of his hands. And we've found no motive for him to harm Izzy.'

'Unless she dumped him,' Paul said like a dog with a bone. Alison ignored him.

'Other suspects,' she went on. 'Simon Banks, English teacher. The note he sent Izzy was suspicious. We've heard he invited boys up to his place from time to time, maybe Izzy knew something about that, maybe that's what he was asking her to keep quiet about.'

'He's got a pretty decent alibi though,' Paul said.

'Decent but not foolproof,' Mick interrupted. 'He left

the classroom for a while, right?' Alison nodded, but didn't want to get into it.

'There's also Dan Humphreys,' she said, continuing her rundown of suspects. 'Izzy may have been about to out him as gay, or he could have been acting for revenge over his sister's death all those years ago. He left school sometime in the afternoon for an appointment with a counsellor. We're not sure of timings, so it's possible he could have been on the Beamsleigh.'

'He'd need to be pretty cold though,' Paul said. 'To kill Izzy and march into a counselling session calm as you like. The counsellor said he was his usual self on Tuesday, not overly upset or agitated.'

A brief pause.

'I also want to look at Dom Mills. His mum found the body. He and Izzy were pretty close last summer, sleeping together. He got home from uni for a break last week. It's just possible this whole thing is as simple as a jealous ex-boyfriend losing his temper.'

'But our man must have planned the attack if he had a weapon with him,' Mick asked.

'I think the murder weapon could have been found up there,' Alison said.

She looked to Paul for confirmation.

'I spoke to Jenny McBride,' he said. 'The injuries are consistent with the sort of wire you might use in a rabbit trap. So then I spoke to the local community support officer, Carol Burgess, and she told me there's been a lot of that recently.'

'So you reckon that lass was strangled with a rabbit wire?' Miles asked.

'The weapon was bugging me, Miles,' Alison said. 'Having a weapon with you means premeditation, but if you were planning to kill someone would you do it there? Beamsleigh Hill isn't exactly isolated, anyone could wander by.'

'Makes sense. Killer isn't planning to kill her, but they fight, he knocks her out and the weapon's there so he uses it.'

'That's my thinking,' Alison admitted.

'So we're spinning in circles,' Miles said cheerfully enough. 'Plenty of suspects, no real evidence.'

It was a succinct summary.

'So tomorrow we get evidence,' Alison said. 'I want Izzy's phone found. See if anyone's tried to sell one like it. I want another search of the area for Izzy's maths journal. It's the closest thing she had to a diary. Let's see if she made any notes in there that give us a motive. We'll chase forensics over the pills in her stomach and the ones her stepdad found in her room. And I want the CCTV from behind the school.'

'They say the glitch should be fixed by tomorrow,' Holly said.

'Well, if it isn't I want you over there first thing and put a rocket up 'em, OK? And I want whoever Andrea Mills saw up there found. She's done an e-fit so we'll get that out everywhere tomorrow.'

They all nodded, a little dejected. They wanted this one closed quickly.

'OK. Thanks, everyone. Go home.'

They drifted away slowly, none of them really wanting to go home, but there was nothing more to do tonight. The phone on Alison's desk rang. It was Debbie on the front desk.

'OK. I'll be there in a minute.'

Henry Chapell was in reception, dressed in a dark suit and giving her a smile that was a gift wrapped in silk.

'Come in, Mr Chapell,' she said in welcome.

'Sorry to call so late,' he said as she led him into a nearby meeting room. 'I found something. I think it might be Izzy's.'

He reached into his pocket and pulled out a mobile in a spotty purple cover.

'Just put it on the desk,' Alison said, not wanting to touch it.

'Oh God, oh sorry… I shouldn't have touched it, should I? I am such a fool, contaminating evidence. Should I wipe it down?'

He pulled a neatly folded handkerchief from the breast pocket of his jacket.

'No,' Alison cried. 'No. Just leave it. There might still be fingerprints or other evidence.'

'But there'll be my prints too. Oh lord, am I going to be a suspect? How thrilling.' Alison couldn't help smiling.

'We'll take your prints for elimination purposes,' she said.

'How exciting.' He almost clapped his hands together, but stopped himself. 'Sorry, I keep forgetting that this is real. I keep forgetting poor Izzy.'

He looked crestfallen, all the joy gone from his features. He was a like a young child, or a puppy, all his emotions close to the surface.

'You say you found this? Where?'

'By the edge of the beck,' he said. 'I was having coffee… the kitchen looks out over the river, you see… so I was looking out and, well, it was just a glimpse. Just something catching the sun. Ordinarily I would have ignored it, but I suppose somewhere in my mind I was thinking of Izzy. And I knew her phone had that case on it. So I looked again. And then Angela and I went down, and Angela sniffed it out straight away. It was half buried in the mud and… oh…'

'Mr Chapell?'

'Well, I wiped it off. Took it into the kitchen and wiped it clean with kitchen roll. I didn't think.'

So any physical evidence was likely wiped away. OK, but there were still the contents of the phone itself. That might be worth something.

'Did you switch it on?' she asked.

'No. I recognised the case and thought it was probably Izzy's, so I brought it here.' Alison took a deep breath. She knew she should hand it off to forensics, but the phone had been in the river and in the mud, and then Chapell had wiped it clean. She would hardly be disturbing pristine physical evidence. She pulled a pair of latex gloves from the front pocket of her bag, put them on and pressed the power button.

Nothing.

She dug a charger out of a drawer, and plugged it in.

'I should have worn gloves,' Chapell was saying, watching Alison's hands. 'I've seen enough shows, CSI and everything. I really should have known.'

Alison said nothing.

'I mess things like this up. I am not the brightest. My mother always said so.'

'People make mistakes,' Alison said absently.

'Izzy used to say that.' Chapell smiled. 'She was always trying to cheer me up, make me feel better about myself.'

'And do you need cheering up?' Alison asked, curious despite herself.

'I have the curse of the artist, I'm afraid. Self-centred and yet ultimately insecure,' he laughed. 'Look at me, but not too closely lest you see my flaws. Love me, admire me, but if you do then you must necessarily be a fool for I could never be worthy of your love.'

'Wow,' Alison said. 'It sounds exhausting.'

He didn't seem to pick up the irony in her voice.

'It is. How I envy ordinary people. Without that drive to create, to make beautiful things. What must it be like to simply be able to feel contentment at the ordinary world? To be dull and humdrum? You have no idea how hard it is to be so sensitive to the ugliness of the world. To so crave aesthetic perfection. I suffer, truly, as is the way with all artists. We must suffer and in our suffering hope to bring forth something powerful.'

Alison was taken aback for a long moment. His pretension was either hilarious or highly offensive. He envied dull, ordinary people. People like her, she supposed.

'Even Izzy didn't understand,' Chapell went on. 'People like Izzy and Niall, they're clever in a very linear, very easy way. My mind works on a different plane entirely. I see things other people don't begin to imagine… I may not be clever in that conventional way… but my vision… my artistry…'

He sighed theatrically.

'I suppose it's the way of the artist not to be appreciated in his own lifetime,' Alison said, not entirely able to keep the sarcasm from her voice.

'I *have* been appreciated,' Chapell shot at her. 'I am. One of my works sold to an American gallery – although they haven't yet found room to display it. There are some people who appreciate what I do, although needless to say not in this town.'

'Small towns can be hard places to live,' Alison said.

'Tell me about it,' Chapell said, smiling again now. All charm. 'I grew up in the smallest town in Devon. Single mother, so I was already an oddity. And my sexuality didn't help. Mother was determined to prove them all wrong. Her boy was going to go to university, get a stellar job, show the lot of them.'

'But you chose to be an artist.'

'It chose me,' Chapell said simply. The pretension sat heavily in the room.

'She was ashamed,' he said after a moment. 'Ashamed that I was gay, that I didn't have the conventional academic success. But then I met Niall. And Niall is so clever in that dull respectable way mothers like. And he was so successful in a way that she could understand.'

'He's still successful,' Alison felt compelled to say. 'Headteacher is a good job.'

'When he gets the job in Harvard that will be something to be proud of. That will satisfy her, I'm sure.' *And you? And Niall?* Alison didn't ask.

The phone on the desk between them buzzed to show it had taken enough charge to be switched on. Suddenly Henry Chapell and his pretensions as an artist became far less important to her. Izzy Johnson was calling her back. There was work to do.

Despite the time it had spent in the water the phone

seemed to work. The welcome screen appeared and Alison swiped to open it; there was no pin protection. She pressed the phone icon. The last call made from the phone was to Robbie Smith. That tied in with what he had said and meant nothing.

Alison pressed the icon for text.

There was a string of messages between Izzy and Robbie. Short and inarticulate. Arrangements to meet. Missing you. Blunt sexual innuendos and reminders of 'what we got up to last night'. She'd have to read them all more closely but they looked like typical teenage communications; there was no indication that the relationship was ending.

There were fewer texts to Dan Humphreys, but what there were were friendly and non-committal. Quite a lot of 'cover for me tonight' and 'do you want me to say you were with me?'. The last text in the string tallied with what Dan had shown them on his phone: '*Soz for today. I won't drop u in it if ur not ready.*'

No texts from Banks. Alison found herself disappointed. She looked up suddenly.

'There's a text from a Henry here. Is that you, Mr Chapell?'

'Probably. What does it say?'

Alison read aloud.

'You still on for Sat? About 9.'

'Oh God, I'd forgotten about that. Yes. I sent that… It must have been… God, yesterday.' He pulled out his own phone and looked at it.

'I never got a reply.'

Alison looked back at the phone in her hand.

No wonder. The text had come in at two twenty-nine. Izzy Johnson was almost certainly dead by then.

'You were arranging to meet her this weekend?' Alison said, scrolling through the earlier texts. Henry had invited Izzy on a dog walk. She had accepted. He had texted her again on Tuesday to remind her of the arrangements.

'Yes. We sometimes walked Angela together. I liked her company. And Niall is always so busy. It gets a little... well, it gets a little lonely.'

There were tears in his eyes. Alison was unsure whether they were for himself and his loneliness or for Isabella Johnson.

'Should I have told you we were meeting?' he asked theatrically. 'Have I done wrong again? I am so trying to help.'

Alison smiled reassuringly.

'No, you haven't done wrong,' she said. 'It's just best always to tell us everything. Let us decide what's important.'

She was scrolling through the phone again. All the usual stuff. Most of the names she recognised. Friends, mum, school, granny, dad. She checked this last; it was clearly Bob Johnson. There were no communications between Izzy and her biological father.

One number in Izzy's contacts did not have a name attached. Nor were there any calls or texts attached to it. All communication seemed to have been deleted.

Alison dialled the number from her own phone.

The call went directly to voicemail, an automated voice telling her to leave a message. No indication of who the phone belonged to, or even if it was currently in use. She picked up Izzy's phone. Called the number again. Perhaps the owner of the phone would answer a call from a number they recognised. The same automated reply. One for the tech boys after all. She thanked Chapell for his time and for bringing in the phone.

'I just hope this helps you prove he did it,' Chapell said.

'Who?' Alison asked, although she knew.

'I heard Robbie Smith was arrested. The whole town knows.'

'We haven't charged anyone just yet,' Alison said.

'But Andrea saw him, didn't she?'

'Did she tell you that?' Alison asked.

'No, not exactly, she said she saw someone. And Robbie is, well... I know Niall had a soft spot for him, but he was always a bad lad. Andrea told me it could easily have been Robbie up on that hill. I just assumed...'

'We can't convict on assumptions.'

'Oh yes. God, sorry.'

'Thanks again for your help,' Alison said, ushering him from the room.

'Don't mention to Niall, will you, if you see him... Don't mention that I messed up. Touched the phone, all that. I mean he thinks I'm idiot enough, I don't want to give him proof.' He laughed as he said it, but there was something endearing in his vulnerability.

'I won't,' Alison said, smiling.

'He's a very clever man. I sometimes wonder what he sees in me.' He threw her another of his gift-wrapped smiles, making a lie of the statement. He knew very well what Niall Riordan saw in him.

NINETEEN

Alison got home just as the children were having their tea. Nick was at work. They were supposed to have been holed up in a little lakeside hotel enjoying a romantic couple of days. Instead they were working, but Nick's mother had still come to help with the children. It meant Nick could work overtime and save for a longer trip later. It was called looking on the bright side.

Maude, her mother-in-law, was fussing over Mabel, trying to get her to eat up her vegetables. Alison recognised the set of her daughter's jaw. On her plate sat the evil triumvirate of broccoli, cabbage and sprouts. There seemed little chance Mabel would eat any of them.

Alison put the kettle on and watched Maude battle with Mabel for a while. She found it amusing, the way in which both of them were digging in their heels, both refusing to give an inch. *As if it matters*, she thought. *Three miles from here a girl has been killed.* A girl whose mother probably used to fight with her about eating her greens. Did it matter what bloody vegetables her daughter ate? Did it matter if she had sweets for tea every night and ended up twenty stone with no teeth? Did any of it matter as long as they were all here?

She took a deep breath. It had to matter. She knew people who said you should live each day as if it was your last. She didn't buy it. She wanted to live each day as if she believed in the future. She knew, all too well and from experience, that families could be torn apart at any time. She couldn't live like that. Waiting for the axe to fall. She had to assume that her family was safe, that they would stay safe and well and that her children would grow up and that it would matter that she had made them eat their vegetables. Life had to be ordinary and mundane, otherwise what was any of it about?

She took her tea over to the table, bent and whispered in her daughter's ear.

'Chocolate ice cream if you eat half your veg.'

'Not fair, I ate all mine,' Beatrice said at once.

Mabel smiled and began to plough through her broccoli.

'You get extra,' Alison told Bea, smiling.

'You shouldn't spoil them,' Maude muttered. 'In my day children ate what was on their plate and they were grateful.' Alison ignored her. She had heard enough tales from Nick of meals that consisted of jam sandwiches and crisps to know that Maude's memory was a little selective.

'Finished,' Mabel said. Alison grinned. Less than half the veg was gone, but at least it was something.

'You get the bowls, I'll get the ice cream,' she said, feeling quite smug. She had resolved a family problem and no one had cried or shouted or slammed a door. It was a small victory.

'I got in trouble today,' Mabel said casually as she placed bowls on the table.

'Did you?' Alison said, not really listening.

'Mrs Williams made me miss playtime.' Alison looked up from the freezer.

'What happened?'

'It wasn't my fault,' Mabel said simply, watching Alison spoon ice cream into her bowl.

'You must have done something for Mrs Williams to make you miss playtime,' Bea said smugly.

'It was Georgia,' Mabel said.

'What about Georgia?' Alison asked.

'She had some stickers, only she said I couldn't have one because I'd been playing with Skye.'

'So what did you do?'

'I asked her nicely for a sticker,' Mabel said, all butter wouldn't melt. 'And she said no. So I told her she could just shove it up her arse.' Bea giggled; Alison stifled a laugh as her mother-in-law beside her gasped.

'Mabel, that's not… We don't use that language.'

'Yes we do, Mummy, that's what you said last week when your boss made you do that paper stuff.'

'Paperwork,' Bea supplied.

'Yeah, that. You said he could stick his job up his…'

'OK, OK,' Alison interrupted. 'Let's talk about it later, shall we?' She could feel her mother-of-the-year award slipping from her grasp as she spoke.

Once Mabel was in bed and Maude and Beatrice were happily watching *EastEnders* Alison decided to check email. She told herself it wasn't really working because she was still in the sitting room with her family. She found a message from Ken Varney in tech support.

'*Got this off Banks' computer before we had to give it back. Thought it best to send it to you at home.*'

Alison smiled. Sometimes discretion really was the better part of valour, especially when valour involved facing the wrath of DCI Rogers. She opened the attached file. It was a list.

Batch 41- GLR +

Lucy Jacobs	8
Izzy Johnson	10
Martha Jones	2
Billy King	8
Joe Simons	4
Max Smith	8
Hugo Bailey	1
Dan Humphreys?	
Dominic Mills? –	No

At the bottom of this page it said:
HMW –   £2,500.

Alison went into the kitchen.

She dialled Jenny McBride in the forensics department. It was almost eight but she knew Jenny wouldn't mind the call.

'Calling for a date at last, eh?' Jenny asked jovially.

'Afraid not.'

'Still boringly straight?'

'Afraid so. If anything changes you'll be the first to know.' Jenny laughed her throaty smoker's laugh.

'Old enough to be your mum,' she said.

'Hardly!' Alison said. 'And anyway, when did that ever stop you?' Another laugh from Jenny.

'So, if it's not my body you're after, what can I help you with?' Alison explained the email she had from Ken.

'I just wondered if the initials GLR mean anything to you?' she asked.

'Not especially but I suppose it fits with the initial findings on those pills you gave us. The ones found at the Johnson house.'

'You identified the pills?'

'Not completely. Didn't you get the preliminary report? I sent it over to your guy. You'll get the full analysis in a day or two. I haven't matched the pills to the stomach contents yet but they certainly look similar. I put it in my email.'

'Who did you send the email to?'

There was a pause as she checked.

'Jack Kent?'

Alison swore under her breath.

'Not your favourite man, eh?' Jenny asked.

'You could say that,' Alison said. 'What time did you send the report?'

'Not sure, just after five, I guess.'

Before they had the last briefing of the day. Either Jack had been too bloody lazy to read it or he was holding back on the info, hoping to make a big show of it when the time was right.

Jenny was apologising.

'Sorry, should I have copied you in? He said he was the designated contact... so...' Designated bloody contact, yeah, that sounded like the sort of management speak Jack Kent would use.

'It's fine, Jenny. Not your fault. Could you give me the gist of what you found?'

'Well, a mix of things really, but it looks like a nootropics stack.'

'A what?'

'Basically a smart drug, a combination of things that are supposed to help cognitive function. Some of them pretty basic, like caffeine, others not so much. We haven't even broken down all the elements that are in there. But there were traces of galantamine, levodopa and ritalin. Guess that could be your GLR.'

'Ritalin – isn't that for ADHD?'

'Yeah and levodopa is to treat Parkinson's, galantamine has been shown to help with early onset dementia. But they're also supposed to help kids with exams. Popular on college campuses in America apparently.'

'Legal?'

'Yeah, I'm afraid so.'

'Any side effects?'

'Some, but the real problem is we don't know how they react in combination – they've never been tested. And, of course, these pills could be cut with anything, mixed with anything. The dosage could be all over the place. These kids have no idea what they're taking. No idea of the risks they're taking.'

'Yeah, but they're kids,' Alison said, 'they're going to live forever.'

'Well, this one didn't, did she?'

'Did the drug have anything to do with her death?' Alison asked.

'Not directly, no.'

Alison understood the distinction. The drugs hadn't killed Izzy, but they might be connected to why she was on that hill in the first place.

'I'll keep going with the pills found in the girl's system,' Jenny said. 'I'll see if they're the same combination. Most of the ingredients in these things are pretty generic though, available over the internet, so…'

'I thought we were looking at something exotic,' Alison said.

'No, not really. Just not part of our usual tox screen. And since the combinations keep changing the chemical fingerprint changes. Unfortunately they're not that rare.'

'Thanks anyway,' Alison said.

She looked back at Banks' list. GLR +.

She didn't like the '+'. What the hell else was Banks supplying these kids with? She looked again at the list. There was nothing conclusively incriminating about it. Banks would probably come up with some bullshit explanation for the acronym GLR. Gertrude, Lear and Romeo. Bastard would try to convince her he was talking Shakespeare.

Her phone rang. Caller ID showed Nick.

'Can you come meet me at the pub?'

'What? Now? The kids are in bed and…'

'Just come. Tell Mum you've just had an urgent work call. I'm at the Feathers.'

'What's wrong? You sound…'

'Just get here, will you… Your mate Paul's here and he's pretty drunk.' He had hung up before she could answer.

TWENTY

Shit. Shit. Shit.

Nick and Paul together. The very thing she had wanted to avoid.

Nick had sounded so angry on the phone. The sort of controlled anger Alison found hard to understand. What had Paul said? Why had he had to say anything? Harrogate had been... well, it had been what it was... a disaster... a mistake... inevitable. She had wanted to forget it; she hadn't wanted Nick to know.

Alison saw him the moment she walked into the pub. He was alone.

She thought back to when they had first met. Both of them just nineteen. Now she was forty-one, and she still thought of him as that handsome boy. She thought he was the most attractive man she had ever known. Certainly he was the best man she would ever know. Something she would never tell him.

'What's wrong? Where's Paul?' she asked before Nick could speak.

'He went to the loo. I think he needed to throw up.' He was looking at her closely. Too closely. What had Paul said? She couldn't ask.

'He OK?'

Nick shrugged. Anger rolled off him.

'He's pretty pissed. Said he wanted to talk to you.' Alison said nothing.

'Have you two…'

'Probably just work,' Alison said.

Nick didn't reply.

There was a tension between them, a nervousness. She wondered again what Paul had said. What was making Nick so angry?

'We shouldn't stay long,' Alison said, trying for a normal tone of voice. 'It's not fair on your mum.'

'She loves it. She'll get the chance to bad-mouth us to my brothers. What a terrible wife you are, how you neglect me, how I don't earn enough so that you can stay at home, how the kids are left to their own devices far too much.'

'The same things she says to us about them and their wives then.' Alison tried to laugh.

'Absolutely. The less perfect we are the happier she is.' It was an old joke and he tried to smile but his face was grim.

'And who are we to make her miserable?' Alison asked.

'It's a shame we couldn't get away this week. I've really missed you.' There was sadness in his voice and that underlying anger and a terrible disappointment.

'I've been right here,' she said.

'Yeah, but not really.'

'Work. This case, you know.'

'Yeah.' He looked at her seriously. Letting her know he

knew it was something more. It was great that Nick knew her so well. Except when it wasn't.

She had learnt young that relying on others was not a good idea, that trusting others was not a good idea. She knew she relied on Nick too heavily, trusted him too well.

'What is it, really?' he asked.

'Nothing. Work. I'm just tired.'

He watched her. Not believing her, waiting for her to say more.

There was a loud crash from near the bar. Paul, stumbling back from the toilet, had knocked a bar stool to the ground.

'Sorry, sorry.' He was struggling to set the stool back on its feet and apologising to no one in particular. It should have been comical. Alison didn't feel like laughing.

'Hey, hi… you're here,' Paul said, reaching their table, smiling.

Nick was quiet, watching them.

'D'you think you could get him a coffee?' Alison asked her husband.

He gave her a hard look but left without a word.

'Glad you're here,' Paul began. 'I wanted to talk… I've been wanting to talk… about Harrogate… what happened.'

'Not now,' she hissed.

'Yeah… but when… I mean…'

'You're drunk.'

'I'm not *that* drunk.' And, despite the stumbling, she knew it was true. Not too drunk to know what he was saying. Just as neither of them had been too drunk that night in Harrogate. Not drunk enough maybe.

She didn't want to talk about it. She looked over at Nick

by the bar… He was talking to the barmaid, deliberately not looking in her direction. Not wanting to know.

'OK… you've got until Nick gets back… Talk.'

'You haven't told him.'

'Of course I haven't. Shit, what would I say?'

For a moment he looked hurt.

'I'm sorry,' he said. 'I didn't mean for it… I didn't mean for it to happen like that.' It had been a conference, that clichéd haunt of affairs and confessions, and they had been drunk and the last two at the bar. If she had just gone straight to bed she might have avoided the situation. Except there would have been another time. Some events were just waiting to happen. They found a way somehow.

'I wish you'd never said anything,' Alison said, not looking at him. 'We got on so well, made a good team. Now I'm not sure. I think one of us will have to move on. There are probably regulations and… well, it's probably for the best.'

Paul looked stunned.

'Why?'

'Shit, Paul. What did you expect? That we'd keep going on as usual? That nothing would change?'

'No. I don't want to keep on as usual. I want things to change, just not… I don't see why work has to change.'

Alison could think of nothing to say.

'I thought you would have told Nick,' he said, looking over at him.

'What do you want from me? I have a family. I have children. I can't just disrupt that. I need to know…' She stopped. 'I need to know what I'm going to do before I tell them. Before it messes up their lives.'

'I want to be *in* their lives,' Paul said. 'I want to get to know them.' Alison laughed.

'Speaks the voice of a man with no children.' There was another pause.

'How long have you known?' Alison asked in a whisper.

'More or less from the start,' he said. 'From the first time I saw you I thought… I knew really… I just knew.'

He paused.

'You look a lot like her,' he said quietly. 'I mean I don't remember her, but you look like the pictures of her.'

'You saw pictures?' Alison asked.

'Yeah, my parents were always… they were open about everything. I had an album. I used to look at it a lot as a kid. And I had a picture by my bed. She looked exactly like you.'

Alison shook her head.

People had often told her she looked like her mother. She couldn't see it herself. And now, at forty-one, she was older than her mother had ever been.

'Of course I didn't recognise the name,' Paul went on, 'but it was easy enough to find out your maiden name.'

'Pretty common name, Jones,' Alison said.

'Yeah, but it set me thinking.'

He paused again.

When they had begun this conversation a week ago, drunk and tired at two in the morning, Alison had cut him off, not wanting to know. Now she sat quietly, still not sure that she wanted to know, but waiting for him to talk anyway.

Paul seemed to understand.

'I always knew about you. I mean I knew you existed. My parents were always really honest with me. They told me I had two older sisters and that my mother died when I was two. Father unknown.'

'Abby's dead too. You know that, right?' Alison said.

'Yeah.'

'Drug overdose,' Alison said, wanting to get the worst of it over with.

Paul nodded.

'Mum and Dad told me she died. I didn't know about the overdose until I was older, but I knew she was gone. I knew there was only you left.'

'You call them Mum and Dad? You get on?'

'Yeah, really well,' Paul said.

'They wouldn't let me take you,' Alison said.

She felt tears trying to come, but she held them back. It was a long time ago, and she had long since realised they were right. The faceless social workers who had told her she was too young to take care of her baby brother.

Nick was heading back from the bar. Alison tried to wipe her eyes.

'OK, now you need to tell me what's going on,' Nick said angrily. 'If you're sleeping with him I can cope with that, but if there are tears... if this... if this is serious I need...'

Alison felt laughter mingling inappropriately with her tears. There was no choice but to tell Nick now.

'I'm not sleeping with... Jesus, that's sick. He's my brother. This is my baby brother.'

'Fuck me,' Nick said. And then they were all laughing. The situation seeming so ridiculous, so utterly implausible.

Alison knew she owed Paul something. She hadn't wanted this conversation but now they were here, he deserved the truth.

'When Mum died you were already in care,' she told Paul. 'Mum was a mess and she couldn't look after you. I was away. I got into university. God knows how. They took you into care, and I thought it'd just be for a while. Just to let her get herself sorted out. Me and Abby had been in and out of care.' She paused, shaking her head.

Care had been horrible, worse than the chaos of home. Anything but a place that cared for you. But Paul had been so young, she had told herself that he wouldn't know what was happening. He would be safe while their mother hauled herself back from the brink of destruction one more time.

Except of course that last time Melody Jones hadn't hauled herself back. She had tumbled into the abyss that had been calling her for years.

Alison had woken one morning in college to a knock at the door, two police officers, the news that her mother was dead. Despite everything, despite the drugs and the violent men and the general chaos of her mother's life, it had still come as a huge shock. Until that day she had still believed that eventually it would all come good. One day her mother would get clean. And then her mother died and her belief in fairytales finally died too. Happy-ever-after was never going to happen.

'I offered to take you. Said I'd take care of you. But I was only nineteen and they said I couldn't.'

Paul nodded.

'Probably for the best.'

'Yeah,' Alison said, 'I would have been a shit mum at that age. I'm not that crash hot now, but at least I had the sense to marry a brilliant man.'

She squeezed Nick's hand.

'I don't want anything,' Paul said.

'Sorry?'

'In case you were wondering. I don't need a mother figure. I have a brilliant mother. I have a brilliant family. Being adopted was the best thing for me. I just… I wanted to know where I came from.'

'And you found out it was pretty shitty.'

Paul smiled.

'Yeah, it was pretty shitty. Except you. You grew up in that and you got out and you're OK.'

'OK is a relative term,' Alison said. 'I'm pretty fucked up.' She laughed, trying to make light of it.

Her mind went involuntarily to Ben Adams and she remembered what he had said about the scars showing. There were always people, always had been people, who could see it. People who knew, despite everything she achieved, that inside she was still that fucked-up little kid from the worst family in the town.

Paul took a breath.

'I should have found a better way to tell you,' he said, 'not some drunken declaration.'

'Yeah, it was a bit of a surprise.'

'I want to meet the girls. If that's OK. Be part of your family.' Alison looked at Nick. She knew he would always let this be her decision.

'It's complicated,' she said.

'I don't see why.'

Alison smiled. No, he wouldn't see why. He hadn't grown up like she had. He didn't know how hard she fought every day to keep her life now separate from her life then. How much she feared that some of the taint of it still showed, like mould under a fresh coat of paint. To him it was the past. To her it would always be essential to who she was.

Her girls knew nothing about her childhood. They knew their Nana Melody was dead but not how she had lived. They didn't know about the children their grandmother had abandoned and destroyed in her own self-destructive race to the grave. They had an image of a nana the way nanas are supposed to be: plump and grey and loving. Smelling of lavender and biscuits. Melody Jones had been bleach blonde and heroin thin; she had smelled most of cigarettes and alcohol and often of men.

Alison had wanted, always, to protect her children from that.

But none of that was Paul's fault.

She remembered the toddler he had been. Blond hair and a snotty nose. A smile just for her. She had been desperate then to make life better for him. Better than it had been for her. When her mother died she had asked to take him. She had wanted to make it right.

She had been too young.

But she wasn't young anymore.

'We'll tell them when the case is over...'

Nick interrupted.

'I'm sure they'd love another uncle,' he said simply.

'Shit. Uncle sounds a bit grown up.'

Alison thought so too.

'Shall I get the drinks in? Celebrate?' Paul said.

'I think you've had enough, Sergeant.' Alison laughed.

Her laugh was echoed by a low chortle behind her.

'Well said,' a slow voice said, barely an inch from her ear. 'Can't have our officers drunk in public. The constabulary must be seen to be above reproach, don't you agree?' It was Ben Adams. By his side was Robbie Smith, looking profoundly uncomfortable.

'Two handsome men, DI Dobson. You must introduce me.'

'We were just leaving,' Alison said coldly.

'What a pity. I'd love to buy you a drink.'

Innocent words, but Alison felt Nick tense beside her. He understood a subtext as well as she did. Adams felt like a dangerous man, despite his charm. Alison stood up deliberately and turned to leave.

'Another time perhaps,' Adams purred.

Alison felt him watching her as they left the pub. She didn't look back.

TWENTY-ONE

Holly was waiting for Alison when she got into the station the next morning.

'CCTV from the school's back. You might want a look,' she said.

'Finally,' Alison said. 'They took their bloody time. You seen this already, Holz?'

'Just the stuff immediately around the time Izzy left school,' Holly said. 'I'll look at the rest of it of course, but I want to see what you think.' The recording was set up to play on Holly's computer.

'This is right before Izzy left,' Holly explained. 'The camera sweeps between the fire exit and the back of the bins. Apparently they've had trouble with kids smoking round there so they put the camera in a couple of months back.'

'Did Izzy come out of the fire door?' Alison asked.

'No, look…'

The image was grainy, black and white, but Alison could make out Izzy walking around the side of the building and into shot. She was talking into her phone. Alison checked the time stamp: 2.04. That fitted with Riordan's claim that Izzy left class just after two. She was walking quickly, but not running. The camera seemed to follow her as she crossed the yard, panning away from the building towards the bins and bike shed. Izzy finished her phone call and stopped walking. The camera began to pan back towards the building. Izzy was just in shot when she turned to look back at the building.

'Why's she turned round?' Alison asked. 'Someone following her?' Holly didn't speak, just let the recording keep running. Izzy was out of shot now; the camera was filming the empty space behind her. And then…

'Bastard,' Alison said.

Indistinct as the image was, there was no mistaking the sheer bulk of the figure standing by the doorway, nor the direction in which he was looking. His eyes following Izzy Johnson, his mouth moving as he called out to her.

'Bastard,' Alison said again.

'I've been advised by my lawyers not to speak to you,' Simon Banks said when Alison entered his classroom fifteen minutes later. She had left Holly and Paul watching the rest of the CCTV with instructions to call her if anything else came up. She hadn't wanted to wait before confronting Banks. He offered her a card with his solicitor's contact details. She glanced at it. Hargreaves, Mitchell and Webster. The same firm that was representing Robbie Smith.

'Expensive firm these,' Alison said conversationally.

Banks flushed.

'Seems a lot of effort to go to, hiring a really top lawyer, if you've done nothing wrong.'

'You can't say that,' Banks said, sounding petulant. 'A man can't be judged guilty just for trying to defend himself.' Alison shook her head. He had clearly been listening to his lawyer's advice. He looked like a man who was confident that, whatever his misdemeanours, he was not going to be held to account for them anytime soon.

'Why didn't you tell me you followed Izzy out of school on the day she was killed?' Alison asked.

'What? I… I don't know what you're talking about. I didn't teach Izzy the day she died. I told you…'

'We have CCTV footage of you at the back of the school, just a few feet away from Izzy. That's the last image we have of Izzy and there you are, Mr Banks. Funny how everywhere I look in this case there you are.'

'I… What CCTV?'

'When did you last see Isabella Johnson?'

'I saw her…' he began, then he stopped himself. 'Hold on, no, you're supposed to talk to my lawyer. I told you I'm not talking to you.'

Alison smiled. For a man who wasn't going to talk to her he was using a lot of words. She hoped his urge to explain himself would overcome his caution.

'What were you doing at the back of the school on Tuesday afternoon? I understood you were supposed to be teaching.'

She didn't mention the information she had from the class about his ten minutes' absence, wondering if *he* would.

'I *was* teaching,' Banks said. 'Year 7. I told you this already.'

'And you never left? Never popped out at all?'

'No. What? Why are you asking?' He looked flustered.

Alison waited. 'Oh, wait, I forgot. I did leave. Very briefly. Ryan Thomas was misbehaving as I recall so I went to look for Mr Riordan. It was a disciplinary matter, you see.'

'And did you find Mr Riordan?' Alison asked, already knowing the answer.

'No... I... I gave up and returned to the classroom.'

'Or maybe you didn't find Mr Riordan because you were never looking for him. Maybe you saw Izzy leaving school and took the opportunity to follow her.'

'Of course not. That's ridiculous. Why would you think that?'

'We have you on CCTV. Behind the school. Following Izzy.'

'Don't be preposterous. I wasn't following...'

'You admit you saw her?' Alison asked.

'Well, yes, now you've reminded me. I do remember seeing her.'

'And you followed her.'

'No, no, only as far as the back entrance. I called to her. I wanted to make sure she was alright. She didn't hear me. Or maybe she did... I don't know... She carried on walking anyway. I let her go. Maybe if I'd gone after her... But I didn't.'

'And you didn't think it was worth telling me this?' Alison asked.

'I forgot. I mean it was nothing. Anyway what difference could it make? Izzy left school, whether I saw her or not doesn't really matter, does it?'

'Why did you want to talk to her?' Alison asked.

'What? Well, I mean she was leaving school, I just wanted to make sure she was... I needed to know she was alright.'

'Sixth formers are allowed out of school, aren't they? It's not unusual, so why were you so concerned about Izzy?'

'I don't know. I… Like I say I just wanted to check she was OK. I just wanted to ask why she was, er, leaving.' The words trailed away, as if he knew how unlikely they sounded.

'You just followed her to see if she was OK? It didn't have anything to do with telling her to keep quiet? Nothing to do with the note you sent her asking her to keep your secrets?'

'Oh for goodness' sake, I have explained that note. And if you saw the CCTV, you saw that I didn't follow Izzy.'

'There are other ways out of school,' Alison said.

Banks sighed. 'Look, you really should only speak to me through my lawyer. I have a class to teach.'

Alison nodded, taking a sheet of paper out of her pocket.

'Is Lucy Jacobs in this class?' she asked, reading from the paper.

'What?'

'Or Martha Jones, Billy King, Joe Simons, Max Smith, Hugo Bailey…'

'What? What is that?' Banks asked.

'Just a list of names. Any of them in your next class?'

'What? No, I…'

Alison went on, 'Dan Humphreys is on the list. Is he in your class? Izzy Johnson. Dominic Mills. Any idea what all these young people might have in common?'

'I don't… What is that list? Where did you get…?'

'You tell me, Mr Banks.'

Banks suddenly stood up.

'I'd like you to leave my classroom,' he said, his voice firm but with the hint of a judder. 'If you want to speak to me please call my solicitor. I have been advised that if you continue to harass me I may have grounds for a civil suit. I have nothing more to say.'

This time Alison sensed that he meant it.

She was breathing heavily when she left the room. She slammed the door behind her half deliberately. Niall Riordan was in the corridor.

'I usually give out detentions for less,' he said, indicating the slammed door. He was smiling. Alison felt herself smile too.

'Are you here looking for me?' Riordan asked. 'Have there been any more developments?'

'None I can really tell you about,' Alison said, glancing back at Banks' classroom.

She wanted to tell Riordan that one of his teachers was dealing drugs. But how could she? All she had was a list of names and a few initials. None of it added up to proof. The last thing she needed was to be sued for defamation of character or police harassment.

'You look like you could do with a cup of tea,' Riordan said gently.

'I could do with a gin and tonic to be honest,' Alison said, 'but tea would be nice. There's something I'd like to ask you actually.'

Riordan nodded and led the way to his office. He had a kettle in the corner and made the tea himself.

'One of the few perks of the job,' he told her, offering her a packet of chocolate biscuits. She took one gratefully.

'You enjoy your work, don't you?' Alison asked.

'I love it.' He grinned. 'I can't imagine anything I'd like to do more than this. The admin can get a bit much. I miss the teaching now that so much of my time is spent out of the classroom, but getting to shape the way the whole school runs is a real privilege.'

'Privilege?'

He laughed. 'Sounds pretentious, I know, but there you are.'

'So why are you thinking of leaving?'

'Nothing's certain.'

'Mr Chapell seems to think you're sure to get the Harvard job.'

Riordan laughed again. 'Yes, Henry has unerring faith in me. He was the one who persuaded me to apply. He always wanted to live in the US… and I suppose it *is* teaching after a fashion.'

'Sounds amazing,' Alison said.

'Yes, yes, it does *sound* amazing.'

'But?'

'Sorry?'

'Well, you don't seem too convinced.'

'No, no, it will be amazing,' he said with a smile. 'It's just been a long time since I was in academia. I've had to submit some original work. I've been revisiting the stuff I did for my PhD. It's all a bit daunting, going back to that world.'

Alison shook her head, watching him.

'What?'

'I'm just… well, I'm just wondering how you ended up here, I suppose. After Cambridge, and then a high-flying City job. Designing algorithms or whatever it was.'

'It wasn't for me. I prefer it here.'

'Really?

Riordan sighed. 'It's complicated.' He paused. 'Actually it isn't complicated at all. I used to work for a merchant bank. It was highly paid, glamorous in a way. There was a lot of travel, a lot of champagne lunches. Henry loved it.'

'And you?'

'I had a breakdown,' he said matter-of-factly. 'A little over ten years ago. I just couldn't take the pressure. Henry stuck by me. I can't tell you how hard it was for him. I'm so incredibly grateful that he's still here. And when I was better I decided I wanted a quieter life.'

'And you chose teaching?' Alison asked, unable to keep the incredulity from her voice.

Riordan chuckled. 'Funnily enough I don't find it at all stressful. I love it.'

'So why leave?'

'Henry needs more. He craves the high life.' Riordan smiled fondly. 'His mother thinks he's wasting his life with me. She calls regularly to tell him so. It's hard for him. He gets bored.'

Alison said nothing, sipping her tea.

'That's why Harvard is a godsend,' Riordan continued. 'I owe it to Henry to at least try. Give him something he can be proud of.' He took a sip of his tea, his mind seeming to be a long way away. 'Anyway, this isn't what you wanted to talk to me about. How can I help?'

Alison hesitated. She wasn't quite sure how to proceed. She wanted to put Riordan on his guard around Banks, but she couldn't accuse Banks of anything without proof.

'Have you had any problems recently with drugs?' she asked at last.

Riordan frowned. 'No,' he said. He seemed to recognise the disbelief in Alison's face and smiled. 'I'm not being naive,' he went on, 'I'm sure some of the young people use drugs. But you said *problem*s with drugs. I take that to mean kids bringing them onto the premises, or cases of addiction, or dealing around the school. At the moment I have nothing like that on my radar. You don't suspect Izzy's death has anything to do with drugs?'

'I can't discuss it directly, I'm afraid. Officially I don't know anything.'

'And indirectly?' Riordan asked. 'Unofficially? If we have a drug problem I really would like to know.' Alison hesitated.

Riordan took another sip of his tea. 'You've got a daughter coming into Year 7 soon, haven't you?' he said. 'Could you talk to me as a future parent? For the good of the school?'

Alison laughed. 'You sound like a lawyer,' she said. 'OK. Look, I have no proof but… have you heard of nootropics?'

'What?'

'They're substances thought to boost brainpower. Some are legal, some are banned but can be brought from abroad, others are prescription drugs. We're… There's a possibility that someone is dealing them at the school.'

'Who? Banks?'

'What makes you say that?' Alison asked, wondering if Riordan had his own suspicions.

'You were coming out of his classroom. There was the note he left Izzy. I'm a maths teacher, I can add two and two.'

Alison smiled.

'I can't say who we're looking at,' she said. 'I can't accuse anyone. I just… I wanted you to know… to be on the lookout.'

'You think Izzy was taking these drugs?'

'We're not sure. Her name was on a list.' Alison didn't mention the contents of Izzy's stomach, the pills found at her house. She was saying too much already really.

'A list? Could I possibly see it?'

After only a moment's hesitation, Alison handed him the printout she had taken from Banks' computer.

'These are all good kids. They're some of our best students, or ex-students.'

'Well, they would be, wouldn't they,' Alison said, 'if they were taking drugs to boost their grades?'

'God, what are we doing to our kids?' Riordan asked. 'What the hell has our education system come to when our children will put their health at risk, and break the law, just for a good grade?' Alison nodded her understanding. They were creating a world where to fall behind was to be left behind. Where success was all that mattered and younger and younger children were buying into it. And men like Banks were profiting.

'Do you want me to arrange for you to speak to the children on this list?' Riordan asked. Alison thought for a long moment. She was in the middle of a murder case. Was this the best use of her time? The morning was already gone, and she was getting nowhere. If Banks was dealing drugs, and Izzy had known about it, that could explain the note. It could explain why he wanted her to keep quiet. And if she wouldn't keep quiet it gave him a motive to kill her. But there was still the problem of timing. How could Banks have got to the Beamsleigh and back so quickly and unseen?

The possibility that Banks had killed Izzy was remote, not something Alison should be wasting much time on. Still, she couldn't just let it drop.

Maybe she wouldn't need to talk to all the kids. Just one or two. Leave the rest to Jack Kent. A little lesson in humility via an afternoon spent interviewing teenagers.

'Do any of the names jump out?' she asked Riordan, trying to decide who, if anyone, she should interview herself. 'Any of them been acting oddly or any that you've noticed had an odd relationship with...' she almost said Banks, 'with... any of their teachers?'

Riordan looked down the list again. Then he shook his head, almost as if trying to dispel an idea that had occurred to him.

'What?' she asked.

'It's probably nothing but... Dominic Mills' name is on this list.'

'Yes?'

'Well, he's left the school now, of course. Been gone a couple of years.' Alison waited. And Riordan continued. 'Last year I saw quite a bit of him. He was part of our mentoring programme of course, but also... well, he used to call in. I saw him around the school more often than I might have expected.'

'Talking to anyone in particular?'

'I often saw him with Simon Banks. But Banks is head of sixth form, many ex-pupils come back to see him. I didn't think anything of it at the time. Until the argument.'

'Banks argued with Dominic Mills?'

'No. The argument was between Banks and Andrea Mills.'

'When was that?'

'It must have been about a month ago. They were in the corridor and Andrea was really shouting. I assumed it had something to do with Mary, Andrea's daughter. There have been behavioural issues, accusations of bullying. I've been called in on more than one occasion.'

'And Andrea was arguing with Banks about it? About Mary?'

'That's the thing, now I think about it I'm not really sure. I assumed it was about Mary, but…' He let the words die.

'Did you hear any of the conversation?' Alison asked.

'Not really. Andrea was threatening to report Banks for something. I was concerned that other students would overhear.' He looked sheepish. 'I asked her if she wanted to discuss it in my office, but she refused. I asked Simon about it later and he was evasive. Said it was nothing. I thought it was odd at the time.'

'Did you ever ask Andrea again about the argument?'

'Yeah, I did actually. It was so unusual, I mean Mrs Mills has always been one of the more supportive parents. I spoke to her at the school gates one day. She was… well, she was as evasive as Simon to be honest. She said it was nothing, said it was sorted. But she did ask me if it was possible to make sure Mary wasn't taught by Mr Banks in future. I said I'd see what I could do. That was it. I thought it was odd but I was relieved, to tell you the truth. Parental complaints mean a lot of paperwork.'

'Right,' Alison said, not sure how relevant any of this was, or why Riordan was telling her.

'The thing is – the reason I'm mentioning it really – I haven't seen Dom in school since then. Since the day of the argument. I hadn't really noticed, but now I come to think of it, I saw him a lot and then I didn't. I didn't make the connection until just now.'

'So maybe the thing Mrs Mills was threatening to report Banks for was connected to Dom not Mary?'

Riordan nodded.

TWENTY-TWO

A weak sun was peeking through the clouds as Alison walked towards the Mills' house; she felt the warmth of it against her cheek, lifting her mood. It felt as if spring was making a new assault, determined to win through.

Something white caught her eye as she approached the house. A note pinned to the front door. '*Mum, sorry about earlier. Gone for a walk. Left key in usual place. Hope you have a good run – Dom.*' The house looked deserted but Alison knocked anyway. As she waited she looked speculatively under a couple of the nearest plant pots. The key to the door nestled under the second.

A girl had been killed and still people felt safe enough to leave a key in such an obvious place. She ought to be horrified, but instead it made her pleased. She liked to live in a place where people trusted each other. Even if that trust was often misplaced. Trust was an act of faith in the face of overwhelming fact.

She left the key where it was.

Clearly no one was in. She knew talking to Dom and

Andrea Mills could wait. There were plenty more important angles to follow up. But the sun felt warm on her back and she wasn't ready to be inside again yet. She decided to walk up the Beamsleigh and see if either of them had headed that way. The crime scene had been released and local people were already urging each other to use the area again. Even if Andrea wasn't brave enough to go up there yet, Alison reasoned that Dominic might have chosen it as a route for his walk. It wouldn't be necessary for him to go near where Izzy had actually been killed, there were plenty of other paths to follow.

She headed up Forest Road and onto the Beamsleigh Hill. The whole area was peaceful, much as it had been on Tuesday afternoon. As Alison climbed the first stile the drizzle began again and she had to put up the hood of her coat against the damp. A loud 'caw' made her jump. She looked up to see a number of gulls circling overhead. There must be a sea fret at Scarborough; the bad weather always drew the gulls inland.

She greeted a couple of women with dogs and prams and continued on her way.

Another call. She lowered her hood. Had it been another gull? She smiled at herself. She was getting spooked. She imagined it would be a while before most people in the town could come this way again without feeling a little uneasy.

She rounded the mound from the right.

A third cry.

A man, standing up and suddenly running towards her. Blood. She felt her heart race. Ready to react, ready to protect herself.

Then the cries became coherent. She understood his words.

'Thank God, thank God. She's hurt.'

She realised with a jolt that the man before her was Henry Chapell. He looked frightened, pale and shaking. His voice was high-pitched with fear.

'Thank God,' he said again. 'I shouted but no one came. She's hurt.' Alison looked past him. There was a body on the ground. A woman in a hoody and jogging pants. Blood everywhere.

'What happened?' she asked, already heading towards the woman.

'I don't know. I found her.'

Alison reached the woman, who was unnaturally pale. If she was breathing it was not detectable.

'Shit.'

Alison felt at the woman's neck for a pulse. Blood was everywhere. Sticky against Alison's hand, soaking into the earth, covering the woman's face and neck. Everywhere. Filling Alison's vision. The woman's throat was slit, but Alison found a place to press her fingers. Was there a slight thump against her fingertips? Or was it her own heartbeat in her hands?

She had her phone in her hand. She was taking off her coat. Not thinking, just reacting. The coat bunched up, the cloth pressed against the woman's still bleeding throat. Trying to staunch the flow. The phone to her ear. No signal. Of course. No bloody signal.

'Hold this here,' Alison told Chapell, giving him her coat. 'Try to stop the blood. Talk to her. I'm going for help.'

'Is she alive?'

Alison couldn't answer. She didn't know.

Then she was running, back towards the road, her

phone in her hand, watching for the signal bars to appear. Shit, shit, shit. Like a mantra in her head. Willing herself to move faster. Shit. She couldn't be dead.

Andrea Mills *could not* be dead.

An hour later and the crime scene felt like déjà vu.

What sort of lunatic would kill two people in such an exposed place? A bloody lucky one. Alison had to acknowledge that there was nothing scarier than luck.

The ambulance had gone, taking the body. Alison was wrapped in a blanket, shock making her shake. Her muscles contracting so fiercely that her jaw ached from trying to stop her teeth chattering. Still she was doing her job.

Jenny McBride and her team were getting to work on the scene.

'Same as the other one?' Alison asked.

'Looks like it. Garrotted. Again probably with a thin flexible wire.'

'There seems to be a lot more blood.'

'Carotid was severed this time,' Jenny said matter-of-factly.

'So more force was used?'

'Not necessarily. The wire happened to sever the artery this time. Pure chance.' Alison didn't speak, feeling another wave of cold sweep over her. Jenny went on with her assessment.

'Victim is female again, but this time older. Mid-forties, I'd say. There was no ID on the body, no phone, nothing. Looks like she was out for a run judging by the clothes.'

'It's Andrea Mills,' Alison said.

'The witness who found the first victim?'

Alison nodded.

'Shit,' Jenny said quietly.

Alison felt Paul shift beside her, but didn't look at him. The last thing she needed was his sympathy. He was here as part of the police team, called in with everyone else to investigate. He was not here to comfort her.

'You think the killer targeted her?' Jenny was asking.

'Either that or it's the location he likes,' Alison said, as much to herself as anyone else. But she wasn't buying that. It was a crap location, far too busy to guarantee the killer could act undisturbed. Andrea had not been killed because she happened to be on the Beamsleigh. She had been killed because she was Andrea Mills, and almost certainly she had been killed by the same person who killed Izzy Johnson.

Alison thought of Robbie Smith. If he had done this then she had to take her share of the blame. She had let Robbie go. She had told him that Andrea could identify him, even though it was a lie. And now Andrea was dead. The guilt sat heavily on her shoulders.

'I want Robbie Smith found and brought in as soon as possible. Preferably before he has a chance to get on a train anywhere or talk to any *friends* who can give him an alibi.' Holly made a note. 'And get a warrant sorted to search his house. If he's involved there has to be some forensic evidence somewhere,' Alison went on. Holly nodded and headed off.

Alison couldn't help feeling as if this case had been a fuck-up from the start. Too close to home, too easy to get distracted.

'What happened?' Paul asked.

'I came up the hill looking for her,' Alison said. 'I heard a scream, ran this way. Chapell was running down the hill, calling for help. I checked for a pulse, couldn't be sure. I left him with her, trying to stop the blood. I called an ambulance. She was still warm.' Alison was aware she was rambling and stopped herself.

Jenny McBride nodded her head. 'She probably died around the time you found her.'

'Chapell was definitely trying to help?' Paul asked.

'God yes, yes. He was screaming for help. I wouldn't have got there so quickly if he hadn't been.'

'You want me to talk to him?' Paul asked.

'We'll do it together.'

Henry Chapell was sitting a short way away, looking diminished.

'Can you tell me what happened? How you found the body?' Alison asked.

'God, don't say that. Don't call her a… a body. I tried, oh God, I'm so sorry.' He bent over and retched into the grass, spitting bile onto the turf beside him. Alison passed him a tissue and he wiped at his mouth ineffectually.

'So sorry,' he said again.

'Did you know Mrs Mills?'

'Yes. Not very well but I'd see her plodding around here sometimes when I was walking Angela.'

'Angela is your dog?'

'My Chihuahua, yes.' He waved his hand towards the small dog tethered by her lead to the door handle of a police car nearby.

'When you came up here today did you see anything unusual?'

'Apart from a dead woman, you mean?' he asked. He stopped and shook his head. 'Sorry. No there was nothing unusual. Nothing.'

'So you walked around the hill and…?'

'She was on the ground. And he was sort of standing over her. I yelled at him and he ran off. I don't know what I'd have done if he hadn't run. What was I going to do? Set Angela on him? God, how awful.' He bent over again and retched into the grass. This time nothing came up.

'You saw the assailant?' Alison felt a beat of adrenaline. Here was a chance. Here was something concrete at last.

'Yes.'

'Did you get a good look at him?'

'Yes, absolutely. He looked right at me.'

A proper description. A witness who had seen something at last. The killer's luck running out. Chapell was still speaking, the words tumbling out of him.

'He ran off, and I went to try to help. I called for help. Did you hear me? I called for help. I tried to stop the blood, but I couldn't. I didn't know what to do. I started running down the hill. I just wanted to get help. And I was yelling… and I saw you… and you came. Oh my God, you came. I've never been happier to see anyone. And then you took her pulse, and I was trying to stop the blood. And the ambulance came…' His words finally ran out. He took deep, juddering breaths.

'How long were you with her before I came?' Alison asked.

'I don't know. It felt like ages, it felt like hours, maybe it was ten minutes. I don't know. It probably wasn't even that long. I just didn't know what to do. I didn't know…'

'You did your best,' Paul said kindly.

'I couldn't stop the blood. There was just so much more blood.' Alison looked down at him. He was indeed covered in blood.

'I'll get an officer to take you home and let you get changed. We'll need to take those clothes for testing, I'm afraid.'

'Of course, of course.' He stood up shakily. 'What about Angela?'

'The dog?'

'Can I give her a bath? She's got blood as well. Do you need to test her?' Alison fought an inappropriate urge to laugh. The idea that the Chihuahua might be implicated in the killing was ludicrous.

'I think you can safely give her a shampoo when you get her home.'

'Thank you.'

'We'll want to talk to you in more detail later,' Alison said, 'get a full description of the man you saw.'

For a second Chapell looked stunned.

'But I don't need to give you a description,' he said. 'I recognised him. It was Robbie Smith.'

TWENTY-THREE

'We found Robbie,' Holly said, when Alison answered her phone.

'Was he at home?'

'No,' she hesitated. 'You're not going to like this, boss.' *I'm not going to like it any better if you pussyfoot about for ten minutes before telling me,* Alison thought but, at the risk of sounding like DCI Rogers, she didn't say it. Instead she waited for Holly to continue.

'He's at the police station,' Holly said.

'Good, that's where I want him.'

'No. At Penbury station. He's been here a while.'

'What the… Holly, please explain to me in words of one syllable.'

'OK. I went round to his house like you said. He wasn't there and his mum said she hadn't seen him. So I put a call out to keep an eye out for him. And Carol Burgess, the PCSO here at Penbury, got back to me. She said he's been in custody here since lunchtime.' Alison shook her head. This was making less and less bloody sense. How could Robbie have been in custody since lunchtime if Henry Chapell had seen him attacking Andrea?

'OK. I'll be there in fifteen minutes. Has he got a lawyer with him?'

'No.'

'Alright. Make sure he knows he can get a solicitor if he wants one. He's got some fancy firm in Leeds representing him and I don't want them saying we didn't treat the little arse with due respect.'

'Right, I'll let him know.'

'Fifteen minutes,' Alison reiterated, then she went to find Paul.

He was on the phone, looking pleased.

'Thanks, mate, good to know.'

'What's good to know?' Alison asked.

'Looks like they found a murder weapon this time. Little noose of wire like you might use to make an animal trap.'

Alison felt a buzz of vindication; her guess had been right.

'Anything useful?' she asked.

'There's some blood and other trace. It's getting tested,' he said. 'You got good news?'

'It's the old good news and bad news thing, I'm afraid.' She smiled. 'Holly found Robbie Smith, but it looks like he might have a pretty good alibi for this one.'

'Yeah? Like what? Letter from the Pope saying he was in confession at the time?'

'Better. Copper in Penbury who says he was locked up all afternoon.'

'Shit.'

'We better go talk to him.'

Alison spoke to Carol Burgess, the community support officer, as soon as she got to Penbury station.

'What's the story?' she asked, as she accepted a cup of weak tea.

Carol was a good lass, a solid copper, even if she was officially just a PCSO. Alison trusted her opinion.

'Got a call saying Robbie was dealing drugs up on the Cawpers estate.'

'Call from who?'

'Anonymous.' Carol took a sip of her tea and smiled. 'We don't get anonymous tip-offs generally. Folk around here usually like to be seen to be doing something. I figured it was maybe a kid playing a prank.'

'Did it sound like a kid?' Alison asked.

'Teenager maybe. A lad definitely,' Carol said, and Alison nodded for her to continue. 'Anyway I thought I'd swing by Cawpers and see what it was all about. And lo and behold there's our Robbie.'

'Our Robbie?' Alison asked. It was a common enough phrase, but something in the way Carol said it caught her attention.

'No relation,' Carol said, 'but I've known him since he was a nipper. Used to work with Sharon over at the Baco before I started here.'

Alison nodded again; the bacon-processing factory in Milbury employed a lot of people. It seemed like most of the town had worked there at one time or another.

'OK, so you know Robbie,' Alison said.

'Yeah, and unfortunately I also know his reputation. Drug dealing reported and there's Robbie. Not hard to put two and two together.'

'So you pulled him in?'

'Thought I'd get him in here, see what he had to say for himself. After what happened to that lass he was so fond of, I thought he might just behave himself for a few days. But hey.'

'So you arrested him?'

'Nope,' she shook her head, 'I got him to turn out his pockets. No drugs, no cash to speak of. I think he had about three quid, nothing to suggest he had been dealing at all.'

'But you brought him in anyway?' Alison asked.

'Like I say I've known him from being a kid. I know there's not much chance an afternoon in the cop shop is going to scare him straight but what can I do? Sharon's a mate.' There must have been something sceptical in Alison's face. Carol sighed. 'I know what folk round here think of Sharon Smith. And I know she was a wrong'un when she was younger, but she's pulled herself round, done her best by those lads. I believe in giving people second chances. Whatever Sharon was like as a lass, she doesn't need the sort of crap Robbie brings to her door.'

'Fair enough,' Alison said.

'So I brought him in. I put him in a cell and told him I was investigating.'

'Did he buy that?'

Carol laughed. 'Kid's not daft. He just kicked back and relaxed, told me he had nowhere better to be. Sad thing is that's probably true.'

'What time was all this?' Alison asked.

'Call came in,' she checked her notebook, 'twelve twenty-eight. I went straight up to the Cawpers and picked Robbie up. He's been with me ever since.'

Alison looked down at her own notes. She had called 999 at twelve forty-two. Shit. That was fourteen minutes *after* someone called to say Robbie was dealing on the Cawpers.

'What time did you actually log him in?' Alison asked Burgess. A long pause. 'You did log him in, right?'

Carol flushed, which told Alison she hadn't.

'I know...' Carol said, 'but it's in my notebook. He was here.'

'But not logged in. Nothing official.'

She shook her head.

'OK,' Alison said, suppressing a sigh. There was no point bollocking Carol Burgess. She knew the rules. But she also knew right from wrong, and she had been trying to do the right thing.

'What time did you pick him up? Exactly?'

'I don't know exactly, I was up there a little while looking for him. You know what those estates are like, a right muddle of dead ends and that. But I can't have taken more than ten minutes, fifteen at the most. I'd have been with him quarter to one at the very latest.'

Alison nodded, trying to get a timeline in her head.

Twelve twenty-eight a call came in saying Robbie was seen at the Cawpers. Could be a mistake, or a prank or a deliberate lie to give Robbie an alibi. It was somewhere between, say, twelve forty and twelve forty-five by the time Carol Burgess actually picked Robbie up.

Could he have been on Beamsleigh Hill and made it to the Cawpers by twelve forty-five? Alison herself had called an ambulance at twelve forty-two, but Andrea had been attacked earlier. Henry Chapell claimed to have been with the body for as long as ten minutes. And even when Alison arrived to help it had taken a minute or more before she could get a signal on her phone. That meant Andrea could have been attacked as early as twelve thirty.

If Robbie had attacked Andrea Mills on the Beamsleigh at twelve thirty it was just possible to be at the Cawpers by quarter to one.

Possible but unlikely. Alison hated possible but unlikely.

'We'll go in and talk to him,' she said to Carol, nodding to Paul to come with her.

Robbie was waiting in the interview room, his head resting on his arms on the desk. It seemed to cost him a great effort to look up at her when she walked in.

'I want to talk to you, Robbie. You have the right to a solicitor. Did DC Webster tell you that?'

'Yeah, only I'm alright.'

'You're waiving your right to a solicitor?'

'Can I do that?'

Alison took a deep breath. 'You don't have to have a solicitor,' she said carefully, 'but most people find it helpful.'

'I called her,' Robbie said. 'She told me I *had* to call her if you guys arrested me or anything.'

'You called Ms Mitchell?' Alison asked, trying to keep the dislike out of her voice.

Robbie nodded, looking as if he didn't like the woman any more than Alison did.

'But I can talk to you before she gets here, can't I?' Alison smiled. That would royally piss off Hortence Mitchell, but as the suggestion had clearly come from Robbie himself Alison couldn't see how anyone could legally object.

'Yes, you can talk to me,' she said. Robbie seemed to visibly relax.

'Is this about Izzy again? Cos I told you I...' Alison interrupted.

'Andrea Mills has been found dead,' she said.

'Yeah?' He didn't look very interested.

'Yes.'

Normally she would ask where he was at the time of the murder, but she knew where he had been. Or at least where he would say he had been. At the Cawpers estate and then here.

'Officer Burgess says she got a call to say you were out at Cawpers selling drugs.'

'Yeah, she said. Except I wasn't selling nothing. That's all bullshit, right.' Alison raised her eyebrows.

'Yeah, I know... likely story,' Robbie said, 'but even bad lads can't be bad all the time. Let's just say I'm having a day off. Even entrepreneurs have a day off occasionally.' He tried to smile; it didn't quite make his eyes.

'Is that what you are, an entrepreneur?' Paul asked scathingly.

Robbie didn't look at him. Instead he directed his reply to Alison.

'Me and Izzy used to talk about it sometimes. How one kind of business is OK but another isn't. How they tell us all the time to get off our arses and make something of ourselves, but when we do it's illegal. Kids with money can open a bar, or sell bloody poncey e-cigarettes and they're businessmen. I sell a bit of weed and it's like the world's going to crash around society's ears. It's a way of keeping the poor man in his place.'

'That you talking or Isabella Johnson?'

'She changed my life, Izzy,' Robbie said with a smile. 'Opened my eyes. It's like – fuck, I don't know – it's like once your eyes are open you just see all this shit. All this injustice everywhere.'

'So now you're Martin Luther bloody King, are you?' Paul snorted.

'Yeah, well I wouldn't expect you to understand.' He turned back to Alison, as if to imply she might be different.

'Were you dealing drugs today on the Cawpers?' she asked, sticking to the subject.

'Not today.'

'So why would someone ring the police and say that you were?'

'No idea. Maybe someone doesn't like me.'

'Yeah, or maybe they were doing you a favour,' Paul said.

'What the… What's he on about? How is dobbing me to the cops doing me a favour?' Robbie looked to Alison.

'Well, you see that phone call gave you the perfect alibi for Andrea Mills' murder.'

'What?' Robbie was ashen-faced. 'Wait up. You want to pin that on me? First Izzy and now this Mills woman?'

'Andrea Mills saw you with Izzy Johnson. Maybe you decided you needed to keep her quiet.' It was just a theory, but it fitted.

'Yeah, two problems,' Robbie said, shaking slightly but sounding tough. 'First she never saw me do anything to hurt Izzy, cos Izzy was fine when I left. And second I've been here for bloody ages, haven't I. So how could I have killed anyone?'

He had a point. And yet. Henry Chapell had seen

Robbie. Seen him standing over Andrea Mills' body. About the same time someone else had called the cop shop to say Robbie was up on the Cawpers selling drugs. Someone was lying. Right now it looked like Robbie and whoever had made that call on his behalf.

Robbie was watching Alison through his impossibly long lashes. Something in his face imploring her to believe him. And she realised, with something close to shock, that she desperately *wanted* to believe him. Yet she couldn't. He had been the last person to see Izzy, and Izzy was dead. He had been seen standing over Andrea Mills and Andrea was dead.

What more do I need, Alison asked herself, *a smoking bloody gun?* Robbie seemed to sense her resignation, and it mirrored his own. He let his head fall onto his arms again. He looked destroyed, there was really no other word for it.

'I didn't kill Izzy,' he said with a weariness Alison found exhausting to watch. 'I don't know who did, and I'd probably kill them if I ever found out.'

Alison watched him closely; either he was a very clever actor or telling the truth. The trouble was, some killers really were very clever actors. Wanting to believe someone wasn't enough.

'Tell me about Andrea Mills,' Alison said quietly.

'I didn't kill her.'

'OK. But you knew her, right?'

He nodded. 'I knew Dom a bit before he went to uni. And he's got a little sister too, hasn't he? She's a bit of a cow but still. Poor kid.'

'Andrea didn't like you, did she?' Alison said.

'Can't be loved by everyone,' Robbie said, 'no matter how charming and good looking you are.'

Alison wanted to smile, but fought it.

'She reported you up at the school one time, didn't she?'

Robbie shrugged.

'Lots of people "report" me,' he said. 'Every time anything goes wrong around here it seems like there's some nosy git saying it was me.'

'And usually it is,' Alison said.

Robbie smiled. 'Aye, 'appen.'

'She told Mr Riordan at the school that you were dealing drugs.'

'Did she?'

'You know she did. Your mother had a go at her in the Co-op about it. Threatened to lay into her.'

Robbie's smile was genuine now.

'Good old Mum.'

'So Andrea knew you. She would have recognised you if she saw you?'

'Yeah, and she would have been bloody happy to point the finger. But if she'd done that you would never have let me go, would you? So she never said it was me. You're saying she saw me with Izzy, hurting Izzy, so why would she suddenly go all shy and not say anything?'

'Maybe she was afraid of your mum?'

'Fuck off, that's never stopped her before. You know what she told Mr Riordan? Said the likes of me should be driven out of the town. That's what she said. *The likes of me*. Like, what the fuck does that even mean? She said that they should all get together and make my family leave. Dom told Izzy. He's alright, Dom. He didn't agree with what she said.'

'This was when you were dealing drugs outside the school?'

'Yeah, only I wasn't, was I?'

'Right,' Paul said sarcastically. 'You were too busy reading philosophy and trying to change the world.'

'You ever wonder why Riordan never went to the police if someone was dealing drugs outside the school?' Robbie asked. 'Because he knew I never did anything. And anyway *she* never wanted the police hanging around, seeing it was her kid involved.'

'Whose kid?'

'That Andrea Mills. It was her kid that was up to it, not me.'

'Dominic?' Alison asked.

'Nah, that little brat Mary. I mean, what is she, twelve, thirteen? And there she was trying to score weed off me, telling me she could sell it on to the other kids for me. And all I was doing was hanging around waiting to meet Izzy. Never went up near the school after that. I mean, twelve years old…'

'And your morals prevent…' Paul began.

'Fuck off, I don't sell crap to children,' Robbie said. 'Anyway Mrs Mills jumped to the wrong conclusion. Riordan listened to me though and when it turned out little Mary was involved it all got hushed up. That Mrs Mills still said it was me trying to sell to the kids, but Riordan believed me. Then it all got dropped, no further action, all that shit. And Andrea Mills was still spreading crap about me over the town. That's what Mum was so pissed off about. It was alright for Mrs Mills to bad-mouth me all over town but no one was allowed to say a word about her little brat.'

'Will Mr Riordan support this story?' Alison asked.

Robbie shrugged. 'He will if he's telling the truth,' he said.

'When did you last see Andrea Mills?' Alison asked.

Robbie shrugged again. 'No idea. Probably months ago. Might have seen her up the street, but I haven't had owt to do with her.'

'Someone saw you today with Andrea,' Alison said calmly.

Robbie looked up, shocked.

'Who says that? They're lying.'

'We have a witness who puts you at the scene of her murder,' Alison said again. She didn't smile at her use of 'police speak', she was feeling less and less like smiling as this case went on.

'I didn't do it,' Robbie said desperately. 'You've got to believe me. This is all bullshit.' As he spoke, the door beside Alison opened, and in walked Hortence Mitchell.

'DI Dobson,' she said. 'I did *not* expect to be seeing you again quite so soon. Are you really interviewing my client without legal representation?'

'He expressly asked to start the interview before you arrived,' Alison said.

'Indeed?' Mitchell asked. 'Well, he will no doubt be happy to avail himself of my services now I *am* here.'

Robbie looked terrified, but he nodded his head in agreement. Mitchell was an intimidating woman, but Alison refused to be intimidated. She straightened her shoulders.

'Would you like a few moments with your client?' she asked.

'That would be usual practice,' Mitchell said, sitting opposite Robbie.

Alison and Paul left the room.

'He'll clam up tighter than a diver's arse now,' Paul said.

Alison smiled. 'A diver's arse?'

'Yeah, well, I couldn't think of anything else that clams tight, except maybe a clam?'

'A Yorkshireman's wallet?' Alison said.

'Yeah, but given present company I thought that might be considered racist.' She laughed again. Paul had grown up in the Midlands, he didn't see himself as a Yorkshireman. He was practically a foreigner, which made it all the harder to consider him her brother.

'What do you reckon?' Alison asked.

'Timing's tight but he could have done it. Learned from last time, got his alibi all sorted. If he knew he was going to kill Andrea about half twelve it's a clever call to get someone to ring up before that and say he was at the Cawpers. Then he could leg it up there in time for Burgess to pick him up at quarter to one.'

'Risky,' Alison said.

'Yeah. But possible.'

Alison nodded. She was wondering who could have made that anonymous call to the police. Her mind went to Ben Adams. How far would he go for Robbie? He had said he was infatuated. Would he perjure himself to win Robbie's favour? Help him to commit a murder? The idea seemed far-fetched.

'Calls coming in here would be recorded, right?' Paul nodded.

'So we need to hear that tape,' she said, 'but first let's hear what Robbie has to say now he's got a lawyer.'

'I hope we're not going to have to look into a case of harassment here, DI Dobson,' Mitchell began once Alison had completed the formalities. 'We spoke yesterday about the lack of evidence against my client.'

'Things have changed since then,' Alison began.

'I don't see how.'

'For one thing another woman has died.'

'Very sad, I am sure, but as I understand it my client was picked up around lunchtime after an anonymous tip-off and has been in police custody all afternoon. Given that, I cannot see the connection.'

'He was seen.'

'A witness? How helpful for you, but then I seem to recall you had a witness in the Isabella Johnson case. How's that working out for you?'

Alison was taken aback.

'Witnesses are far from infallible, as you know.' Mitchell went on, smiling, 'They change their minds. They are mistaken. They become... unavailable.' She smiled again. 'You have a witness who claims to have seen my client with Mrs Mills. You also have a witness who saw my client some distance from the murder scene. A witness who called the police. You're not suggesting, I hope, that Mr Smith can be in two places at once.'

'No, of course not...' Alison began.

'Then we have two witnesses, one of whom is *mistaken*, shall we say.'

'Or one of whom is lying.'

'Ah.' Mitchell smiled. 'I thought you might suggest that. The problem of course is proof. How to prove which witness is right and which is wrong. That, I'm afraid, is your problem. Juries do so hate uncertainty, haven't you found?'

Alison took a deep breath, trying to compose herself. Before she could do so Hortence Mitchell continued.

'As I understand it Mrs Mills' body was discovered at around twelve forty-two?'

'The paramedics logged a call at around that time, yes.' How the hell did Mitchell know that? Was someone passing her information? There'd be hell to pay with Rogers if they were.

'And as we have already established, Mr Smith was in the custody of your charming community support officer at that time.'

She spoke of a *community support officer* as one might name a species of particularly vile spider.

Alison's dislike for her grew.

'Mrs Mills could have been attacked ten or more minutes before the call to the ambulance service…' Alison began.

'Even so, that would take us back to… what? Twelve thirty-two? Let us be generous and say twelve thirty. That is still two minutes *after* my client was seen at the Cawpers estate.'

'*Allegedly* seen,' Alison put in. 'It's possible Mr Smith had a friend call in that alibi. It's not far from the Beamsleigh to the Cawpers estate. It is perfectly possible for Mr Smith to have attacked Mrs Mills and made it up onto the estate before Officer Burgess…'

Mitchell interrupted her. 'With due respect, Inspector, we're not dealing in what is *possible*. Surely you understand that it is your job to prove, beyond a reasonable doubt, that my client was involved in this killing. Not that it is possible, or even that it is likely, but that it actually happened.'

'I never…' Robbie began again.

Mitchell held out a hand to silence him. He looked terrified, a schoolboy talking out of turn.

'Did you get someone to call in and say they saw you up on the Cawpers?' Alison asked Robbie.

'God yeah, 'cause I love getting myself into trouble. Don't be bloody daft.' Alison nodded, as if she believed him. 'I never did it. You know I never... I never hurt Izzy and I never hurt this woman.'

Alison felt her old belief in him again. Irrational and strong.

'Who else could it have been, Robbie?' she asked, aware that her voice was almost as desperate as his. 'Who else might have wanted to kill Izzy?'

'I don't...' He paused. 'Maybe...'

'That's enough,' Mitchell said. 'Do you intend to charge my client?'

'I'm still gathering evidence,' Alison said. 'We'll let you know.' Robbie dropped his gaze.

'You've been arrested, Robbie. You understand that?' Alison said. He nodded.

'We're going to move you to Milbury station. I'll need to talk to you again. But if there's anything... if you think of anything that could help...' Her voice trailed off.

'If my client wishes to communicate with you he'll do so through me,' Mitchell said imperiously.

Alison said nothing. She tried to catch Robbie's eye, but he wouldn't look at her. She wanted him to know she believed him. Or at least that she believed *in* him. Which wasn't quite the same but might be more important.

'Shit,' Paul said, checking his phone as they left the room.

He showed Alison the summons from Rogers. The boss was not happy.

TWENTY-FOUR

Rogers was in his usual towering rage when Alison and Paul entered his office. Marianne Downes was with him, looking as elegant and well groomed as before, although Alison noted with some pleasure that there was an edge of panic in her eyes. Things were not going well for media relations on this case. Robbie Smith had been arrested to quite a fanfare, only to be released for lack of evidence and mutterings of police harassment. Now someone else had been killed and Robbie was in the frame again. That was definitely not good PR.

'So?' Rogers asked.

'Sir?'

'Don't give me "sir", I want to know what the fuck is going on and I want to know right away, DI Dobson, because this is looking to me like a shit storm of fuck-ups and at the moment you look like the one flinging the shit.'

Alison wasn't quite sure that she understood the metaphor, but she decided not to push the point.

'We arrested Robbie yesterday, as you know, despite my reservations that we hadn't yet built a case against him.'

Here she looked at Downes, hoping to convey that she was laying this at her door. Downes made no comment. Alison went on, 'Robbie's lawyer argued that we had insufficient evidence to hold him and, given everyone's concerns about media coverage which could be damaging to the force, we release him on bail. Again against my better judgement.' Another meaningful look at Downes.

Rogers interrupted.

'Yes, yes, we get it, Inspector, everything was against your judgement and you yourself are above making mistakes. We were wrong to arrest him and then we were wrong to let him go and you, in your infinite wisdom, were the only person able to see that.' Alison remained silent. 'What I want to know,' Rogers said, his voice ominously quiet, 'is why exactly you told Robbie Smith, a potential killer, that Andrea Mills had identified him as a suspect?'

Alison paused. She had known this was coming and she had no defence.

'I didn't exactly tell him I mean…' She took a deep breath. There was no excuse. 'I made a mistake.'

'Too bloody right you made a mistake. If Smith is our killer, then you as good as put a gun to that woman's head.'

Alison didn't answer. She had thought much the same thing herself, but she wasn't going to give Rogers the satisfaction of being right.

'You think he did it?' Rogers asked.

'I don't know.'

'I know you don't know. Nobody knows except the little shit himself. What I'm asking you is what you *think*. Surely you have an opinion. Use your bloody women's intuition if you don't have any proper copper's instinct.'

Alison bristled at the sexist insult but knew better than to rise to it.

'I don't think he did it, no,' she said. 'It just doesn't feel right. He has no motive at all for the first killing and an almost perfect alibi for the second. I don't believe someone could get that clever that quickly.'

'Why not?' Rogers asked. 'I've seen plenty of supposedly clever people get really dumb really quickly.' He was looking pointedly at Alison but again she ignored the jibe. 'What about you?' he asked, turning to Paul.

'Sorry?'

'What is it with you people and your bloody apologies? I'm asking for your opinion. Did Smith do this?'

'Well…' Paul looked involuntarily at Alison.

'Don't look to mummy like a toddler needing his dummy,' Rogers barked. 'Surely she hasn't got you so tightly by the short and curlies that you can't have an opinion of your own. What do you think?'

'I like him for it,' Paul said, facing Rogers now.

'Because?'

'He was the last known person to see Izzy before she died, then he buggered off to a party which looks to me like a botched attempt to set up an alibi. Henry Chapell actually saw him attacking Mills, so whoever rang to say Robbie was at the Cawpers was lying for him. All the evidence points his way.'

'See,' Rogers said, turning back to Alison, 'a straight answer to a straight bloody question. "The evidence points that way." And what does your gut tell you, boy?'

'I don't trust him. He gives off a dishonest sort of vibe.'

'Yeah, I find drug-dealing criminals tend to do that.'

Roger's sneer was back. 'So all the evidence points to him. Good.'

'Except he has an alibi,' Alison said. 'Someone *did* report that he was dealing at the Cawpers. We can't just ignore that. We've got nothing yet to suggest that anyone lied for him. And Carol Burgess picked him up by quarter to one at the latest. If Robbie was the person Chapell saw attacking Andrea, then he'd have had to leg it pretty quickly up to the Cawpers to get there by quarter to one.'

'So what are you saying? Chapell was mistaken? Or lying? He didn't see Robbie?'

'I don't know. It's possible.'

Rogers turned away and spoke to Paul again. 'First thing you need to do is find out who made that call. You want to prove your case you start by showing me the lad was setting himself up with an alibi. Oh and hope to holy shit that the murder weapon comes back with his DNA all over it.'

Paul began to speak, but Rogers had turned to Alison.

'You want to prove it *wasn't* Smith, then tell me who Henry Chapell saw?'

'I don't know,' Alison admitted.

Rogers nodded as if he expected as much. 'Who else do you have in the loop?' he asked.

'I don't like the English teacher, Banks. There's some evidence he was supplying pills to kids. He didn't like Izzy and there was that weird note he wrote her asking her to meet him.'

'OK, Banks has motive for Izzy, although no real opportunity. But why Mills? Any reason he'd want to kill her?'

Alison knew she was reaching now. 'There's a suggestion

Andrea Mills knew about the pills, about his dealing. She'd been seen arguing with Banks about a month ago. Threatening to report him for… something… we don't know what. That's why I was looking for her today as it happens. To ask her about Banks. He's still a possible suspect.'

'Fat fucker though, isn't he?' Rogers said.

'Sir?'

'God, I hate how you turn that word into a question. What I'm trying to point out to you, DI Dobson, is that Mr Banks is not a good fit for the description Andrea Mills gave of a man she saw running away. Nor could he have been mistaken for Robbie Smith by Mr Henry Chapell.'

'No, sir.'

'No, sir, exactly. Anyone else?'

'Dan Humphreys.'

'Remind me?'

'Humphreys was supposedly Izzy's boyfriend. He's admitted to us it was a sham relationship. According to Humphreys they were only dating in order to mask the fact that he's gay.'

'Is Mr Humphreys' orientation of any relevance? Are we rounding up suspects on the grounds of their sexuality now, DI Dobson?'

'No, sir, not at all. Humphreys has admitted arguing with Izzy the day before her death. She was suggesting he come out about his sexuality. He could have killed her to shut her up. Also his younger sister was killed in the crash up at Whitby. The one caused by Izzy's father.'

'And his motive for killing Andrea Mills would be what? Presumably he was the mystery man seen at the scene of Izzy's killing, and he was afraid Mills could identify him?

I suppose he's a teenage lad, similar height and build to Robbie Smith.'

Alison nodded, preparing to speak. Rogers held up his hand for silence.

'OK, so we have one for and one against. Frankly I don't care who did this. I don't care if it was Mother Teresa or the Yorkshire fucking Ripper. Whoever it was you're going to get him, understood?'

'Excuse me.' Downes cleared her throat and spoke at last. 'I thought we decided, in light of the sensitive nature of this case and the unfortunate lack of judgement shown by DI Dobson...'

'Lack of judgement?' Alison interrupted angrily.

'... in revealing to Mr Smith that Mrs Mills was a potential witness to his earlier crime,' Downes continued.

Alison began to defend herself but Rogers held up his hand again.

'DI Dobson fucked up,' he said, 'no doubt. But everyone in that town knew Andrea Mills had seen someone up on that hill and she hadn't yet identified him. It was hardly a fucking state secret even if Dobson shouldn't have been broadcasting it.'

Downes took a deep breath, composing herself. 'Nevertheless, we discussed the sensitive nature of this case, the huge amount of media attention which it is generating. I understood that the decision had been made, in the light of all that, to enact a change of personnel. In order to give the right impression. Show how open the force can be in the face of criticism, willing to take on board necessary changes, that sort of thing.'

'Let me make one thing clear, Ms Downes,' Rogers said

with menacing calm, 'whatever you "understood", I make my own decisions about my investigating officers. However convenient it might be to scapegoat DI Dobson for the fuck-ups so far in this case, I'm not going to do it. Dobson stays.'

'Thank you, sir,' Alison said, feeling an unexpected surge of affection towards him.

'Sod that, Dobson,' Rogers said, 'I don't want "thank yous", I want this case solved. I want it solved quickly and I want it done right. Bringing someone else in now would just cause delays and we can't afford that. I don't care who did this, I want no more deaths and I want the right person charged, got it?'

'Yes, sir.'

'This conversation is giving me a terrible sense of déjà vu and you know how I hate the French. Do not make me repeat myself again.'

'No, sir.' She waited for him to say more.

'OK then, fuck off, get some bloody work done for a change.'

'Yes, sir.'

She left the room before he could change his mind.

'I could have done with your backup in there,' she said, rounding on Paul.

'I said what I thought. I'm sorry but I think Robbie did it. I think you're being soft on him because he reminds you of...'

'Who the hell is that?' Alison asked, interrupting him. She had glanced out of the window as she made her way down the corridor. A hooded figure was leaning up against her car, looking as if he was waiting for her.

TWENTY-FIVE

By the time Alison got to the street Dominic Mills was sitting on the edge of the pavement beside her car. Waiting for her and looking as if he could wait for days.

'You looking for me, Dom?' she asked.

'Sorry, yes, I... Yes.'

'You want to come in?' she asked, gesturing to the police station.

'I couldn't face it. I came to talk to you. To tell you... Only when I got here I couldn't face it.' Alison nodded, understanding. Grief was exhausting. Sometimes for weeks and months afterwards.

'You want to go for a drive? Or a walk? And we can talk?'

'A walk, yeah. Thanks.'

She held out a hand and helped him up. He smiled and blushed at her, reminding her again how very young he was. He still looked like a teenager. Too long in the limb, a little too thin, the muscle not yet fully developed across his chest and upper arms. It shocked her to think that Nick had been a boy like this when they had first met. They had been children playing at grown-ups. That was the same impression she had of Dominic Mills now.

Alison had been about his age when her own mother died. Although in many ways she had been much older. She felt sometimes as if she had been an adult all her life. For her, losing her mother had meant the removal of a worry, the end of chaos. She doubted it would be like that for Dom. Alison's heart broke a little as she watched him trying to be strong.

'I called to see your mother just before…' she said. 'This lunchtime I mean. There was a note on the door. It said something about you being sorry.'

Dominic nodded. 'We had a row.'

'When was that?'

'Just before she went out for her jog. It was all petty stuff really.'

'Can you tell me?' Alison asked as gently as she could.

There were tears in Dom's eyes but he was ignoring them.

'It was nothing really.' He rubbed his eyes with the heel of his hand, refusing to succumb to the sobs which so clearly wanted to come. He was determined to be stoical. Alison waited, knowing he would speak in his own time. 'It was just one of those stupid rows,' he said at last. 'She had a go at me for not doing some washing-up that I'd said I'd do. She said I treated the house like a hotel. Then I went mad at her for borrowing my college sweatshirt to run in.'

'People argue,' Alison said, 'it doesn't mean anything.'

'She drove me mad borrowing my stuff, like, I don't know, like she was young or something. Izzy borrowed that sweatshirt once, it reminded me... only I didn't say that to Mum. I said some awful stuff, about her being old and fat and... I really lost it with her.' He paused. 'If I'd known it was the last time I'd ever see her... If I knew...' He shook his head, trying to sound angry with himself but just sounding painfully sad. 'She said, "I love you". Even though we'd just had this stupid row. She said, "I love you", like she always did when she went out of the door.' Alison smiled. She did that. Every morning as the kids got on the school bus. 'Love you', just flung out into the world. Mabel usually said it back, but Alison sometimes caught the derision in Bea's eyes. Ten years old and already embarrassed by her mother's love.

Alison sometimes wondered if she was the only mother who was pleased by that. Pleased that her love was so taken for granted as to be an embarrassment. Her own mother had rarely even been conscious in the mornings to see her to school, let alone embarrass her with 'I love yous'.

'I didn't say it back,' Dominic said. 'I could've said it back, but I was just so pissed off over being asked to do some washing-up, and over some stupid shirt that I probably hadn't even worn for six months.'

'We all get angry over stupid things,' Alison said, 'it's family life. Your mother understood.'

'I called her pathetic,' Dominic said, determined to berate himself. 'I said she looked ridiculous out waddling about at her age.' Andrea Mills was barely older than Alison. She forgot sometimes how ancient that was to someone so young.

'She knew you loved her,' Alison said. 'You stayed at home to be with her after she found Izzy's body, you were there for her.'

Dominic nodded, fighting the tears again.

'Is this why you came to see me?' Alison asked. 'To tell me about the row?'

'No. I… You asked about drugs.'

'Yes?'

'I didn't exactly tell you the truth. They weren't street drugs or anything so I didn't think… But now… well, I just want to tell you everything. I know I should have just told you from the start.'

'Told me what?' Alison asked.

'He told me they were legal, that they were perfectly safe,' Dominic said quietly. 'I wouldn't have taken them otherwise.'

'What were safe, Dominic?' Alison asked.

'The tablets.'

'Someone was selling you tablets? Who?'

'Mr Banks.'

He looked up at her from under his long fringe. A little boy caught with his hand in the cookie jar. Alison kept walking. It was easier, sometimes, for people to talk when they walked. She didn't look directly at Dominic when she spoke.

'Do you know exactly what they were?' she asked.

'No idea. They were supposed to be for Alzheimer's or something, but apparently they make you think quicker and clearer. They're supposed to make you smarter.'

'And did they?'

'I thought so.'

Alison walked and waited.

'Before Izzy came along I was the star pupil. I wasn't close to her league, but I was smart enough.'

'Go on,' Alison urged.

'There's always one or two of us every year that they think can make it to Oxbridge. And we're given special treatment, extra tuition, let off games or assembly or whatever if we say we need to study. Before Izzy I was one of the brightest maths students they'd had for a while.' He blushed. 'I'm not showing off… I mean God knows now I'm up at Cambridge I realise I'm nothing special. There are lots and lots of people cleverer than me.'

Alison smiled at him. 'You must be pretty clever to be there at all,' she said.

He shook his head, not wanting the compliment.

'Anyway, Banks was head of sixth form when I was there,' he continued, blushing. 'I guess he still is?'

Alison nodded.

'So the A-level results were his responsibility. I mean obviously each subject reflected on the teacher of that subject, but overall the results reflected *his* sixth form. And he wanted better results every year.'

'So he gave you drugs?'

'He *sold* us drugs,' Dominic corrected. 'He said they were fine, totally legal and everything. It was just that doctors in the UK wouldn't prescribe them to students. So all these students from the Far East and from America were taking up top spots in UK universities while we were falling behind. And it had nothing to do with ability or teaching or work. It had to do with these drugs.'

Fear and unfairness mixed with a touch of xenophobia. It was a clever marketing technique.

'He gave out free samples, only to a few of us, to those he thought had the best chances and those he could trust to keep quiet about it.'

'And did it work?' Alison asked.

'I thought it did,' Dominic said again. 'I felt sharper, clearer. So I started taking the pills, just to get me through my A-levels. And I got the grades I needed, and so Banks was happy and I was happy.'

'You said you *thought* they worked.'

'Yeah, well people at uni, they take things like this quite a lot, I mean it's quite prevalent.'

'OK.' Alison tried to hide her shock. Street drugs she got, party drugs, drugs to numb the pain, but drugs to make the super bright just that tiny bit brighter? She couldn't honestly say she understood that.

'So I have this friend who wanted to investigate, wanted to see if they really work. She got me to get some pills, from Banks, and she did this experiment. Gave me a test before and afterwards.'

'And the drugs didn't work? You didn't get better results.'

'No, that's the thing. I got way better grades afterwards. After I took the pills.'

'OK, so whatever Banks was selling did help make you smarter.'

'No, you see my friend hadn't given me the drugs, she'd made up a placebo – just sugar and colouring – and I'd still got better grades.'

'So Banks' pills did no good?'

'They did some good, but it was all in the mind I think. I did better because I expected to do better. But that wasn't the problem. This friend of mine was a chemistry student. She was able to find out what exactly was in the stuff Banks was selling. And she found out there was some stuff in the stacks Banks was giving us that wasn't even tested on humans, not even for Alzheimer's or anything. It was pretty bad stuff. She found out it had been shown to have some bad side effects on rats. Cancers and shit like that.'

'Did you tell Izzy this?' Alison asked.

Dominic hesitated.

'We know Izzy was taking the drugs.' She didn't give details of the pills found at the Johnson house or those in Izzy's stomach.

Dominic nodded.

'I told her when I was home at Christmas. She said she was going to confront Banks. She was going to tell everyone to stop taking the pills.'

'Do you know if she did it?' Alison asked.

'I never asked her. I just wanted to forget about all that stuff. I was a bit embarrassed to be honest.'

Alison waited a moment.

'Your mum found out about the pills,' she said, not really asking. 'She confronted Banks.'

'She went ballistic. Marched up to the school all ready to talk to Mr Riordan, get Banks sacked, go to the police… everything. She'd read some old emails between me and Izzy. That's another thing we always fought about, her reading my email. Anyway, she'd read this stuff and figured out what Banks was up to and she went apeshit.'

'But she never did report it to the police, or Mr Riordan, did she?' Dominic shook his head.

'Banks persuaded her not to. He told her they'd kick me out of uni if they found out I'd taken pills to help me get in. He persuaded her to keep quiet about it. Told her he'd stopped selling the drugs anyway, learnt his lesson or something. I don't know if she believed him, but she wouldn't risk reporting him if it got *me* into trouble. Me being up at Cambridge is a big deal to her.'

'And to you? Is it a big deal to you?' Alison asked.

'Yeah, I guess. University felt like the only chance I had to get out of this town.' Alison nodded. She knew that feeling. The need to escape no matter what it took. She imagined that even a neat house in a pleasant town could feel like a prison when you were young. Even loving parents could be a burden.

'And Banks went on supplying?'

'I don't know. I know Izzy stopped taking the pills though. After what I told her at Christmas.'

Alison nodded, although she knew different. Izzy had been found with pills in her stomach the day she died. Why had she continued to take them if she knew they were dangerous?

'I don't know if this has anything to do with Mum and Izzy. I just wanted you to know.'

'Thank you, Dom, you did the right thing.'

'I heard you arrested Robbie again.'

'I can't really talk about it,' Alison said.

'It's all so bloody pointless. I mean if he killed Mum because he thought she saw him with Izzy that's so ridiculous. She couldn't say who she saw.'

'Robbie wouldn't know that though, would he?'

'If she was going to identify him she would have done it already. She was just saying to Henry yesterday that she wished she *could* say it was Robbie.'

'Henry?'

'Yeah, Mr Riordan's partner. He dropped by yesterday, just to see if she was alright. I found them talking about what

Mum had seen. She said she couldn't say for sure but she felt like if it had been Robbie she'd've recognised him. Henry said the whole town was talking about it and everyone thought it was Robbie. Mum was adamant though, she definitely couldn't say who she saw. There was something familiar about him, she said, but she couldn't place it.' Dom shook his head, then went on, 'I know people say all sorts of shit about Robbie, but he's really not that bad. And if Izzy spent time with him… She was a good judge of character, Izzy. If she trusted him…'

'You don't think Robbie could have harmed Izzy?'

'What do I know?' he said, running his hands through his hair. 'Mum saw someone in a hoody, that's all she could say for sure. She thought maybe he looked familiar but it could have been anyone. They might not have had anything to do with Izzy being killed. Could have been one of old Banksy's crew for all I know.'

'Banksy's crew?' Alison asked.

'Yeah, you know one of the lads he gets to do little jobs for him. Could have been a kid he'd sent out to get him some fags or booze or whatever.'

Alison remembered Dan Humphreys talking about lads doing jobs for Banks.

'You know the names of any of those boys?' she asked Dom.

'Sorry, I don't know.'

They had doubled back now to the front of the station and Alison could see Holly waiting anxiously for her on the front steps.

'You want to tell me anything else?' Alison asked Dom, trying to sound patient, not wanting to rush him.

'I should have gone with her,' he said, his voice low. 'I was going to go, before we had the row, I was going to go with her. I know it's morbid but I sort of wanted to go up there and be near Izzy one last time. I had this mad idea that maybe I'd find something, like her phone or her journal, or, I don't know, a clue. And I wanted to keep Mum company on her run and keep her safe and… I don't know, just…'

'You couldn't have stopped this,' Alison said. 'It wasn't your fault.' He ignored that.

'I was the one who suggested going up there. To look for a clue or to prove we had nothing to fear. Only then I didn't go. We fell out and I didn't go.'

'It wasn't your fault,' Alison said again. 'Everyone thought it was safe to go up the Beamsleigh again. No one knew.'

'Henry didn't… he didn't think it was safe. He said we should all stay away. Me and Mum laughed. I mean, I know what happened to Izzy, but we laughed. Because it's just the Beamsleigh, isn't it. Nothing to be scared of. Still, I should have gone with her.'

He finally let the tears come.

Alison had nothing to say; she put her hand on his shoulder and let him weep. It was the only comfort she could give him.

'We're all really sorry for your loss,' she said lamely.

'Thank you,' he muttered.

He would get used to saying that over the weeks and months, Alison knew. Thank you. Polite, meaningless but important.

She separated from Dom at the steps of the police station, and watched him walk wearily in the direction of home.

Holly hovered until Alison snapped at her.

'What?'

'Sorry, boss, it's just… We've got the tape of the call that came in to Penbury. The anonymous caller who said they'd seen Robbie dealing.'

'Right, let's hear it.'

Back upstairs Holly opened the attachment on her computer and they listened to it together.

'Oh for fuck's sake…' Alison said after only a few seconds. 'What the hell is *he* playing at?'

TWENTY-SIX

'You know why we're here, Dan?' Alison asked.

Alison had recognised Dan's voice as soon as she heard the recording of the call to Penbury station. They had come down to the school and pulled him out of a biology class. Now they were talking in Riordan's empty office.

Riordan had gone home to be with his partner.

Dan Humphreys looked petulant, annoyed rather than nervous.

'No,' he said.

'You made any anonymous phone calls recently?' Paul asked impatiently.

'What?'

'I'm getting sick to death of all this bollocks,' Alison said. 'Did you ring Penbury police station earlier today?'

'What if I did?'

Alison took that as a yes.

'And did you report someone dealing drugs on the Cawpers estate?'

'I might have…' He paused, seeing the look on Alison's face. 'OK, yes I did.'

'And did you actually see anyone dealing drugs up there?' Humphreys shrugged.

'I need an answer, Dan.'

'Not exactly,' he said.

'So what exactly *did* you see?'

'I saw Robbie Smith heading up that way. Just thought I'd let the police know.'

'What time was that?'

'I don't know. About half twelve?'

'And it was definitely Robbie Smith you saw?'

'Yes.'

'And *was* he dealing drugs?'

'Probably. He's always dealing drugs.'

'You ever buy drugs from Robbie Smith?'

Dan shrugged.

'Dan.' There was a warning note in her voice.

'Maybe, once or twice. Just a bit of dope.'

'You ever buy drugs from anyone else? Anyone in school, for example?' Dan didn't answer at first. Alison waited.

'Robbie Smith's the only drug dealer I know,' Dan said with a hint of his old swagger.

Alison decided now was not the time to ask him about Banks.

'I want to be really clear on this. Did you actually see Robbie dealing today?' she asked.

Dan shrugged again. And again Alison waited, although her patience was wearing thin.

'Look,' he said eventually, 'he got away with killing Izzy, and you lot weren't going to do anything. So we all decided... We thought we'd make his life a bit difficult.'

'We? You and who else?'

'A few of Izzy's friends. Me and Lucy and Sarah-Jane and Billy... You know, the whole crowd.'

'Did Robbie Smith ask you to ring the police?'

'What? No, of course not.' He looked genuinely confused.

'OK,' Alison said, 'so tell me exactly what happened.' Humphreys took a deep breath, letting her know exactly how much effort this was costing him.

'I was in town at lunchtime and I saw Robbie heading up that way, towards the Cawpers. I... Look, I just wanted to piss him off. Make his life hard, get him stopped by the police or whatever. So I said he was dealing.'

'You sure it was Robbie?'

'Yeah, course. I mean, who else wears a bloody old tracksuit like that? It was him.'

'Anyone else see him? The people you were with I mean.'

'I guess. Yeah, we all saw him.'

'Whereabouts in town were you?'

'Near the Co-op. We were buying lunch.'

'And Robbie was heading along the road to the Cawpers? He wasn't heading into the woods?'

'No. He was going up Flint Street.'

A route that would lead him away from Beamsleigh Hill and onto the Cawpers estate from the east.

'What time did you see him?'

'I don't know, like I said it was lunch so probably about half twelve, maybe just after.'

'You know wasting police time is an offence, don't you?'

'Yeah, but that's why I never rang 999 or nothing. I looked up the local number. I figured they're never doing anything important.'

'D'you know Andrea Mills?' Alison asked.

'Dom's mum? The one who found Izzy?'

'She's been killed. Her body was found on the Beamsleigh this afternoon.' His face went pale, but he didn't speak.

'You see her at all this afternoon?'

'No.'

'You anywhere near the Beamsleigh this afternoon?'

'We cut across that way out of school, but just down the path. I didn't go round the hill or nothing. Then on the way back we went up the road. Billy needed to pick up his PE kit and his house is up that way.' Alison nodded.

'I'll need the names of all the people you were with. Anyone else who might have seen Robbie.'

Dan nodded and reeled off a list of names.

'Don't know why you're wasting time with me,' he said, 'instead of getting the bastard that killed Izzy.'

'I'll be in touch, Dan,' Alison said.

They checked with Dan's friends. They all said the same. Robbie was in town, heading up Flint Road towards the Cawpers. Nowhere near Beamsleigh Hill when Andrea was killed.

None of it seemed to make sense. Everything pointed to Robbie, except all the things that didn't. He could have killed Izzy, but he had no motive. He was seen attacking Andrea, except he was also seen on the other side of town. But if Robbie wasn't their man, then who was? Simon Banks? He was a bad man with plenty of motive, but there was nothing to tie him to either murder scene. He had teenagers on his payroll, but it was a long way from doing odd jobs for cigarettes to carrying out two vicious murders.

Everything was going round in circles. She felt as if her head was about to explode.

'Next?' Paul asked.

'A gin and tonic and a hot bath?' Alison asked hopefully.

'Sure. Let's just get the case solved, shall we?' he said.

She smiled.

'Let's talk to Henry Chapell then,' she said, 'see if we can't sort out this sighting of Robbie that couldn't have been Robbie at all.'

It was already almost dark when they got to Chapell's flat, although it was barely four o'clock. Another day of the investigation was almost gone.

They could hear raised voices from the corridor outside as they approached the door. Or rather one raised voice, that of Henry Chapell. Riordan's replies were quiet, sounding calm and measured.

'Should we knock?' Paul asked.

'Yeah, we don't want a case of domestic violence on top of everything else,' she said.

'You never think of me,' Chapell was yelling. 'Never. After all I've done for you... You have no idea what I... what I've been through.'

Alison banged loudly on the door.

'And who's this? One of your precious students no doubt. You think more of them than you do of me. Don't answer it... I'm talking to you... Don't...'

Riordan opened the door before the sentence was complete.

'It's the police,' he said needlessly to Chapell who was right behind him in the hallway.

'Oh God.' Chapell covered his mouth. 'I have all this

to face, Niall. I have all this. What happened to Andrea...
everything... and you choose today to ruin my life.'

'You're being dramatic, Henry,' Riordan said calmly.

'Is everything OK?' Alison asked.

The scene before her was unsettling. Chapell was
close to hysterics and yet there was an indulgent smile on
Riordan's face.

'Everything's fine,' Riordan said, stepping aside to let
them in.

'Everything's fine?' Chapell shrieked. 'Everything's fine?
My life is over. My life is ruined, and I saw a dead body
today, Niall. An actual dead body.'

'I know,' Riordan said, trying to take his partner's arm.
Chapell shrugged him off. 'I'm sorry. I didn't mean that. Of
course that isn't fine. Poor Andrea.'

'Poor me,' Chapell pouted.

'Would you like to tell me what's going on?' Alison
asked.

Riordan looked as if he would demur.

'Tell her, Niall. Tell her what you've done. Tell her how
callous you are... How cruel.' Riordan shook his head. When
he spoke he was addressing Chapell as much as Alison.

'I've been trying to explain,' he said. 'I just told Henry
that I turned down the Harvard job...'

'You see. Turned it down. Like that! Without talking to
me. Without asking me. So what am I supposed to do? Tell
me that. What am I supposed to do now?'

'I was rather hoping you'd come back to London with
me.'

'What? So you can work in some horrible slum school?
God, is that it? Your vocation...'

'So I can work at Emersbys again,' Riordan interrupted. 'What?'

'Matt called a couple of days ago. They've been wanting me back for a while. And he made me an offer. Fewer hours, more money. I'd have time to do some voluntary work, tutoring maybe. You'd be nearer your mum. I thought…'

Before he could finish the sentence Chapell was in his arms, raining kisses onto his face. All anger gone. His face radiating joy.

Alison was reminded, as she so often was with Henry Chapell, of a toddler. Immersed completely in his mood of the moment. The tantrum forgotten the second it was over, the adults left with the emotional fallout.

'I take it this is good news,' Paul said with a dry smile.

'God yes.' Chapell beamed. 'When Niall worked for Emersbys before it was amazing. We were so happy then. It was so much fun.'

Alison remembered Riordan telling her how the pressure had led to a breakdown. It hadn't sounded much fun. She hoped things would turn out better this time.

'I'm sorry to spoil the mood, but we need to ask you some questions about today,' Alison said reluctantly.

Predictably the change in Chapell's demeanour was complete.

'Oh God. Oh God, yes. It was awful. God. Here I am celebrating. And she's…' He held his hand to his mouth. 'God. I feel so bad.'

'Go sit down, Henry,' Riordan said quietly. 'I'll make us all coffee.' Alison followed him into the kitchen.

'Sorry about all the drama,' he said with a smile that slipped from his face before it really took hold. 'I think this thing with Andrea has upset Henry more than he's letting on. I thought I'd cheer him up with the news about the Emersbys job. That backfired spectacularly.'

'He seems happy enough now though,' Alison said.

'Yes, that's Henry all over. A man of the moment. His moods are mercurial, to say the least. He had his heart set on Harvard, and I knew I couldn't let him down but I just… I couldn't face it. So when this City job came up… I made a bit of a hash of telling him, that's all.'

'He's happy you'll be back in the City?'

'Yes. It'll make him very happy.' He looked almost defeated.

'You OK?' Alison asked.

'Yes, yes. I'll be fine. It's been a hard few days,' he said with a sad smile. 'And on top of that I'm short of staff at the school.'

'Oh?'

'We sent Simon Banks home early after a parent raised some concerns.' She knew he was letting her know he had acted on the tip-off she had given him about Banks dealing smart drugs.

'What time did Banks leave school?' she asked.

'About lunchtime,' Riordan said. 'I met with the governors this morning and they felt it was best if he was removed from teaching while we investigate.'

Lunchtime. So Banks had no alibi for the time that Andrea was killed. But there was no way Henry Chapell could have mistaken Banks' bulk for Robbie Smith. Whoever he had seen it must have been someone similar enough to Robbie's physical type for his brain to be fooled.

By the time she and Riordan took Chapell his coffee he was calm. It was as if the anger and euphoria of a few moments ago had never happened. He was sitting looking out at the river edging by below the window, his small dog curled on his lap.

Paul was sitting in a chair opposite him. They were not speaking. Paul was evidently waiting for Alison.

'Mr Chapell, I need to ask you about the statement you made earlier today.'

'Oh my God, I'm so shaken. I mean, it was awful, just absolutely awful. I didn't know it was Andrea. When I first saw her… I didn't know.' He shivered, and the dog on his lap shivered as if in sympathy. 'I think that's why I overreacted, when Niall said he wasn't taking the job. All this stress isn't good for me. I think my nerves are shot… I've been through a lot today and on top of that Niall announces…'

'You knew Mrs Mills I understand,' Alison said, not wanting to let Chapell slip back into an explanation of the row they had just witnessed.

'I didn't know her very well. We weren't friends exactly, but yes I did know her. I'm something of a curiosity around here. A novelty, I suppose.'

'Hardly,' said Riordan, bringing over coffee on a tray, and offering them cream and sugar.

'Well, there's hardly a thriving *scene*, is there. I think some of the locals find me a bit exotic.' Chapell smiled at her and she found herself forgiving his arrogance.

'Andrea liked to make a bit of a pet of me I think,' he went on, 'so she could say, "my gay friend", you know, that sort of thing.'

'I don't think it was like that at all,' Riordan said. 'I think she was just a nice woman. I think she just liked someone to chat to.'

'Yes, OK. You're probably right,' Chapell said, 'and she was nice. We would always talk. Just for a minute or two if she was out jogging. I think she liked the excuse to stop and get her breath back.'

'You went to see her yesterday, I understand?' Alison asked.

He shot her a calculating look, but he answered placidly enough.

'Yes. I called in, just to see if she was alright. After finding that body – Izzy I mean – I said I couldn't imagine what it was like. I wish I still couldn't.'

'Did she say anything to you yesterday? Anything that sheds any light?'

'No.' He stroked the dog absently. 'She kept going over what had happened, what she'd seen. I asked her about seeing Robbie running away, and she wasn't a hundred percent sure it was him. But we're sure now, aren't we? Now that I saw him too. He *is* in jail, isn't he?'

'He's in police custody,' Alison confirmed.

'Henry's a little nervous…' Riordan began.

'You'd be nervous, Niall,' he shot back. 'Andrea saw him and now she's dead. Now I've seen him… I'm just glad he's behind bars.'

'Can you explain to me exactly what happened this lunchtime?'

'I was walking Angela. I decided to go up on the Beamsleigh. Everyone's been saying we all need to keep using it, not be afraid and all of that. Obviously I didn't want to go where Izzy… So I went the other way, and as soon as

I rounded the bend there she was. On the ground, and he was standing over her. I yelled and he ran. And then I went to see if she was OK. Which of course she wasn't. I tried to help, but I don't really know first aid or whatever. So I decided to run down and phone for help. There's no signal up there, you know. So I was running down the hill to get help when I saw you…'

'You told me the man you saw standing over Andrea was Robbie Smith.'

'It was. I'm sure… That is I think… it looked like him.' Alison looked at Riordan. He seemed to read something in her eyes.

'You need to be sure, Henry,' he said.

Henry pouted. 'I *am* sure, Niall. My God, I know what I saw.' Alison tried to make her voice as gentle as possible.

'Robbie has an irrefutable alibi for the time of the killing,' she said. 'He was seen elsewhere. He can't have been the person you saw on the hill.'

'There's a mistake,' Chapell said, 'there has to be.' Alison thought for a moment.

'It couldn't possibly have been Robbie,' she repeated.

Unless Dan Humphreys and all his friends had lied to give Robbie an alibi. And why would any of them do that?

Chapell shook his head.

'It was him. I feel certain. When I close my eyes I see him. At least it looked like him. I was sure, but I suppose… He had his hood up, so…'

Alison nodded. Understanding.

Chapell and Andrea had talked about Robbie being Izzy's killer. That made Robbie a killer in Chapell's mind. So when he saw a man attacking Andrea, he saw what he expected to see. He saw the only killer he knew. He saw Robbie Smith. His eyes had seen something briefly and his mind had filled in the blanks. There was no tape he could rewind and check. All there was was a fleeting impression and what his brain decided to create from it.

Chapell hesitated for just a minute.

'You've arrested Robbie though, haven't you?' he said. 'Didn't I hear on the radio that he's been arrested again?'

'He's in custody at the moment, yes,' Alison said carefully.

Chapell nodded, took a long draught of his coffee. Alison could see that his hand was shaking slightly.

'Can you describe the man you saw?' Alison asked.

'He looked like Robbie Smith,' Chapell said quietly. 'I remember him from when Niall first started at the school. Smith was a trouble causer, constantly in bother. Niall tried to take him under his wing, but there was no changing him. "Bad will out," my mother always says. Said it about me once or twice, in fact.' He gave a nervous smile.

'He wasn't a bad kid,' Riordan said, defending Robbie. 'He had a tough life, and he made some bad choices.'

Alison had heard this before.

'I really thought I saw him,' Chapell said. He closed his eyes a little dramatically. 'I can still see him... But you say it can't have been.'

'What did he look like?' Paul asked. 'Talk to me as if I didn't know Robbie Smith and just describe the person you saw.'

This was a good tactic, but it yielded only generic results. A teenage boy, slightly above average height. Hooded jacket, brown hair.

Could be anyone, almost literally.

Anyone except Robbie Smith. Or Simon Banks.

'I can't believe I got it so wrong,' Chapell said, holding his hand to his mouth as if he was going to be sick again. It was as if the shock of being mistaken about Robbie was worse than the shock of finding a dying woman. Alison supposed the realisation that you couldn't trust your own eyes was a scary thought.

'Can you think of anyone with a grudge against Mrs Mills?' she asked Chapell, bringing him back to the moment.

He shook his head.

'Like I said, I didn't know her that well.'

'OK. What about people who might have known she would be up on the Beamsleigh this lunchtime?'

Another shake of the head.

'She often jogged up that way, and I suppose someone could have seen her but... I don't think she had a schedule or anything.'

'OK, thanks.'

She turned to Niall Riordan.

'I spoke to Dominic Mills earlier. He may be willing to help with that governors' inquiry you were talking about. He knows something about Mr Banks and his *behaviour*.'

Riordan nodded. They were talking in code but he fully understood.

'How is he?'

'Upset, of course, but holding it in. He blames himself... He was going to go up on the Hill and look for some of Izzy's things – her phone and her journal – and he thinks if he had, if he'd been up there with his mum...'

'But you found the phone,' Riordan said.

'Yes. But Dom didn't know that. And we still haven't found the journal. I'm not sure that's significant though.'

Riordan took a characteristic pause to think.

'You're probably right. I mean, I doubt there is anyone in this town who would even understand it. I suppose it's possible someone might think it's connected to dealing perhaps. They might mistake the numbers for formulas or orders? I'm clutching at straws…'

'Oh God, I'm going to be sick…' Chapell suddenly stood up, tumbling the dog onto the floor and lurching for a door which Alison assumed led to the bathroom.

'I'm so sorry,' Riordan said, 'this has hit him very hard. I know he comes across as an old queen, but I think he was more fond of Andrea than he let on. It's not easy for him living in a small town. He misses the drama of the City.'

'Well, he'll have that again soon, won't he,' Alison said.

Riordan looked grim but his smile returned as Chapell came back into the room.

'We were just saying you'll be glad to get back to London,' Riordan said.

'I'm so glad my genius is getting back to where he belongs,' Chapell said, squeezing Riordan's hand but addressing his comments to Alison. The excitement was palpable through his body. Riordan smiled indulgently at him, rather as one would at a young child. Alison felt suddenly as if she was intruding on a private moment. Then Chapell seemed to pull himself back into the room. He shivered ostentatiously and pulled a throw from the back of the chair over his knees.

'The shock has been awful,' he said.

Alison sympathised.

'We'll go,' she said. 'If I have any further questions I'll be in touch.'

'You were asking about Izzy's notebook, weren't you,' Chapell said sharply, his eyes on Riordan. 'I meant to tell you, Niall, I saw her burning it the other day.'

'Burning it?'

'Yes. She was out the back of the school, near the bins, where the children go to smoke. It was that day I came in with a picnic lunch, remember?'

'The day she died?' Alison asked, remembering Riordan had said he'd had lunch with his partner that day.

'No, the week before that. I try to get in and have lunch with Niall at least once a week.' He smiled affectionately at his partner but Riordan was frowning.

'It was Thursday or Friday last week that you came in,' he said. 'That's when you saw Izzy burning her journal?'

'Yes. I went to throw all the rubbish from the picnic in the school bins and Izzy was there setting fire to her notebook.'

'Why would she do that?'

'I don't know,' Chapell said.

'You didn't ask her?'

'And get my head bitten off? No, I just left her to it.'

'She could have started a serious fire.'

'Well, she didn't, did she… so…'

Alison stepped in before a full-blown argument ensued.

'How do you know it was her maths journal she was burning?'

'It was very distinctive. Pink with a picture of a purple owl on the front. You know the sort of lurid crap teenage girls like. I suppose she could have had an identical book for something else, a diary or something, but it certainly looked like her maths journal.'

'And you had seen it before because…?'

'She would come around sometimes to discuss her ideas,' Riordan said. 'Chapell was forever finding us with our heads over that journal, with Izzy trying to explain something to me.'

'Explain to you?'

Riordan laughed softly.

'Maths is a young subject,' he said patiently. 'It doesn't rely so much on experience, so it is often the case that great maths minds can come up with ideas when they are very young that older people find hard to understand. Once you have the basics, maths really is about free thinking. So yes, Izzy very often had a lot to teach me.'

'But you've got a brilliant mind too,' Chapell interjected. 'You're still coming up with new ideas.'

Riordan smiled.

'I still have the odd flash of inspiration,' he said. 'That's why Emersbys are prepared to offer me the big bucks.' He tried to smile, but the comment made Alison feel inexplicably sad.

She'd need to check the CCTV around the school, see if Izzy really had burned her journal, but she couldn't see that it was important. Except that it was odd and odd things always intrigued her. Still, it wasn't a high priority.

'I don't think we have any further questions at the moment,' she said. 'We'll let ourselves out.'

Alison's phone trilled just as they were leaving the building.

'Holly,' she said as she answered.

'He wants to see you,' Holly said.

'Rogers? What's happened?'

'No, not Rogers. Robbie Smith.'

'Robbie? What does he want to talk about?'

'I'm not sure. He's really agitated and he's calling for you and says he won't talk to anyone else.'

'OK. I'll be there as quickly as I can.'

TWENTY-SEVEN

Holly was waiting for them when they got back to the station. She looked anxious.

'What is it?' Alison asked. 'Has Robbie said anything?' Holly shook her head.

'But he asked to see me?'

'Yes, only… I… Well, I'm not sure I should have called you. DCI Rogers told me not to. He said to let Robbie stew. I just thought… What if he wants to tell you something? Confess or something.'

'Is his lawyer with him?' Alison asked.

'No, he says he doesn't want to see her.'

Alison thought for a moment. Rogers was probably right. It would do Robbie good to stew for a bit. But Holly was right too. What if he wanted to tell her something useful? And if he didn't want to have his lawyer present? Well, that was his choice.

She took a deep breath. 'You did the right thing, Holly,' she said slowly. 'I'll go see him.' Holly looked a little more reassured.

'Don't let Rogers bother you,' Alison said. 'His bark is

worse than his bite.' She had no idea if that were true, but Holly was going to need to toughen up if she was going to last long in this job. They all had to get used to dealing with some unpleasant characters, and DCI Rogers was near the top of that list.

On her way to the custody suite Alison called Miles for a quick update. He had been talking to all of the kids on Banks' list. So far none of them were willing to talk about the smart drugs. All of them were claiming ignorance. They only had Dom's word so far. And some names on a list, which meant nothing.

'You want me to push it?' Miles asked.

She thought for a moment.

'Nah,' she said, 'it's almost certainly got nothing to do with Izzy or Andrea. We'll let the school handle it.' She ended the call as she reached the custody desk.

'How's my boy?' she asked the custody sergeant, Martin Roberts.

'He's been shouting his head off about how he wants to see you and won't talk to no one else,' Martin said. His smile told her he was the one who had asked Holly to call her. He wouldn't face up to Rogers himself, but if someone was causing a stink in his cells then he was sure as shit going to do what he could to shut them up.

'I'll go in and have a word, shall I?' she asked.

'He's quietened down now as it happens,' Martin said. 'A bit of grub and a visit from his brief has done the trick.'

'His solicitor has been in to see him?' Alison asked. 'I thought Holly said he didn't want to see her.'

'Yeah, but she turned up about ten minutes ago. He said to let her in… so… She didn't stay long and since Holly had already rung you…' His voice trailed away. 'You still want to see him?'

'How was he after the solicitor left?' Alison asked.

'Quiet as a lamb. Sitting on his bunk, never moved. I left him some tea even though he said he wasn't hungry.'

'OK,' Alison said, 'I'll see what all the fuss was about. Since I'm here.' She wondered if there was any point in her talking to Robbie now that Mitchell had spoken to him. She would have advised him to go 'no comment' all the way, convinced him that silence was the best policy. Alison couldn't say she was wrong. Given the confusing nature of the evidence they had so far, Robbie didn't need to clarify things for them. He just needed to keep quiet and trust to reasonable doubt, of which there was a shedload.

She looked through the peephole, into the holding cell.

'It's DI Dobson.'

There was no sign of Robbie.

Prisoners often sat with their backs to the door. It was the one place where they couldn't be seen from the peephole; it was their one chance at some privacy. In newer cells there was now CCTV, but at Milbury police station they usually only dealt with drunks, drug addicts or petty thieves. A peephole was enough.

'Come on, Robbie,' Alison said, 'let me see you so I can open the bloody door.' It was then she spotted it. Dark, dark red, almost brown. And spreading. A pool of it, on the floor. Blood. It sent a visceral shiver through her limbs. Her body knew before her mind did.

'Shit.'

She banged on the door. A stupid impulse. Robbie couldn't open up even if he wanted to. She had the keys;

there was a handle only on her side. She fumbled with the keys, shouted for Martin. Her heart was banging in her chest, her pulse racing.

'Shit, shit, shit,' she mumbled to herself as she finally turned the key.

The door was heavy; she struggled to move it. Then Martin Roberts was beside her. He added his weight to hers and they pushed the door open wordlessly.

Robbie was on the floor, pushed onto his side by the opening door. His body had made a smear in the blood pool beside him. His eyes were open. Alison bent to check his pulse and pulled back. His wrist was mangled.

He had hacked at it, opening up a vein. This wasn't a clean cut but the raw meat of skin and sinew. Blood was still oozing from the wound.

Fuck.

Robbie's breath was so shallow that Alison could barely hear it. But he *was* breathing. She elevated his arms, hoping it might stop the bleeding. Not that there was much bleeding now. It was as if even his blood had given up.

'Come on, Robbie,' she said, sitting down beside him in the blood, 'come on, lad. Nothing's that bad.'

Martin had called an ambulance; now he pulled a sheet from the bed and wrapped Robbie's wrists, staunching what little blood there was left.

'Come on, Robbie,' Alison said, 'it's going to be alright.' Robbie's eyes swivelled in her direction. She didn't know whether he recognised her, or whether he could understand her, but her words seemed to give him comfort.

'Izzy,' he said so quietly that Alison could barely hear him.

'It's DI Dobson,' Alison said. 'I'm here. Like you said, like you asked me. I'm here.' He didn't respond.

'I'm here,' Alison said.

'Izzy,' he said again.

Alison didn't correct him this time, hoping it gave him comfort. His breath was slowing. She felt him becoming a dead weight against her. Almost a literal dead weight.

'The ambulance will be here in a minute, Robbie,' she said, 'you're going to be fine.' She caught Martin Roberts' eye as she said it and knew she was lying. It felt as if there was nothing for Robbie now. It felt as if he was already gone.

He tried to speak again, but no words came. Alison held him to her like a child, stroking his hair. Telling him pointlessly that he was fine.

There was a horrible frothing sound in his throat; his breath rattled into his chest.

'It's OK, Robbie,' Alison said stupidly, because it so evidently wasn't OK. 'I'm here.' He closed his eyes. He was shaking violently and then he wasn't. She no longer knew if he was alive or dead. Still she held him, elevating his wrists, hoping it wasn't too late.

And then the paramedics were there. And then they weren't. She wasn't aware of how it happened, but they took Robbie from her. Took over the responsibility. There were drips and masks and a stretcher. There was a blanket around her shoulders for the second time that day. There were words but she couldn't make them out.

Robbie was still alive. She realised this was a shock to her. She realised that she had believed he would die. In her heart she had already thought of him as gone.

But the paramedics had taken him and he was still alive.

She wanted to ask what his chances were, but she found the words too slow to come and the ambulance too quick to leave.

She seemed to sit on the floor for the longest time. *This is shock*, she thought quite calmly. *This shaking and light-headedness. This inability to move. Shock and adrenaline. A natural physical reaction. This is what it feels like to have no idea how to react.*

And yet she had seen worse. She had seen bodies and beatings, accidents and deaths.

She forced herself to her feet. Forced herself to do her job.

'What the fuck happened?' she asked Martin, hoping for anger in her voice but hearing only sadness.

'I don't know.'

'What did he even use?'

Martin pointed to a pen shaft on the floor in the pool of Robbie's blood.

Alison blinked back a tear. How desperate must he have been to hack away at himself with the broken shaft of a cheap pen? How long must it have taken to get down to a vein? How much must it have hurt? She shook her head, fighting her tears.

'Where the hell did he get that?' she asked.

Martin looked pale, shocked and also frightened. This would be his career on the line. There would be an inquiry, public scrutiny, the family would probably sue.

'He was searched when he came in,' Martin said.

Alison nodded, as if she believed him. Then she took a deep breath. She was still a fucking police officer, if she couldn't do this right then what the hell could she do?

'OK,' she said, glad to hear the calm authority in her voice, 'we'll need forensics. They'll want your clothes and mine, I expect. Then get yourself home, get yourself cleaned up. Write it all down as soon as you can, make sure you're clear on everything you did.'

'What will you do?'

'I think I'd better speak to Robbie's solicitor,' Alison said. 'She was the last one to see him. He got that pen from somewhere and if he didn't bring it in with him...'

'He didn't,' Martin said, sounding certain.

'Then Ms Mitchell has some explaining to do.'

TWENTY-EIGHT

Alison knew it was more hope than expectation that made her believe Mitchell had left the pen in Robbie's cell. She wanted someone to blame for the way he had hurt himself, and she would love that someone to be Hortence Mitchell.

As soon as she had changed clothes and cleaned herself up she called Mitchell's mobile. The solicitor told her she was having dinner at the Masons Arms.

'I'll be there in five minutes,' Alison said, without waiting for an invitation.

Mitchell was alone at a table when Alison walked in. Two wine glasses in front of her, one empty, the other half full. Had she been dining with someone or were the waiting staff just slow to clear the glasses?

'Have a good chat with your client this afternoon, did you?' Alison asked, sitting herself down opposite Mitchell without being asked.

'You know I can't possibly comment on that. I'm sure you've heard of a little thing called client confidentiality.'

'I have,' Alison said. 'I wonder if you've ever heard of

professional diligence, safeguarding vulnerable prisoners, just being bloody responsible for your own actions?'

'Excuse me?' Mitchell said imperiously.

'I'm here to inform you, since you are his lawyer, that Robbie Smith attempted suicide this afternoon. Shortly after you left him.'

'Attempted?'

'Suicide, yes. It means he tried to kill himself.' She adopted Mitchell's own condescending manner. 'More precisely he hacked at his wrists with a broken pen. A pen which *someone* left in his cell.'

'Oh dear, and in police custody too. That won't look good.' Mitchell didn't look shocked, if anything she looked a little bored.

'You don't give a shit, do you? You haven't even asked how he is.'

'I assume, since you used the term *attempted* suicide, that his attempt failed. Am I incorrect?'

'He's alive. Just barely. If I hadn't... hadn't gone to see...'

'You went to see him?' For the first time Mitchell sounded interested. 'Did you speak to him?' she asked.

'No, I... When I got there I found him...' Alison found she couldn't finish the sentence. She started again, trying to recapture her anger. 'He had been very seriously hurt. If I hadn't got there when I did...'

'But you did. You were fortunate enough to play the hero.'

'Luckily for Robbie.'

'Luckily for you and your colleagues, I'd say. A death in custody rarely does anyone's career any good.'

'I'd be looking to my own career if were you,' Alison said

spitefully, 'given that you saw your client approximately five minutes before he tried to take his own life. You made no mention of his troubled state of mind to the custody officer and it seems likely you were the source of the weapon he used to cut himself.'

Mitchell raised herself up haughtily.

'Those are serious accusations,' she said coldly, 'so let me rebut them. I saw my client a little over an hour ago. When I left he was in good humour, a little subdued but not unduly so given the seriousness of the charges he is facing. The custody sergeant was about to give him a meal. I believe he referred to it as "tea". I assume that happened?'

Alison nodded.

'So,' Mitchell went on, 'I very clearly was *not* the last person to see Mr Smith before the incident. That would have been the custody officer who, incidentally, is also the individual with supposed expertise regarding, and a requirement to check upon, my client's mental state. If *your* custody officer saw nothing wrong with Mr Smith's state of mind I fail to see how I could have deduced a suicidal tendency.'

Alison wanted to respond, but really there was nothing to say. Mitchell was so cold, so unconcerned by Robbie's suffering and her logic was impeccable. Alison found herself hating the other woman.

'You don't even seem to care,' she said weakly.

'It isn't my job to care,' Mitchell said.

Alison was taken aback by the iciness of the response.

'So,' Mitchell continued, 'I think I have absolved myself of any responsibility for assessing the mental state of Mr Smith. However, you also implied that I was responsible for his acquiring a weapon of some sort. Again I would like the opportunity to set the record straight. What exactly am I accused of doing? Providing Mr Smith with what? A knife? A razor blade?' There was almost a laugh in her voice as if she considered the situation too ridiculous for words.

'It was a pen,' Alison said. She wished it had been a razor blade, imagining the clean cut instead of the hamburger of mangled meat that had been Robbie's wrist.

'A pen?' Mitchell asked.

'Yes,' Alison said petulantly. 'Your client, who seemed in good humour to you, was so desperate to die that he hacked at his wrists with the broken shaft of a pen. It must have taken some effort and determination.'

'And you suspect I gave this pen to him?'

'You went to see him,' Alison said. 'Are you telling me you didn't take notes?' Mitchell paused. Then she smiled.

'Do you have any idea how much money I make?' she asked.

'What? What does that have to do...?'

'I would estimate I make at least five times what you do. Maybe more.'

'What the...'

'I make that money because I am *very* good at my job and I am inordinately clever. Yet you think that I am stupid enough to leave a potentially dangerous object in a cell with a client? Even the duty solicitor, even the kid on their first case out of university, knows better than that. Yet you think I would...' Mitchell shook her head. Then she laughed lightly. 'It has been a very long time since anyone underestimated me, DI Dobson. Thank you. It reminds me of being young.'

'You're saying you didn't leave a pen with Robbie Smith?' Alison said stubbornly.

'Oh, sorry, do you need me to spell it out in single-syllable words? I did not leave a pen with Robbie Smith. I am not an idiot.'

'How can you be sure? Everyone, even inordinately clever people, makes mistakes.' Mitchell opened her expensive handbag and pulled out an equally expensive-looking fountain pen.

'Rather nice, isn't it,' she said, as if Alison had said something admiring. 'My grandmother gave it to me when I graduated. I use it at *all* times. I am very careful to never lend it to anyone, or to leave it where clients might get it. And as you can see by the fact that it is still in my possession, I certainly did not leave it in a cell with Robbie Smith this afternoon.'

'You were the last person to see him,' Alison began.

'Far from it,' Mitchell said. 'By your own admission two others saw him after me. Your custody sergeant, and yourself.'

'Are you suggesting…?'

'As I said before, failure in your duty of care tends not to be good for a career. I quite understand that one might wish to apportion blame elsewhere. I suggest you find a more credible, or at least a more gullible, scapegoat.'

Alison said nothing. Her head was spinning uncomfortably. The fact that Mitchell owned an expensive pen didn't mean she couldn't use a cheap one. It didn't mean she *hadn't* left a pen like that with Robbie. It was impossible to prove, however. Martin Roberts was a decent copper, but we all make mistakes. He could have failed to search Robbie properly. The pen could have been in the cell; God knows they weren't cleaned as often as they should be. It could have fallen out of someone's pocket and lain there for days.

It was all going to shit, and suddenly the anger left her. Suddenly the adrenaline drained away and she was exhausted. She slumped back in the seat, unable to keep her upright posture a moment longer.

'Are you OK, Inspector?' Mitchell asked. There was no concern in her voice, rather a sort of bored politeness.

Alison shook her head. The image of Robbie swam in her head; he was blood-soaked and pale, his wrist and lower arm a mass of raw meat. For the first time she wondered why he had done it. Was it an admission of guilt or an indication of innocence? A boy like Robbie would never trust that innocence alone would protect him. He knew that it was possible to be blamed, to be punished, even when it wasn't your fault. He knew, as all kids who had grown up like him knew instinctively, that life wasn't fair.

But bloody hell. He had a good lawyer. Hadn't he realised that everything was starting to point to his innocence? Dan Humphreys had confirmed his alibi for the time that Andrea was killed. Henry Chapell was willing to admit he *could* have seen someone other than Robbie. Alison was fighting for him. Didn't he see that Alison was fighting for him?

No, of course he didn't. The police were the enemy to kids like Robbie. Alison was the last person he would expect to be on his side.

'Why the hell did he do it?' she asked, not expecting an answer.

'Guilt can eat away at people,' Mitchell said unexpectedly. 'I see it a lot. People who are determined to fight, professing their innocence, sometimes for years, and then suddenly...

Well, suddenly they get to a point where they can't do it anymore. They can't face what they've done. I find it often leads to a confession, but occasionally it leads to this sort of unpleasantness.'

'Did Robbie tell you he was guilty?' Alison asked.

'As I have already explained to you, Inspector, I cannot discuss what my client may or may not have told me. I am speaking purely hypothetically.'

Alison eyed her suspiciously. Was Mitchell trying to tell her something? 'I know you can't tell me. I know, but... Did he kill her? That's all I need to know. Because doing this... the way he did this it looks a lot like...' Mitchell gave a tiny, almost invisible nod of the head. So small and quick that Alison felt she almost hadn't seen it. Then she said calmly,

'A gesture like this looks like guilt. Of course any solicitor worth her salt would say that it also looks like grief. The act of a grieving young man.'

'He didn't say anything? You didn't have any idea?' Mitchell raised an eyebrow, not even deigning to answer.

Alison realised that whatever Robbie had been so desperate to tell her, he had probably told Mitchell instead. And Mitchell would never say. This whole conversation was pointless.

'I need to go,' Alison said.

'When can I see my client?' Mitchell asked, her tone all business again.

'Sorry... What?'

'I assume Mr Smith is currently in hospital. When can I see him?' Alison shook her head, she genuinely didn't know.

'You'll have to speak to the doctors. I don't... speak to the hospital.' She had to make an effort to keep her back straight as she walked away. She was exhausted, and no closer to knowing what had happened to Izzy or Andrea. Or Robbie for that matter. They were united now in her mind. A triumvirate of victims.

Alison went back to the station. She had showered of course, she had changed her clothes before she spoke to Mitchell, but still she felt as if she smelled of despair, as if Robbie's blood was still on her.

Her hair had dripped red into the shower as she washed Robbie's blood off herself. She had cried. Cried for his sadness and his pain, but also for herself. Cried because she lived a life that meant she could end up with blood in her hair from holding up a man's hands to try to keep him alive. A boy really. She cried because her children lived in this world and this wasn't the world she wanted for them.

She had cried in the shower, but that was over. There would be no more tears today. She was a professional and this was just another day at the office.

Rogers was waiting for her, inevitably.

'About time,' he said. 'Got your tights in a knot, did you?'

'It took a while to wash the blood and gristle from my hair, sir,' she said calmly. She knew he was squeamish and enjoyed watching him squirm. The word gristle made her think of the hamburger wrist again and she felt her stomach roil. She kept her face impassive though, as if none of it affected her.

'It's a right royal fuck-up,' Rogers said. Alison said nothing. 'I hear he wanted to talk to you,' Rogers said.

'Apparently,' Alison replied.

'Any idea why?' Rogers asked.

'Afraid not,' Alison said. 'He was a bit too busy bleeding

when I got there to answer any questions.' She smiled to cover the insubordination.

'Maybe if you hadn't been putting on your makeup you might have got there in time for once.'

Alison bit her tongue. *Maybe if you hadn't told Holly not to call me*, she thought, but she said nothing.

'There'll be a bloody inquiry, of course.'

'Yes, sir.'

'What're they gonna find?' Rogers asked.

'Sir?'

'Come on, Dobson, you were there. Martin Roberts is a pen pusher,' he gulped, perhaps aware of the inappropriateness of the phrase, 'he's a decent guy – no imagination, no ambition – but he knows how to do his job. So what I'm asking you is, did he fuck up?'

Alison shook her head. 'I don't know,' she began. She saw the thunder in Rogers' eyes. He didn't like not knowing, he liked answers. She took a deep breath. 'Roberts was checking on Robbie regularly, every fifteen minutes or so, because he was young, vulnerable. He was doing his job.'

'Any reason to suspect he was a suicide risk?'

'None, Roberts was just being thorough. The solicitor had only been gone five minutes when I got there. Roberts had been in to give Robbie some food after that. He can't have been alone for more than a couple of minutes.'

'In which time he slashed his wrist with a pen?' The word slashed made Alison pause. People were always described as having *slashed* their wrists. She wished, for Robbie's sake, that it was an accurate description. A slash would have been quick, clean, deep. Better than the desperate hacking she could only imagine from the damage on his wrist.

'Looks like he used the broken shaft of a biro,' Alison clarified. 'Roberts spotted it in the cell. It was quite sharp, but it still must have taken some effort for Robbie to cut himself, sir.'

'So where did he get it?'

'Roberts says he searched Robbie properly for weapons and I believe him. If he brought that pen in with him it would have had to be well hidden.'

'And why the hell would a kid like that have a pen shoved up his arse?' Rogers asked. 'He put it up there this morning, did he? Just in case he got arrested and needed to try to kill himself?'

Alison shook her head. 'I don't think so, sir.'

'I should hope you don't bloody think so,' Rogers said. 'So if he didn't have it on him when he came in…?'

'Either it was left in the cell, overlooked somehow,' Alison said, 'or someone gave it to him.'

'The solicitor,' Rogers said with something like glee in his voice.

'She says not. Says she only uses a posh fountain pen and never lends it to anyone.'

'Bollocks,' Rogers said. 'She can prove that, can she?'

'No, sir, but we can't prove otherwise. She's the most likely source of the pen. She probably took some notes when she visited Robbie and left it behind, but she's not going to admit it and short of getting hold of her notebook and comparing inks…'

'Which I'm sure she'd be delighted to let us do.'

'Well exactly,' Alison said, acknowledging the sarcasm.

'Let the inquiry worry about where he got the bloody pen,' Rogers said. 'What I want to know is did the lad say anything before he did it? Deathbed confession?'

'Not to me, sir. He said Izzy's name, that's all. Mitchell says he didn't tell her anything significant either, but then she would say that.'

She omitted to mention the hint Mitchell had given about Robbie's guilt. Mitchell would deny it. Rogers didn't need to know.

Rogers let out a low noise through his nose like a walrus.

'Skinner tells me Robbie couldn't have been at the scene when Andrea Mills was killed. That right?' he said.

'It's watertight, sir. Dan Humphreys saw him in town, made that anonymous call to Burgess at the Penbury station. He was trying to get Robbie into trouble for dealing drugs.'

'And accidentally gave him a perfect alibi,' Rogers said. 'Could they be working together?'

Alison shook her head. 'Dan hates Robbie. Blames him for killing Izzy. Even before that he didn't like the idea that Robbie knew he was gay, he was afraid he'd tell the whole town.'

'Could young Mr Humphreys have been mistaken? Seen someone else?'

'His friends confirmed it. So I don't *think*…'

'Well, be sure, will you, because a suicide attempt looks like guilt and Robbie certainly had a motive to kill Andrea Mills.'

'Only if he killed Izzy,' Alison pointed out, 'and he had no motive to kill Izzy.'

'Not that we know of at least,' Rogers corrected her.

Alison nodded. *Not that we know of.* But then what the hell did they really know? Rogers was speaking again.

'If Robbie didn't kill Andrea he probably didn't kill Izzy, right?' Alison nodded and Rogers went on, 'Are we still assuming Mills was killed because she saw someone at the Izzy Johnson murder scene?'

'Yes.'

'Fabulous. Only problem is, who the fuck was it?'

'We're still looking into the drugs angle.'

'Yeah, trouble is your bloody "drugs angle" means a fat old teacher selling the kids stuff that strictly speaking isn't even illegal.'

'I know but…'

'Of course you *know*, DI Dobson. Like most women I imagine you think you know everything I'm about to say before I say it, but I would appreciate a chance to finish my own sentences.' He paused provocatively.

Alison said nothing.

'As I was saying,' Rogers went on, 'the trouble with the "drugs angle" is that there's no clear connection between Banks possibly selling pills to kids and any real motive to kill Johnson or Mills. And our portly Mr Banks is a long way from fitting the description of our assailant at either scene.'

Alison remained silent.

'Right,' Rogers said decisively, 'you go home. Rest of the day off, all that benevolent boss shit.' He held her eye as if daring her to mention that it was already long after the end of her shift. 'I don't want to see you before ten tomorrow,' he went on. 'But then we start again. Look at Izzy Johnson's killing as if we don't know anything, which to be bloody honest is close enough to the truth. Examine the evidence. Where was she found? How was she killed? Forensics? Look for anything we missed. All that crap. Look at Andrea Mills with fresh eyes too. Talk to everybody again. Start with Dan Humphreys, make absolutely sure he saw what he's saying he saw. I want to be a hundred percent sure it wasn't Robbie on that hill.'

'With respect, sir,' Alison said, 'we did all that…'

'With respect,' Rogers said, his voice dripping with sarcasm, 'you can do it again. I know you believe yourself infallible, but it's just possible you missed something. Start again and try to do it with an open bloody mind.'

'Yes, sir.'

'Go on then, bugger off home.'

Alison paused.

'What is it?' Rogers asked, cross as usual.

'How is he, sir? Have we heard anything?'

She expected his usual pedantic answer, 'That sentence needs a more specific subject. To whom are you referring?' Instead Rogers was direct.

'He'll live,' he said simply. 'Pretty poorly, but they've transfused some blood and he's young. He should make a good recovery. Looks like you saved a life today, Dobson. Good job.'

She felt the tears spring to her eyes at his unexpected kindness.

'Now fuck off out of my office. Unlike you, some of us have work to do.'

TWENTY-NINE

Alison slept badly, with images of Izzy and Andrea and Robbie floating in her head. All mixed up together. Connected in ways she didn't understand.

She woke early, her head too full to think, and decided to go for a swim. She hoped that the repetitive motion would free her mind from the case for an hour. A sort of reboot for the brain. But her mind was too full and she was unable to find her flow. She had the feeling she had missed something. It wasn't just that nothing added up or that nothing made sense, it was the feeling that it *did* make sense if she only looked at it the right way. She felt as if she knew the answer, she just didn't know what it was yet.

She thought through the options, the possible solutions to her puzzle.

Robbie Smith. A jealous boy, a petty criminal with a record for minor assault. Killing a girl for rejecting him, killing a woman for seeing him kill the girl, attempting suicide because of the guilt. The blood and the ruined flesh and the pain it must have cost him only really made sense if he was guilty. Even his solicitor had hinted at his guilt with a single nod of her head. As a solution it was neat, it was simple. It was destroyed by Dan having seen Robbie at the other side of town about the time that Andrea was killed.

Dan Humphreys. Another teenager and one with a temper. Begrudging Izzy her golden life. Sisterless, motherless, struggling with his sexuality. Killing Izzy because she could expose him and destroy the image he had worked so hard to create. Killing Andrea because she was a possible witness. Except he had been at the other side of town when Andrea died. By making that anonymous call to the police he had not only given Robbie an alibi but also himself. Half a dozen friends were with him when he made the call. Would they all lie for him?

What if they were in it together? Robbie doing the killing, Dan providing the alibi. His friends all backing Dan up. But why would Dan help Robbie? Dan hated Robbie. Blackmail? Robbie threatening to expose Dan unless he made that call?

So why Robbie's suicide attempt? Could a boy be so manipulative one minute and racked with guilt the next? It was possible, but it didn't feel right.

So who else?

Simon Banks. Asking Izzy to meet him so he could explain something. Dealing drugs to children. According to Dominic Mills, Izzy had threatened to expose Banks. Andrea Mills had definitely threatened to stop his dealing. Was that really reason enough to kill? After all, as Rogers pointed out, the drugs weren't strictly illegal. And there was the bigger problem. They had two descriptions of possible assailants now. The hooded teenager Andrea Mills had seen and the young man Chapell mistook for Robbie Smith. Banks couldn't be further from that physical type.

A paid accomplice? Even with the drugs connection the idea felt ludicrous. They were talking pills readily available on the internet, not international cocaine smuggling.

With each length Alison swam the puzzle seemed further from a conclusion. Rogers had said start again, but she felt like she had no firm footing to start from.

When she had swum a mile, she got out of the pool and dressed quickly. She didn't feel better.

As she headed towards her car she heard raised voices. Robbie's house was visible across the road from the pool. She could see his mother, Sharon Smith, hands gesticulating wildly. Her voice was raised to a shout but even so Alison could not make out the words from this distance. A man was standing in front of Sharon, too close, his fists clenched by his sides.

Without thinking Alison headed across the road towards the arguing couple. As she drew closer Sharon's words became audible.

'You can shove it up your arse,' she was yelling for all the world to hear. 'It's the likes of you got us into this fucking mess.'

If there was a reply, it was inaudible.

'I told you to fuck off. I won't say it again.' A pause. 'You don't scare me. And you don't fucking impress me. I'm not some kid who thinks you're a big man because you've got a fancy bloody car and a few quid in your pocket. Now fuck off like I told you to.'

'Everything alright?' Alison asked, approaching the

man. There was something vaguely familiar about him, although she was sure she hadn't met him before.

'None of your business,' he said curtly.

He was much taller than Alison and powerfully built. The sort of physique that screamed powerlifting and steroids. But he was dressed in a softly tailored suit and his watch looked like it cost more than Alison's car. If his appearance was a mixture of fierce and sophisticated his stance was all aggression.

'What the fuck's it got to do with you?' he went on, taking a half-step towards Alison.

She stood her ground.

'He was just leaving,' Sharon said, her body language daring the man to contradict her.

'I'm not going anywhere, Shaz. Let me in. I'm trying to help.' His tone was neither conciliatory nor helpful.

'I told you where you can shove your help.'

'I can make you feel better. You know that, right?'

'You offering me drugs, Carl?' Smith asked, mocking him. 'In front of an officer of the law?'

'What?' The man turned to look at Alison fully for the first time.

'DI Dobson,' she said coolly.

He turned back to Smith.

'You're a dick, Shaz, you know that?'

'Fuck off.'

'I just want to talk to you.'

'I told you to fuck off.'

He reached out as if to take Smith's arm. Alison stepped between them.

'I think you probably ought to leave,' Alison said.

'I'm just talking to her,' he said petulantly.

'She asked you to leave,' Alison said again.

'Yeah, that's what fuck off means, Carl,' Sharon said, 'it means leave. Got it?' For a moment he looked as if he might explode with fury, but he contained it. Wordlessly he turned and got back into his car.

A convertible sports car. Deep blue. As the man reversed down the street Alison made a mental note of the registration and the car's BMW badge. It was a habit most police officers shared.

'Everything alright?' she asked Sharon, inclining her head to the retreating vehicle.

'I can handle Carl if that's what you mean,' she said with a hard laugh.

'Looked like a pretty heated argument.'

'God, woman, if that's what you call heated you've lived a pretty sheltered life. Look, Carl's not a problem. I told him to fuck off and he's gone. End of.'

'Who is he?' Alison asked after a short pause.

'A not very nice man I used to know,' Sharon said with a dry laugh. 'I haven't always been a model citizen. You might have heard that on the grapevine.'

Alison didn't answer.

'Like I say, Carl's a pretty bad man,' Sharon lit a cigarette, looking away from Alison in thought, 'but I can handle him.'

'Anything we need to know about?' Alison asked.

'No offence, love, but I've never been one for the police. Not gonna start now.' Again Alison nodded.

Sharon turned to her. 'I suppose you want to come in and talk about our Robbie,' she said.

'If that's OK.'

Sharon gave a dry laugh. 'Nothing's really OK today, but you coming in or not in't gonna make any difference to that, is it?'

Alison didn't reply, she had not really considered how hard it must be for Sharon. Her youngest son accused of murder and now lying in a hospital bed having tried to kill himself.

She followed Sharon back into the small living room. It was hard to believe it was only a few days since she had been here. Nothing had changed, except everything. The atmosphere was colder; the room was empty even though it was as cluttered as before. There was a hush, as if anyone who came in knew to speak in quiet voices. This was the third house she had visited this week where silence draped life.

'I'm sorry about Robbie,' she said.

'Aye, I bet you are. Your lot'll be in the shit over this.'

'There's no reason to suppose any police misconduct or mistakes,' Alison began. She stopped, aware of how defensive she sounded.

'Aye, well you would say that, I suppose.' Sharon shrugged. 'I've already had bloody ambulance chasers on the phone offering to represent me if I want to sue the police.'

Alison bit her tongue. She really shouldn't be discussing this.

'They said you were the one,' Sharon asked, 'the one who... found him?' Alison nodded.

'They told me you saved his life.'

'Is he OK?' Alison asked. 'Have you seen him?'

'Saw him last night but he was still out of it. Our Rita's

gonna come over later, give us a lift in. They say he's gonna be fine.'

'Good,' Alison said, meaning it.

'I've seen you with your kids round town,' Sharon said suddenly. 'Couple of little girls, isn't it?'

'Yes. They're six and ten.'

'Nice ages those. Past all that toddler crap and not old enough to start giving you grief yet. You make the most of it. You enjoy it while you can.'

'I will,' Alison said seriously.

'Thing is, even once they're grown they're still kids to their mum. Our Robbie is still my little boy. Curly brown hair, a permanent snotty nose, always up to mischief and then crawling on me knee at the end of the day for a cuddle and to say sorry. That's the Robbie I see, even though he's a man and a bloody nuisance now. To me he's still that little lad.'

Alison smiled at that.

'He never hurt that lass,' Sharon went on. 'I'm not saying he's an angel, far bloody from it. But the way he was with that lass, soppy as a bloody puppy he was, there's no way he'd've hurt her.'

'I can't really discuss it,' Alison said.

'I know. I just wanted to say. You've got them lasses right, so you understand. You know your own kids. Our Robbie said he never hurt that lass. I believe him. When I talked to him last night, he was adamant…'

'You spoke to him? When was this?' Alison asked. 'Did he come round… regain consciousness… after…?'

'No, no. This was before. When he rang me up. After you arrested him that second time. Said he needed me to know he didn't hurt her. He said, whatever happened I had to understand that it didn't mean he'd done anything to Izzy or that bloody Mills woman.'

'He *rang* you up?' Alison asked, sure that there was no record of a phone call from Robbie to his mother.

'Yeah. Yesterday like I say. Not long before… he did what he did.'

'Was it a call from the police station?'

'No, the bloody Bahamas!'

'Sorry, of course, that's not what I meant. I meant was it official? Did someone speak to you first? Did a police officer tell you Robbie was calling from the police station?'

'No, I don't think so. It was a mobile number I think. Yeah, it was "number withheld" because I nearly didn't answer. I mean it's usually crap, isn't it? Trying to sell you something, some sort of scam. Anyway, for some reason I answered it yesterday and it was our Robbie.'

A withheld number? Probably a mobile. So where had Robbie got it? Alison's thoughts turned to Hortence Mitchell again. The solicitor had been in Robbie's cell before he died. She was probably the source of the pen he had used to cut his wrists. Now it seemed she had allowed him to call his mother. What the hell was going on?

'Tell me exactly what he said,' she said.

'Like I say, he said he never killed Izzy and whatever happened I had to keep on believing that.'

'Did he sound depressed?'

'Course he sounded bloody depressed. His girlfriend was dead and you lot were telling him he was going down for a double murder.'

Alison nodded, although she was more confused than ever. Sharon Smith was still speaking.

'When Robbie was growing up I got called into school a lot… I mean, like, every other day. He'd hit a kid, he'd spat at someone, he'd nicked a kid's dinner money. I got called in once because he'd eaten a worm. I mean, for fuck's sake… I said to them, if he's eaten a fucking worm don't you think that's punishment enough?' She smiled at the memory. 'Anyway, I got called in all the time. Thing was, Robbie never tried to say it wasn't him. If he did it he'd tell you. Sometimes he was sorry and sometimes he wasn't, but he never lied about it.'

'Murder is different…' Alison began.

'If he'd killed that girl he'd've told me,' Sharon said simply. 'I know he wouldn't hurt her. You've got kids. You understand. Some things you just know.'

'If he didn't do it, we'll find out who,' Alison began.

'No offence, love,' Sharon said, 'but we both know it doesn't work like that. You've got someone in the frame, you stop looking.'

'I'm not like that,' Alison said.

Sharon looked at her appraisingly. Then slowly nodded before she said, 'I hate fucking ambulance chasers. I don't want to sue anyone. But I need you to promise me you'll find out what happened. Find out why he did this to himself. I need you to look after my boy. Daft beggar doesn't even know he needs looking after half the time.'

There was a smile on Sharon's lips even as the tears slid down her face.

'I'll do what I can,' Alison said.

'Just find out the fucking truth. I know it wasn't my lad, I just need you to find out who the fuck it was. Not too much to ask, is it?'

THIRTY

Paul was outside Alison's house when she got home.

'What is it?' she asked. 'Am I late? Rogers told me to come in at ten.'

'I know, I know. I just came to see... You alright?'

She forced a smile. 'I'm fine.'

'Is there anything I can do?'

'I need a check on the owner of a car.'

'OK,' he said, 'but I meant...'

'I know,' she said, dismissing his concern. 'Here's the reg number.' She recited the number and watched him write it down.

'Urgent?'

'Everything's always urgent, isn't it?' she said. 'But I don't think this is life and death if that's what you mean. Just belongs to some bloke I saw arguing with Sharon Smith this morning.'

Paul gave her a long look but didn't comment.

'OK, I'll see it gets done.' He paused. 'You really OK?'

'Yeah.'

'I know you've got a soft spot… for Smith I mean.'

'Rogers wants us to talk to Dan Humphreys again.'

'Why?'

'He thinks Robbie's suicide attempt means he's guilty. If there's any doubt about Humphreys seeing him across town, or what time he saw him… If there's any chance at all that Robbie could have killed Andrea Mills, Rogers wants to know. So I'd like you to go talk to Dan Humphreys for me.'

'Sure. What are you going to do?'

'I need to speak to Robbie… I just… His mother's convinced he's innocent.'

'You've spoken to Smith's mother?' Paul asked.

Alison chose not to answer.

'Jesus, boss,' Paul went on, 'he tried to top himself. That's practically a signed confession.'

'Except he can't have been at the scene of Andrea Mills' murder.'

'Unless Dan Humphreys got it wrong. Or lied.'

'Which is what Rogers is hoping. Wouldn't it be lovely and convenient? Dan says he made a mistake, he never saw Robbie. All Dan's friends had lied to back him up. Henry Chapell was right all along. Robbie was the one who killed Andrea. He killed Izzy and he tried to kill himself.'

'It'd make sense,' Paul said.

Alison shook her head. It did make sense. And she realised she had been trying all night to convince herself that it was the truth. But none of it *felt* right.

'He rang his mother before he did it. Before he cut himself.'

'Rang her? There's no log…'

'Used a mobile phone. Told her that whatever happened she had to believe he never killed Izzy.'

'Where did he get a mobile? How did he?'

'Not making so much sense anymore, is it?' Alison said. 'Where did he get the mobile? Where did he get the pen to cut himself with?'

'It must be Mitchell.'

'Yeah.'

Paul hesitated.

'Look,' he said, 'the inquiry will get into all that.'

'What if Mitchell gave him that pen? What if she knew what he was going to do, and that's why she let him ring his mother?'

'Why would she do that?'

'I don't know… maybe…'

'What?'

'Maybe it suits her somehow if Robbie looks guilty.' She saw the sceptical look on his face and shook her head.

'OK, OK,' she said, 'that doesn't make sense. I don't know, I just… It doesn't feel right. I don't think he was suicidal.'

'He slashed his wrists,' Paul said gently. 'I think that's a pretty good indication he was feeling suicidal.'

Alison had no answer to that. People who weren't suicidal didn't cut into their flesh the way Robbie had. The act had been deliberate, decisive. Robbie had been alone in that cell. He had chosen to harm himself. It had been his choice, no one else's.

'I just want to talk to him, OK? Find out what his explanation is.' Paul opened his mouth in protest; Alison stalled him. 'And then I'll be a good girl. I'll talk again to

Dan Humphreys, I'll come into the office and start again from the beginning like Rogers wants, OK?

'OK,' Paul conceded. 'I'll start without you, shall I?' She smiled her thanks.

'Oh, by the way, who's heading up the forensics on Robbie?' she asked.

'That's an internal investigation,' Paul said.

Alison waited. Her question still stood.

'You're a witness, you can't get involved.' There was a hint of warning in Paul's voice.

Still Alison waited.

'Jenny McBride,' he said at last.

Alison smiled.

'She can't tell you anything,' Paul said. 'It's a matter for the IOPC now.'

'I know.'

As soon as Paul had gone Alison called Jenny McBride.

'Well, fuck me, I wondered when I'd be hearing from you,' McBride said, a smile in her voice.

'Officially I'm not involved.'

'Aye and officially I'm supposed to work forty hours a week, take a lunch break and two twenty-minute coffee breaks a day. Since when did officially have anything the fuck to do with anything?'

Alison smiled. Jenny McBride was one of her favourite people. Almost sixty, she was supposed to be an elder statesman, or woman, in the forensic department. Trouble was, no one seemed to have told Jenny that. She swore like a navvy, drank like a sailor and intimidated young officers for fun.

Jenny didn't ask why, or how, she just asked what. What

was there, what was missing, what could have happened, and what couldn't. She wouldn't tell Alison why something happened, she wouldn't hazard a guess as to who was responsible but she would give her the facts. This is possible, this is likely, that is impossible. No speculation.

'You had a chance to look at the pen yet?'

'Just removed the gloves from my dainty hands.'

'And?'

'And I'm about to head out for breakfast with a very nice young woman I met on an internet dating site.'

'I'm pleased for you, I hope you have a lovely time and it leads to true love,' Alison said.

'Thank you. To be honest I'll be happy if it leads to a quick shag.'

'OK then,' Alison laughed, 'but, as I think you know, I was asking whether you found anything on the pen?'

'The pen which is evidence in a case you're officially not a part of? The one that is being passed to the IOPC? The case in which I am supposed to determine whether there was any negligence on the part of the police, and which by its very nature *you* should not be involved with at all?'

'Yes, that one.'

Jenny was the one to laugh now.

'The one that *looked* like a suicide attempt?' she said.

'Looked like?' Alison asked.

'For fuck's sake, Alison, you were the one who found him, weren't you? Wrists hacked to buggery, blood all over the floor. Wouldn't you say it looked like a suicide attempt?'

'Yes,' Alison said, waiting.

'Aye, and maybe half the numbnuts working in this department would have put it down to a suicide attempt too. Which is why they're bloody lucky I haven't succumbed to the dubious lure of retirement just yet.'

'You found something on the pen?'

Jenny chuckled her throaty smoker's chuckle.

'I found plenty on the pen, most of it unspeakable, but nothing unexpected given that it had been used to hack at a young man's flesh.'

Alison felt her skin crawl, but she kept quiet.

'One interesting thing I didn't find on the pen was... the rest of it.'

'Sorry, the rest of what?'

'The rest of *it*, rest of the pen. Smith used the broken shaft as his weapon of choice, and the team found two pieces. But no actual pen if you see what I mean. That little plastic straw with the ink in and the nib attached.'

'The inside of the pen was missing?'

'Yeah,' Jenny said. 'Of course that doesn't necessarily mean anything. Smith could have found a broken pen discarded somewhere, or more likely the other bit got kicked about, stuck in someone's shoe, picked up with the stretcher, whatever. Doesn't mean it was never there.'

'But?' Alison prompted.

'Always were impatient,' Jenny chuckled again. 'OK, look, odd stuff makes me think. So the fact that part of the pen was missing got me thinking.'

'And?'

'Took an awful lot to get through the skin to the veins on that lad's wrist. I mean, you saw it, didn't you? Must have caused a lot of pain. You wonder at all how he managed it?'

'I'm trying not to think about it, to be honest,' Alison said.

'Local anaesthetic.'

'Sorry?' Alison said, unsure she had heard properly.

'I could give you all the detail of my genius and how I figured it out, but basically I was confused by the amount of damage that boy had managed to do to himself without making a sound, without crying out. And quickly too. By all accounts he only had a few minutes alone. So no time to hesitate, no time to get up his courage. And he's in a police cell so no booze, or pills to take the edge off.'

'He had to have been determined,' Alison said.

'More than that. Lad needed balls of steel to do what he did and not cry out. It didn't seem likely to me so I went up to the hospital last night and took a closer look. And every cut was deep. There was no hesitation, no tentative first steps. So I took a swab of the skin. Call it a hunch. And lo and behold, topical local anaesthetic.'

'Shit. Is that hard to get hold of?'

'You'd need a prescription but it's not hard to get. Lots of GPs prescribe it when people need to have a needle stick, a jab or a blood sample. It could have come from almost anywhere.'

'How quickly does it take effect?'

'Pretty quickly. Your skin would be pretty numb in five minutes or so. It's not gonna take away all the pain, that lad would still have felt every cut. But it would take the edge off.'

'And how long would the effects last?' Alison asked.

'Couple of hours maybe.'

'So Robbie couldn't have applied it before he was arrested?'

'Not if he wanted it still to have any effect. He had to have put it on right before he made those cuts. Which means he got it in the cell, which means someone gave it to him. And someone had to take the tube away afterwards. Question is who? And why? Attempted suicide it might have been – but it wasn't without help.'

'Shit. OK. Thanks, Jenny.'

'Yeah. Only you haven't heard this from me, have you. Seeing as how you're not involved in this case.'

'Absolutely,' Alison assured her.

THIRTY-ONE

Alison pulled into the car park at the hospital, prepared for a long search for a space, but just as she drove up the first row a car in front of her reversed out. Maybe her luck was changing.

She sat in the car and made two phone calls. The first to Sharon Smith.

'Did Robbie have a prescription for any sort of local anaesthetic?' she asked after a brief preamble.

'You what?'

'Anaesthetic cream, the sort you rub on the skin.'

'Not that I know. Our Robbie isn't much for doctors, can't remember the last time he went, so no… I'd say no. If he needed owt to take away the pain he usually had his own sources, if you get my meaning.' Alison did but she didn't want to go into it.

'Thanks,' she said, ending the call.

Next she rang Holly and asked her to check with Robbie's GP. It was possible he had been planning this. Possible that he had had the cream and the pen with him and had smuggled them into his cell somehow. Possible. Unlikely. Like everything else recently.

At the hospital reception Alison asked for Robbie and was directed to the high-dependency unit. The doctors assured her he was on the mend; however, they were monitoring his heart after so much blood loss. He was in a room by himself. There was an officer on the door. Alison nodded to the young policeman, showing him her warrant card.

'Any visitors?' she asked.

'Mum and brothers came last night,' he said, 'no one yet this morning. Oh no, hold on, his solicitor did call but he was having some sort of tests, so...'

'She didn't get to see him?' Alison clarified.

'No, said she'd be back later. Asked me to pass on a message though.'

'Which was?'

'She said to tell him, "Nothing's changed, I'm still your solicitor." She said she wanted to reassure him.'

'Sounds more like a bloody threat to me,' Alison muttered to herself. She nodded to the officer and went into Robbie's room.

Robbie was sitting up in bed. Drips attached, monitors, all the usual shit. His arm was bandaged, but there was no blood. No sign of trauma.

'You look a bit better than last time I saw you,' Alison said with a smile.

He smiled back reluctantly. He looked like a child, tucked into bed after a hard day. Scrubbed clean. Young. Innocent.

'You feeling up to a little chat?'

'I don't have to talk to you without my solicitor,' he said belligerently.

'You wanted to talk to me yesterday,' Alison said.

'Yeah, but… I'm supposed to have a solicitor.'

'I'd have thought you might have seen enough of her for a while.' Robbie looked at her thoughtfully for a moment, then shrugged.

'I saw your mum this morning,' Alison said. 'She's coming in this aft with your Aunty Rita.' Another shrug.

'She told me she knew you hadn't hurt Izzy. Said she believed you when you told her that.' Yet another shrug.

'When you rang her yesterday.'

'Don't know what you're talking about.'

'Where did you get the phone, Robbie?'

'No idea what you mean. I don't remember anything. Must be the blood loss.' He was trying for cocky and Alison didn't press him, knowing if she did all she'd get were more shrugs.

'Gave me a nasty shock yesterday,' she said. 'Never thought you'd be the suicidal type. Never thought you'd give up that easily.'

He laughed without humour. 'Looks like you got that one wrong, eh,' he said, lifting his bandaged wrist.

'Were you really trying to kill yourself, Robbie?'

'No, I was writing myself a shopping list and the pen slipped. What do you think?'

'I think maybe it was a call for help. A way to make me take notice. To tell me you're innocent.'

'Fuck off,' he said, 'I'm not a nutcase. If I wanted to tell you I'm innocent I'd tell you I'm innocent not slash my fucking wrists.'

'So you were trying to kill yourself? You really wanted to die? You still want to die?'

'Jesus, what are you, a bloody shrink? No, I don't want to die. It was a moment of madness, it won't happen again.' His voice was flat, as if the words were rehearsed.

'What if I let Hortence Mitchell in here with her anaesthetic cream and broken pens?'

'She's not here, is she?' Robbie asked, something close to panic in his eyes. Then he seemed to realise that was the wrong response. 'I don't know what you're talking about.' His words were unconvincing.

'Mitchell sent you a message,' Alison said, ignoring Robbie's last remarks. 'Did the officer tell you? She came by this morning, while you were having tests. She wanted you to know nothing's changed. She's still your solicitor.'

'Fuck that,' Robbie said, but without conviction.

'What happened, Robbie?' Alison asked. 'What made you feel like… like that was your only choice?'

'God, I don't know… Maybe the fact that the most amazing girl in the world is dead, and you lot are hounding me saying I did it. And then that other woman gets killed, and I'm suddenly in the frame for that too. Puts a bit of a downer on your day, don't you think?'

'Who gave you the anaesthetic, Robbie?'

He shook his head. 'Don't know what you're talking about.'

'There was anaesthetic cream on your wrists.' He shrugged.

'Where did you get the pen shaft?'

'Found it.'

'It must have hurt. Even with the cream. I saw those

cuts. I saw what you did. It must have taken a lot of determination. You must have had to be brave.'

'Brave?' He faltered. 'It wasn't brave, it was stupid. You want to see brave? OK. Here's brave. I'm gonna face it. I'm gonna tell you I killed Izzy and that other woman and I'm gonna take the blame. How's that for brave?'

His face was determined and yet utterly defeated.

For a second Alison sat in stunned silence. He had just confessed. As simple as that. He had just confessed.

'You're telling me you killed Isabella Johnson and Andrea Mills. Is that what you're saying?'

'Why not? You've been saying it for days. Why the hell won't you believe it when I tell you the truth?'

'OK. OK,' Alison said. 'So tell me why.'

'It's like you said, me and Izzy argued. I lost my temper. I hit her, with a rock. I strangled her.'

'Strangled her?' Alison asked.

'Yeah. There was an old rabbit trap up there. I used that.' Robbie's voice was a monotone. 'That Mills woman must have seen me. So yesterday I followed her up on to the Beamsleigh. And I did the same to her. Strangled her. Then I ran up onto the Cawpers.'

'How was that possible? You were seen heading to the Cawpers just after half twelve. You were arrested up there. You couldn't have had time to kill Andrea and get up to the Cawpers by the time you were picked up.'

Robbie shrugged.

'Not that far from the Beamsleigh to the Cawpers. I'd just got there when the cop car pulled up. And as for whoever says they saw me, I just got lucky I guess. They must have seen someone who looked like me. Like I say, I followed the Mills woman, then I ran up to the Cawpers. Whoever called old Aunty Carol did me a favour. Except I'm confessing so I guess not.'

Alison shook her head.

'Why run to the Cawpers? Why not go home?'

'Maybe I'm just a bit thick.'

Alison watched him in disbelief. One thing she knew for certain was that Robbie was far from thick.

'You had no blood on you. Your clothes were clean.'

'Yeah, well, like I say, I got lucky.'

Alison didn't believe him. Everything he said was plausible, but she knew he was lying. So how did he know all these details? They hadn't released the information about the rabbit-trap wire used in both killings. Robbie could only know that if he was the killer or he had seen the killer or knew the killer. Here he was giving her an explanation. Telling her something that fitted perfectly. And still she didn't want to believe it.

'Why?' she asked again.

'I told you why,' he said, 'I lost my temper.'

'I'm not sure I believe…' Alison began.

'That other copper'll believe me. Everyone in this piss-ant town will believe me. Robbie Smith, loser, lowlife. Why not? Why wouldn't I do something like this? Prime suspect, right?'

Alison watched him. He was angry and scared and hurt.

'I saved your life yesterday,' Alison said, suddenly feeling her own anger rising.

Robbie shrugged.

'I never asked you to.'

'Yes you did,' she said, suddenly sure of it. 'You asked

them to call me, you knew I was coming. You knew I'd be there to save you.'

'Yeah, cos I have that much faith in the police,' Robbie said sarcastically.

'I nearly didn't make it in time,' Alison said, feeling faint at the thought. 'I nearly decided to let you wait.'

'Maybe you should have done,' he said. 'Maybe I'd be better off dead.'

'I don't think so,' Alison said vehemently.

Robbie watched her for a long moment as if trying to catch her in a lie.

'You heard me arrive, didn't you?' Alison said, hoping it was true, hoping he had waited for her. 'You waited until you heard me talking to Sergeant Roberts, before you... before you did it.'

'No idea what you're talking about.'

Suddenly it mattered fiercely to Alison that she was right. That Robbie hadn't really wanted to die, that the terrible damage he had inflicted had not been meant really to end him. She needed to know, no matter what else happened, that he had not abandoned all hope.

'I had to throw out a perfectly good shirt,' she told him. 'There was no way I'd be able to get the blood out. So the least you owe me is the truth.'

Robbie gave a half-smile. 'Sorry about the shirt,' he said.

'I only bought it last week.'

'I'd offer to buy another, but I reckon my shopping opportunities might be a bit limited for a while.'

He smiled again, the saddest smile Alison had ever seen.

'You don't believe me?' Robbie asked. 'What I said about killing Izzy and Mrs Mills?'

'No I don't,' Alison said decisively. Robbie smiled.

'I never had anyone not believe me when I said I *did* something wrong before. Plenty times people don't believe me when I say I never did it, but usually everyone's quick to believe the worst.'

'You loved Izzy,' Alison said simply.

Robbie nodded. He was silent for a long time.

'I've confessed, right,' he said at last. 'You have to report that, right? I confessed, and I'll do it again on tape or whatever.'

'OK,' Alison said.

'I'll keep saying what I've said. Only if you don't believe I did it, you need to prove it.'

'Bloody hell, Robbie, how am I supposed to do that? Do you know who it was? Do you have any information?'

'Yeah, it was *me*, remember. That's what I said, that's what I'll keep saying. Next question.'

'Where did you get that pen and the anaesthetic for your arm?'

'Found the pen, under the mattress in the cell. I never had any anaesthetic, someone got that wrong. Or maybe the doctors put it on me later. Couldn't tell you. Next question.' His voice was deliberately toneless. Goading her.

'No more questions,' Alison said, annoyed. 'You know how the system works, Robbie. You confess and we stop looking. You plead guilty and everyone's happy.'

'Yeah, I know. You stop looking and *everyone's* happy.' He gave her a significant look. 'But what can I do? I've got to say what I've got to say.'

'Why do you have to say anything if it isn't true?'

'Sometimes you need to do things. You need to do the best for your family, you know?'

'Is someone threatening your family? Is that what this is about? Who, Robbie? Come on, help me out.' He didn't reply. There was a knock on the door.

'His solicitor's here,' the young officer told Alison.

'You OK to see her?' Alison asked.

Robbie looked frightened, but took a deep breath and nodded his head.

'Let's make it official, shall we?' he said.

THIRTY-TWO

The room exploded with applause as Alison entered the station.

'Well done, boss.'

'Good work.'

Pats on the back, literally and metaphorically. Handshakes. Smiles. It was the usual reaction to the end of a case. Alison usually took a bow. Relishing the moment. Today she had never felt less like bowing. She made her way directly to Rogers' office.

'Bloody hell,' he said on seeing her, 'you look like shit. We got the bastard, you should be celebrating.'

'I know…' Alison began.

'Well, you could tell your face,' Rogers went on. 'You look like you lost a bloody tenner and found a turd. What's the matter? Too bleedin' straightforward for you?'

Alison shook her head; straightforward was the last thing it was.

There was a knock at the door; Paul entered without

waiting. Alison expected Rogers to bellow, but he simply said, 'Yes, Sergeant?'

He really must be in a good mood.

'Some further forensics, sir,' Paul said, beaming. 'They've finished analysing the contents of Izzy's stomach. Quite a mixture of stuff, all consistent with these smart drugs. Only odd thing is, there were tiny traces of speed too.'

'Speed?' Alison asked. 'How was that missed on the first tox tests?'

'Tiny traces – too small for the initial testing to pick up,' Paul said.

'So...'

Rogers interrupted. 'Another link to Smith, isn't it? Supplying Izzy with drugs. Makes sense.'

'Sorry, sir, but how does it make sense?' asked Alison. 'We're pretty sure it was Banks supplying the smart drugs. And there's been no suggestion Izzy was using speed.' It was Paul who answered.

'Lucy Jacobs said she thought Izzy had started taking drugs, remember. If Robbie was supplying her with speed then their whole relationship makes a lot more sense.'

'Good work,' Rogers said. 'Both of you.'

'But what about Banks?' Alison asked.

'What about him?' Rogers asked, before relenting. 'OK, I'll concede that maybe the drugs are connected to Banks. Doesn't detract from Smith as our killer, does it?'

Alison took a deep breath. She had to say it now or she would never say it.

'Did you speak to Dan Humphreys this morning?' she asked Paul.

He looked sheepish, but nodded his head.

'And?'

'He's sticking to the story. Says he saw Robbie heading for the Cawpers at about the time Andrea Mills was killed.'

'So Robbie couldn't have...'

'Mistaken identity,' Rogers bellowed, 'happens all the time. Smith confessed. It's done. Case closed.'

'I don't think he did it, sir.'

'Jesus, Dobson, what do you want? You want it tied with a ribbon? He confessed, didn't he? Gave details we hadn't released to the press, all that shit?'

'Yes, sir, it's just...' She paused. She knew she had to speak but she was not sure how to articulate her certainty. Robbie hadn't killed those women, she was convinced. 'It was the way he said it, like it was rehearsed. Like he was saying what he'd been told to say. And I don't trust that lawyer. And yesterday he tried to kill himself.'

'Because he's guilty...' Rogers said.

'I don't think...' Alison began.

'When will you understand, DI Dobson, that I do not care what you *think*. I care what you can prove. And as far as I'm concerned we can prove Robbie Smith killed Isabella Johnson and Andrea Mills.'

'It doesn't make sense...' Alison tried again.

'It makes perfect bloody sense,' Rogers said. 'He was seeing Izzy Johnson and she got sick of him. It's easy to see why she would, I'm getting sick of him myself. She dumped him. Maybe she was going to report his dealing, who knows. We've got DNA putting him at the scene at the time she was killed, he has no alibi... oh and yes... he's confessed.' This last word was dripping with sarcasm. 'He gets arrested, gets a fancy lawyer thanks to some mug in Leeds, who has a frankly incomprehensible crush on the lad, and we let him go. Oh, but of course you have conveniently told him the name of a witness who may or may not have seen him killing Izzy. Next thing Andrea Mills is dead. This time there's no DNA linking him to the victim, but he has a strong motive and... what was it... oh yes... he confessed. You see where I'm going with this, Dobson?'

'Yes, sir, but what about the timing? He couldn't have been with Andrea Mills when she was killed. He was seen.'

'Except he bloody confessed,' Rogers said again. 'Humphreys got it wrong. Why is that so hard for you to believe? And remember we have another witness who said Robbie *was* at the scene. Why are you so ready to believe that Henry Chapell was wrong? Why couldn't Chapell be right and Humphreys be wrong?'

Alison thought for a moment.

'Chapell was in a state of shock. He'd just found a body, a woman he knew. He knew Robbie was a suspect in the first killing and his mind leapt to a conclusion. Humphreys had no reason to get it wrong, and his friends all confirmed...'

'When I spoke to the friends again today they admitted none of them got a really good look,' Paul said, 'they were backing Dan up. They all thought it *could* have been Robbie but...'

'But Dan Humphreys is sticking to his story,' Alison said belligerently, 'even with you trying to sow doubt in his mind.'

Paul glowered at her and she knew she was being unfair. But why couldn't any of them see what she could see? Why were they taking Robbie's confession at face value?

'However much young Mr Humphreys sticks to his

story, witnesses are unreliable,' Rogers said. 'Everyone knows that.'

'So are confessions,' Alison said. Rogers scowled at her. 'I'm sorry, sir, but it just doesn't feel right.'

'I am not conducting an investigation based on the quivering of your womb, DI Dobson, do you understand?' Rogers yelled. 'You got a result... Whether by luck or judgement or fucking magic I don't care...'

His rant was interrupted by another knock at the door. They could all see Holly waiting on the other side of the glass.

'Come,' Rogers bellowed.

'Sorry to interrupt, sir,' she said quietly. 'DI Dobson asked me to...' Her voice trailed off.

'What is it, Holly?' Alison asked firmly before Rogers could intervene.

'I contacted Robbie's GP – no prescription for anaesthetic cream.'

'OK, thanks.'

Holly paused.

'Yes?' Rogers bellowed.

Holly kept her eyes on Alison.

'CCTV came in from the high street. It's a bit grainy, but we've got an image that looks like Robbie at around the time Dan Humphreys says he saw him.'

'Great,' Alison said.

'Means nothing,' Rogers said. 'Grainy image could be anyone.' Alison ignored him. She could tell Holly had more to say.

'Holly?'

The young officer took a deep breath.

'The tech guys have got some more info off Izzy's phone. I thought it might be useful.'

Alison rushed into the main office. Jack Kent had the information up on his screen.

'They managed to retrieve some deleted messages, to and from a pay-as-you-go phone.'

'Any idea whose number it is?'

Alison checked her notebook as she spoke. This was the same number she had tried to dial when Henry Chapell first handed her Izzy's phone.

'No,' Kent said, 'but take a look at the content. It's pretty interesting.' Alison looked over the thread of messages.

'*Can we just talk about it. I can explain.*'

This was sent to Izzy Monday morning. The day before she died.

Izzy's reply read:

'*OK – one chance to explain. I'll see you at school.*' Before the exchange on Monday there had been a string of incoming messages which Izzy seemed to have ignored. Alison scrolled up, reading each one.

'*Please let me explain.*'

'*You really have nothing to worry about.*'

'*You have as much to lose as I do. Try to be reasonable.*' Alison scrolled further back.

She reached a date not long after Christmas.

'*You seem to have the wrong idea about what's going on. Allow me to explain.*' There was a response from Izzy this time.

'*I really don't want an explanation. The only reason I'm not reporting it is for Dom's sake.*' It was the last message to the unknown number from Izzy until the day before she died. Alison smiled at Holly.

'I think we can guess who these messages are from, eh, Holz? You fancy giving him a ring?'

'Is he likely to answer?' Holly asked.

'I doubt it,' Alison said, smiling. She gave Holly the mobile number while she dialled a landline.

The phone Alison was calling rang twice before a man answered. In the background she could hear the insistent ringing of another phone.

'Good afternoon, Mr Banks,' Alison said smoothly. 'Don't you want to pick up the other line. It might be important.'

THIRTY-THREE

Paul was not pleased that they were going to talk to Banks and he let her know as they drove out of town. 'The case is closed. Robbie confessed. Whatever was going on with Banks and Izzy it's none of our business. Let the drug boys and girls have it.'

Alison ignored him. Robbie had confessed, but he had also asked Alison to find out the truth. The case was far from over. From the start this case had stunk of Simon Banks. Now Alison was determined to get to the bottom of why.

They saw Banks through the window of his living room as they pulled up to his cottage. He was sitting in an armchair by the fire reading a book. Alison could hear some classical music as she got out of the car and walked up the path to his door.

'Nice work if you can get it,' Paul said, 'suspended on full pay.' Alison banged loudly on Banks' door. He must have heard them arrive but he took his time answering.

'You think this is a wild-goose chase, don't you?' Alison said to Paul, as she knocked again.

'I think we have better things to do with our time.'

'Indulge me, will you? Like you keep telling me, Robbie's confessed. He's not going anywhere and the paperwork can certainly wait. I just have a bad feeling about this.' Paul's reply was cut off as Banks finally opened the door. Alison walked past him into the living room without invitation. He didn't try to stop her, although he looked far from happy.

'My solicitor said I wasn't to speak to you unless she was present,' he said.

'Oh yes, your solicitor,' Alison said, 'Hargreaves, Mitchell and Webster. The same people who are representing Robbie Smith as it happens. That's a coincidence, isn't it?'

Banks didn't speak.

'Of course you're welcome to call Ms Mitchell,' Alison went on, 'but I'm not sure I'd be so keen given the state poor Robbie ended up in after her last visit to him. You'll have heard about that, have you?'

'I heard he tried to kill himself,' Banks said, looking uncertain.

'Absolutely,' Alison said, 'that's what it looks like.' She put as much inflection as she could on the word 'looks', hoping to imply something more sinister.

'I'm sure you're quite right to trust Ms Mitchell. Absolutely. Like Robbie did. Feel free to call her, and while we're waiting for her to arrive we'll just arrest you and handcuff you and take you out of here in a police car with the sirens going and lock you in a cell at the station for a while.' Alison smiled serenely at Banks, as though she were inviting him to tea, as she took a seat without being invited. 'Alternatively we could avoid all that. We could just ask you a couple of questions. Here, quietly with no neighbours looking on. It's up to you of course.'

'I don't have to speak to you. I told you I had nothing to do with Izzy's death. I explained that note you found. And you had no right to search my laptop.'

'Your laptop. Yes, I'd almost forgotten. I'll be honest, Mr Banks, I thought we might find some porn on there. Single man, physically repulsive, working all day with these young girls…'

'And boys,' Paul said.

'And boys of course. We thought that laptop might just contain… well, you can imagine what we thought.' Alison paused. 'It's probably what everyone else will think when we haul you out of here in a police car. People talk.'

'Are you threatening me?' Banks asked.

'No.' Alison looked innocent. 'Threatening? DS Skinner, did you hear me make any threats to Mr Banks? No, I was just pointing out what can happen. No threat, absolutely not. Shall we go then?' Her tone remained pleasant, conversational even, but she accompanied the words by taking out her handcuffs. 'You can call your solicitor from the station. I'm sure she'll be a great comfort to you – like she was to Robbie.'

Banks shot her a look of deep dislike, but there was fear there too. 'What do you want?' he asked.

'Let's start with the drugs, shall we?'

'What drugs?'

'The ones we found in Izzy Johnson's room. The ones we found in her stomach. The ones on the order list on your computer. The ones you sold to Dominic Mills. You need me to go on?'

'You've got no proof. It's like I told Riordan, kids make stuff up. You can't believe a word…'

'Yeah? Well, I think people *will* believe the word of a dead girl, don't you? Especially one like Izzy Johnson. Maths genius, sports star, head girl?' She took out Izzy's phone in its evidence bag. 'We have texts on here confirming that you sold her those drugs.'

'I never texted her. You can check my phone.'

'Oh, we know you never texted her from *that* phone,' Alison said, dismissing the mobile Banks was holding out to her. 'These are from the one I heard ringing in the background when I called you earlier.'

'I don't know what you mean,' Banks said smoothly.

Alison knew he would have destroyed the phone by now but she was confident they would find it. Or at least enough of it to make a match. For now she just wanted to rattle Banks.

Unfortunately he seemed to be holding his nerve.

'I didn't text Izzy,' he said, 'and even if I had, which I didn't, there can't be any proof I sold drugs to her or to anyone. Besides, those sorts of drugs are freely available on the internet. They are, in fact, perfectly legal.'

'Not when they're laced with speed they're not.' Banks looked shocked but quickly recovered. 'I don't know anything about speed,' he said determinedly.

'We're not messing about anymore,' Alison said. 'This is a serious offence. Dealing carries a custodial sentence. We're not talking about some cosy school inquiry anymore. You're looking at being the focus of a full criminal investigation. And given that one of the girls you were dealing to is dead, I imagine a lot of eyes are going to be looking your way.'

Banks flinched but his voice was calm. 'I never harmed Izzy. I never knew anything about any speed. If the students at the school were taking cognitive enhancing drugs, and note I say "if", then those drugs are not illegal. Nor are they harmful in any way.'

'That's not what Dominic Mills thinks,' Alison said.

'Yes, well, he's entitled to an opinion. Thousands of people take those supplements with no ill effects.'

'And do those same people lace them with amphetamines and sell them to children?'

'I told you I don't know anything about that.'

'Supplying amphetamines is a serious offence,' Alison said calmly. 'And if Izzy was going to expose what you were doing I'd say that gives you the perfect motive for killing her.'

'Robbie Smith killed Izzy. Everyone knows that. Why else would he try to kill himself? Why else would he confess?'

'Who told you Robbie confessed?' she asked, knowing it had to be Mitchell.

'I… He tried to kill himself, that's as good as a confession, isn't it?'

Alison wasn't at all convinced. 'Where did you get the drugs, Mr Banks?' she asked.

'I'm not admitting to having anything to do with any drugs, but as I have said those drugs are freely available on the internet.'

'You're telling me you bought speed off the internet? And you cut it with Alzheimer's medication yourself? Then you laced it with speed just to see what would happen? I thought you taught history not chemistry. Where did you get the speed?'

'I told you I don't know anything about any speed. And I'm not saying I bought anything, I'm just saying you can get... that is to say *one* can find...'

'You cannot get the sort of mix of chemicals found in Izzy Johnson's system from the internet. You need to know the right people, have the right contacts or the right skills.'

'I'm sorry, but do I *look* like the sort of man who has "contact" with drug dealers. I'm a schoolteacher, Ms Dobson. I probably wouldn't know a drug dealer if I saw one. Except, of course, Robbie Smith and I have certainly never bought drugs from him. Now if you don't mind.' He stood to show them out of the door.

Alison was furious. She knew he was lying, but she had no way to prove it. Izzy's phone provided circumstantial evidence at best. Dominic Mills would confirm that he bought nootropics from Banks, as might some of the other students given a little pressure. But so what? Dominic had never mentioned speed. All he knew about were the ineffective smart drugs. It was a misdemeanour at best. It wasn't motive enough to kill. And Robbie, like an idiot, had confessed. She didn't know what sort of pressure had been applied to make him do it. Still the confession remained.

Reluctantly she followed Banks to the door.

'Thank you for your time,' she said smoothly as he opened the door for her. Politeness was her default when she was beyond rage.

Banks smiled uncertainly at her.

'By the way,' Alison continued, 'don't worry that you wouldn't know a drug dealer if you saw one. Just take a look in the mirror from time to time.' With that she strode out onto the path, glad to see an elderly woman walking her dog along the lane. Listening covertly.

'What's he been up to then?' the woman asked as Alison reached the pavement.

'We're just asking a few questions,' she said, although she wanted to say more.

'We don't often get police up here,' the woman went on conversationally, 'and it's the second time this week, isn't it?'

Alison didn't comment, just smiled.

'Mind you, it makes a change from the usual sort he has knocking at the door all hours.'

'What sort's that?' Alison asked.

'Young lads a lot of the time. Smoking and drinking some of them, which you think he'd put a stop to being a teacher. Then the other night it was some ungodly hour of the morning he had someone banging at the door.'

'Very antisocial,' Alison sympathised.

'Yeah, we like a quiet life up here.'

Alison nodded, looking around. Quiet to the point of comatose.

'I almost called the police as it happened,' the woman went on, 'but, well… I don't like to make a fuss.'

'It's not really a crime, I'm afraid,' Alison said, 'having late-night callers.'

'No, no, of course. It was more the way he drove through the village. You know the way they do when they have a fancy car. Think they own the place.'

'What night was that?' Alison asked.

'Night after that lassie got killed. Would have been Tuesday, or I suppose Wednesday morning by that time. About half past four it was.'

'Could you describe the car?' Alison asked, not holding out much hope.

The old lady laughed. 'Couldn't see much of it. Was a dark thing, blue or black. Has a really loud engine, I know that. One of those convertible roofs,' she said, smiling. 'Not much of a description, you'll think I'm useless.'

Alison just smiled.

'Miriam up at the pub would probably know. She heard it too. Right kerfuffle it was. We talked about it the next day, what a nuisance he is. And him a teacher.'

'I'll have a word with Miriam, shall I?' Alison asked. 'See if we can't do something about it. We don't want maniacs racing through the streets.'

'Well… if you're sure. It was a nuisance… and the language…' Alison smiled again.

'We'll see what we can do,' she said. She headed for the pub.

'What you playing at now?' Paul asked.

'Call it community relations.'

'What? If we can't get Banks for dealing drugs we're going to give him an ASBO, are we?'

'Just bear with me, will you?'

Miriam at the pub knew a lot about cars.

'BMW 5 series, soft top. Couldn't give you the reg but it was an 08 plate. And there was a second guy, couple of minutes later. Another Beemer, 7 series I think. He wasn't driving so fast though, seemed like he was there to sort of calm things down.'

'There were two cars?' Alison clarified.

'Yeah, but like I say, second fella wasn't causing any trouble.' Alison nodded.

'Thanks,' she said, 'that's very useful.' She pulled her notebook from her bag, then called Holly to confirm.

The phone call lasted a little over a minute.

'Thanks, Holz,' she said, 'that's great.'

'What?' Paul asked.

'Wouldn't know a drug dealer my arse,' Alison said with a satisfied grin as she headed back to Banks' house.

THIRTY-FOUR

'Do you know a man by the name of Carl Adams?' Alison asked, before Banks had even fully opened the door.

His face went very pale and for a moment he held the door for support. He recovered quickly though.

'No,' he said, with a slight quiver in his voice.

'You sure about that? Sure he wasn't here on Tuesday night? Him and his cousin Ben?'

'Never heard of them.'

Alison pushed past him into the house.

'Really? How odd that both their cars were seen up here on Tuesday night. Or more precisely the early hours of Wednesday morning. Social call, was it? Bit of an odd time to call, especially if you don't know either of them.'

'I don't know what you mean.'

'I saw a blue BMW soft top outside Sharon Smith's house this morning,' Alison said. 'The man in it was having a somewhat heated conversation with Sharon. I checked the plate. Came back to a very nasty little man by the name of

Carl Adams. Mr Adams has numerous convictions, some of them for drug dealing.'

'So?'

'So, a car meeting that same description was seen here, outside your house in the early hours of Wednesday morning. The night after Izzy Johnson was killed.'

'Coincidence,' Banks said. 'There are a lot of BMWs. I have a number of friends who drive them.'

'I find that hard to believe,' Alison said, 'that you have a number of friends I mean.'

Banks flushed, but said nothing.

'A second car was also seen outside your house that night. A car that fits the description of one belonging to a Mr Ben Adams.'

'I don't know him,' Banks said.

'Of course you don't,' she said sarcastically. 'Unlike Carl, Ben Adams doesn't have *any* criminal convictions. He is apparently a legitimate businessman. I say apparently, because of course appearances can be deceptive.' She gestured around Banks' cottage as if to imply he himself was not all he seemed. 'Now, Ben Adams just happens to be Carl's cousin,' she went on, 'and by an amazing coincidence he drove Robbie Smith home from Leeds that very evening. The evening after Izzy Johnson was killed. We thought he was doing a favour for a friend. But maybe he had business to attend to.'

'Not with me,' Banks said.

'You deny you know either of these gentlemen?' Alison said coolly.

'As I say, I have a number of friends who drive BMWs, and one car does look much like another in the dark.'

Alison said nothing.

'I apologise if my friends disturbed the neighbours by calling late at night,' Banks continued, 'but I assure you I have nothing to do with these Adams people.'

'Fair enough,' Alison said. 'It's possible your neighbours were mistaken. As you say, one car can look much like another – your elderly neighbours could easily have been confused. Would you say the same of South Yorkshire Police?'

'Sorry, I...'

'Would you say trained officers from South Yorkshire Police are unlikely to know one car from another?'

'I don't see what that has to do...' Banks stammered.

'Well, you see when Ben Adams first came forward as a possible alibi for Robbie, we did a quick check. Routine really. As I said, Mr Adams came up clean.'

'So?'

'Well, the same couldn't quite be said of his car.' Alison smiled. She referred to her notebook, but it was for show, she knew the details. 'A little over two weeks ago that same car, a BMW 7 series, was pulled over in the red-light district of Sheffield. Two men inside. The guy driving admitted he'd borrowed the car from a cousin. The guy gave his name as Carl Adams. His story checked out. The other guy, the passenger, claimed he was called Simon *Baines*.'

'As I say, I don't see...' Banks said again.

'People usually use similar names to their own if they have to come up with something quickly. Simon Baines does sound remarkably like Simon Banks, wouldn't you say?'

'Could have been anyone,' Banks said. 'I can't see how a case of kerb crawling can be relevant to anything.'

'That's the funny thing about police work, Mr Banks. Everything is relevant.' Alison smiled, taking her time. Enjoying herself for the first time. 'Mr Adams, Carl Adams I mean, hired a lawyer to deal with the police on his behalf over the kerb crawling. Can you guess? Of course you can. Hortence Mitchell. Is that just another coincidence?'

'Coincidences do happen.'

'Very true,' Alison said, opening her notebook very deliberately and reading a page. 'Here's yet another coincidence. The description of the passenger. 'White male, mid- to late-thirties, mousey brown hair, considerably overweight.' Sound like anyone you know?'

'Could be anyone…'

'Of course, of course. Could be a coincidence. But I don't think it is. I think when we get those police officers up here to identify the man they saw that day they're gonna be pointing the finger at you. And your little speech about not knowing anyone who deals drugs is going to start to look very shaky indeed. Wouldn't you say?' Alison asked.

'I need to make a phone call,' Bank said, his face ashen now.

'I'd have thought your solicitor was the last person you need now, given she's working for Adams,' Alison said.

'I don't want to talk to Mitchell I want to talk to DCI Hathaway.' Alison was taken aback. 'Who?'

'DCI Hathaway. Leeds. Let me call him. Or better still, you contact him. Tell him I'm ready to talk. Tell him I'm ready to make a deal.'

Alison was stunned.

Banks looked terrified but determined.

Alison looked at Paul in shock. This was the last thing

she had expected. 'Just tell me first. Tell me how the Adams boys are connected to all this? Are they responsible for Izzy and Andrea's deaths?'

'I'm not saying anything else. Take me to the station. Just keep me safe until Hathaway gets here. Please.'

It was the last word that persuaded Alison.

THIRTY-FIVE

Alison watched out of the police station window as a car pulled up and a large man got out. Immaculate suit, short hair, his shoes polished to a mirror shine.

She rushed downstairs to greet him.

'DCI Hathaway,' he said curtly to the desk sergeant. 'I'm expected.'

'I'll show the DCI in,' Alison offered.

He turned and looked at her without interest.

'DI Alison Dobson,' she said, holding out her hand.

He looked down at her for a moment, then he took the proffered hand for the briefest of seconds. It was like shaking a dead hand. Alison suppressed a shiver.

'It was my sergeant, Paul Skinner, who contacted you. I'm sure Paul explained that we were speaking to Simon Banks when he clammed up, refused to say more, asked to speak to you.'

'Good,' Hathaway said tersely.

'We're in the middle of a murder investigation here,' Alison said, annoyed by his tone.

Hathaway didn't respond.

'This way,' she said tersely, leading him up the stairs. Paul was in the incident room. 'DS Skinner, this is DCI Hathaway.'

'Pleased to meet you, sir,' Paul said, reaching out a hand.

Alison had to look away. If she caught Paul's eye during that weak handshake they were bound to giggle like schoolboys.

'So, fill me in,' Hathaway said, sitting at Alison's desk.

She pulled up a chair opposite and gestured for Paul to do the same.

'We're investigating the death of Isabella Johnson, you may have read about it.'

'Pretty girl, nice town, the papers have been full of it. You've had a second murder since, and the attempted suicide of a suspect I understand. Not often we find ourselves upstaged by you guys in the sticks.' He didn't smile. 'So what exactly does Simon Banks have to do with it?'

Alison quickly filled him in. The note that she had found from Banks when Izzy died. His almost perfect alibi teaching a classroom full of kids. The pills found in Izzy's stomach contents. The initials GLR found on Banks' computer which matched the compound elements in those pills. The texts on Izzy's phone that led her to question Banks again.

'So you accused him of dealing in so-called "smart drugs"?' Hathaway asked.

'Yes.'

'And that's when he asked to speak to me?'

'Not exactly,' Alison said. 'It was only when I mentioned Carl and Ben Adams that Banks decided he needed to speak to you.'

'You found a connection between Banks and the Adams boys?' Hathaway asked, sounding really interested for the first time.

'Yes.'

'Bloody hell, I've been trying to do that for months. How did you…?'

'We did our jobs,' Alison said, not liking the surprised tone of his voice.

Paul interrupted. 'Ben Adams was on our radar because Robbie Smith, our suspect, was with him the evening after Izzy was killed. One of our PCs checked him out. He doesn't have a criminal record, but his car had been logged during an operation in Sheffield a few weeks earlier. His cousin Carl was driving, with a passenger matching Banks' description. Carl Adams was also seen arguing with Robbie's mother this morning. So when a neighbour of Banks mentioned two BMWs seen in the village the night after Izzy's death…'

'You jumped to conclusions,' Hathaway said.

'We made an educated guess,' Alison corrected, 'and asked Banks about the connection.'

'Fuck me, I've been trying to link him to those bastards for months and you just stumble across a connection.'

'Hardly stumbled…' Alison began.

'OK, OK, call it inspired police work if you like,' Hathaway interrupted. 'It doesn't matter how you did it, what matters is the arsehole has agreed to talk to me.'

'And why is that so important?'

He looked at her for the longest time, as if deciding whether she was worthy of a reply. Eventually he spoke.

'Ben Adams is a clever man. Carl not so much. He's the muscle. It's Ben who's the brains behind it all.'

'Behind what?'

'We've had some odd drugs activity over the last few years.'

'Odd how?' Alison asked.

'Leeds is a big city,' Hathaway said, 'we always have drugs. But we've started having… well, let's say it's not been the usual suspects. It's been good kids, high-achieving kids getting into trouble. Petty theft, dealing, that sort of thing. All to fund drug habits.'

'Even good kids can get involved with drugs,' Alison said defensively.

'Quite, quite. But we had kids acting like addicts when they swore they'd never so much as smoked dope. We'd pick a kid up for shoplifting and they'd be clucking for a fix, but when we asked them what they were on – what they needed to help them with the withdrawal – they told us they didn't do drugs.'

Alison bit back the 'well, they would say that', which was on the tip of her tongue.

Hathaway held up his hand as if in surrender.

'I know, I know. But an addict will usually tell you when they need a fix, they'll do anything to avoid that pain. And like I say, these were good kids. I know the politically correct bollocks about drugs are everywhere and anyone can be affected. But you know as well as me, there are certain lowlifes you expect to arrest and others you don't.'

Alison said nothing. She didn't agree, but she wanted him to keep talking.

'You know how it is, Inspector. You work an area, you get to know what to expect. A crime happens, you know where to look. This wasn't like that. None of the youth workers or the social workers or the people working in the shelters had seen any changes. The usual addicts were still the same as ever and none of the usual dealers on the street had anything new to report. But there was this whole new batch of problems, all around the top colleges and the university. And one name kept popping up.'

'Ben Adams?'

Hathaway nodded.

'So Adams was the new dealer on the block?' Alison said. 'Muscling in, trying to take over?'

'Yeah. Only he wasn't taking over the old markets. He was targeting a whole new market. Or at least he was targeting an old market in a new way.'

Alison waited.

Hathaway sighed, as if explaining to her was more effort than it was worth. But she was buggered if she was going to hand Banks to him without knowing what it was all about.

'Speed,' he said at last.

'OK, well that's hardly new,' she said. But he had her attention.

'The way it was distributed was.'

'Inside smart drugs? Nootropics stacks?'

Hathaway smiled.

'You've been doing your homework,' he said. 'Yes, the kids were taking what they thought were cognitive enhancing pills, only to find someone had spiked them with amphetamine sulphate – or speed to me and you. A clever idea really. The buzz would let them work a bit harder, study longer, get the better grades they were after. And of course it's profitably addictive for the dealers.'

'So what? They upped the dose and upped the price as the kids got hooked?'

'That's the idea, yes. We got a few of the low-end dealers, students and a few lecturers at the college. But we knew there was more to it. The whole thing felt too organised.'

'Banks says you can get the stuff off the internet,' Alison said.

'Yeah. But these are bespoke pills we're talking about. I've no doubt they're manufactured in China or somewhere, but it's the importing that takes organisation. And the distribution. Logistics. That's where the money is. Logistics and marketing. Criminal enterprise is no different from any other business in that respect.'

'And Ben Adams was behind the logistics?'

'We had a couple of guys ready to give evidence against him last year. Low-level dealers ready to make a deal. Only the case collapsed.'

'What happened?'

'Hargreaves, Mitchell and Webster. They were hired to represent one of our guys and suddenly his story changed. He wanted to plead guilty, he was in it alone and he'd never heard of the Adams boys. Then the other defendant killed himself while on remand. Left a note saying he couldn't live with the guilt. We didn't have enough for the CPS to justify charges against either Ben or Carl Adams after that.'

'So where does Banks come in?'

'We've got a pretty good idea of the Adams' MO. Basically they recruit someone local. Sometimes a street dealer, but more often a lecturer or a tutor. They persuade them to sell the smart drugs, and as far as we know they're pretty straight to start with. For a few weeks or months. It's only later that they introduce the "special stuff".'

'The stuff cut with speed you mean?'

'We've been monitoring internet activity on some of the sites that sell these smart drugs,' Hathaway continued, nodding. 'When Mr Banks began to buy in bulk we decided to ask him a few questions.'

'And let me guess, he denied all knowledge.'

'Said his computer had been hacked. And we had nothing concrete to connect him to Carl or Ben.'

'Until now,' Alison said with a smile.

- - -

In the interview room Banks was sweating gently.

'You have to protect me,' he said. 'All that stuff you promised. You need to keep me safe.'

'You'll be fine, Simon,' Hathaway said casually. 'As long as you tell me the truth. *All* of it. OK?'

'OK.'

Banks talked for over an hour. Telling his tale with relish. He had met Ben Adams through a school fundraiser; his business had sponsored the football team for a while. They had socialised a few times. Ben took him to a nightclub in Leeds, wined and dined him, supplied him with ecstasy and introduced him to a young woman.

'I had no idea she was, well, you know... I didn't know Ben had paid.'

'And let me guess, you'd never done drugs before either,' Alison said sarcastically.

'It was only an E,' Banks spluttered, 'but... well, I would have lost my job.'

'So what happened then?' Hathaway asked, his tone a study in boredom.

'Ben said he had a business deal. I thought it was harmless… and I knew… I mean, he didn't say but I knew I couldn't really say no.'

'Because of the prozzy and the drugs,' Alison said, unable to resist the dig.

Bank said nothing, sweat rolling into his collar.

'What about Carl?' Hathaway asked.

'He came up occasionally. To keep an eye on me I think. That trip to Sheffield was his idea. He called it a treat. I knew I had to go along. I couldn't stop. You have to believe me.'

Alison didn't believe a word of it. The lying sack of shit would love to think of himself as a gangster. Paying for sex was probably the only way he could get any woman to go near him. But he wouldn't care because he didn't want a woman. He just wanted a warm place to put his dick.

Banks painted himself as an innocent victim, too frightened to stop. It didn't matter if it wasn't the truth, what mattered was that he kept talking. What mattered was that he gave them Carl and Ben Adams.

'I didn't want any of this,' Banks said. 'People are winding up dead. That's not what I signed up for. Izzy and Mrs Mills. And what they did to Robbie. I don't want… You have to make sure that's not me.'

Alison looked away from him in disgust. He wouldn't have cared if the people who were dead were teenagers who had overdosed on a drug they thought was safe. It was only when his own skin was at stake that he suddenly grew a conscience.

'Hargreaves, Mitchell and Webster?' Hathaway asked.

'What about them?'

'How do they get people off? Intimidation? Bribes?'

'I don't know,' Banks said. 'I've told you all I know.'

'Right. I think I'm done,' Hathaway said suddenly, turning to Alison.

'You have to protect me,' Banks said pathetically.

'You answer this young lady's questions, like a good lad. And you testify against Ben and Carl and then we can think about getting that protection you're so keen on.'

'Who killed Izzy Johnson?' Alison asked, deciding to be direct.

'I don't know.'

Hathaway gave a loud tut.

'Not very helpful, Simon. I'm not very impressed.'

'I honestly don't know,' Banks said, 'but...' he paused, licking his lips and sweating again, 'I told Carl Adams that she was being awkward. Telling people that the pills didn't work. Trying to get people to stop taking them.'

'You told Carl that? When?'

'Couple of days before she died. He said to persuade her to take some of the new batch. Explain to her that these were a new formula – that they would *really* work. They were the first ones with the extra ingredient. I didn't want to but I did. That's what the note was about.'

'*Meet me as usual. I can explain,*' Alison said, quoting the note they had found on Izzy's body.

'Tuesday morning was the usual time for... well, all the kids knew Riordan got in late on a Tuesday. I sent Izzy the note and she came to the classroom. I had to get her to take something. I couldn't risk her stopping the other kids taking stuff. I couldn't risk making Carl angry.'

'So she took some more tablets? When was that?'

'The day she died. I told her it was a new formula, asked her to try it out properly, scientifically.'

'And she fell for that?'

'For all she was clever, Izzy wasn't really very streetwise.' Paul sneered.

'Maybe she didn't expect her teacher to be trying to get her hooked on speed. Not an unreasonable position to take I would think.'

Banks didn't reply.

'Do you think Carl Adams killed Izzy?' Alison asked.

Banks looked terrified, glancing from Alison to Hathaway and back.

'I don't know. He rang me Tuesday afternoon. Told me to make sure there was no way I could be connected to Izzy. That was before I even knew she was dead. That's when I wiped everything off the computer and off my other phone. Then him and Ben came to see me, that night. To make sure.'

'Make sure of what?'

'I don't know exactly, just… They just said this better not come back on us.'

'You've no proof either of them killed Izzy?'

Banks shook his head.

'Did either of them tell you directly that they wanted Izzy killed?'

'No, no. They just came round that night… after… after she died. They said I needed to make sure they weren't implicated in any way. They were furious when I said you'd taken my laptop, even though I told them I'd wiped it. Carl said I should have taken a hammer to it, but it was nearly new…'

'Did Carl tell you Izzy was dead? Did he say he killed her?'

'No. When he rang he just... he said she was a liability, that he was worried she'd go to the police and for me to make sure there was nothing connecting her to the drugs or to me.'

'How did Hortence Mitchell get involved?' she asked.

'They said they needed the laptop back, just to be sure there was no link to Izzy. So they sent Mitchell in as my lawyer. Once I got it back Carl made me destroy it. Stood over me while I did it. Cost me 800 quid that laptop.'

'Poor you,' Paul said unsympathetically.

'What about Andrea Mills?' Alison asked. All along she had assumed Andrea was killed because she witnessed the first murder.

'Andrea was always poking her nose in. She had a go at me once, threatened me with the police. But I sorted it. I told her Dom would be in as much trouble for taking the tablets as I was for selling them. That shut her up. But I told Carl at the time, and then when Izzy was killed and you were asking questions about drugs and... I suppose maybe Carl or Ben got worried that she'd cause trouble. Or maybe she really did see more than she told anyone the day Izzy died.'

'So Andrea was killed because she might have gone to the police?'

'That's what they do,' Banks said. 'That's why you have to make sure...'

'Yes, yes,' Hathaway said in his bored drawl, 'we'll keep your precious hide safe.'

'Once Robbie was arrested they set him up? Told him to confess?' Alison asked.

'It was the best way to keep the focus away from me, and away from them. They gave Robbie a choice. He could confess and go to jail, or he could top himself. Either way everything would point at Robbie and no one would be looking at them. They told me it's worked before. Only Robbie couldn't even kill himself properly.'

Alison felt her temper rise, but she held it in check.

'What if he didn't agree to that choice?'

'I don't know. They knew where his mum was and his brothers, didn't they... so...'

'Did Carl Adams tell you that? About Robbie having a choice? About the threat to his family?'

'It was Ben. He was quite upset actually. I think he quite liked Robbie. But business is business. That's how they operate.'

Alison thought of Robbie faced with a choice that was no choice. So sad and so desperate that he had wanted a way out no matter how messy or painful. She was thankful again that she had got to him in time. Whether he had waited to hear her arrive, or whether he had really meant to die, she would never know. All she knew was that now he had decided to live, Robbie had trusted her to help him find a way out. He had confessed in such a way that he knew he'd never be believed. He had trusted Alison to find the truth, and now she felt like she was finally getting there.

There was a knock at the door. A quiet PC Alison barely knew said, 'Excuse me, ma'am, there's a woman...'

Before she could finish her sentence Hortence Mitchell burst into the room.

'I expressly told my client not to speak to you without my presence,' Mitchell said imperiously.

Banks looked plainly terrified. It reminded Alison of the look on Robbie's face when Mitchell had turned up to defend *him* at Penbury station. It certainly wasn't the face of someone who felt their saviour had arrived.

'Oh, I'm afraid Mr Banks isn't your client anymore,' Alison said smoothly. 'He has asked for new representation.'

'Are you sure you want to do that, Mr Banks?' Mitchell said significantly, watching Banks. 'I have been authorised by my firm to represent you for as long as it takes.'

'And which firm would that be, Ms Mitchell,' Hathaway asked, 'Adams and Adams?'

Mitchell said nothing.

'I don't want you,' Banks said at last, his voice quivering.

'Don't worry,' Alison said smoothly, 'given what Mr Banks has just told us I'm sure you'll have plenty of other clients to keep you busy.'

Mitchell gave no reaction other than to turn sharply on her heel and leave.

- - -

'Police in Leeds have pulled in the Adams boys,' Paul said, finding Alison in her office an hour later. 'So far they're denying everything.'

'What a surprise,' Alison said.

'The drugs charge will hold up,' he said. 'Banks gave Hathaway enough verifiable facts. And you know how these things are. Once it's clear they've been toppled there'll be other informants desperate to give their side of the story.'

Alison nodded.

'Once Robbie knows they're going to be spending some

serious time inside he's bound to retract his confession,' Paul continued.

'I'll make sure he knows he and his family are safe,' Alison said, but she was shaking her head. 'None of it proves they killed Izzy and Andrea though, does it? All we've got is hearsay.'

'The bastards did it,' Paul said.

'Yeah, but we can't prove it.'

'They'll do jail time,' Paul said. 'That's something, isn't it? They could get up to fourteen years for the speed, more if we can prove coercion and perverting the course of justice.'

'Yeah, only you know how it works. Big men on the outside, big men on the inside.'

She felt depressed suddenly. They had found the truth, but that wasn't justice. Her job was to find out what happened, to find out who did it and then to bring them to justice. She felt like she had barely done half a job.

'Maybe Robbie knows more than he's saying?' Paul said hopefully.

'Yeah. But it's likely to be his word against theirs, isn't it?'

'Things change all the time,' Paul said.

'Meaning?'

'There might not be any useful forensics at the moment, but Carl and Ben Adams will be inside for a while, and science moves on.'

'So I need to be patient?'

'Basically.' Paul smiled.

'Bollocks to that,' Alison said.

THIRTY-SIX

Alison decided to visit Robbie again. Maybe Paul was right and he would have something useful to tell her. Maybe she just wanted to know he was alright, to know she had done something right in this whole case.

Robbie was sleeping. She was surprised, when she arrived at the hospital, to find Niall Riordan at his bedside.

'How is he?' she asked Riordan.

He put down his book and looked up at her. 'They say he's going to be fine. Just tired. We had a bit of a chat, but he just sort of drifted off. I didn't want to leave him… so…' He indicated the book.

'I'm surprised to see you here,' Alison said.

'I wanted to see how he was. I heard he confessed. Is it true? Was Henry right about what he saw after all?'

'I can't talk about an open investigation,' she began.

'Of course, of course. I just… I can't believe he could have killed anyone if I'm honest.' Alison nodded, unsure what to say. She hated the idea that Riordan believed Robbie was a killer, but she knew it was too soon to reveal what

Banks had said. For now Robbie had confessed and Alison had to go along with it.

'He looks so young and helpless, doesn't he?' Riordan went on. 'And I know his mother has to work, so… I didn't like the idea of him being alone. I know he's no longer a pupil, but I can't help feel… well, I suppose I feel like the school let him down. Like *I* let him down.'

Alison nodded; she felt much the same way.

They sat quietly for a while. The silence between them companionable.

'He was a nice kid, you know,' Riordan said at last, gesturing Robbie. 'Bit cheeky, bit naughty, but I always liked him. He was bright, too. I could never understand why his grades were so low.'

'Not academic I guess,' Alison said.

'Yeah. It's a shame isn't it that kids think they're dumb if they just can't jump through the hoops we expect of them. It's one of the things I've always regretted about teaching, the fact that I spend so much of my time trying to reach government targets and as a result I fail kids like Robbie.'

'You haven't failed him. He had a chance, he could have taken it. He chose not to.'

'It's a lot harder for some children,' Riordan said. 'Not all children come from stable homes. You'd be surprised by how many children haven't even had a decent breakfast when they get to school. It's hard for them to concentrate, or to do well, when their home lives are chaotic.'

'Hard, but not impossible,' Alison said, with a smile.

Some people saw her childhood in her, and some people didn't.

It was hard to go to school with no breakfast. It was

hard to go when you'd had to clean up your mother's vomit before you could get into the kitchen. It was hard when you had to try to get your little sister and baby brother out of bed. Harder still when you had to leave that little brother with a mother you doubted was fit to care for him. Hardest of all was when your mother hadn't come home for days, there was no food, no nappies and you had to make the decision to call the social workers.

It *was* hard but it could be done. There was always a choice, always a chance. Some kids had a better chance, easier choices to make. But survival was always a decision.

'There was a point,' Riordan was saying, 'when I thought Robbie might turn it around. He'd been a bit of a handful at primary school apparently, but when he came up in Year 7 it was like he wanted to turn over a new leaf. Then there was all that trouble at home and things went downhill again.'

'What happened?' Alison asked absent-mindedly.

'Oh, the mother got a new boyfriend. Let's just say Mr Adams was not the most salubrious of men. Bad influence on Robbie.'

'Adams?' Alison asked. 'Did you say her boyfriend was Adams? Can you remember his first name?'

'Sorry, no, I could get my secretary to…'

'No, it's fine it doesn't…' Alison's voice trailed away.

She thought of Carl Adams shouting at Sharon in the street. The familiar way he had called her Shaz. Could he have been her partner once?

'I need to go,' Riordan said, looking at his watch. 'Always work to do. I feel better leaving him with someone.'

'You're a good man,' Alison said.

Riordan dismissed her with a wave of his hand. The way good men do.

As soon as Riordan had left the room Alison shook Robbie gently to wake him. She didn't have the time, or the patience, to wait by his bedside like a loving relative.

'Izzy?' he asked groggily as he awoke. The look of disappointment on his face as he reached full consciousness broke Alison's heart.

'I need to ask you a couple more questions,' she said gently.

'For fuck's sake,' Robbie said, 'I confessed. I told you I did it. What do I have to do to get left the hell alone?'

Alison didn't answer, instead she said, 'We've taken Simon Banks in for questioning.' Robbie looked terrified.

'What? Why? Does Mitchell know?'

'Banks didn't want her there,' Alison said, not really answering the question.

'Fucking hell. Where's my mum?'

'Robbie, calm down,' Alison said. 'It's OK.'

'Don't tell me it's OK,' he said. 'You've got no idea.'

'So tell me.'

'I killed them, OK. I confessed, right? Remember that. So why are you arresting Banks?'

'We haven't arrested him,' Alison said, 'he's helping us with inquiries.'

'Bloody hell, is he mad?' Robbie said. 'Doesn't he know how those people work?'

'Which people?' Alison asked.

'No one.' Robbie was the sullen teenager again.

'No one, like Ben and Carl Adams?' Alison asked.

Robbie looked shocked, shook his head, said nothing.

'Banks has told us about the drugs. That it was Ben and Carl Adams supplying them. They've been arrested. Both of them.'

'Jesus, what is Banks playing at? These people don't mess about.'

'Neither do I,' Alison said. 'I just came to tell you that no matter how powerful they think they are, no one is above the law. Trust me.' Robbie laughed without humour.

'You don't trust me?'

'I don't think you know who you're dealing with,' Robbie said.

She smiled. Why were so many people determined to think she had never come across bad men before? As if she had been born middle-aged in a small rural town. 'OK, so enlighten me.'

Robbie didn't speak.

'Alright,' Alison said, 'I'll guess, shall I? You tell me when I'm a million miles off the mark.' Again Robbie didn't speak.

'Carl Adams used to date your mum. Maybe that's how he got to know the area. Maybe he did a little bit of drug dealing up here, mixing business and pleasure. So when the little scheme him and Ben have going in Leeds goes pear-shaped it makes sense to move operations up here. I mean, who's going to stop them? Everyone knows the police are all country yokels, right?'

Robbie laughed without much humour.

'Of course they needed a local contact and that's where Banks fits in.'

'Dickhead thought it was his idea,' Robbie said as if he couldn't stop himself.

'So what happened, Robbie? I know Izzy found out the

original stuff was useless, what about the new stuff, the stuff laced with speed?'

'What?'

Alison didn't elaborate. The shock on Robbie's face told her he knew nothing about the new merchandise.

'What happened, Robbie? The day Izzy died.' He didn't say anything.

'We've arrested both of them. They can't touch you.'

'Arrested is a long way from charged and charged is a long way from convicted and sent down,' he said at last.

'They're going down, Robbie. Banks isn't as dumb as he looks. He taped conversations, saved emails and texts on his phone. I think he knew it might come to this and decided to get himself some insurance.'

Robbie nodded. 'Insurance is useful,' he said. 'I confessed, remember.'

'Yeah, and I didn't believe you. Remember?' He smiled. Still he said nothing.

'Look, this is off the record,' Alison said. 'Just you and me. Did they do it? Did Carl or Ben kill Izzy?'

'I don't know.'

Alison looked sceptical.

'No, really I don't know. I knew they were pissed off with her. She'd threatened to report Banks to the police. She didn't know... she didn't know anything really... about Carl and Ben... about the sort of men they are. She thought... she thought if you told the truth nothing could hurt you.'

He smiled fondly at the memory.

Alison nodded. Both she and Robbie knew the truth wasn't always enough. That was the difference between people like them and people like Izzy. They knew, first-hand, that life wasn't always fair, that doing the right thing or telling the truth didn't keep you safe.

'Why did she take the drugs the day she died?' Alison asked.

'She needed a new batch, to take to the police. Her old man had confiscated the last lot. She told me she was going to get some more off Banks. I guess he made her swallow one in front of him. Like he didn't trust her or something.'

'So she *was* planning to go to the police?'

'I don't know. I tried to persuade her not to.'

'Is that why you argued the day she died?'

Robbie nodded sadly. 'It started off so lovely that afternoon. She called me and I met her and we… got together. She was in a funny mood though. She started going on about Riordan, about the row they'd had.'

'The reason she left school?' Alison asked.

'It was summat and nowt. She'd realised he'd got a calculation wrong and he wouldn't listen or something. Normally she wouldn't give a shit, but that day she was going on and on and she was talking twenty to the dozen, raving. It makes sense now you've said about the speed, but I didn't know. I just thought she was being weird. Then she was talking about Banks, how she was going to get him done, all that. I tried to tell her to be careful, but she wouldn't listen.' He paused, remembering, shaking his head. 'She got really pissed off when I said I was going to Leeds. Told me to "just go"… and I did. I left her… I just walked away.'

'It's not your fault,' Alison said.

'I told Ben that she wouldn't go to the police. I spent the whole bloody evening with him, letting him perv all over me and pretending I was flattered or something. I wanted to distract him, and all the time, all the time it was already too late. I should have known they'd do something, him or Carl. They were proper pissed off. I thought I could keep Ben sweet. I thought that'd keep Izzy safe. Bloody idiot, right?'

'Had you seen either Ben or Carl up here that day? Before Izzy died?' Robbie shook his head. 'No. That's not to say they weren't here, only I never saw either of them.'

'But Ben offered to give you a lift home that night, after the party.'

'Said he had some business,' Robbie confirmed.

That *business* was seeing Banks. Making sure everything was cleared up and any connection between himself and Banks and Izzy was eradicated.

'I never thought they'd kill her,' Robbie said, 'I would never have left her.'

'But you thought they'd do something,' Alison said. 'You knew she might be in trouble? That's why you warned her?' Robbie dropped his head, crying.

Now the suicide attempt suddenly made sense. Guilt. Not for having killed Izzy, but for having left her. He had known that Adams would seek to silence her, hurt her, possibly quite badly, and he had walked away. He had been a coward. He had been a little boy.

Guilt.

That was the only thing that could explain the ferocity and conviction of those gouges in his skin. He didn't want to die, but he *did* want to suffer.

'I haven't even got anything to remember her,' Robbie said. 'I had pictures on my phone, loads of pictures. But the bloody thing got stolen.'

Alison doubted that. She was certain now that Ben

Adams had removed the phone to make sure there was nothing on there to link him to Izzy.

'We have *her* phone,' Alison began. 'Once the case is over...'

'She never kept any photos of us on her phone,' Robbie said. 'Her mum used to check it all the time. She couldn't risk it. I don't think Mrs Johnson would exactly think of me as perfect boyfriend material.' Alison said nothing to that.

'Have you found her journal?' Robbie asked. 'There was a picture in the front. I told you, didn't I? A photo of us...'

'I'm afraid Izzy burnt it,' Alison said softly, 'a few days before she died.'

'Bollocks. Izzy'd never do that. Bloody Carl Adams probably has it, probably thinks there's some formula for a new chemical compound in there or something. Chimp's so bloody dumb he wouldn't know an equation from a hole in the ground.' Alison nodded. Glad to see Robbie angry. He'd need the anger to get him over the grief.

'When you're ready I'll need you to retract that confession, tell me the truth officially,' she said compassionately.

'When I know Mum's safe,' he said.

'OK.' Alison was about to leave when a thought occurred to her. 'When you confessed, Robbie, you gave details. About how Izzy and Andrea Mills were killed.'

'So?'

'They were details we never released to the press. How did you know?'

'Off the record?'

'For now,' Alison agreed.

'Mitchell,' Robbie said softly. 'She told me what to say.'

'I suppose she was passing on the information Ben or Carl Adams had given to her?'

'Dunno. I doubt it though. They never trusted anyone, can't see them giving Mitchell details of what they'd done.'

'So who gave her the information?' Alison asked.

'All I know is she told me if I told you all the details she gave me then you'd believe me. She said old school friends could come in handy.'

Alison nodded. A conversation in a corridor. Jack Kent greeting Mitchell warmly. 'We really must catch up'... 'We were at school together.'

Bastard.

Back at the station Rogers was in his usual good mood.

'Managed to palm this one off onto someone else, eh, Dobson?' he said.

'Sir?'

'Jesus, you can't even be bothered with the "sorry, sir" now. I presume rather than "sir" you meant to ask me what I was referring to.'

'Yes, sir. The inflection in my tone was intended to indicate that I had not understood fully what you were implying and that I wished you to clarify. I merely hoped that by using shorthand we might save time.'

Rogers gave her a grudging smile. 'Very good, Dobson, very good,' he said. 'What I was referring to was that the whole shooting match has now been passed to DCI Hathaway and the glory seekers in Leeds. We do the bloody graft, they get the bloody arrests.'

'Yes, sir,' Alison said.

She was disappointed, but really this was inevitable. They had been after Ben and Carl Adams for a long time.

And the drugs offences were the ones that would get those boys real prison time. Unless some new forensic evidence came to light or a witness suddenly came forward it seemed unlikely either Carl or Ben Adams would ever be charged with murdering Izzy Johnson or Andrea Mills.

Two families would never get a chance of their day in court. None of it felt right. There was nothing she could do.

'You want a couple of days off?' Rogers asked unexpectedly. 'You were due leave when this came up, weren't you?'

Alison was halted for a moment by the reasonableness of his tone, but she shook her head. She couldn't go off and relax. She could think of nothing she wanted to do less. She needed to get straight back into work. Straight on to the next case. One that hopefully would end more satisfactorily.

'No thank you, sir,' she said to Rogers. 'I'd like to keep working.'

'Fair enough,' Rogers said. 'The rate you work it's almost like you're on holiday anyway.' Alison smiled, glad that he was back to his cantankerous self.

'It's almost four,' Rogers said, looking at his watch. 'Finish now and I'll see you in the morning.'

'Thank you, sir.'

'And tell Skinner the same. He's no bloody use without you anyway, mooning around like a faithful puppy.'

'Yes, sir,' Alison said.

She didn't move, making a decision.

'Well, what are you waiting for? You need it in writing? Fuck off home.'

'Yes, sir... I just... I need to tell you something.' Rogers sighed.

'OK, go on.'

'Remember when Robbie confessed you pointed out that he knew details about the murder that we hadn't released to the press.'

'Yes. I assumed at the time it was because he was guilty. Now I assume his friends Mr and Mr Adams told him.'

'Robbie's sticking by his confession for the time being.'

'Make your point, Dobson,' Rogers said, but without real heat.

'He told me, off the record, that it was Mitchell, the solicitor, who gave him those details.'

'How terribly unprofessional of her,' Roger said grimly. 'And I suppose she got the information from Carl or Ben Adams.'

'Robbie says it was an old school friend. Of Mitchell's.'

'I assume you have a point, Dobson, please make it.'

'Jack Kent went to school with Hortence Mitchell.'

'Fuck,' Rogers said quietly. He was silent for a long moment. 'Leave it to me,' he said at last. 'Bugger off home and I'll clear up all the shit. That's what I get paid the big bucks for after all.' Alison didn't need telling twice.

She would go home to her family. She would get drunk with her husband and tomorrow there would be a new case and life would move on. Her life at least, not those of Izzy Johnson or Andrea Mills.

THIRTY-SEVEN

Alison expected the house to be empty when she arrived home; instead the whole family were there. The girls were eating fish-finger sandwiches while Nick drank a cup of tea. Her mother-in-law had left that morning and the house felt like theirs again.

'What're you doing home?' Nick asked, standing up to make Alison tea.

'I was going to ask you guys the same question,' she said.

'Dad picked us up straight from school,' Mabel said. 'We didn't have to go to out-of-school club at all. I mean not even a bit.'

Her excitement made Alison smile and tore at her heart at the same time. Such a small thing to make her daughter so happy.

'It's my open evening tonight,' Beatrice said. 'Is that why you've come home early? You said you'd come too if you could.'

'Of course,' Alison said. 'I got off early especially.' Bea leapt up from the table and threw her arms around her mother. It was an increasingly rare show of affection from the ten-year-old. Alison held her tight.

'You girls go wash your hands and faces then we'll get going,' Nick said.

They trooped out of the room.

'Open evening?' Alison asked as soon as they were gone.

Nick laughed.

'You really aren't going to win that mother-of-the-year badge, are you?' he said.

Alison smiled.

'It's the open evening up at the Penbury High. Bea gets to go and look around, find out who her form teacher will be next year and all that shit.'

'Was that actually on the invitation? All that shit?' Alison laughed.

'Yes, I distinctly remember that's what it said.' He smiled. 'You don't have to come if you don't feel up to it.'

'Are you kidding? Did you see the excitement on her face? Besides, it'll be good to see around the school.'

Nick smiled and put his arm around her. 'You home early because this case is over?' he asked.

'Sort of,' she said. 'I'll tell you about it later. It's all pretty shit to be honest.' Mabel burst in, carrying the largest teddy she owned. 'Can I take Biggy Bear?' she asked.

'I think he's a bit big,' Alison said. 'We don't want him getting hurt.' Mabel looked as if she was about to cry. She was very good at looking as if she was about to cry. Alison and Nick generally ignored her.

'That's shit to be honest,' she said, turning on her heels and walking out.

Alison burst into laughter.

Bad mother.

'I had a phone call from Mrs Williams today,' Nick said, grinning. 'She said Mabel had called one of the other girls a dick.'

Alison giggled.

'She was concerned that Mabel was exposed to "inappropriate language".'

'Oh for fuck's sake,' Alison said, laughing again. 'What did you say?'

'I told the silly old trout to go screw herself.' Alison shook with laughter.

'Really?'

'Well, no. Really I said I couldn't imagine where she had picked up a word like that and I said that I would have a word with her about what language was appropriate for a six-year-old.'

'It doesn't seem to have sunk in,' Alison said, still smiling.

'I blame the parents,' Nick said.

'Oh God yes, me too.'

'I'll go speak to her, shall I?'

'No, I'll go. I'll just get changed quickly then I can be in full mummy mode.'

Once she was in jeans and a clean shirt she knocked on Mabel's door and went in. Mabel was quite happily reading a book to all her bears. No sign of tears now there was no audience to see them. Alison gave her the old speech about how swearing wasn't nice, how it wasn't clever and just meant that people couldn't think of anything more original to say.

Mabel listened through it all.

'You said it, Mummy.'

'I know I did, and I was wrong.'

'Does that mean you're not very clever?'

Alison smiled.

'I suppose it does,' she said.

'I don't want to be clever,' Mabel said.

'Of course you do,' Alison replied. 'Why wouldn't you?'

'That big girl at Penbury High was clever and then she got killed,' Mabel said.

Alison took a deep breath. She faced the worst that people did to each other every day, but she still believed most people were good. Almost everyone was decent and just trying to get along. She wanted her children to believe that for as long as they could. There would come a time when Mabel needed to know about all the bad things that people could do to each other. A time when she needed to learn to be careful and cautious and suspicious. But not yet. Not at six.

'That big girl's name was Isabella,' she said. 'She was really unlucky that she met some very bad people and they hurt her. It had nothing to do with being clever. And we've caught the men now so they can't hurt anyone else.'

'Olly Green says if you come top in maths the bogeyman will get you. He says that's what happened to that girl.'

'Isn't Olly Green the one who ate a blue crayon once?'

'Yeah.'

'Well, if he thinks crayons are a tasty snack I don't think we have to take anything he says too seriously, do we?'

Mabel giggled. 'He is a bit of a dick,' she said, smiling with feigned innocence at her mother.

Alison pretended not to hear her. 'Come on,' she said,

'let's get going. Are you excited to look around Bea's new school?'

'Yeah, I'm going to be going there soon, aren't I?'

'No, I've told you,' Alison smiled, 'you're never growing up. You're going to be in Year 2 for ever and ever.' Mabel giggled again.

'I'm *so* not. I'm going to be in Year 3 really soon.' It made Alison's heart ache, this eagerness her daughters had to grow and change when all she wanted was to keep them the same.

'I can't find a bobble,' Beatrice shouted from her bedroom.

'Just wear your hair down,' Alison said.

The instant sigh told Alison she had said the wrong thing.

'I can't... Oh my God you've got no idea... I look like an idiot.'

'I'll sort it,' Alison said, heading into the bathroom and looking in the drawer where the bobbles were kept.

Predictably there were no bobbles.

'We'll improvise,' she said desperately. She found a little pile of tie-wraps in Nick's office. He often used them to tidy cables. Alison grabbed a handful.

'You cannot be serious,' Bea said.

'Trust me.'

She made a ponytail of her daughter's hair and used a tie-wrap to hold it in place. A small section of hair twisted around to disguise the plastic wrap and the disaster was averted.

'Thanks, Mum,' Bea said, kissing her on the cheek.

Alison felt her spirits lift. There were times when life

could be so simple. When problems could be so easily solved.

If only all times were like this, she thought, as she slipped the rest of the tie-wraps into her pocket.

'Let's go see your new school,' she said cheerfully.

'It's massive, Mum,' Bea said as they made their way into the hall of the secondary school.

'You'll soon find your way around,' Alison said, giving Bea's hand a squeeze. Her daughter smiled up at her uncertainly.

They took their seats and the head boy and girl gave speeches. Alison realised with a pang that it should have been Izzy Johnson up there talking. If it weren't for Carl and Ben Adams and Simon Banks, Izzy would have been the one giving a speech. Anger bubbled in her at the injustice of it. What they had done and the fact that she hadn't yet been able to prove that they had done it.

She looked down at Beatrice beside her and wanted to cling on to her so tightly that she would never grow up. While Beatrice was a child she could keep her safe. Once she was grown, who knew?

Bea was sensible, she was clever, surely that would help. Alison thought again of Izzy. A clever girl. A genius some had called her. It hadn't kept her safe.

Nothing could keep Alison's children safe really. All she could do was cross her fingers and hope for the best. Protect Beatrice and Mabel as best she could and hope for luck. Because in the end that was all there was. Izzy had had bad luck, ultimately it had been nothing more than that.

After the talks in the hall some of the Year 7 children came to show the younger ones and their parents around the school. Beatrice immediately spotted Skyla, a slightly older girl from her dance class, who agreed to show them around. She was proud of her school and keen to show it off.

'This is the maths room,' Skyla said happily. 'I'm in top set with Mr Riordan.' His name brought a joyous blush to her cheeks.

The classroom wasn't like any Alison had had as a child. Every desk had a laptop and at the front was an interactive whiteboard. Children were gathered around the whiteboard attempting impossible-looking puzzles. There was a young man offering help and showing the kids what to do.

'Where's Mr Riordan?' Skyla asked, obvious disappointment in her face.

'He's at a meeting,' the young man said. 'I'm in charge.' Beatrice was immediately absorbed with the whiteboard. She loved Maths and she loved technology. This was going to be her second home. Mabel on the other hand was getting restless. It might have been a bad idea to bring their younger child but somehow Alison wanted them all to be together tonight.

'Mabel, come here,' Nick called.

Alison looked up, just in time to see the stack of papers and books on the desk topple.

'Oh for God's sake,' Nick said.

Half of her wanted to laugh. Half of her was embarrassed. The whole room had turned to look at them. Some of the children were giggling. Nick had stooped to pick up the fallen books, red in the face.

'Come here, Mabel,' Alison said firmly. 'That was very naughty, those are Mr Riordan's books.'

And then she froze.

She wasn't even looking at Nick, she was looking at Mabel, but still she saw it. In his hand as he picked up the books. A flash of purple went off like an explosion in her head. The way you see a car speeding towards you when you're about to step out into the road; the way you sense when someone walks into a room, even with your back turned. Her mind saw it before her eyes registered what she had seen.

'Can I just have a look at that?' she asked, her voice trembling slightly.

'You OK?' Nick asked, holding out the book towards her.

'Not sure.'

Here it was in her hands. Purple with an owl on the front. The sort of thing she might buy for Beatrice or Mabel. The sort of notebook she would have chosen herself when she was a teenage girl.

Inside the paper was plain, unlined, and about half the book had been filled with equations, squiggles, strange marks Alison didn't even know the meaning of. It was like a foreign language. The language in which Izzy Johnson had been so fluent. The language of maths.

As she flicked again through the pages she found the photograph. Izzy and Robbie, arms around each other, smiling up at the camera.

There could be no mistake. This was Izzy Johnson's maths journal.

Why, she wondered, did Niall Riordan have Izzy Johnson's maths journal on his desk? And why had he lied to her about it all this time?

Turning to the last used page, she thought she found the answer.

THIRTY-EIGHT

Alarm bells were sounding in Alison's head as she made her apologies to Nick and left.

She had thought it was over. She had thought the puzzle was solved. Now there was another piece and it changed everything.

She called Paul. Voicemail.

'Meet me at Niall Riordan's flat if you get this. There's something not right.'

Henry Chapell opened the door to her a couple of minutes later.

'Can I speak to Mr Riordan, please?'

'Niall isn't in,' Chapell said. 'Can I help?'

Alison thought for a moment.

Chapell had told her Izzy had burned her notebook. She had meant to check on the CCTV, but then she had been called to see Robbie. There had been blood and flesh and drama. She had forgotten. She had messed up.

'Do you recognise this?' she asked, holding the book under Chapell's nose.

'Is that Izzy's?'

'You told me you saw Izzy burning this. Last week. You sat in this very flat and said you saw her burning it.'

Chapell nodded his head.

'Why did you lie to me?' Alison asked.

'For Niall,' Chapell said simply.

'Niall Riordan asked you to lie for him? Asked you to say Izzy burned this book?' She remembered now. Chapell had been sick when she mentioned the book. Physically sick. She had assumed he was in shock. It was the day he found Andrea Mills' body after all. But it had definitely been when she mentioned the book that he had gone to the bathroom to throw up.

Then he had come back and told her that Izzy had burned the book. 'What does this mean?' Alison asked, turning to the last page on which Izzy had written. 'Rebuttal of Mr R's proof. Fatal error.'

'I don't know. I'm not a mathematician.'

'I'm not a mathematician either,' Alison said, 'but it's pretty bloody obvious to me that Izzy found something wrong with the work Riordan was doing.'

Chapell shook his head.

'Did Niall show Izzy his work?'

He nodded reluctantly. 'He said she was remarkable. He wanted to share it all with her. I think he wanted someone to reassure him. Some of it was really complicated and he wasn't sure, he wasn't *quite* sure, he had it right.'

'And when Izzy looked at it she found a flaw?' Alison pressed. 'That's what this is in her journal – his work, not hers, and she's found an error in it?'

He shook his head again, then broke down in tears, sudden and silent.

'Do you have something you'd like to tell me, Mr Chapell?' Alison asked quietly.

'I don't know. I didn't understand any of it. I mean, Niall is very clever and he'd been working so hard on his dissertation. He was so close to finishing that PhD, before he went off to work in the City. And then there was the chance to finally finish it and a chance of a teaching post in Harvard.'

'And Izzy put paid to that?'

Chapell shrugged.

'But Niall had another job lined up. He didn't need the Harvard gig.'

'I don't know. I think the whole thing at Emersbys came up after. Later... after what happened to Izzy.'

'Did Izzy ever show Riordan this book? Did he know about the error?'

'I don't really know,' Chapell said. 'She came round that Thursday night. The Thursday before she died. They were together for ages, huddled together. And when she went, he was in a towering rage. He can get very angry.' Alison thought of the man at Robbie's bedside. A man who had seemed so gentle. But you never really knew what people were like behind closed doors.

She thought of the row she had interrupted between Riordan and Chapell. Chapell verging on the hysterical and Riordan so very calm. She had taken it for patience. Could it have been the ice of a man with all the control? A man who held his anger only so long and then exploded.

He had lost his temper with Izzy the day she died. Bellowed at her in front of all the class. Had that been just a hint of the true depth of his fury?

'You think he saw this book? That Thursday?' Alison asked.

Chapell nodded.

'You had lunch with him the day Izzy died, didn't you? How did he seem?'

'He was fine, totally fine. Only...' He stopped. 'Nothing, nothing at all.'

'Please tell me, anything at all could be useful.'

'Well, he wanted to keep Angela with him. Our dog, you know. That wasn't unusual. She sometimes stays with him and sleeps in the office, then he walks her at the end of the day. But this day he called and said she'd been hurt and could I take her to the vet.'

'What time was this?'

'No idea, sorry. The vet will know surely.'

Alison thought of her friend Milly, chattering on about a dog brought in to the vet, covered in blood but not really that badly injured. She hadn't really listened. It had been just another distraction. But the dog must have been Angela. Covered in blood not from a barbed wire fence, but from Izzy Johnson. Yapping and terrified and covered in a teenager's blood.

'What did he say happened? To Angela?'

'Said he was walking near the Beamsleigh and Angela got caught in a trap of some sort. I never thought anything... then when the police started asking questions he asked me to say I was the one walking her.'

'And you were prepared to do that? To lie to the police.'

'I never had to. You never asked me. But yes, I would have lied. I would do anything for Niall,' Chapell said seriously.

'What about the journal? Riordan asked you to lie about that too?'

'He said she had given it to him. To check some figures. But he wanted me to say she'd destroyed it. He said it had nothing to do with anything and, if the police wasted time trying to understand it, it would just take the focus off finding her killer.' How convenient. Izzy was dead. Riordan had her journal. Now no one would ever know his mistake.

Except. Surely the people at Harvard would know. Was that why he had suddenly given up on academia, gone back to a job in the City?

Could he really have killed Izzy just to keep his mistakes hidden? It was hard to believe and yet it made a kind of sense.

She needed to speak to him.

'Where is Riordan now?'

'He's at a meeting in Whitby. Local school liaison.' Shit. Shit. Alison rang Paul again. Voicemail again.

'Shit.'

'I could take you,' Chapell said. 'I'm sure Niall can straighten all this out.' *And you'd rather not be here alone with him if he gets back unexpectedly,* Alison thought. She felt the fear almost tangibly rolling off him. She wondered if she had missed it before, or if it was a new thing born of his growing realisation of what Riordan was capable of.

She hesitated over accepting a lift. She probably should call for backup, but what would she say? She'd found a book. It wasn't enough to reopen the case. It might mean nothing at all.

She needed to speak to Riordan. Hear what he had to say. She wanted to drive straight to Whitby, but her car was up the hill at the school and Nick would need it to take the kids home.

Should she wait? Speak to Riordan later? She was probably overreacting. Ben and Carl Adams were responsible for Izzy and Andrea's deaths, weren't they? They had pieced it all together. It all fitted.

Except there had been one piece missing. The book. Mabel's words came back to her. Izzy had died because she was so clever. And Holly, days ago, saying Izzy was extraordinary and yet they were looking at ordinary motives for her murder. Alison had said it was a good point but she had dismissed it.

They had heard hooves and thought horses, and all along Izzy had been a zebra. Or maybe even a unicorn. Extraordinary and rare. Could the reason for her death be that extraordinariness?

Alison knew she couldn't wait to find out.

'Ring Riordan,' she said to Chapell. 'Don't tell him I'm here. Tell him… I don't know… tell him the dog's sick and he needs to come home. Just get him here.'

Chapell nodded, taking out his phone. Alison watched him.

'No reply,' he said after a moment. 'There'll be no signal. You know what it's like over there.' Alison swore quietly. She tried Paul again. Voicemail.

'I'm heading to Whitby. Niall Riordan's over there. I found Izzy Johnson's journal and I want to talk to him about it. I don't know if it's important, but… Oh look, just call me, will you?'

She turned to Chapell.

'Let's go.'

Chapell didn't speak as he led her down to his car, a surprisingly modest hatchback. Alison was glad of the silence. She needed the space to think.

The case Hathaway was putting together against the Adams' seemed so logical. Could it really be entirely wrong?

She thought of Niall Riordan. She had liked him from the start, even begun to trust him as the case went on. Now she needed to assume that everything he said was untrustworthy and see the case in a whole new light.

Riordan had been keen from the start to paint Banks in a negative light. Could it have been a distraction? The gap in Banks' alibi was the ten minutes when he had left his classroom to look for Riordan and been unable to find him. In the end they had dismissed that gap because Banks couldn't have run up to the Beamsleigh and back in that time. But what if the gap wasn't in Banks' alibi but in Riordan's?

Niall Riordan was younger and fitter. He could have run up to the Beamsleigh and back in five minutes. And he would have been coming back to an empty office with no one to notice if he was out of breath, with time to change his clothes and clean himself up. Hell he even arranged to have the damn dog with him, so he'd have an excuse for being out there if anyone saw him.

She thought of Andrea Mills. Mills had seen someone. She said she couldn't recognise him, but she had talked about that figure looking familiar. She had told Henry Chapell as much when he visited her. Could Chapell have passed that information to Riordan, however innocently? Could it have been enough to get Andrea killed? The path from town onto the Beamsleigh was visible from Riordan's office. What if Riordan saw Andrea heading up that way and seized his chance?

Then there was the compassionate visit to Robbie's hospital bed. Was Riordan checking his wellbeing, or making sure Izzy hadn't shared her findings about his 'fatal error'?

Alison shook her head. Was she really considering the possibility that Niall Riordan had committed two murders? And all for a job? A job he didn't even take in the end.

Yet even she knew it was about more than a job. It was about esteem and self-worth and maybe even keeping his relationship alive. It was about being the man he was destined to be. It was mad of course, but then a lot of human behaviour was mad. It didn't make it inconceivable.

'I saw her the day before she died,' Chapell said unexpectedly.

'Izzy?' Alison asked.

'Andrea.'

'I know, Dom told me.'

Chapell was silent for a minute, watching the road as he negotiated the roundabout and took the Whitby turning. 'I went to see how she was. I mean, we weren't friends but... I felt for her.'

Alison felt her curiosity twitch. 'Did she say anything to you?'

'It's awful that she's dead,' Chapell said mechanically.

'What did she say?'

He was still watching the road, concentrating even though it was straight and practically empty of traffic. 'She didn't say anything.'

'Did she recognise him?' Alison asked. 'Did you tell

Riordan that Andrea might have recognised him as Izzy's killer?'

'I feel awful that she died. Honestly. She didn't need to die.'

'Neither of them *needed* to die,' Alison said quietly.

'Niall's a good man.'

They were out of town now. Open moorland flanked the road on either side. The dark here was truly impenetrable. The light of an oncoming headlamp filled their vision and then they were plunged again into darkness. Chapell's headlights lit a little of the road ahead, but it was like being in a cocoon, or spaceship. The world outside was alien and threatening and dark beyond imagining.

'No one ever expects things like that in a town like ours,' Chapell said. 'This is more like the setting for a murder.' He gestured to the darkness with his gloved hand.

Alison shrugged; she wasn't in the mood for inconsequential small talk. If Andrea hadn't told Chapell anything then there was nothing to say. She was still piecing together what had happened. There was a simple explanation.

Izzy had found Riordan's mistake and he knew if it was made public his chance at a new life was over. She was innocent, or maybe arrogant, enough to confront him. He knew he was going to kill her. Why else arrange to walk the dog? Maybe he planned to ask her to walk it with him. That didn't happen; instead she stormed out of his class and met Robbie on the hill. Maybe Riordan followed her, maybe he went onto the Beamsleigh a little later. Either way he waited until Robbie was gone. He…

'Izzy was supposed to meet me up here this weekend,'

Chapell was saying. 'Take Angela for a walk. She loved that dog.'

Alison ignored him, he was interrupting her train of thought.

Once Izzy was dead Riordan must have headed back to school. Andrea Mills saw him. She mistook him for a teenager. Easily done, he had the build of a younger man. Maybe she confided in Chapell that the man she saw could have been Riordan. Maybe Riordan just didn't want any loose ends, either way...

'It would have made a nice walk. I would have made sure she had a good time.' Alison wished he would stop talking. She was trying to think.

Of course once he knew his work was flawed there was no way Riordan could continue his application to Harvard. But maybe he used it as leverage to get his old job back. Bosses could be like ex-boyfriends that way; nothing made them want you more than the idea that someone else was interested.

'She liked to walk Angela,' Chapell said.

The car was slowing. There was a tight bend in the road.

Izzy had confronted Riordan on Thursday night. So why wait until Tuesday to kill her? *Thursday night.*

Chapell had said Izzy came round to the flat and told Riordan he had made a mistake. Dominic Mills had said the same. He said he was supposed to meet Izzy on Thursday, but she had cancelled because she needed to see Riordan.

Thursday night, *last* Thursday night.

Last Thursday night Alison had been stuck in the school hall of Penbury Primary for almost four hours. There had been a power cut and the electronic security doors had locked them in. The bloody transition meeting for Bea's move to Penbury High. Details of uniform and equipment requirements. A talk about how great the GCSE results were last year.

And giving the talk – Niall Riordan.

No way Riordan had got home in time to talk to Izzy.

No way Izzy had told him about any mistakes.

Another memory came back to her, about what her friend Milly had told her. The yappy dog brought to the vets on the day Izzy died. Covered in blood that must have been Izzy's. Her owner too, covered in blood, described by Milly as one of those *proper gorgeous* men.

'Riordan never saw Izzy's book, did he?' Alison said quietly.

'He'd have given up everything. He'd have thanked her. I couldn't let him. He could be so much more. I wasn't going to let a silly little slut like her…'

'She came to see him. Last Thursday.'

'He wasn't in. I took the stupid book, told her I'd show it to him. Told her he'd be able to explain.'

'Only you never showed him?'

'He couldn't understand why she was so angry with him. Of course, she thought I'd told him, about the mistake, and he was refusing to acknowledge it. She was furious with him and he didn't know why. I was never going to tell him about that mistake. As if I would. As if I was going to let her, the clever little bitch, ruin everything for me.'

'She was a child.'

'She was going to ruin my life.'

'So what did you do?'

'I arranged to meet her here,' Chapell said, gesturing

out of the window. 'I said we could take Angela for a long walk. We could talk about Niall, how to get him to speak to her about the problem she had found. She even offered to help. The arrogant bitch thought she could find a solution. Only I knew Niall was looking for any excuse not to push forward with the application. Anything to stay in this shitty little town.'

'That isn't true,' Alison said. 'He found another job. He's taken a job in the City for you.'

'He owes me,' Chapell said flatly.

'So what about Izzy? You didn't meet her here.'

'Didn't have to. When I saw her that day, leaving school early, I followed her up to the Beamsleigh. That boy was there for a while… and then he left and… and suddenly we were alone and… well, sometimes the gods smile.'

'But Andrea Mills saw you,' Alison began.

'No. She's blind as a bat, Andrea, without her contacts. I never wanted Andrea to die.'

'So what happened? Why did you kill her?'

'I thought it was Dominic, of course.' He said it as if it was the most obvious thing in the world. As if Alison was a fool not to see it. 'I saw her from behind and I thought she was him. He had told me he was going up there. To look for the bloody book. He was obsessed with that bloody book. He talked about it like it was some sort of holy relic. Izzy's legacy. He said the ideas in there needed to be preserved. I knew he'd never let it lie. So I thought… I needed to shut him up. And I went up to the Beamsleigh, and I saw… I thought I saw him, I mean the silly cow had a university hoody on.' Alison nodded. Dominic and Andrea had argued, because she was wearing his hoody.

'You screamed when you saw it was Andrea,' Alison said. 'You weren't calling for help, it was just a shock.'

'I didn't expect anyone to come, and then suddenly you were there running towards me. I thought I'd had it then. But you comforted me. Remember that? You comforted me, told me it wasn't my fault. Then you asked me if I'd seen anyone.'

'And you decided to blame Robbie Smith.'

'Why not? Low-life scum, who'd care?'

The car swerved as Chapell rounded another bend too fast.

'Why didn't you destroy the book?' Alison asked. 'Get rid of the proof?'

'I was going to. And then he got the job at Emersbys and there was no need anymore. They wouldn't care about some stupid theoretical error. So...'

'But once Riordan saw the book, weren't you afraid that he would realise...' She stopped herself. 'You wanted him to know,' she said, 'you wanted him to know what you'd done for him.'

'I *need* him to understand how far I'm willing to go for him, for us, to get us out of this crappy place.' It was madness. Utter madness. A madness with its own internal logic.

'You expected him to forgive you?'

Chapell looked shocked. As if the idea that he might not be forgiven had never crossed his mind. 'He loves me,' he said simply.

Alison didn't reply.

'This was the spot I chose,' Chapell said, slowing the car. 'Secluded. Rather beautiful in a bleak way.'

'People knew you were meeting. They knew she was

going to be with you.' Chapell laughed softly. 'Actually they didn't. It was our little secret. Teenagers love secrets, don't they? All I would have had to do was delete that text. As it happened I let you see it. Why not? Izzy wasn't killed on the moor, so what did it matter? Shame to waste the perfect spot though, don't you think?'

'This is madness,' Alison said. 'My colleague knows I'm out here with you.'

'No, he doesn't,' Chapell said, smiling. 'What you actually told him was that you were heading for Whitby to speak to Niall. My name was never mentioned.' As he said it, he reached into the side pocket of the car door. Alison saw the glinting blade of a kitchen knife.

He pulled the car off the road onto the soft verge where the moorland dropped away sharply to the left. Alison knew that just a couple of feet from the road they would be completely invisible even if a car did happen past.

'Get out,' Chapell said.

'I'm not going to do that,' Alison said steadily.

'Yes you are. Just one last loose end and I'm done.'

'If I worked it out someone else will.'

'You didn't work anything out though, did you? You thought it was Niall. As if Niall has the guts or the ambition. As if he has the nerve.'

'You did all this for him. And what? Now you're going to let him take the blame?'

'I want a better life. He promised me a better life.'

'Why didn't you just leave him?' Alison said. 'Make your own life. Or hitch yourself to someone more successful. Or were you worried that no one else would have you? Getting old? Losing your looks?'

'Hardly,' Chapell said coldly. 'I get offers. Lots of offers.'

'But you stay with Niall,' Alison said.

'This isn't a fucking therapy session,' he said. 'Just get out of the car.'

'Why? So you can kill me at your own pace?'

'Get out of the car or I will cut you.' He held the knife close to her throat.

She forced herself to laugh. 'And get blood all over your perfect interior? I doubt it. Why don't we have a little chat instead? You can tell me about your childhood. It usually comes down to that with psychopaths. Mother didn't love them, or father abused them. Which was it? Both maybe?'

'My mother loves me,' Chapell said, almost like a child.

'That's right, you told me. Single mother. She adored you. Until she found out you like fucking men.'

She forced herself to laugh at him. A hard false sound, but mercifully devoid of fear. She needed him to lose control. She needed this to come to a head here, in the car or by the roadside where she had a chance. She couldn't let him force her out onto the moor where she might never be found.

'She didn't love you so much then, did she? When she found out you like cock. And when she found out how stupid you are. When you failed all your exams and told her you wanted to draw pictures for a living. She didn't think much of you then, did she?'

'Shut up.'

'Did she call you a loser?' Alison asked, feeling she had touched a nerve. 'Is that why you had to stick with Niall Riordan? Because you couldn't admit you'd made another mistake? Failed again. You had to make him into a winner at any cost.'

'Shut the fuck up.'

Suddenly he was upon her with his hands at her throat, the knife clattering into the footwell at his feet. He was shockingly strong. His whole weight was above her, pressing her back into the seat. She was struggling for breath. The edges of her vision darkened. She was about to black out. Her fingers were grappling with his, scratching at the back of his hands, trying to loosen the grip he had on her throat. The pressure on her windpipe increased. He was still talking, spitting words at her, but she could longer make sense of them. Her vision was narrowing. The sound seemed to be coming from further away. There wasn't much pain, just the inability to breathe and the closing down of her senses.

Was this how she would die? In a car with a madman? It didn't seem so unexpected to her. It didn't feel far from the life she had started out with. Drug-addict mother. Scruffy, underfed kid. Attitude problems. In and out of care. Strangled. Murdered. Gone.

There was almost a poetic logic to it.

Except she wasn't just the daughter of a drug addict anymore. She was a copper. She was a wife. A mother. This couldn't be her daughters' destiny. They couldn't become motherless. Life couldn't be that circular.

She let her arms fall to her side. Closed her eyes, surrendered to the lack of air. Still Chapell pressed against her, his weight and his strength and his madness massed against her.

She lay still. Not fighting. Pretending not to be, the way she had when she was a little girl. When the noises and the men had frightened her. Giving in but not yet giving up.

The weight lifted just a little. The pressure eased. Maybe he was tiring; maybe he thought she was already dead. Passed out at least. She forced herself not to gasp for air. Waited. Her lungs were burning for oxygen. She waited another heartbeat. His weight against her eased a fraction more.

She launched herself.

As fast and as hard as she could.

She pushed up against him with all her might. Her fingers no longer sought to loosen his grip, but flew to his eyes. She tried to prise her fingers in under the eyelids, into the soft jelly of his eyeballs. His hands flew from around her throat and caught her wrists, twisting them as he pulled her fingers away from his face. She felt something snap and suspected a broken bone. The pain seared through her. Adrenaline surged.

Air rushed into her lungs and she felt light-headed, worse than she had before. She barely had time to take a breath before he was pushing her back again, forcing her wrists down by her sides. Trying to straddle her, trying to pin her hands against her body with his knees. She turned sharply to the side, throwing him off balance. At the same time, she slumped low in the seat. Scrabbling with her left hand on the floor. Feeling for the discarded knife.

Chapell's hands had found her throat again, but her fingers were touching the ice metal of the knife. She grabbed it by the blade. It cut deep into the soft cushion of her palm but she brought it up and slammed the tip into his thigh. He gave a yell of pain and grabbed his injured leg. Alison stabbed him again, closer to the knee. Again a scream of agony. Suddenly he was scrambling to get away from her.

She felt herself laugh in relief.

'Where are you going, Mr Chapell?' she asked, reversing their positions. Now she was pinning him to his seat, straddling him and feeling the blood from his bleeding thigh and knee warming her through her clothes.

She felt in the pocket of her jeans and found the tie-wraps she had used earlier on Bea's hair.

Chapell twisted his body suddenly, trying to throw her off. At the same time he lunged for the knife. She was too quick for him, plunging the blade down again, into his side this time.

As he crumpled with the pain, she grabbed at his hands, pulling his wrists together. Within seconds she had secured them with the tie-wrap. Another wrap soon tethered his hands to the steering wheel.

Watching his face still contorted with pain, Alison scrambled back into the passenger seat, wet and sticky with blood. Chapell was whimpering softly. Alison was glad to find she felt no sympathy.

A car passed, its headlights shining into the window for just a moment. Then it was gone.

Alison held the knife to Chapell's throat.

'You have to get me an ambulance,' he said, suddenly pathetic. 'I could bleed to death.'

'That's very true. I hear that can take hours. And you know how bad the signal is up here.'

'You have to get me help. You're the police. You have to…' Alison laughed bitterly.

'It always amazes me how people like you think you're the only ones who can break the rules. I have to help you. I *have* to? You just tried to kill me, you little shit. You think I *have* to do anything?'

'OK, arrest me… I'll admit everything… just… Fuck, my leg really hurts.'

'Does it?' Alison asked. 'How awful.'

She put her hand on his injured leg and applied pressure. He screamed. She felt nothing.

'Please help me,' Chapell said. 'You're the police you're not going to…'

'Not going to what?' Alison asked. 'Kill you? Why not? Because I'm a nice middle-class police lady from a nice middle-class town and I'm not a psychopath? Is that what you think?' Chapell said nothing.

'You know fuck all about me, Mr Chapell. You don't know where I've come from or what I've had to do. And you have absolutely no bloody idea what I'm capable of.'

'Please don't…' Chapell began.

'Fuck off,' Alison said, disgusted. 'Did you listen when Izzy said please or Andrea? Did you care? But you think *I* care? You think I'm not like you?' She laughed, glad to hear how mad she sounded. 'I'm more like you than you know.'

She held the blade lightly to his throat. 'I could slit your throat now and never have a single sleepless night over it. Not one.'

'Please…' he said again.

'You tried to make my children motherless,' Alison spat at him. 'You think I'm just going to let that go?'

She weighed the knife in her hand, then pressed it against his throat again.

One deep slash and he would be gone.

This man who had killed two people and tried to kill her. He would be gone and she could say it was self-defence and no one would know any different. And she would not have a single sleepless night. She was sure of that. She felt his skin give a little as she pressed against it.

One deep slash would be enough.

THIRTY-NINE

'I don't get it,' Nick said, not for the first time. 'He did all that for a notebook. He killed two people.'

Alison nodded, pouring herself another glass of wine and holding the bottle up to Paul and Nick. They both shook their heads. Alison took a long, slow sip. She was still having trouble swallowing and had some impressive bruises around her throat but other than that she had come out of it pretty well.

She smiled at the sight of Paul and Nick side by side on the sofa. Paul had come round for dinner. The first time. Alison hadn't told the kids yet that they had a new uncle but she thought it would do no harm for them to gradually get to know him.

It had been a success on the whole. Mabel had played her recorder and Paul had managed not to cover his ears. Bea had talked and talked about her new school and he had been able to feign interest.

The girls were in bed now. Both had protested loudly, but they were quiet at last and Alison hoped that meant they were asleep.

Now the adults' talk had turned, as it had so often over the last week, to the case they had just closed.

'Still doesn't make any sense to me,' Nick said. 'If a teenage girl could spot the mistakes Riordan had made surely the people at Harvard…'

'She wasn't *just* a teenage girl,' Alison said, 'she was a genius where that stuff is concerned.'

'Still, aren't the people at Harvard geniuses?'

'You're right, of course,' Alison sighed. 'But Chapell was desperate. Not thinking straight.'

'And then Riordan dropped out of the Harvard job anyway. So the mistake would never have mattered,' Nick said.

'What you're forgetting,' Paul said, as if explaining something immensely complicated, 'is that Henry Chapell is stark raving mad.' Alison laughed.

'Do *not* let his defence team hear you saying that, they'd love to claim diminished responsibility.'

'No, I don't mean clinically insane. I mean just your common or garden nutter.'

'Well, obviously,' Nick said, 'but he can't have thought no one else would notice…'

'He was desperate,' Alison said again. 'He saw the job in Harvard as a sort of redemption and he saw Izzy standing in his way. Any rational person would know other people would spot the mistake too, just like any rational person would see that Riordan could always get another job if the Harvard thing didn't work out.'

'I heard he's not going to take that new job after all,' Paul interrupted.

Alison hoped it was true. She liked Niall Riordan. She would be glad if he stayed on at the school.

Nick shook his head again. 'I still don't get it,' he said.

Alison smiled. Nick never really understood crazy.

'Chapell wasn't thinking rationally,' she told him. 'He panicked. He overreacted. Basically he's a nutter, like Paul said. Izzy showed him the mistake in that book and all he could see was his chance of a new life being taken away from him.'

'Why didn't he just leave?' Nick asked. 'Get a job of his own if he hates it here so much?' Alison shook her head. Chapell was a beautiful man, used all his life to being admired and looked after. She imagined the idea of work and self-sufficiency had never even occurred to him.

She shrugged; it was too hard to try to explain.

'OK,' Nick went on, 'so he killed two people to keep Riordan's mistake a secret. But he kept the notebook. He kept the evidence of the error Riordan had made. Why? Why not just destroy it?'

'He needed Riordan to *know*,' Alison said. 'It's the same reason he gave me Izzy's phone. He was hoping Riordan would piece it all together. He wanted to show him his warped idea of love and loyalty.'

'The phone was genius actually,' Paul said. 'It led us to Banks and, because Chapell had sent a text to Izzy after she died, it diverted suspicion from him.'

'Not that we ever suspected…' Alison began.

'I just don't get how he thought he'd get away with it,' Nick said. 'How could he think Riordan would work it all out and still forgive him?'

'Because he's a nutter,' Alison and Paul piped up together.

Nick laughed. Then his face fell. 'The thought of you up on the moor on your own with him…' he began, putting a hand on her leg.

'I'm fine,' Alison said. 'You should see the other guy.' The two men laughed without real humour. She understood the masculine guilt they both felt. For different reasons, they both felt that they should have been there to protect her.

Of course she had not needed their protection.

There had been a chance, a pretty good chance, that she was going to kill Henry Chapell that night. Not because of what he had done to Izzy or Andrea, although she wanted justice for both of them, but because of what he had almost done to her girls. He had almost made them motherless. She could never forgive that.

In the end she had stopped herself. She wanted to be better than him. She needed it. She had flagged down a car and asked the driver to ring the police and an ambulance as soon as he got a decent signal. She had waited with Chapell and, every second, she had questioned her decision to let him live.

Now he was in Armley Prison on remand. She'd heard he was having a hard time coping. She was glad. Niall Riordan had not been to see him.

'OK,' Nick said, 'at the risk of sounding super thick, why did he kill Andrea again? Because he mistook her for Dominic?'

'Andrea took Dominic's hoody that day. She's a tall woman, he's a very slight young man. From behind, in the rain, Chapell made a mistake. He was expecting to see Dominic. He'd heard Dominic saying he was going up to the Beamsleigh to search for that notebook.'

'But why kill Dominic? Chapell knew he wasn't going to find the book up on the hill.'

'True, but Dom kept going on about it. He mentioned it

to me and he kept saying he thought it might be important. Chapell didn't want us asking questions about it, he didn't want any focus on him and Riordan. We were so conveniently focused on Robbie and Simon Banks. Chapell wanted to keep it that way.'

'So he meant to kill Dominic not his mother?'

'Yeah. He kept saying to me that he didn't know it was Andrea. The day she was killed. He said it again and again. I just didn't put it together.' She looked sour, blaming herself.

'There's no way you could have known,' Paul said.

Alison ignored him. 'He'd got away with a killing on the Beamsleigh once, I suppose he thought he could do it again.'

'But that's...'

'Insane?' Alison smiled. 'Yeah, it is.'

'Like I say, he's a complete headcase,' Paul noted.

'I think he freaked out when he saw that it was Andrea. I think he genuinely liked her.'

'And he nearly got rumbled, you nearly caught him.'

'Yeah, if I'd just been a bit more observant. Realised he was killing her, not trying to save her.'

'There was no way you could know...' Paul began.

'Nice try, mate,' Alison said, 'but I should have seen it. I just assumed he was calling for help and he was quick thinking enough to go with it. He twisted the whole thing and tried to pin it all on Robbie.'

'Which would have been genius, except that Robbie had a perfect alibi.'

'Yeah, if it hadn't been for that we'd've had an open and shut case.'

'Especially since Robbie confessed,' Paul said.

'And why *did* he do that?' Nick asked.

'Because the Adams cousins wanted an end to the police investigation. They needed a scapegoat and Robbie fitted the bill. A bit of pressure, a threat against his mum, and Robbie was persuaded to take the fall. I'm not sure how culpable that solicitor Mitchell was in all that. It was after her visit that Robbie cut his wrists. I think he saw it as a way out. Better than spending his life in prison. When the suicide attempt failed he knew he had no other option but to confess. He put his faith in me to find out the truth.'

'He thought the Adams' had killed Izzy?'

'I think so. And ironically I think they assumed Robbie had done it. That's probably why Robbie's phone went missing that night. Ben Adams wanted to get rid of any evidence of a link between Robbie and Izzy. That way he could keep us away from looking at him or Carl or the drugs. And he probably believed he was protecting Robbie too.'

'But we had DNA,' Paul said, 'so Robbie was in the frame from day one.'

'Yep,' Alison said, 'so Ben and Carl moved into self-preservation mode. Getting Robbie to confess must have seemed like the best way to shut down the investigation quickly. The last thing they wanted was us poking around anywhere near their drugs business.'

'If Dan Humphreys hadn't seen Robbie and called the police…' Paul began.

'We'd've believed his confession. Robbie would be headed for prison and Chapell would have got away with it.'

'So it's luck,' Nick said.

'Life's pretty much about luck, isn't it?' Alison said. 'Everything's just chance. If Izzy hadn't chosen the one night Riordan was out to go and tell him about his mistakes, if she hadn't decided to trust Chapell with the information instead, if Robbie had turned back when they had that row instead of leaving her there. Any one of those things might have saved her.'

'If she hadn't taken the smart drugs, or whatever you call them, she might never have been clever enough to spot Riordan's mistake in the first place,' Nick said.

Alison smiled. 'So we get to blame the drugs in the end,' she said. 'I like that.'

'It's always about the drugs,' Paul said. 'Don't you read the papers?' Alison smiled. She'd like to blame the drugs. It was a comforting narrative. Stay away from drugs and you'll be fine. But she thought it probably was more about luck than anything else. Izzy and Andrea's bad luck, their own good luck in catching Chapell.

Life was luck really, both good and bad.

Even the way Alison had escaped her early life had been more luck than determination.

She could have gone the way of her sister.

She remembered the week after her mother died. She had been at university, where she thought of herself as independent and clever and free. Then her mother died and she came back home to her old life and found it still waiting for her. Her mother was gone and she was desperate and sad and alone. Filled with a grief that felt like dying and unequipped to deal with it. She had smoked heroin with Dave Sparks in his grotty bedsit in Seacroft; she had woken up to find him having sex with her.

And she had been lucky.

She didn't like the heroin too much; she didn't get pregnant; she didn't pick up an incurable disease. She made a mistake when she was desperate and sad and young and she got away with it.

Her sister Abby wasn't as lucky. Within a year she was dead of an overdose. It had nothing to do with character. Sure there were strong people and weak people, but there was also just chance.

Two people had died in her town this week. It was down to the behaviour and the decisions of Henry Chapell and he would be held to account. But it was also down to the vagaries of chance and that was what scared her.

She could keep her children safe from the dangers she could see and understand, but the chance danger of speaking to the wrong man, being too clever, understanding too well? How was she supposed to keep them safe from that?

Paul said he had to go and she saw him to the door.

'Come for lunch on Sunday,' she said.

'Are you sure?'

'Yeah, Sunday lunch is for families.'

'Thanks, sis.'

She laughed. 'Don't let me catch you saying that at work, Sergeant.' He smiled, kissed her lightly on the cheek and left.

She went back to Nick, who was sitting in the living room and had turned on the news.

'I like him,' he said.

'I invited him to Sunday lunch.'

Nick just nodded; he was already half asleep.

Alison sat on the sofa beside him and lifted his arm around her shoulders. With her body pressed against his side she felt as if nothing could go wrong.

She knew it was an illusion but sometimes illusions are all we have.

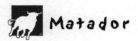 Matador

For exclusive discounts on Matador titles,
sign up to our occasional newsletter at
troubador.co.uk/bookshop